CHILDREN OF THE HUNT

CAROLYN GLASSHOFF

INDRI PUBLISHING

This is a work of fiction. Any names or characters are fictitious. Any resemblance to actual persons, living or dead, or actual events is purely coincidental.

Children of the Hunt

Copyright © 2023 by Carolyn Glasshoff

All rights reserved.

No part of this book may be reproduced in any form or by any electronic or mechanical means, including information storage and retrieval systems, without written permission from the author, except for the use of brief quotations in a book review.

Indri Publishing

Formatted using Vellum

Cover art by MiblArt

ISBN 979-8-9886980-0-5 (trade paperback)

ISBN 979-8-9886980-1-2 (ebook)

CONTENTS

1

I wiped at the sweat dripping down my face, took a deep breath, and tried to run faster. Not fast enough. Not far enough. Not that long ago, I could run a 5k on a whim and twice that if I pushed, but now I felt like collapsing after a half mile. Another minute and I had to slow down before my lungs burst. Back to walking. I slowed the treadmill as my phone beeped that my twenty minutes were up. In the locker room, I stood under the steaming shower and closed my eyes, trying to forget life for a few minutes as my body relaxed with the heat.

Moving across the country with only a five-year-old for company hadn't seemed as daunting when I planned it, but reality had been harder than I'd anticipated. I'd managed to at least unpack basic necessities, but my little apartment was still filled wall-to-wall with boxes, and I didn't want to go back to staring at all that cardboard. I knew I would have to deal with it soon. Or not. Maybe I could just move James into my room and stuff all those boxes in the second bedroom and forget about them. That's what a responsible adult would do, right?

A bell chimed, a signal that the gym was closing soon, and I jumped, realizing I had lost track of time. Cursing lightly, I toweled off as quickly as I could and pulled on my jeans and shirt, the fabric sticking uncomfortably to my damp skin. Another thing I hadn't anticipated when I moved from the west coast to Florida: the extreme humidity meant I never felt completely dry. I wrapped my hair up into a dark, wet bun, not wanting to take the time to dry and braid it, and ran out into the lobby to flag down the woman who had checked me in earlier.

"Hey..." I tried to get a look at her name tag again without it being too obvious. I was pretty certain I failed in the subtlety department, but her chipper smile didn't waver. "Kelly, if it won't take too long, can I go ahead and sign up for the membership we talked about? Today was the last day of my trial," I said.

"Sure!" Kelly positively beamed, her long, blonde ponytail swinging as she looked around for a pen and fished a small paper packet out from behind the counter. If she'd noticed me reminding myself of her name, it didn't seem to bother her in the slightest. "It only takes a few minutes. You had a kid, right?" I nodded. "I'll phone downstairs to childcare and let them know you'll be there in five minutes."

"Thanks," I said, then noticed the clock behind her. "Wait, I thought you don't close until ten."

"Oh, there was a sign on the door." She pointed at the swinging glass doors behind me that led out into the central atrium of the commercial plaza we were in. I looked back and saw the paper taped to the door, handwriting in permanent marker bleeding through to the backside. "Private event tonight, so we're closing the gym early to the public. Back to normal hours tomorrow, though, don't you worry!" she continued cheerfully. She picked up the phone while I started filling out the packet. A responsible parent would probably have their preschooler home and in bed before ten at night anyway. I heard her say "Jessica? Paige is just filling out some forms, so she'll be down for James in a few minutes." How did she remember both of our names so easily? I wished I had that ability.

As I began filling out the papers, I mentally congratulated myself for finally remembering my address without copying from my new license, even if I stood there thinking about it longer than I should have. Wait, did I remember it right though? Maybe those last two numbers were backward... I dug it out anyway to double-check. Behind me, I heard the scrape of metal chair and table legs on the tile floors as employees began setting up for whatever private thing they had going on. Probably some wellness guru giving a talk about yoga or a recipe seminar on a hundred things to do with kale. Those seemed like the sort of things that someone who rented a gym for a private function would find interesting. I handed the packet back and she thumbed through it.

"You don't have a local emergency contact," she said, pointing to a blank spot on one page.

"Yeah... working on that," I admitted with a shrug. Her smile turned from gym-trainer-chipper to something softer.

"New to Orlando, then?"

"Yeah, about a month or so," I said.

"And you moved here alone?"

I shifted uncomfortably. "Just me and James downstairs in the playroom," I admitted. I wasn't sure if I felt weird admitting this because I felt like I was oversharing with someone who wasn't interested in my life story or because telling a mostly-stranger that I didn't have anyone checking in on me seemed like a safety hazard.

"Where did you move from?"

"Chico, California."

She whistled. "That's a long way. Well, if you'd like some ideas or a local guide sometime, I'm happy to show you around a bit. We're all new at some point," Kelly said. She seemed sincere and I thanked her. I appreciated the gesture, but I'd never be able to take her up on it without feeling like I was intruding. The last thing she needed was a customer taking up her time outside of work. But I did feel a little less "stranger danger" anxiety. "Don't worry about that part of the form," she added. "If you're here, we'll make sure you're watched over if anything happens."

"Thanks. Really," I said, meaning it. I was starting to realize this was the longest conversation I'd had with someone other than James since moving. As much as I loved my son, he wasn't exactly a stellar conversationalist yet. I needed to get out more. But that was what I was doing now, right? I was out of my apartment, talking to actual grown-ups. "I'll see you tomorrow," I said, grabbing my bag. Behind me, a surprising number of people were leaning on the plastic tables and chatting or helping to set out cheap metal fold-up chairs. Maybe it was a private event, but it didn't look like anything lavish. Then again, they had rented out a gym, not a ballroom.

"Kelly, is she the last one?" a man's voice called from across the room.

"Yep, that's it. Everyone else left a while ago," Kelly called back. Multiple pairs of eyes suddenly found me and watched my short trek across the room. Great. That wasn't awkward. Maybe I wouldn't come back to the gym, after all. I stared ahead and tried to ignore the feeling of holes being stared into my back. When I got to the door, I looked behind me to see that everyone had returned to their conversations.

Ok, maybe it wasn't as bad as I had worried. Most of them probably wouldn't be here at the same time as me most days, anyway. Or may not even be members of this gym at all. With that happy thought, I pulled the door open and almost collided with a tall man with shaggy, dark blonde hair who seemed shocked to find me in his way.

"Sorry," I muttered. He smiled, the surprise leaving his face.

"No worries. I wasn't paying attention. You'd think I'd notice someone standing on the other side of a glass door," he said. I smiled back and stepped out, then held the swinging door open for him and motioned him through. "See you around," he said as he passed me, followed by a small gaggle of children of various ages. As they trooped past, one of them playfully shoved one of his peers who collided with me, her foot coming down with what seemed like an extreme amount of force for someone so small. I groaned as I tilted slightly to get off my suddenly throbbing foot.

"I'm so sorry, miss!" the little girl said, "Trevor pushed me, I'm so sorry!"

"That's ok. Accidents happen," I assured her as the tall man came and gently pushed her through the door, also apologizing profusely on her behalf. She must have been wearing steel-toed boots or something from the way my foot was throbbing. I might not be back tomorrow after all. I glanced at her feet to see what had been so heavy and almost started laughing.

What I saw peeking out from under her jeans weren't shoes, but brown fuzzy slippers with huge claws. I didn't know if this was a fad, part of a summer camp ritual, or her own unique style, but I thought briefly that I'd have to figure out more about what kids thought was cool as James got older. Luckily, since he was only five I still had total control over his fashion sense, but I apparently had no idea what sort of things his peers might be into soon. The girl seemed like she was at most a couple of years older than James. Only a few children were left in the hallway when the open-air atrium in the middle of the building began rumbling and the walls and floor around us began to tremble.

I was thrown back against the door as the ground shifted under me, the movements becoming suddenly more violent. Was this an earthquake? Does Florida have earthquakes? Pieces of the walkway overhang started to crack and flakes of plaster started raining from overhead. There was a crashing sound and dust started rising from the first floor of the atrium in a thick cloud.

James! My thoughts were suddenly panicked. I let go of the door I had been using to prop myself up and started for the stairs leading to the bottom floor of the plaza.

"Everyone get in here, now!" the same voice that had asked Kelly about me yelled. The man the voice belonged to was running toward me from inside the gym, shoving the few remaining, suddenly screaming children into the doors behind me. He reached me and grabbed my arm. "You, too! It's not safe out here!"

"My son is downstairs!" I yelled, snatching my arm back.

"We'll make sure he gets out, just come..." he cut off with a curse as I yanked my arm away and ran for the stairs. I stopped dead in my tracks on the top step, almost losing my balance, and grabbed for the rail just in time. The bottom half of the stairwell was gone, rebar sticking out of broken concrete, the lower stairs lying broken in the hole that was opening up in the ground in the middle of the building. I spun and looked for an emergency exit. Around me, pieces of the building started to rain down as the building continued to shudder apart. I heard the man yelling after me as I ran for a door marked with a glowing exit sign in the wall further down the walkway. *James. I have to get to James. I can't lose him, too!*

I got to the door and shoved as hard as I could, but it was jammed shut, something on the other side holding it closed. I pushed harder, hoping desperation would give me extra strength. Apparently, that's only something that happens in movies. The door shifted slightly but didn't open. The air was filling with dust, and I coughed, tears streaming down my face as I realized I wouldn't be able to save the one person in the world who depended on me.

"Come *on*," the man yelled again, coming toward me, holding out his hand. He was moving slower now, looking for all the world like he was trying to catch a skittish cat. "We can get out, but not this way," he said. The panic was starting to ebb away and I realized that he probably had a better idea of how to find another exit than I did. As I started toward him, his eyes suddenly went wide and he broke into a sprint toward me. I looked up to see a huge chunk of concrete falling toward my head. Right before it struck, something warm and heavy slammed into me, knocking me to the floor. My head bounced hard on the tile floor and I saw a flash of light, then my mouth filled with dust and everything went black.

My body ached and my mouth felt like I'd tried to eat ashes. I groaned and tried to sit up, but my head throbbed and I felt a hand gently hold me down. My back wasn't against a hard floor but on something soft. My eyes flew open

"James! Where's James?" I cried, suddenly remembering why I was hurting so bad and trying to jump to my feet. The man who had chased me into the atrium grabbed me as I collapsed instead, stars flashing across my vision, and laid me back gently onto the couch. I groaned as my head and back protested the attempted movement. "Where's my son?" I asked, staring at the man looking down at me, daring him to tell me that they hadn't been able to get my child out like he'd promised. His brown eyes were filled with concern as he looked me over, seeming to assess my condition and not liking what he saw.

"He's fine. He's out back with Jessica. She was with him in the childcare center and got him out. He's fine." I closed my eyes and took a deep breath, then started coughing. How much dust had I swallowed in that disaster?

"Here," I felt a water bottle pressed into my hand and I gratefully took a few sips then downed half the bottle. The man stared at something past me for a moment, then his attention snapped back to me. "Jessica is bringing James inside now. She said he was a very brave little guy." I heard a screen door slam.

"Remember, she got hurt, so don't jump on her, ok?" a teenage girl's voice whispered from across the room behind the couch.

"I know." My heart clenched at the small, worried voice. They did get James out. He was safe. He came around the side of the couch and the man who had been sitting with me stood up and stepped back. I stared at James, at his blonde hair, his big green eyes looking at me with a mixture of awe and fear. I grabbed for him and held him close, a sob escaping from me. He hugged me back, but when he squeezed I groaned, bruises igniting even from that little hug. James stepped back and inspected me closely.

"They said you were ok but had to sleep. You're ok?" he asked. I nodded.

"Just fine, baby. Nothing a bath and some sleep won't fix." I eyed him all over. He had a couple of small bruises but seemed to be fine overall. And by some miracle, he wasn't acting terrified or traumatized. The man, now standing a few feet away, cleared his throat.

"You might need a little more than sleep, although a bath wouldn't hurt," he said. "You've been out for nearly a full day."

I snapped my head up to look at him and immediately regretted it. I leaned back again as pain shot up my neck and head.

"At the very least you've got a concussion and extensive bruising. I'm not convinced you didn't break a rib too, but our doctor tells me that you're just banged up." He frowned at me. "I told you we had him. What were you thinking?" he demanded.

"I've never seen you before in my life," I said, hugging James to me, who was looking between us, wide-eyed. "I was thinking I needed to save my kid from getting hurt in the..." I paused, frowning. "earthquake? Was that an earthquake? Do you get earthquakes here?"

"We don't normally have earthquakes, no," Kelly said, coming around and crossing her arms. "The north part of the state sometimes does, but people barely notice them. They don't happen this far south, though. If there had been an earthquake like that, it would have made national news."

"So... sinkhole?" I guessed again.

"That's how we'll spin it for the public," Kelly said, frowning.

"Kelly!" the man hissed.

"She almost died..." Kelly started, fire in her eyes.

"Because she didn't listen when we tried to get her to safety," The man interrupted.

"*She* is right here, you know," I snapped. Kelly and the man both stopped and stared at me for a second, then Kelly's eyes drifted to James, who had started squirming in my vise grip. I sighed and loosened my hold on him. "Sorry sweetie," I mumbled. "Do you want to go play some more?"

"You'll be ok?" James asked, eyeing me warily.

"I'll make sure she's well taken care of, ok, hun?" Kelly said to him. She held her hand out and gave him a reassuring smile. He looked between me and Kelly and I nodded at him.

"I'll be fine."

"Ok," James said reluctantly. He dropped a kiss on my cheek. "Feel better, Mommy," he said, then ran around the couch and I heard the screen door slam again. I leaned back on the couch. I felt like I should be getting up and trying to assess my situation more, but every inch of me was screaming to lie down, go back to sleep. I had no intention of losing consciousness again, at least until I knew where James and I were, but lying down seemed a reasonable compromise–at least until my stomach grumbled loud enough that James probably heard it from outside.

"Can you stand up?" Kelly asked gently. I closed my eyes and nodded slowly.

"Yeah, I can." I sat up again and groaned. Kelly looped her arm through mine and helped me to my feet.

"Kitchen's through here. Let's get some food in you," she said. I leaned on her and followed her through to a large kitchen with yellow countertops lined with food in tin foil serving containers, like a potluck buffet. I closed my eyes and inhaled the smells coming from those containers. I was absolutely starving. "You sit and I'll grab you a plate," Kelly said, steering me away from the counters. "Kyle, move!"

I realized that we weren't the only ones here. A large

farmhouse-style table was surrounded by a group of men and women in various stages of finishing their own meals. More leaned against the walls, I guess having already finished eating. There had been a low buzz of conversation when we came in, but it stopped as they all stared at me. Great. Not only did I not know where I was or who they were, but I was also clearly an outsider here.

A man with shoulder-length light brown hair and a dark tan, Kyle I guessed, got up and took his plate to the opposite side of the table, shoving his way onto the end of a bench next to a tall red-headed woman who looked displeased at being squished. Kelly sat me in the chair Kyle had abandoned and then rushed toward the counter and started filling a plate for me. I could feel the eyes of everyone in the room on me, but instead of acknowledging them, I rested my head in my hands. After a moment, the low hum of conversation started back up around me, but with an air of caution, as if they were being careful not to say something I shouldn't be hearing.

"She looks like shit," I heard a man's voice say softly, then the sound of someone getting smacked and an "OW!" I ignored it. My head was still throbbing too much for me to concentrate on anything other than staying upright. I felt a hand rest on my back and I sat up. A plate overstuffed with an assortment of barbequed meats, veggies, and macaroni and cheese was set in front of me.

"Here," Kelly said, then frowned. "I didn't think to ask if you're vegetarian or something. Are you?"

I shook my head slowly. "Nope. This looks great, thanks," I said, meaning it sincerely. Kelly smiled again.

"Excellent! If you want more, let me know. I'll grab you more water," she said and wandered off. She really was the perfect person to work in customer service. I winced, realizing she was probably unemployed now. As I started to eat, I looked around at the others at the table, who were all trying not to stare at me as they talked to each other. They kept shooting furtive glances my way then looking away suddenly if I caught their eye. If I hadn't been so famished it probably would have made me lose my appetite.

I felt a sudden jolt of recognition as I analyzed the group. They were the same people who had been gathering in the gym right before the (apparently non-earthquake, non-sinkhole) disaster. But unlike me, none of them looked like they'd had to escape a collapsing building. I didn't expect them to be covered in dust or anything considering they had apparently had plenty of time to get cleaned up while I slept, but I didn't see a single cut or bruise among them. Certainly, nothing that suggested anyone other than myself had suffered any actual injuries. They all looked extremely fit for a random group of people, but I guess I should expect that from a group of people who were spending their free time at a private gym function. Now that I thought about it, I hadn't noticed any injuries on Kelly or the man who woke me up, either. And I knew he'd been out in the thick of it because he had run out after me. Yet another thing I didn't have the mental bandwidth for at the moment, though. I concentrated on my food, feeling slightly more awake and aware with each bite.

"I'm glad you're up and able to eat, at least." The man who woke me up sat in a chair next to me. "We were pretty worried about how long it took you to wake up."

"We?" I asked, glancing around the room and then at him. "Who are you, exactly?"

"Oh, right." He ran a hand over his short brown hair like he'd been reminded of something he should have remembered. Then he smiled, a customer-service grin to match

Kelly's, and held out a hand. "I'm Devon. I guess we hadn't actually had time to make introductions yet. Although with how long you've been sleeping on my couch, I feel like you're practically part of the family now." A few people shot shy grins my way and I tried to smile back but it felt like a grimace. Was I coming across as grateful or angry? Some weird combination, probably. This was starting to feel even more awkward.

"Why exactly have I been sleeping on your couch?" I asked.

"We didn't have anyone else to call," he said. "Kelly said you just moved here and didn't have anyone listed we could contact. We could have dropped you off at your apartment, but considering the only person you had to watch over you was a five-year-old and you weren't waking up, we didn't think it was the best option."

Oh. Right. I had just finished telling Kelly why I didn't list any emergency contacts on my membership contract when everything fell apart. Did I still have to pay for a membership to a gym that didn't exist anymore? I immediately felt guilty for thinking of something that seemed so trivial in light of what had happened.

"Why not just drop me at a hospital?" I asked, then winced. "Not that I'm not grateful. I just don't want to be a burden on anyone."

"We didn't want to put you into medical debt. You just moved to a new town to start over," Kelly said. I raised my eyebrows. "No one moves to a new town with no connections at all who is trying to build on their past," she explained. "And we didn't know what they'd do with James and we figured you'd want him nearby."

"We have a physician in the family," Devon added. "If you were in real danger, we would have taken you to a hospital. Honestly." I gulped down the mouthful I was working on and nodded.

"Well, I do appreciate it," I said.

"Plus, the official story is that no one was in the building when it exploded," Kyle cut in, "and we'd have to explain what happened to—hey!" He cut off suddenly with a jump and glared at Devon, who glared right back at him. I recognized his voice as the one that had commented on my appearance earlier and made a mental note that he was probably the one who would accidentally explain things to me if Devon didn't want to.

"Exploded?" I looked around the room at the dozen or so faces that were suddenly looking anywhere except at me. Devon was still glaring at Kyle, who scowled down at his plate.

"When the sinkhole made everything collapse. More of an implosion, really," Devon said, now glancing around at the others, who were grumbling about places they needed to be as they slowly moved toward the door.

"No one says 'explosion' when they mean 'sinkhole,'" I said. Devon turned that searing look on me suddenly, an intensity in his brown eyes that made me want to stop pushing, but I stared him down, refusing to break eye contact. I didn't know what sway he held over the others, but I was not going to be cowed into submission. *Explosion. I almost lost James to a bomb.* I put my fork down, my appetite gone, as the thought swept over me. Kelly hovered, nervous energy radiating off her. "Why would anyone bomb a small shopping center? There weren't even that many businesses in there, certainly nothing high profile," I asked.

"You still hungry?" Kelly asked, leaning over me.

"No," I snapped. She winced and I sighed, guilt washing over me. "Sorry. No, I'm good now," I said more softly.

"Maybe let's head back to the den," she said as she grabbed my plate and took it to the sink. Kyle muttered something under his breath and Devon sighed and squeezed the bridge of his nose like he was trying to hold himself together. Kyle shot him an exasperated look, then took his plate to the sink, dropped it unceremoniously in, and stalked out the back door with what sounded like a growl, the last few people left at the table watching him. As he passed through the door, I caught a glimpse of a small group of children playing in a large yard, James right in the middle of them. I hadn't lost him. He was safe, and I was safe, thanks to Devon and Kelly and whatever this little group was.

I took a deep breath as I stood and started walking back toward the room with the couch, which I assumed was the den Kelly had mentioned. I had only taken a few steps, though, when I started to feel wobbly again. Kelly was suddenly there, looping her arm in mine, looking for all the world like we were just walking along as close friends rather than that she was acting as a crutch to keep me from falling to the floor. While I was still hurting, I didn't get any more searing flashes of pain, and I considered that a good thing. We sat on one side of the L-shaped sectional couch together, and Kelly fussed and situated brightly-colored pillows around me, chatting about things I might be interested in around town—restaurants, the children's museum, parks, tourist attractions—and I let her talk and nodded along. I wasn't sure if she was trying to distract me or trying to get her own nervous energy under control. Either way, I understood she was trying to establish some calm for at least one of us, and I let her do it.

"Sorry about Kyle," Devon said as he followed us a few

minutes later. "He opens his mouth more than he should and says stuff he doesn't mean."

"Like that I look like shit?" I asked, teasing. Devon smiled at that.

"Yes, like that," he said. He leaned his head back and sighed then looked back at me. "He's a good guy and brilliant. He just doesn't have as much of a filter as most people might consider necessary."

"I've had people say that about me before, too," I admitted. With that, the tension in the room seemed to dissolve. Kelly relaxed and leaned back on the couch beside me, and Devon dropped into one of a pair of armchairs facing us.

"Look," he said, "it was a freak accident. A bad one, but an accident. We only wanted to make sure you were ok. Truly."

"And I do appreciate it," I said. I gestured around me. "Do they all live here? This place doesn't seem quite that big."

"Some of them. Kyle, Xavier, Jessica, Hannah, and Trevor live here with me. Jessica is the girl usually running the gym daycare in the evenings, so you've met her. And you met Kyle. Everyone else has their own homes," he said. "It's a sort of halfway house for certain people whose families and friends have turned their backs on them and they need somewhere to go." My eyes widened.

"There's a lot of people here."

"Yes, well, the people who need us find us," Devon said. He was studying me now, and I started to feel a tingle of uneasiness. Kelly was watching me, too, and I realized I was squeezing my hands together tight enough to cut off circulation to my fingers. I forced myself to relax.

"How... fortunate for them," I choked out. His intense stare softened.

"They don't stay permanently, usually. Just long enough to get established. Most of them," he waved his hand toward the kitchen that was now empty, although I could hear discussions and laughter coming from other parts of the house, "have apartments or houses nearby."

"Why were you all meeting at the gym?" I asked. "Why not meet here?"

"Call it a reunion," Kelly said, her eyes sad. "We hadn't seen some of them in years. You know, life happens and one day you realize how long it's been since you've seen someone. We missed having everyone together. We can't fit everyone in the house at one time. Some of them traveled here from pretty far away."

"You were having a reunion and rented a gym?" I asked. These seemed like stupid details for me to get hung up on, but I hoped that something would leak out if I could get them talking.

"We didn't rent it. It's... well, it was my gym," Devon said.

"Oh. Oh, I'm so sorry," I said. He shrugged, trying to seem nonchalant, but his shoulders were tense.

"I have insurance. We'll rebuild," he said. The words were casual, but I could feel a wave of emotion riding behind them, something I didn't quite feel ready to face. Not as I was still reeling over how close I'd come to losing my son. *But I didn't. He's safe. We're safe. We're safe.*

"Look, I know you're probably anxious to get home," Kelly said, her words directed at me, but her gaze directed at Devon. He nodded and she turned to look at me. "But considering what you just went through, maybe you should stay here tonight. To make sure you'll be ok."

"I... I don't... I mean... you don't have to," I stammered. Kelly smiled at me. I didn't know how she turned on what seemed like pure sunshine whenever she wanted to, but it worked.

"It's no trouble. And I did tell you that you'd be watched over if anything happened. I wasn't expecting anything like this, but the sentiment still holds." She put a hand on my shoulder. "One night, ok?"

I nodded. It felt like an imposition, but I really wasn't sure that I should be alone with James if I wasn't even able to stand upright alone for more than a few minutes. "Thank you," I said quietly, and she beamed.

"We have a room upstairs you and James can use," she said. "And we always have extra clothes on hand. I'll get you something that should fit while you can bathe and relax." She stood and pulled me up after her. "You told James a bath and sleep would fix you right up. Let's work on that." I followed her down a hallway, glancing back over my shoulder once, eliciting a twinge in my neck that had me facing forward again. Devon was staring at the floor, leaning over his clasped hands and frowning as if he were trying to piece together a puzzle he couldn't solve.

2

I woke up the next morning with James sprawled across the full-size bed, shoving me to the very edge. He rolled over and I gasped as he kicked me in the side and it felt like I had been stabbed. Maybe Devon was right about the cracked ribs. I was a mess. I rolled out of bed and stumbled to the door, grabbing the new toothbrush and travel-sized toothpaste that Kelly had produced last night after my shower. I softly closed the door behind me and headed to the bathroom down the hall. How long would I still be tasting dust from the building collapse? Maybe it would never go away.

I started to push the bathroom door open, then yelped as it slammed shut again. "Sorry!" I called out through the door, mortified. How many people were living here right now, and I didn't think to knock first? I started turning to head back down the hallway when a man with black hair and eyes almost dark enough to match opened the bathroom door. He was wearing nothing but loose cotton shorts and had a towel draped around his shoulders. The towel caught some of the drops from his wet hair, the rest trailing down his arms, leaving glistening trails on his light brown skin. He stepped into the hallway and held the door open for me, grinning.

"All yours," he said, gesturing toward the bathroom. I blushed and hoped my face wasn't turning too noticeably red.

"Thanks," I mumbled. "Sorry I didn't knock first. I didn't..." I trailed off.

"I should have locked it," he said with a shrug. "It's so late I didn't figure anyone else would still be needing to get in there. You had a big day yesterday, though." He held out a hand toward me. "I'm Xavier."

"Paige," I said, shaking the proffered hand.

"I'll let you get to it. Come down to the kitchen when you're ready. I'll get breakfast set out for you and... Joe?"

"My name is James." I nearly leapt out of my skin at the voice behind me and every bruise felt like it lit up again. I hadn't even heard him come up behind me.

"Well, James," Xavier said, now looking down with a smile, "Get your... mom?" he glanced at me and I nodded. "Get your mom all cleaned up and bring her downstairs for breakfast, ok?"

"Yes, sir!" James gave a little salute. Xavier saluted him back with a grin and headed toward the end of the hall.

"I didn't think I woke you up," I said. "Did you get your toothbrush?" James held up the toothbrush he'd grabbed on his way out the door. "Let's get ready for the day then, shall we?" I said, ushering him into the bathroom. After cleaning up and changing clothes, we found our way back to the kitchen. I held onto the stair rail tightly, worried that I might fall based on how my head was spinning. Kyle and Xavier were sitting at the table, heatedly discussing something that came to a sudden halt when they noticed me. Kyle grabbed his plate, muttered something toward Xavier, and nodded a greeting at me as he dropped his plate in the sink and left the room.

"Well that wasn't awkward," I mumbled. Xavier motioned toward two chairs where plates of eggs and toast were waiting. I sat down and James plopped down beside me, barely hitting the seat before he grabbed a piece of toast and started shoving it into his mouth. "Hey, don't choke," I said, handing him a fork. He nodded and started taking smaller bites.

"Don't mind him," Xavier said, nodding toward the door Kyle had run out of. "He's young."

"Not that young," I said. He hadn't seemed much younger than me.

"Well, he's been here a while, but he still feels like he's relatively new to the family, anyway," Xavier said with a shrug. "We've all accepted him, but he still feels like he needs to prove his place here sometimes. And he can be very protective," Xavier said. The way he looked at me made me suddenly feel self-conscious, as if he were trying to analyze me and figure out what my place here was.

"We don't have a family right now. It's just us," James piped up. "If he can be new when he's a grown-up, maybe we can be new, too." I almost choked.

"James!" I said, trying to shush him, "We don't... invite ourselves into families." It sounded weird even as I said it. Xavier laughed and James shot me a grin. "Finish your breakfast, ok?" I said, nudging his plate closer to him, and he obediently started shoveling eggs into his mouth.

"Weren't you at the gym yesterday?" I asked Xavier. I was pretty sure I remembered seeing him there. His expression darkened, all traces of laughter gone.

"Yes, I was," he said. "Most of our family was there."

"Did... did everyone get out ok?" I asked.

"Yeah, we did. We have contingencies for... well, let's say we're good planners."

"Like scouts!" James said enthusiastically through a mouthful of breakfast.

"Swallow your food before you talk, please," I said, and he bent down toward his plate again and downed the last bite.

"Can I go out back now?" he asked.

"I don't know what's back there," I said.

"It's all fenced in and there's a swing set, toys. He was back there all day yesterday. He'll be fine," Xavier said.

"Pleeeeease?" James asked, giving me pleading puppy eyes.

"Let me look first," I said. James grabbed my hand and yanked me from my seat, but the world swayed when I stood up and I grabbed the table. Xavier was by my side before I even noticed him move.

"If you insist, I'll help you out there. But I promise he'll be safe. We have a camera back there and I can turn the feed on to the TV in the den so you can watch him and relax." He looked genuinely worried and James was bouncing on his toes, his eyes darting from me to the back door.

"Go play..." I started, and he was out the door before I could finish saying "But be careful." I sighed. "A good mom would still go see where her five-year-old is going, right?" I asked.

"You are. Just through the magic of electronics," Xavier said, leading me back to the couch I woke up on... was it yesterday? I felt like days had passed since then. He fiddled with some remotes and the screen lit up with an image of a grassy backyard with a tall privacy fence and enough toys to look like a daycare. Behind the fence, tall trees surrounded the yard, and I wondered how far we were from the city.

"You have lots of kids over often?" I asked.

"Big family," Xavier said with a smile. He checked his watch. "I gotta get going. You ok?" I nodded and leaned back against the couch, watching James run in circles with a toy plane held up over his head.

"Thanks," I said.

"No problem," Xavier said. He tilted his head slightly and seemed to be looking through me for a second. I shivered, remembering a similar look on Devon's face the night before, but the look was gone so quickly that I wondered if I imagined it. He smiled again and waved as he left. "See ya around," he called.

I picked up a fantasy book that had been left on the coffee table and tried to read a bit, but my head started pounding after a couple of sentences, so I set it back down and watched James run and swing and act like a kid who didn't have a care in the world and who certainly had not almost been crushed to death recently. Maybe he had gotten out before realizing the extent of what was happening. We had both passed out so quickly last night that we didn't talk about what was going on. I sighed. I still didn't actually know, though, so I wasn't sure what to tell him.

"Good morning!" Kelly bounded into the room, grinning and holding out a steaming paper cup and a brown paper bag. "I brought you some tea and donuts!" She said, dropping the bag in front of me and holding out the cup.

"Thanks," I said, suddenly more cheerful than I'd been yet today. I took a sip of the tea and felt my body relax as the warmth filled me. "This is perfect." Kelly beamed and plopped down next to me on the couch.

"He's having fun," Kelly said, motioning toward the TV and pulling a donut out of the bag.

"That kid can have fun anywhere," I said, pulling another donut out. "He's the happiest kid I've ever met. Even after all he's been through, he's always cheerful and looking for someone or something to play with." I smiled, watching him, still with the toy airplane, pumping high enough on the swings that the chains slackened at the top of each arc.

"So," Kelly said, and her hesitant tone made me go on alert. I shot my eyes over to her but she looked as composed as ever. "Is there anyone that we can call to let them know what happened and to check in on you?"

I shook my head and she frowned. "No one at all?"

"Nope."

"I mean, I get that you don't have any local contacts, but surely you have family somewhere who you would want to contact in case... well, in case a building falls on you or something," Kelly said. "Siblings? Parents?"

"Only child, and my parents and I haven't talked for... almost six years."

"Six years... oh," Kelly's eyes widened. "James is five?"

"Yep," I said.

"So I take it they weren't happy about you having a baby?" Kelly frowned. "You're, what, twenty-seven? It's not like you were a high schooler or something. What was the problem?"

"How did you know how old I am?" I asked.

"Your gym application. I have a good memory and you wrote down all the important stuff, like your birthday" she said, grinning. "So why was your having a baby as a full-grown adult a problem?"

"They didn't like his dad," I admitted with a shrug. "Like, hated him. Tried really hard to get me to leave him. Said I was moving too fast and was too young to be making decisions that would affect my entire life."

"You were twenty-something. Not fifteen," Kelly said.

"I told them the same thing," I laughed. "But they kept trying to get me to 'see reason' and focus on finishing my degree and getting into grad school and tell him I didn't need to be in a relationship. The day I told them that not only had we moved in together, but I was pregnant... well, it didn't go well. Lots of yelling. Said they were disowning me. I thought they just needed time to cool down and when James was born they'd realize what a good thing this was. But they did cut me off. I sent pictures of him and everything. He was the most adorable baby ever and I got no response." I shrugged and sipped my drink again. "So that was that."

"Well, then where's your husband?" Kelly asked, then backtracked, "I mean, if you don't want to talk about it..."

"No, it's fine," I said. "Not husband. We didn't get a chance to get married. We meant to, but I was trying to finish up undergrad and then we had the baby and things got busy with a newborn and work and grad school applications, and then," I took a deep breath. Years later this still wasn't easy. "He disappeared."

"He left you? After your parents disowned you for him?" For the first time since I met her, Kelly looked angry enough to punch something.

"No. I mean, yes. But no, he didn't leave me, not like that. He didn't pack up and go, there was never a fight or anything. One day he didn't come home from work. I called his office and they hadn't seen him that day. He didn't call in, and that wasn't like him. I called the cops, called all our friends, went driving around to all the places we usually went. He was just… gone." I started to choke up. "I still don't know what happened."

"Shit," Kelly whispered.

"And when I went to my parents' house, desperate to see if he'd told them anything, they basically said 'told you so' and slammed the door in my face. I mean there was no chance but I had to cover all my bases," I sighed. "James was so small he probably doesn't really remember him now other than from pictures."

"I'm so sorry," Kelly said. I took a deep breath.

"It's fine. I'm fine. Well, I mean it's not *fine*. The cops closed the missing person case and told me he'd probably run off with some other woman. Bastards," I grumbled. "But it's been a long time. I tried to believe he was still out there somewhere but James was upset enough that his daddy was gone when it happened, and my obsessing over every detail I could for years wasn't healthy for either of us. Eventually, even I had to admit that if he hadn't come home yet…" I sighed, not finishing the thought, trying not to get sucked into my old fears, all the horrible things I'd imagined had happened to him.

"Anyway, I realized I had to focus on James. I tried to stay in the same town, so that if anything did come up I'd be there, but everything reminded me of him. And our friends started avoiding me or didn't know how to act around me. Most of them were single or in new, happy relationships and didn't know how to deal with having a newly single mom friend, much less someone whose partner was missing. They all just sort of dropped off. And it became too much living completely alone where everything reminded me of him and what things should have been like, and it was getting harder to believe he was still…" I swallowed, choking on the last word. "Alive. So we left." I waved a hand around me. "And now here we are."

"How long has he been missing?" Kelly asked.

"About four years," I said, sipping on my tea again.

"That's..." Kelly frowned, then shook her head and seemed to shake some thought loose, "That's not how people normally wind up here but it's a heck of a story," she said.

"How do people normally wind up here?" I asked.

"I mean your parents turning their backs on you is pretty par for the course, but your partner disappearing isn't typical. And having a shopping center dropped on you certainly isn't." She grinned at me and it felt both like she was trying to lighten the mood and like she was trying to steer the conversation away. I didn't have the energy to try to figure out what she was avoiding, so I asked the first thing I thought of.

"How's Devon?"

"How's Devon?" Kelly repeated, her eyebrows going to her hairline.

"I mean, he just lost his place of business and his income... Oh." I looked at her closely, "And you did, too."

Kelly waved a hand dismissively. "Like he said, we have insurance. And we have enough of a backup that we're good for a while until the insurance comes through. We're fiscally responsible business owners around here. Plus our family takes care of each other. We're good." I looked at her skeptically, not able to imagine being so casual about what seemed like such a huge loss. "Seriously," she said. "We're fine. I'm more worried about you since you were the only one who couldn't... who got seriously injured."

"Which wouldn't have happened if she'd listened to me

in the first place," Devon said, wandering into the room and sinking into a chair.

"I couldn't..." I started, but Devon waved a hand to cut me off.

"I don't blame you," he said. "I would do anything to protect my family, too. But sometimes you have to trust people around you to help you, especially in a crisis." The intensity of the gaze he directed my way as he finished the thought was unsettling. How much of the previous conversation had he heard? "And I'm fine, by the way," He added with a wink and I flushed. He'd heard at least the end.

"So what now?" I asked.

"How are you feeling?" he asked.

"Sore, but mostly ok, I think," I said. Kelly snorted.

"She'd be ok if she had someone to go stay with her for a couple of days, but she doesn't," Kelly said. I glared at her and she shrugged. "As soon as you try to stand up, he'll know it, too."

"We're not going to kick you out, you know. We don't do that," Devon said. "You can stay as long as you need."

"I do appreciate it," I said. "But I don't want you to have to worry about me. You don't even know me."

"We don't need to know anything except that you need help. That's what we do," Kelly said, putting a hand on my arm. I almost teared up at that. How long had it been since I had an actual support system? Friends who didn't look uncomfortable when they mentioned their partners in front of me, or who didn't look at me like I might implode at any second? People who asked how I was and actually expected to hear more than *I'm fine*?

"I should get home, but maybe you could come over for lunch for a few days?" I said to Kelly. She grinned.

"I think you should stick around here a little longer, but I'll take that compromise," she said.

"Oh, crap," I said, wincing. Kelly and Devon both looked like they were ready to catch me if I fell over. "Nothing physical. I'm fine," I said, and they both relaxed. "I can't get into our apartment. My key was in my gym bag and I have no idea what happened to it. And the complex office is closed on the weekend so I don't know who to contact to get the door open. The emergency number is in my kitchen." It occurred to me that it was probably an important number to program into my phone once I got back into my apartment. I could call a locksmith, I supposed.

"I can help with that," Devon said. He left the room for a moment and came back holding a very crushed and dirty gym bag. I blanched. When had I dropped it... and how long had it been between when I dropped it and when it looked like the roof had caved in on it? I felt like I could feel the ground shaking again, taste the dust in the air. Kelly's hand landed on my arm again, grounding me enough to pull me from the memory.

"You good?" she asked.

"Yeah..." I shook my head to try to dispel the images. *We got out. We're safe.* "Just hit me again what actually happened."

"You're safe," Kelly said, her hand tightening comfortingly. Considering what she'd told me about this place, how often did she have to say those words? I put my hand over hers and squeezed.

"I know," I said. She smiled at me and turned to Devon.

"Anything in there salvageable?" She asked.

"Doesn't look promising, but I haven't looked inside yet," he said. He held it out to me. My hands shook as I took it and set it on the coffee table. *Safe. We're safe. James is safe.* I pulled out my cell phone and wallet, both of which looked like they'd been crushed by bricks. That didn't make much of a difference to my wallet, but the phone had clearly seen its last day of life. I sighed. One more thing to deal with. But my apartment key was still tucked inside the wallet.

"When did you get this?" I asked.

"I've been back a few times since the incident," Devon said, and Kelly rolled her eyes.

"*The incident.* Sounds like insurance-speak," she cut in. Devon just glared at her and continued.

"And I found it this morning," he finished.

"Thank you," I said. He was going into his own ruined business and managed to grab my one bag from who knows where.

"No problem," he said. He stood up. "Again, you're welcome to stay, but if you want to go home, Kelly or Xavier can drive you."

"So um, did the parking lot wind up ok?" I asked.

Devon winced and I figured out I was out of a vehicle before he spoke. "Parts of the building fell onto the cars out front. It was mostly cars from people who were with us. I guess one of the unaccounted-for vehicles was yours."

"At least I have insurance," I said with a sigh.

"If it doesn't cover it, let us know," said Devon.

"I appreciate the hospitality, but I'm not going to let you pay for my car," I protested.

"We'll figure it all out starting tomorrow," Kelly said, cutting off whatever Devon had been going to say. She shot him a look and he closed his mouth and sighed.

"Good idea," he said, smacking his knees and standing up. "Stay as long as you like, but if you'd like a ride home, we can do that, too."

"Thanks," I said again. I didn't feel like I could thank

them enough at this point. Devon nodded and left. Kelly dropped my ruined gym bag onto the floor and propped her feet up on the table, settling back onto the couch.

"So what's the plan?" she asked.

"I honestly don't know," I said, leaning back next to her.

"Stay for dinner, and then I'll take the two of you home and make sure you get settled in," Kelly said.

"Sounds like a good plan," I said, closing my eyes.

WHEN I OPENED my eyes again, Kelly was gone and the sunlight was coming through the windows at a different angle. The TV was still on, and I could see that there were a few more kids playing with James in the backyard. In the corner of the screen, I recognized Jessica's head of thick brown curls next to another teenage girl with bright blue and purple shoulder-length hair. They laughed together, occasionally calling out to the group of children. My neck was stiff and I groaned as I sat up. I hadn't meant to fall asleep again. My head at least felt a little clearer, even if I did still feel like I had been hit by a car. Maybe I really did just need more sleep.

"Oh good, you're up. I was wondering if you'd sleep right through dinner." I jumped and felt my body tense in a fight-or-flight response. Xavier laughed from the armchair. "It's ok, just me," he said. "I fed you breakfast, remember? Although apparently you're a hobbit since Kelly brought you second breakfast." I laughed, relaxing.

"Hi," I said, stretching. He watched my face as I winced with the movement but didn't comment on my reactions.

"Hi," he replied. "Scintillating conversation."

"I just woke up. Give me time," I said, leaning forward. "Has James been out there all day?"

"Yeah. Kid's a ball of pure energy. He's actually keeping up with our little pack of mutts. I'm impressed."

"He's always been like that," I said. "Constant, non-stop movement. He's like a perpetual motion machine."

"Sounds exhausting."

"He is, but the good kind of exhausting."

"Everyone else already had lunch. You hungry?"

"A little," I admitted. "How long was I out?"

"It's four in the afternoon," he said. My eyes widened. "You're still in recovery mode. You needed it," he added gently. "Come on. Let's get you a snack."

This time I managed to stand up without wobbling at all, although Xavier looked ready to jump over to catch me if he needed to. Everyone in this house treated me like I was going to fall over. Then again, I couldn't blame them since even I wasn't completely sure that I wouldn't. He followed me into the kitchen and I stood awkwardly for a moment in the middle of the room. I felt weird having others make food for me and watch my son, like I was taking advantage of them. On the other hand, I was a guest here and didn't feel comfortable raiding their fridge either, even if my stomach had finally gotten the memo that we'd slept the day away and was now grumbling uncomfortably.

A boy who looked about ten years old was standing in front of the open fridge, taking his time browsing the contents. From the back, I noticed he had the same thick brown curly hair as Jessica's. "Trevor," Xavier said. The boy didn't respond. Xavier walked up behind him and flicked Trevor on the shoulder. Trevor jumped and took an earbud out of his ear as he turned to see Xavier behind him. "Get what you need and close the door," Xavier grumbled at him. Trevor rolled his eyes, grabbed a can of Mountain Dew, shut the refrigerator, and wandered out the back door. "Eventually the cute five-year-old turns into that," Xavier said, pointing a thumb toward the slamming door. "You'd think he's already a teenager from the attitude."

"I'm not even emotionally prepared for James to start kindergarten," I said, laughing. Xavier opened the fridge again and pulled out sandwich ingredients.

"Ham and cheese sound good?" He asked.

"Sounds great... but I can do it," I said, shifting on my feet uncomfortably.

"Give it another day and you'll be foraging through here like anyone else. For now, sit down and enjoy your last day of being considered a guest," he said, pulling a paper plate out from under a cabinet.

"She finally leaving?" Kyle asked. I turned to see him sitting at the table, leaning back in a chair and watching me, a pile of papers spread out before him.

"Be polite," Xavier said, pointing a mayonnaise-covered knife at Kyle.

"I'm always polite," Kyle said, attempting a look of wide-eyed innocence. Xavier snorted and went back to putting together an absolutely huge multi-layered sandwich.

"I'm going home tonight," I told Kyle, sitting across from him. "Kelly is taking me home after dinner."

"Probably a good plan," Kyle said, narrowing his eyes at me.

"Polite," Xavier said without turning around. Kyle shrugged and went back to sorting through his stack of papers. From where I was sitting it looked like a mix of spreadsheets and printed web pages, but I didn't feel like striking up another conversation with him. Xavier brought over my sandwich and a cold can of Sprite then sat down next to Kyle with two Cokes, handing one to Kyle in what seemed to be an offering of peace. Kyle nodded to Xavier and took the can, clinking cheers with him before popping it open and taking a big sip.

For a few moments there was a comfortable silence as I ate and Kyle and Xavier looked over the paperwork that it turned out was related to their insurance. The sound of kids and teens laughing drifted in from the backyard, and despite the situation that had landed us here, and despite Kyle's unexplained dislike of me, I felt peaceful for the first time in years. It was almost enough to make me feel like maybe things would be ok.

3

James lay limp, breathing deep in Kelly's arms as I wiggled the key in my lock and shoved the door open. Dinner had been a large and cheerful affair. Some of the people from the gym had shown up again, along with a couple of new faces, and people had grabbed food buffet-style from the kitchen and settled to eat in the kitchen, backyard, and den. It turned out that the only reason some people had been standing to eat in the kitchen that first night was because I had been taking up the den, and I felt guilty about that until Kelly pointed out that since I'd been unconscious, I hadn't exactly been the one to make that decision.

James had played himself silly, then stuffed himself with spaghetti before falling asleep draped unceremoniously across Jessica's lap. He'd attached himself to her, showing her toys and rocks all day, and then sticking close to her side during the meal. For her part, she seemed to be enjoying him.

The red-headed woman who had been sitting next to Kyle at dinner the first night turned out to be the family doctor ("Just call me Maria. No formalities when we're at the house," she had said when I asked her last name). She took me up to the guest bedroom I'd slept in, checked me all over, and declared that I was ok to return home as long as someone checked in on me daily, and I took it easy for a while to let the concussion heal. Kelly assured her that was already the plan, and Maria gave me her number and said to text if I wasn't feeling better soon or just wanted to check in. I'd forgotten to mention that my phone had been smashed into a paperweight but took the business card she gave me and put it in my pocket.

"Where should I put this one?" Kelly asked, nodding down toward James.

"His room is through there," I said, waving toward the bedroom near the back of the apartment. She disappeared for a moment, then came back out, closing the door gently behind her. I unloaded the bags of leftovers I'd been sent home with and started stacking containers in the refrigerator. Kelly sat down on the inflatable camping couch I had set up in the living room and looked around at the boxes still stacked against the walls and the two upside-down boxes that I was using as temporary tables.

"How long have you been here again?"

"I know," I said, sitting next to her and handing her a glass of water. "I've been trying to find work and make sure James is comfortable and getting settled in. And... there's a lot of memories in some of those boxes that I honestly don't want to deal with just yet."

Kelly nodded. "I understand that part," she said.

"Plus I need bookcases. That whole stack is boxes of books, and the cases at my old place were built into the wall so I couldn't bring them." I pointed toward the two stacks of boxes in the corner that nearly reached the ceiling.

"Well that's easily remedied," Kelly said. "I'll have some of the guys bring some over tomorrow."

"You don't have to do that," I said. "You've all done so much for me already."

"We don't have to but I want to," Kelly said. "Most of us know what it's like to start over after running from your past. You know at this point that our family is basically a big group of runaways. We hold each other up," she said.

She looked around the apartment. "And while Devon and Kyle figure out the next steps for the gym, I don't have anything to do, so I need a project. And you aren't supposed to do anything for the next week." I realized that the look in her eyes wasn't so much judging as planning. It looked like I'd gained an interior decorator.

"I have questions," I blurted out. Kelly's expression changed quickly from assessing to wary as she turned to look at me.

"I bet you do," she said with a sigh. "Look, Devon's not here to fuss at me so I'll try to answer what I can but I think you've figured out by now there's some stuff that I can't talk about just yet."

"That doesn't make sense."

"It doesn't now. Eventually, it will."

"Well, what can you tell me?" I asked, exasperated.

"What do you want to know?"

"Why did Kyle say there was an explosion and Devon is determined to insist it's not?"

Kelly winced. "That's a tough one," she said.

"I'm decently smart. I don't think it will totally stump me," I said. She nodded slowly.

"We don't know exactly what happened yet, but we're fairly certain at this point we were targeted and bombed," Kelly said. "But we don't want to bring attention to ourselves. Most of our family came here to rebuild and restart. Some of them have run away from some pretty bad situations. The last thing any of us want is to be on the news."

"But surely there's an obvious difference between a bombing and a sinkhole?" I said. "I mean, this is my first time dealing with either of them but a lot of stuff went upwards and I'm pretty sure sinkholes go downwards."

"We have contacts who deal with public information. I'm not sure exactly how they'll spin it, but when Devon wants something to seem one way to the outside world, he finds ways to make it happen."

"But I was there, so why is he insisting I be told it's a sinkhole?"

"Yeah, I don't agree with that part," Kelly sighed. "But we don't really know you yet. You said that yourself. He gets protective. Honestly, he'll probably soften up soon and quit trying to spin it for you but in the immediate aftermath, he's trying to protect all of us. Especially since we don't know for sure who did it or why."

"He thinks I had something to do with it?"

"Definitely not!" Kelly said. "It would have been pretty stupid of you to put your own kid at risk if you knew what was going to happen and the way you reacted when things started falling apart... No, you're not a suspect. But you're also not one of us, so you're in this weird in-between place right now."

"Why does Devon get to make all the decisions? Why is he in charge?" I narrowed my eyes. "Kelly," I asked softly. "Are you in a cult?" Her eyes widened and she stared at me a moment, then burst out laughing.

"Oh, man, no! I can see how it looks that way, but no," she choked a bit as she tried to quiet herself, glancing toward James's bedroom. "No," she said, breathing normally again. "I promise. We're a safe house, not a cult. And Devon doesn't make all the decisions alone. He does sometimes steamroll people, I admit. But he, Xavier, Kyle, and I generally work together. We've been together a long time, and we all trust each other to do the things that we're good at. And Devon is really, really good at seeing the big picture. We trust him for that and this is one of those moments where a lot of decisions may have long-term consequences."

"What's your role?" I asked.

"Call it customer service and HR," she said. "Now," she said, getting up and taking my water glass from me. "It's your bedtime." As she pulled me to my feet, I realized I was so tired my body didn't want to get up from the couch. But I let her lead me into my bedroom where she stopped in the doorway and stared for a moment. I had a mattress on the floor, and in lieu of a dresser I had put some boxes sideways and stacked them to make temporary shelves for my clothes.

"Do you actually have furniture?" she asked.

"It's in storage," I said. "When we moved I didn't have a place so it all went into storage while we were in a hotel for a bit. I haven't gotten around to hiring someone to help move it here yet."

"We'll have to fix that," she said.

"You don't have to..." I started before she waved a hand to shush me.

"We've been through this. I'm going to be bored and you need help. We're a perfect match." I collapsed on the mattress, too tired to dig out pajamas. She grabbed the blankets that I had left crumpled at the bottom of the bed (how many days ago?), pulled them up over me, and patted my head as if I were a child.

"I'll leave some breakfast out for James for the morning so you can rest. I'll see you tomorrow."

"See you tomorrow," I mumbled through a yawn. I fell asleep before I even heard the click of the front door.

I WOKE up the next day with James snuggled against me, strawberry Pop-tart crumbs covering his mouth, and a Lego car he had built clutched in his hands. I heard a knock on the apartment's front door and then the door opened. Before I could react, Kelly called, "Just me!" I relaxed back into the pillows and James nuzzled into my side. "Afternoon," Kelly said, coming into the bedroom and sitting on the bed gently so that she didn't wake up James.

"Seriously?" I asked.

"Well, almost. It's nearly noon. Here, brought you something." She handed me a new phone.

"This is... these models cost a thousand dollars! I can't take this," I said, trying to hand it back to her.

"Xavier just got a new phone. This is his old one," she said.

"This thing is brand new!"

"It's last year's model. He takes good care of his tech. They came out with a new model and he's had this lying around for a month now. He'll never remember to resell it anyway. I already put your SIM card in there so it works, but we couldn't transfer any of the data. Your phone was pretty smashed up."

"I've got everything backed up online," I said faintly.

"Perfect!" She grinned. "Now, you stay in here and relax and ignore the sounds out there."

"What sounds..." Just as I started asking, I heard a man's voice cursing and a loud thud.

Kelly got up and poked her head out of the bedroom door. "Hey, language! There's a little kid in here!"

"Sorry," the man grumbled. "This thing is heavy!"

"Just... umm... deflate the couch and move those boxes over there, then we'll set up the bookcases over there. Those should be the easiest boxes to unload and then they'll be out of the way," she said, pointing to various points around the room.

"What are you doing?" I asked, sitting up slowly and trying to peer around her.

"I may have rummaged around in your kitchen last night and gotten your storage unit information and key. We'll have you set up in no time," she said.

"That's... you don't..." I stammered.

"Don't start," she said, narrowing her eyes at me. "I'm not going to let you live with a cardboard dresser and no kitchen table when you have perfectly good stuff available and the only thing stopping you is not having enough hands to move it."

"Thank you," I said quietly. Kelly smiled again.

"You're welcome." From the living room, the man started to curse again, then stopped halfway through and just grunted.

"Are *all* these boxes full of books?"

"Yep!" Kelly called cheerfully. I heard a familiar laugh.

"Is that Xavier?" I asked.

"Xavier, plus Ben and Greg. I don't think you've met them yet. And Jessica came along in case you want to get James out of the house for a bit since you're supposed to be laying low and little kids aren't exactly relaxing."

"Jessica's here?" James's sleepy voice sounded from behind me and he sat up, rubbing his eyes. "I ate breakfast and played and took a nap so you can get better," he said, looking at me proudly. I squeezed him and kissed the top of his head.

"You did perfect, baby," I said

"Can I go play with Jessica now?" he asked, wiggling out of my arms.

"Put on some daytime clothes first," I told him. I sniffed his face and added, "And brush your teeth."

"Ok!" he jumped out of bed.

"Wait, don't get in anyone's way!" I called, imagining him tripping up someone trying to lug an entire bookcase into the room.

"I'm careful!" he called back across his shoulder as he darted out of the room.

"Hey there, James!" Xavier called.

"Where's Jessica?"

"She'll be right back. She went to get some coffee."

"Ok, I'll be ready! I bet she gets me a big one."

"You're not getting any coffee."

"I might!" Then James slammed his bedroom door shut, presumably to get dressed.

"Last thing that kid needs is coffee," I grumbled. Kelly laughed and stood up.

"I'll let you get dressed, too," she said. "We'll get the living room furniture put up first and then you can move out there while we do the bedroom." She bounced out the door, calling out instructions. I sat in bed for a moment trying to process what was happening. Only a few days ago I didn't know a single person in this city, and now I had people bringing me coffee, babysitting, and moving my furniture. And somehow, they already felt like friends.

I pushed out of bed, grabbed some purple leggings and a green t-shirt, and headed into the bathroom. After a quick shower and back into my own clothes again, I was feeling better than I had since I'd gone to the gym. My head was pounding, so I took some ibuprofen before poking my head out of the bedroom door.

Through James's open door, I heard him proudly giving a tour of his prized rock collection and Jessica's voice encouraging him. I could imagine the preening look on his face as she complimented his favorite specimens. Kelly saw me and came over with a steaming cup.

"Decaf," she said, handing me the cup. "Maria said no caffeine for now because of the concussion."

"I remember," I said, taking a sip. "This is still great." Kelly shoved a paper bag into my hand and shooed me back into the bedroom.

"Here's some brunch. You stay in there. There's nowhere to sit out here right now." I looked around and saw that she was right. An armchair and two dining chairs had been brought in, but they were covered in boxes, as was my real couch that had now replaced the blow-up one. I sat on the end of my bed, munched on the egg and bacon bagel sandwich I'd pulled from the bag, and watched through the open door as Kelly directed Xavier and two other men to move furniture around the room, eyeing placement, then redirecting them.

As she called out directions, I realized Greg was the blonde man I'd almost run into when I'd left the gym before everything went crazy. He was built like a bodybuilder but was one of the softest-spoken men I'd ever met.

Ben was smaller, with dark tan skin, black hair in a bowl cut, and eyes that lit up with laughter as he came up with colorful and exceedingly ridiculous alternatives to cuss words as he moved my furniture around. I had a feeling he only seemed small next to Greg and Xavier because he was much stronger than I would have expected from looking at him.

Occasionally James poked his head out of his door and gave them advice or encouragement then disappeared again. In less time than I would have expected, the living room looked like an actual living room instead of a storage area. Once enough boxes of books had been unloaded onto shelves, Kelly herded me to the non-inflatable couch.

"If you get tired or your head starts hurting, right back to bed," she said firmly. I nodded obediently and she started directing more books to be unpacked and pulled Jessica and James from the bedroom to start unpacking in the kitchen. Jessica let James show her where he thought things like silverware and dishes should go. Watching them work together, I began to tear up.

"Hey, you ok?" Kelly asked, noticing my expression. "Need to go lie down?"

"No, I'm fine," I said, wiping my eyes. Kelly looked unconvinced, and I noticed Xavier glance over from where he was working on attaching my TV to the wall. "I'm good," I insisted again. "It's just... we haven't really had anyone else around much for a long while now. It's... it's a little over-whelming." Kelly's expression shifted from concerned to understanding.

"Ah," she breathed. "And you said this is the first time you've moved since..." she trailed off and I nodded. From the kitchen, I heard James's small intake of breath and knew he was listening. Kelly seemed to sense it, too, because she whirled back into motion, mouthing "We'll talk later" as she started calling out directions again. I caught James's eye and blew him a kiss and he smiled and turned to help Jessica unload pots and pans into a cabinet near the stove.

Before long, I did go lie back in bed, sensing that I

needed less visual stimulation. I napped, and James woke me up by bursting into my room declaring that he and Jessica had gone to pick up lunch and he had gotten to choose what kind of sandwiches to order all on his own. I smiled and followed him back out into the living room and stopped in the doorway.

There was still a small stack of boxes in one corner of the room, but otherwise, we'd been completely moved in. The bookshelves were filled with books, my desk had been set up by a window, and my curtains had been hung. The men were sitting on the couch and armchair eating sub sandwiches, drinks sitting on coasters on my actual coffee table instead of a cardboard box.

Kelly stood in the kitchen texting and muttering to herself and waved toward the dining table, where subs and glasses of water were set out in front of two of the chairs. James jumped into one of the chairs and pointed at the other place setting. "I got your seat ready, Mommy!" he declared. I sat and held my drink up to him.

"Cheers to you for working so hard today!" I said. He beamed and clinked glasses with me before taking a big bite of his chicken tenders sub. We sat and ate, making small talk, and for the second time in as many days, I felt a sense of peace that I hadn't felt since James and I had found ourselves on our own years ago.

"All that's left is your bedroom," Kelly declared after lunch had been cleared away. "James's room was already pretty well set up."

"Yeah, that was the first thing I did," I said. "I wanted to make sure he felt at home here."

"We did it together, right, Mommy?" James said, grinning. He turned to Xavier. "I told her where to put everything like Kelly did to you."

"Very impressive management skills," Xavier said, giving him an approving nod.

My phone dinged and I looked down to a text message from a new number:

> This is Jessica. Ok if I take him to a movie? Didn't want to say it out loud yet until you said yes.

I looked up at her and nodded.

"Hey, James. Want to go to a movie?" Jessica asked. James leapt to his feet.

"Yes! Mommy, can I?" I nodded and he ran to grab Jessica's hand and drag her toward the door.

"Here," I said, grabbing a couple of twenties from my wallet and handing them to Jessica. "Thanks for keeping him occupied today."

"No problem. He's a good kid," Jessica said, letting him pull her out the door. "I'll share my location with you so you can check in on us." A minute after the door closed, I heard another ding and looked down to see a notification that a friend had started location tracking. I watched the icon move out of the parking lot, then added Jessica's name as a new contact and put the phone in my pocket.

I looked up and noticed that Kelly had moved into my room and flipped one of my shelf boxes right side up and was shoving all my clothes into it. Xavier moved to help her but she pointed a finger at him.

"You stay there," she said. "You guys can come in once all her private stuff is packed up." Xavier didn't say anything, but he put his hands up and backed up, then sat back down to chat with the other two. I moved toward the bedroom and she repeated the point. "You stay put, too. This will only take a minute. You're resting." I sat back down at the table and took a sip of my water. I was starting to get antsy. I wanted to do something, anything, although I could feel my body protest at the thought.

"You look like you're going to burst right out of your skin," Xavier commented. Ben chuckled, but Xavier shot him a look and he quieted down. I wasn't sure what was so funny about the comment because that's exactly what I felt like.

"I'm not used to other people doing things for me," I admitted.

"It can take some getting used to, but it's worth it in the end when you find your pack," Greg said. Ben sucked in a breath and Xavier gave Greg a look I couldn't identify.

"Yeah, it is worth it," Xavier said. Ben relaxed again and Xavier looked back at me. "You just have to make the decision. Where do you want to belong?" My mouth went dry. Where did I belong? What did I really know about these people? It seemed like each moment brought some new mystery, and I didn't like being kept out of a loop that I wasn't even sure existed.

I was starting to feel paranoid. Then again, no one had taken care of me like this in years. The friends I had thought were steady back in California had all drifted off when things got stressful. This group had taken me in during a crisis and was making sure James and I had a full support system. I'd moved here for a new start. Crisis notwithstanding, maybe this was it. Kelly certainly felt like the closest thing I'd had to a friend in a long time.

"I... I don't know," I whispered. Xavier smiled at me.

"Give it time. You'll figure it out."

. . .

OVER THE NEXT couple of weeks, Kelly, Xavier, and Jessica made routine stops at my apartment. Jessica would bring over kids she was watching to play with James in his room, the sounds of children's laughter making me smile while Jessica and I talked about her college plans and how she wanted to be an elementary school teacher. I learned she'd been taking care of her brother, Trevor, since they'd run away from home when she was ten and he was three. Thinking about what might prompt a ten-year-old to legitimately run from home with her little brother in tow made my heart break for her. When I asked about how she found her way here, her face darkened and she changed the subject, and I knew better than to push her.

On other days she would take James on outings to local parks or to the house, where he played in the huge backyard with the pack of children who seemed to descend on the place every evening when their parents came to have dinner. I noticed more of the kids seemed to be fond of animal-feet shoes so I ordered a pair of bear-foot slippers online for James. When they came in, he said thank you but had an odd look on his face as he looked at them in the box. The next day when Jessica came to take him to the house, he showed her his new shoes. She complimented him, then gave me a look that seemed to be a mixture of confusion and amusement before herding him out the door.

Kelly or Xavier came by for lunch most days, and we'd spend the afternoon chatting about my plans for the near future. I'd need to register James for school soon, so I asked about local schools. We talked about local jobs I might be able to apply for soon, something that I was waiting for Maria's blessing to get started on after the concussion. I had enough saved up to last a couple of months, but I didn't like just eating into my savings if I didn't have to. Kelly asked if I still wanted to go to grad school, but it wasn't something I was prepared to discuss, much less take action on at the moment.

Most days I'd ride home with Kelly or Xavier to eat dinner in the comfortably crowded and cheerful kitchen. Devon generally kept his distance but seemed to be watching me. Any time I approached him he was polite but aloof. He did tell me that they'd filed insurance that should cover replacing my car and I could start shopping soon, so that was good news. Kyle didn't hide his continued dislike of me. He scowled at me any time we were in the room together and I learned to ignore him. Xavier said that once Kyle accepted someone into his circle he was much more pleasant to be around, but I figured I'd need to trust him on that one because Kyle showed no sign of warming up to me.

Somehow, despite the move, James's still-missing father, and the fact that I'd almost been blown up, life started to feel normal again, like we'd finally landed somewhere we could build a home and a life. Finally, after years of feeling lost, alone, and scared, I was starting to feel hopeful when I thought about the future.

4

A week later, I was driving to the house in my new-to-me car. Somehow, I'd gotten far more for the car that had been buried by a wall than I'd ever expected. Kelly said that Kyle was the financial brains of their group and that he had negotiated with the insurance company to get me a good payout. I doubted Kyle's willingness to go to bat for me but had to admit that if anyone was stubborn enough to fight with an insurance company, it was probably him.

I drove up the long driveway to the house, thinking about how I'd never realized that such rural areas surrounded Orlando before I'd moved here. I'd thought it was city and tourist stuff right up to the beach, but it wasn't a very long drive to areas like this where people still lived on acreages that were somehow still a fairly quick drive to downtown. Jessica had come to get James earlier that day, and I'd gotten bored so decided to come hang out with the others earlier than I'd planned. I came in the front door and almost called out, but froze at the raised voices coming from the kitchen.

"Look, I know you all like her. I get that. She's a good person. I like her also, really. But she's not one of us!" Kyle said. I closed the door as quietly as I could and tiptoed to the side of the room so I wouldn't be seen through the kitchen doorway.

"She needed help. That's what we do. When they come to us for help, we help," Kelly said, her voice icier than I'd ever heard it.

"But just our kind! We can't afford to take in every human who has a sob story. We've met plenty over the years, and we've never taken them in until her."

"She was bombed with us, for god's sake!"

"That wasn't our fault!"

"We've never turned someone away because of their blood before and we won't start now," Devon's voice cut in.

"We've never needed to because we've never opened our door to one of them before. We've never made ourselves vulnerable like this," Kyle growled.

"What exactly do you imagine she's exposing us to?" Kelly asked.

"I don't know," Kyle admitted. "I just know that since she showed up, things have gotten dangerous. We can't risk the entire pack for her sake."

"Then why did Greg see her?" Kelly asked. "Greg clearly saw her. When she showed up at the gym, he confirmed it was her. If she's not one of us, then why were we led to her? Maybe she doesn't trust us enough yet."

"If she could shift we'd know it by now," Devon cut in. "No one's ever hidden it this long before. I think Kyle is right about that, at least."

What the hell? I thought. They were clearly talking about me, and the argument had made a modicum of sense until now—Kyle had made his dislike of me clear from day one—

but things were taking a turn that was making me want to run.

I heard the back door open and close and a chair scrape on the floor.

"Do you need something?" Devon asked. "We're kind of in the middle of something."

"Yeah, I know. I can hear you out back. She's not a shifter," Jessica's voice said. "James is."

I felt the blood drain from my face.

"That's who Greg saw," Jessica continued. "He saw Paige too because she was always with him. But she wasn't who he was really seeing. It was James this whole time. You all seriously didn't know?"

"Then she's one of us, at least by association," Kelly said. "We can't exactly take him in and kick her out."

"Yeah, I'm pretty sure that would be called kidnapping," Jessica snorted.

I had to get out of here. I had to get James out of here. I'd thought we'd found a safe place, but they'd been targeting us. Whatever they wanted him for, whatever they thought he was, they couldn't have him. He was mine, and I was not giving up anyone else I loved. I backed up slowly, keeping an eye on the kitchen door.

"Going somewhere?" a voice asked behind me. I spun around to see Xavier looking at me with a mix of assessment and sympathy. "I think we owe you an explanation," he said gently.

I SAT on one end of the couch with my hands clasped in my lap, trying to calm my breathing and flicking my eyes between each of the others. Jessica had gone back to the backyard with the kids at a pointed look from Devon when they'd all filed into the den after I'd been outed by Xavier. Kyle sat in one of the armchairs and Kelly and Xavier sat on the other end of the couch, both of them looking at me like they expected me to bolt and wanted to keep me calm enough to stay put. Devon stood directly between me and the front door, his arms folded across his chest. He wasn't even going to pretend that I was here of my own free will. He had no intention of letting me leave.

"How much did you hear?" Devon asked.

"Kyle still doesn't want me here. You thought I was… something. I can't remember. I'm not what you thought. But you think James is, and you want him." My breath caught in my throat and my heart started pounding so hard I thought it might burst from my chest, but I put every ounce of motherly defensiveness I had in the next words. "But you are not taking my son."

Kelly made a distressed noise. "Paige, we have no intention of stealing James away from you. We would never dream of doing that to either of you." She started to reach across to grab my hand, but looked at my face and hesitated, then sat back again.

"The things we told you before were true," Xavier said. "We're a safe house for people like James. You've seen yourself that it's not always safe for us in the world. Most people don't have their places of business bombed or have… well there have been other incidents recently. There's a lot of fear directed at us, and we tend to gather together both for comfort and safety. Usually, with a pack as big as ours no one messes with us."

"But there's been a huge increase in attacks in the last five years or so, and they've picked up more in the last few weeks," Devon took up the story. "We don't know why, but it's not only here. It's all over. Running somewhere else won't make it stop."

"I have no idea what you're talking about," I said, looking between them all. "James is just a regular kid. I don't know what you mean by 'people like you' but he's five. He hasn't had time to make any connections, join any networks or religions, or anything like that."

"It's not something he's done. It's just who he is. How he was born," Kelly said.

"I'm his mom. I have a pretty good idea of his pedigree," I snapped.

"Do you?" Kyle was leaning forward now, his grey eyes intense on me. "What do you know about his father?"

"We were together for two years. We had a child together, started building a life together. I knew him pretty well, thank you. It wasn't a one-night stand or something," I snapped.

"I wasn't suggesting it was," Kyle said. His tone was softer now, probably the nicest he'd ever spoken to me, and it threw me off guard. "But even if you'd been together for a while, how well did you know his family? His past?"

"I..." I paused, the first bloom of doubt taking root. "I never met his family. He was an only child, like me, and he said when he moved out, he left on really bad terms, so they weren't talking. They hadn't made up yet when we met and considering my own parents' behavior, it seemed plausible."

"Did you ever meet them?"

"No." My mouth was starting to feel dry and my heart was racing. Xavier got up and went to the kitchen, and I heard the refrigerator open.

"Did you ever do any genetic testing when you were pregnant with James? Anything pop up that seemed off?" Kyle pressed.

"No. We did the usual blood tests. Checking iron levels, glucose monitoring, all that. I didn't think to ask... I just did what they suggested. I didn't know anything about having a baby. And there wasn't any question of paternity. We knew it was ours." I felt a hand on my shoulder and looked up to see Xavier standing next to me holding out a cold can of Sprite. I took it, my hands shaking, and he sat down next to me.

"What exactly are you suggesting? Is something wrong with him?" I asked. My voice was no longer fierce, but sounded terrified. I tried to take a drink but nearly choked and set the can down on the coffee table instead.

"Nothing's wrong with him," Devon said fiercely.

"Well, that we know of," Kyle cut in.

"Not helpful," Kelly hissed at him, and he held up his hands in a surrendering motion.

"I'm just saying what we're talking about right now... there's nothing wrong about it. But it may be a bit of a shock to hear about," Devon said.

"This doesn't mean he's in danger or that he's not still himself," Kelly said soothingly.

"You literally just said it was dangerous to be whatever you're claiming he is," I snapped.

"It's not dangerous for him to be himself," Kelly said. "There's a lot of prejudice from others that comes with it, but just being him isn't dangerous to him. It's not like we're going to tell you he's got a shorter life span or a higher risk of cancer or anything. I promise this doesn't change him."

"What exactly *are* you going to tell me?" I asked. I tried to sound intimidating, but it came out as a whisper.

"Do you remember the term we used when we were trying to figure you out just now?" Kyle asked. I closed my eyes and tried to remember through the frantic thoughts racing through my mind.

"Shifter." I opened my eyes. "What is that?"

"We can shift forms," Devon said.

"We're werewolves," Kyle said, staring at me with a grin on his face. Devon sighed and pinched the bridge of his nose.

"Yeah... traditionally that's what we've been called. But 'werewolf' feels dehumanizing and historically has been used as a slur and a reason to hunt us down," Devon said.

"I like it," Kyle said with a shrug, still grinning.

I looked between them, waiting for one of them to break and tell me this was all a joke, but Devon, Kelly, and Xavier were watching me with looks of grave concern. Kyle looked positively giddy.

"You're..." I took a deep breath. "You're telling me that you're a group of mythical beasts, made-up legends meant to scare children."

"We're clearly not made up. We exist," Devon said. "As for what stories have been told of us," he shrugged. "We can't control what other people say and think."

"*You* exist, but you can't... you're talking about dressing up or something," I said.

"Kyle, don't!" Xavier suddenly snapped, and I looked over to the armchair to see Kyle's face transforming. His ears moved toward the top of his head, his nose elongated, and his face started sprouting dark grey fur. He opened his mouth and I saw sharp, pointed teeth that definitely weren't human. I screamed and leapt to my feet at the same time that Devon snapped "Damn it, Kyle, you're going to give her a heart attack!"

Strong arms came around me, holding me back against someone's hard chest. I didn't know if my body was planning on running or collapsing but I could feel myself straining against the hold. Mentally, I had gone blank, instinct taking over completely. Kelly appeared in front of me and put her hands on my face, making soothing sounds. I think she was actually saying something, but it didn't register. Her face took up my entire field of vision, so I couldn't see Kyle anymore as he said in a much more guttural tone than usual, "At least she'll believe us now."

I flinched at the sound of his not-quite-human voice. "Not helpful!" Xavier growled at Kyle over my head and gave me a quick squeeze as if to comfort me.

"It's ok. You're fine. Nothing's changed except now you have more information. You're not in danger, James isn't in danger," Kelly was saying, her words finally getting through my brain fog, her hands pressed to my cheeks giving me enough physical input to drag me back into the world. "You're still safe."

I closed my eyes and started forcing myself to take deep, slow breaths, six counts in, six counts out, willing my body out of fight or flight mode. Normally, I would start trying to notice sights and sounds around me to ground myself, but in the circumstances that seemed like a bad idea. I felt myself if not fully relax, at least quit straining against Xavier's hold.

"You ok?" Xavier whispered into my ear. I took a deep breath and nodded, and he gave one more squeeze before dropping his hold on me.

I was trembling as I sat back down and dropped my head into my hands, continuing to breathe deeply. The couch moved slightly as Kelly and Xavier sat down on either side of me, and I could feel all their eyes on me as I sat there trying to make the world stop spinning. Finally, I looked up again. Kelly and Xavier smiled encouragingly. Kyle had an uncharacteristic mischievous grin on his now human-looking face. Devon looked like a kindergarten teacher who was trying to keep his patience with a class of uncooperative kids.

"So all of you can..." I trailed off as they all nodded. I swallowed. "And you're telling me that he," I pointed toward the five-year-old digging in the sand pit on the screen where we had the backyard camera displayed. "He's a... a werewolf?"

"More like a werepup at this point," Kyle said, earning an eye roll from Devon.

"Yes, he's a werewolf. A shifter," Devon said. I stared at the screen, trying to see what they'd seen. But all I could see was my son. A perfectly normal kid. Aside from his dad missing. And the crazy energy. But this was James. My baby.

"Surely I'd know if I birthed a werewolf... um, shifter?" I said.

"You're not one, right?" Devon asked.

"Obviously," I said.

"Not necessarily then. If both parents are shifters, it's clear from the beginning. The babies start out being able to shift and learn from their parents how to control it. They learn it just as they learn walking or talking. If only one parent or if it's dormant in both parents, then it doesn't necessarily manifest immediately, or ever." He pointed toward the screen. "Now that he's around others of our kind, he's going to start shifting more. He'll see what others are doing and his body will start to sense that it can do the same and start reacting and experimenting, especially since he's so young."

"He's going to change into a wolf?" I asked, incredulous.

"Puppy," Kyle said gleefully. I glared at him and he grinned back at me. He was enjoying this far too much, but at least he'd stopped attacking me and arguing for my banishment.

"Will he..." My brain felt like it might implode with all the questions suddenly bearing down on it and I said the first random thought that formed into actual words. "Will he get fleas?" As soon as I said it, my face turned crimson. My son was a werewolf, and that was the first question I asked? Kyle, Xavier, and Kelly burst out laughing. Even Devon looked amused.

"I'd like to say I'm offended that you think we're all flea-ridden mongrels, but the honest truth is yes, he will probably get fleas at some point. We all go through it. It's like lice for human kids," Devon said, his eyes twinkling.

"They weren't shoes," I muttered, thinking of the kids' feet I'd seen and feeling more than a little ridiculous for buying James that pair of bear-foot slippers. Xavier looked at Kelly and raised an eyebrow, and she shrugged. I stared at the screen, trying to see something new in James, some sign that he was different. Everyone else in the room waited, watching to see how I'd react. I took a deep breath.

"So what now?" I finally asked. "What do I... what do we do?" With those words, I could feel the tension in the room leak away. Kelly reached over and squeezed my knee encouragingly.

"Well first," Devon said, "unless anyone objects," he paused and made eye contact with the other three in the room, who one by one nodded their agreement with whatever question was in his eyes. "Welcome to the family."

"You do understand that Kyle will be insufferable now," Kelly said, nudging me. "You were getting off easy when he just didn't like you."

"Why?" I asked, looking at Kyle.

"I don't know why she's saying I'm insufferable. I'm delightful," Kyle said, leaning back and folding his arms over his chest.

"I mean why have you been so against me and now all of a sudden you're ok with me?" I asked. Kyle let out a long sigh and let his hands fall onto his lap.

"You didn't follow the usual patterns. Usually, when a new shifter finds their way to us, it comes out pretty fast. They recognize what we are and are usually relieved to be able to let loose. You never did notice. You never shifted, never hinted that you suspected we were anything other than what we appeared to be. You showed up right before we got bombed and there wasn't anyone else new at the time, so it seemed like a strong coincidence."

"For the last time, no one would be stupid enough to bring their kid to a building that was going to be destroyed," Kelly said, exasperated.

"She didn't have to know when it would happen in order to be feeding information about us to someone so they'd know where we were and when to strike," Kyle responded. From Kelly's eye roll and sigh, it was clear they'd had this conversation before, multiple times.

"I wouldn't ever..." I started, going pale.

"We know," Xavier said. "At least the rest of us knew. And now Kyle knows, too."

"So why don't you think I'm some kind of spy now?" I asked, looking back at Kyle again.

"I knew you weren't a shifter but I never thought about your kid being one. If he's a shifter and you're here with him, then you could belong here after all," he said. "We've never had a shifter kid brought here with a non-shifter parent before, but there's a first time for everything." I thought about Jessica, at ten years old, trying to keep her little brother safe all on her own and shuddered, imagining James finding his way here completely alone.

"If you thought I was here to hurt your family, I do understand why you'd want me out," I said.

"I know you understand. I've watched you with James. I know what you'd do to keep him safe," Kyle said, looking serious for the first time since we'd started the conversation.

"And now that's what we'll do, too. He's one of us, and that makes you one of us," Devon added. "If you want to be."

I looked around at the circle of people who had just turned my world upside down, but who had also been my first safe landing place in years. The people who had made sure that James and I were safe and looked after, even when they didn't know if we could ever really be let into their world. Kelly squeezed my hand encouragingly as I drew a breath and said, "Yes, I do want that. Very much."

5

Kelly offered to stay over with us that night, citing Kyle's overdramatic display and its effect on my mental health. Honestly, I thought she just wanted to make sure I didn't run overnight, but I agreed.

"When was the last time you had a girls' night sleep-over?" she asked once we'd tucked James into bed and settled on the couch.

"Umm, I have no idea. Probably college, but we were roommates."

"Doesn't count if they live with you."

"Maybe high school?"

"Then we'll have some fun tonight!" Kelly exclaimed. "Wait right here. Don't go anywhere." She fixed me with a meaningful look and ran out the front door. She came back with plastic shopping bags full of candy, caramel popcorn, and soda.

"Oh, James is going to be so upset he missed this!" I laughed as she spread out the offerings across the coffee table.

"We can stay up late and gossip," she said, tucking her feet underneath her.

"I do have a lot of questions, but I'm not sure this counts as gossip," I said. Kelly's expression sobered.

"I promise, we weren't going to disappear on you and we definitely weren't going to take James from you," she said softly. "I wouldn't let that happen. You don't need to go through that again."

"Do they know why I'm here in the first place?" I asked. Kelly shook her head.

"If they know somehow, it's not from me. That's your story to tell. I did tell them that you had everyone in your life turn their back on you, similar to what many of us had gone through, but I didn't say why. Devon seemed to think that was a point in your favor and at the time, Kyle said the fact that you didn't have anyone we could check up with was suspicious." She rolled her eyes. "As if we hadn't almost all been in that exact situation at some point."

"What about you?" I asked, then immediately wondered if I'd overstepped.

"Oh, my story's more boring than many of theirs, or yours," she said. "Both my parents are shifters. They live in Manhattan. I go visit them around Christmas every other year and they occasionally pop in down here for a visit. But I saw what it was like for some of my peers who didn't have my support network as I was growing up, and I wanted to help them. I wandered around different packs for a few years, seeing how different groups structured themselves. Most packs will take in lost shifters if they can show they fit in with the group, but Devon and Xavier are the only ones I've met who actively go looking for shifters who need help. I liked that, so I joined up with them."

"Not Kyle?"

"Don't let him fool you. He's hard to win over, but he'll fight like hell once he's on your side. He had it hard before he found us and is really distrusting of non-shifters in general. He's probably more dedicated to finding lost shifters than Devon and Xavier, especially kids. Don't take it personally."

"I mean you didn't mention him when you said that you joined the pack."

"Oh, he's newer than me. I've been with the pack about..." she squinted, thinking. "Ten, eleven years now? Kyle's been here four or five years. Somewhere in there. He wasn't here when I showed up."

"You said that Greg saw me somehow?" I asked, switching tracks. "What does that mean? Does he stalk people or something?"

"No, no, nothing like that!" Kelly said. "Greg is a sweetheart. He wouldn't do that."

"Wait, is this the same Greg who moved my furniture and likes to watch kitten videos on YouTube with the kids after dinner?" I asked.

"Yep, same Greg," Kelly said, nodding. There was something ironic about a werewolf who was addicted to online kitten videos, but I wasn't in the mood to dwell on that.

"How exactly did he see me?"

"When shifters relatively close to him are in trouble or distress, he sort of senses them," Kelly said. "We call it visions, but it's not like he has a crystal ball or anything. He gets a general sense of where they are, sometimes gets a glimpse of a face or two, usually the shifter and someone they're strongly connected to if they aren't alone. Just enough for us to know what to look for. Sometimes he gets a sense like a compass. It's how we know who to reach out to."

"Why only when they're in trouble?" I asked.

"We don't know," Kelly shrugged and grabbed a chocolate bar from the table. "My guess is because negative emotions send out a stronger signal for him. But your guess is as good as mine on the 'why' part."

"Can all of you do that?" I asked, frowning.

"No. Greg is the only one in our pack who senses other shifters in that way. But some of us have other abilities. Devon can communicate mentally with others in our pack while he's human, but it's not full telepathy or anything. More like he sends intent, and we interpret what he means."

"So can any of you read my mind?" I asked, trying to sound light and teasing. I felt like I was coming across as accusatory though. Her expression darkened briefly with what looked almost like grief, and I thought I'd crossed a line somehow.

"Well... we knew one person who kind of could do that, but he left years ago and we haven't heard from him since," she said. "Those of us who can do things like that while human usually can communicate just one direction or in vague flashes like Greg. Most of us can't do anything like that unless we're wolves. Then we can all communicate with each other in what you'd normally think of as telepathy, but only with members of our own pack."

"So you don't know what I'm thinking right now?" I asked, poking her shoulder and hoping to lighten the mood. It worked.

"I'm sensing..." She closed her eyes and waved a hand in front of my face. She opened her eyes. "That you want ice cream and to watch a show that isn't child friendly."

"God, yes," I said. "Did you bring ice cream?"

"I may have stashed some over here a few days ago for an emergency," she said with a grin and she jumped up and headed for the kitchen.

"An emergency involving ice cream?" I asked, raising an eyebrow.

"Absolutely. Any emergency calls for ice cream. Especially when the emergency is that you don't have ice cream and are about to have an impromptu movie night," she laughed.

THE NEXT MORNING I woke up to Kelly and James laughing in the kitchen as Kelly flipped pancakes on the stove. She'd slept on the couch, so I guessed that James had gone for her first when he woke up and wandered out of his room.

"Mommy! Good morning!" he said when he saw me, his face lit up with happiness. "I told Kelly that pancakes are your favorite breakfast, and she taught me how to make them! It's really easy!" I saw the box of just-add-water pancake mix on the counter and almost laughed at Kelly's conspiratorial wink.

"Only two ingredients, right James?" she asked.

"We should have more ingredients," he said, frowning.

"Oh?" Kelly asked, testing the pancake she was currently cooking.

"Like blueberries! Or chocolate chips!"

"Or bananas?"I asked.

"Oh, definitely balamas!" He said.

"Did he say..." Kelly started. I made a cutting motion across my throat and she nodded and turned back to the stove to pull finished pancakes onto a plate. James didn't have many words that he still mispronounced, and I wasn't in any hurry to lose the few baby words I had left.

"You want to go hang out at the house today?" I asked him. Kelly smiled, looking relieved. I wondered what she had thought my next decision was going to be.

"Yeah! Can I take Barksie today? I want to show Milly," he said. I hesitated.

"You'll take super good care of him?"

"Promise. The best care," James said solemnly. I nodded and he whooped and leapt to his feet. "I'm going to get dressed!" he said, running to his room and slamming the door.

"Who's Barksie?" Kelly asked as she set a plate in front of me and sat down with a cup of coffee.

"It's that stuffed dog he sleeps with. His dad bought it for him when he was a baby and..." I suddenly trailed off, making the connection. I rubbed my temples. "A stuffed dog. His dad got him a dog. He knew..." I closed my eyes.

"He may have known about himself, but he may not have known that James was a shifter, though. Recessive, remember?" Kelly said. I frowned, trying to remember basic genetics.

"But if it's recessive that means it's somewhere in me, too, right? I mean for James to... to be a shifter." The words felt like lead coming out of my mouth, like saying it out loud was making some pronouncement, was changing the course of our lives. Maybe it was. Kelly seemed to understand what I was feeling because she took my hand and squeezed sympathetically. Then she straightened up and picked up her coffee mug.

"The short answer is yes. But how far back, I couldn't tell you. If your parents know..."

"I won't find out from them. That's a closed door," I said.

"Well, does it matter? I mean for you."

I sighed. "Probably not. If I were a shifter I'd definitely know, right?"

"Yeah, you'd know by now," Kelly said. "Kids can start shifting as babies if they're around it and know what to mimic. But even if they've never met another shifter, it'll come out by puberty at the latest. We get a lot of young teenage runaways," she said, taking a sip from her cup. "Some people hide it until they're older and go looking for others like us as adults, or manage to hide it until we find them. But there's no one that I've ever heard of who didn't know what they were by the time they were sixteen or so."

"So... how do I parent this?" I asked. "I have no idea what he's going through, what he will go through. What do I do?"

"You don't know what it's like to be a little boy either, but here you are parenting one of those," Kelly pointed out.

"It's not the same thing," I said.

"In some ways, it is," Kelly replied. "Look, you don't have to change anything. He's going to figure himself out. But unlike some of the others, he'll still have you to be there for him and to love him. All those kids he plays with? Half of them went through some serious trauma the first time they shifted at all. Some of them lost everything. He won't have to deal with that. He'll still have his mom, and he'll have the rest of us to walk him through the shifty stuff."

"Shifty stuff?" I couldn't help but laugh. "Please promise me you only mean the werewolf stuff and not things like sneaking out in the middle of the night."

"I can promise for myself but can't vouch for Trevor or Kyle," Kelly said. I smiled for a moment, then sobered as a thought crossed my mind.

"Do you think he already knows?"

"The way Jessica was confident makes me think that yes, he has some idea," Kelly said.

"Ummm... Mommy?" My eyes widened as I realized he was listening in. I plastered a smile on my face as I turned to

James, dressed in yellow shorts and a Star Wars t-shirt, hugging Barksie to his chest.

"What's up?"

"I... I'm..." He fiddled with Barksie's ear.

"What is it, baby?" I asked encouragingly. I tried to keep my face calm, but I could hear my blood racing in my ears, thinking about what he was so nervous about telling me. He glanced over my shoulder at Kelly and his eyes grew wide. Then he smiled at her, nodded, and fixed his eyes on mine again. I wondered what she had done but didn't want to turn away from James.

"I can do stuff. Weird stuff. Like grow more hair," he said. Ok. That was one way to interpret what he was experiencing.

"Do you want to show me?" I asked. He nodded, then closed his eyes and scrunched his face in concentration. I watched with a mixture of awe and fear as his toenails grew longer and formed into tiny claws and his legs sprouted dark yellow fur. When he opened his eyes, he had long, canine-looking feet and fur from the knees down.

He grinned down at his achievement and giggled, then looked at me, his face serious and searching mine for a reaction. "That's really cool!" I said, smiling, and he grinned and bounced on his furry feet. I mentally facepalmed again over buying him fake bear feet and wondered what was going through his mind when I handed them to him.

"It is, isn't it!" he said excitedly. "Everyone else can do it, and Trevor taught me how!" He beamed with pride.

"Go brush your teeth," I said, dropping a kiss on the top of his head. He skipped into his bathroom and closed the door. I looked at Kelly.

"I told you I couldn't account for Trevor," she said with a shrug. "You did amazing, by the way. That right there is exactly what he's going to need. Your acceptance and support."

"What did you do that made him move forward with telling me?" I asked.

"Don't scream?" She asked. I nodded. Her ears moved toward the top of her head and sharpened into wolf ears covered in light brown fur, and her nose changed into a wet brown muzzle. By the time I blinked again, she was back to normal. "Gave him some moral support," she said.

I leaned back in my chair, mentally exhausted. "Thank you," I said.

"Don't mention it," she said, waving her hand dismissively. "We all love him. He's adorable. And we love you, too, and we want you both to thrive."

"I can see why you were so good at getting people to sign up for gym memberships," I laughed.

"It's a particular talent I have," she said. "Signing up people for workout routines and werewolf packs."

"Speaking of, how's the gym coming along?" I asked. I needed to think about something else. As long as I didn't think too hard about why they were rebuilding the gym, I figured I'd be ok with this topic.

"I don't know if we're reopening the gym," she said with a sigh. "Kyle wants to do something completely different so it's not obvious it's still us. He thinks if we reopen the gym, we'll get targeted again. Devon thinks if we blatantly reopen the same thing again they won't dare touch it because a repeat would start a media investigation that neither side wants to happen. So we're at a standstill for now, which is fine because Kyle is still fighting insurance tooth and nail to get as much as we can back so that when we do decide our next step, we have all the resources we need. Whatever it is, we'll want something public facing that draws people in. It's one of the ways we can connect with lost shifters. It's much easier to convince someone to come to a Zumba class as a first step than to dinner at a shifter safe house." She smiled at me conspiratorially. "As I'm sure you're aware now."

I narrowed my eyes at her. "I didn't choose that gym randomly, did I?" I asked.

"Nope. That free trial offer only went to one person," she said, pointing at me.

"How did you know I'd come?"

"We didn't." Kelly sipped her coffee. "If you didn't bite, we'd have tried other ways to connect. But you did show up, and here we are. Although I admit that it didn't go quite as planned. We meant to bring you in much more... gently."

"The reunion?

"Ah, no. That was a coincidence as far as you being there. We'd been planning that for months. We only knew about you for about a week before we reached out."

"I'm ready!" James flew out from the bathroom and body-slammed into the front door then stood there jumping up and down, holding Barksie over his head.

"Hey, shift back, kiddo," Kelly said. "Only do that here and at the house for now, ok?"

"Oh... right. Ok," James said. He closed his eyes again and his legs and feet snapped back into human shape, the fur disappearing back into his skin. "I guess my shoes will fit better this way, too." He said, wiggling his toes.

"Yep. And your paws aren't like shoes, ok? They're stronger than your regular feet, but they can get hurt, too. Shoes are good," Kelly said.

"Mooooommy!" James whined, suddenly looking me over. "You're not dressed yet! I got dressed and brushed my teeth already!"

"I needed caffeine first, ok?" I said, holding up my cup for him to see.

"Ugh! Grown-ups!" he grumbled and flung himself face down onto the couch. I couldn't help but laugh and felt some relief. He hadn't changed. It was still James, had always been James. Kelly was right. Nothing was different, I just had more information now, had more of an idea of who he was and who he was growing into.

"Ok, I'm going, I'm going," I said. I downed the last gulp, shoved one last bite of pancake in my mouth, and headed back into my bedroom while Kelly started clearing the dishes.

"Hurry, please," he called, his voice muffled by the couch cushions.

I heard Kelly and James chatting in the living room as I changed and got ready for the day, and then James's voice quieted and the only sound left was the clink of dishes and the running water of the kitchen sink. By the time I came back out, Kelly had gotten the kitchen completely cleaned up. James was sitting on the couch munching one of the left-over candy bars from last night, suddenly content to wait for me. That explained why he had uncharacteristically stopped talking for any length of time. When he saw me, he leapt to his feet again and tilted his head questioningly.

"Yes, yes, I'm ready," I said, grabbing my keys. "Let's get going." He was across the room faster than I could track and obediently waiting by the door. The entire ride, he barely contained himself in his seat, to the point I had to tell him to quit kicking the back of my chair. But as I looked at him in the rearview mirror, I couldn't help but feel like something had finally gone right. I couldn't remember ever seeing him smile this big, and he seemed to be sitting up a little taller, a little more confidently.

With a pang, I realized that he was looking far more like a kid and less like a baby than he ever had. I didn't know if finding out something new about himself did it or if this was an age where this transition seemed more pronounced, but it felt like I was watching him grow up at an astounding rate suddenly.

We pulled up to the house and I shut off the car. I expected him to bolt, but he sat in the back for a moment, thinking. "Hey, Mommy?" he finally said.

"Yeah?"

"I'm glad we have new friends now."

"Me too, sweetie." I blinked back tears that were threatening to form.

"Love you, Mommy."

"Love you too, James. Forever."

With that, the spell of tranquility was over. He unbuckled and, Barksie in tow, ran as fast as he could for the house and disappeared through the front door without so much as slowing down to knock or announce his arrival. As if he were running to see family. As if he were finally, at long last, home.

6

"It's no problem. Trust me, you don't want a shifter kid who knows he's a shifter kid at a public school," Jessica said, trying to stand up straight as James put his full weight into hanging on her arm.

"You and Hannah are going back to school in a couple of weeks, too. You both need to focus on your own studies, not worry about a kindergartener," I said, trying to use a stern-mom voice. Jessica, as usual, seemed immune to any attempt on my end to try to pull a "you're just a kid" argument. I had to admit, she had good reason for being independent and confident enough in her choices to stand up to every adult in this house. But despite that, she was still a high schooler.

"And you really don't want him in daycare where they're paying less attention to what he's doing," she added, a mischievous spark in her eye. "We're all a bunch of show-offs."

"I'm not a show-off!" James protested.

"Your favorite phrase is 'watch this,'" Jessica countered, laughing.

"I don't say that unless I'm really, really good at something," James said, sticking out his tongue at Jessica.

"I rest my case," she said, rubbing his head with her free hand and raising her eyebrows at me. I rubbed my temples and sighed.

"Seriously, it's your senior year, Jessica," I said. "You said you want to go to college, and this year is going to be busy preparing for that. I don't want him distracting you."

"I won't be the only one here," she said. "I won't even be the one in charge once school starts. Brenda and Denise are here all day, and they're the ones who watch the little kids. And it's not like he's the only one or even the one who's going to make everything tumble into chaos. Group home-schooling is normal for us. And you said yourself that you need to find somewhere else for him to be during the day while you work now."

I only knew Brenda and Denise from brief snippets of conversation when they had come to dinners a couple of times. Brenda had never struck me as a woman who would willingly take charge of anyone under the age of eighteen. She was always put together like she was on her way to a photo shoot, not a hair out of place or a wrinkle in her clothes. I wasn't sure I'd ever seen her crack a smile.

Denise, on the other hand, I had to admit seemed particularly well-suited for the endeavor. Every kid in the family flocked to her every time she came to visit. At first, I thought she was just good-humored about being overrun with kids every time she showed up, but I'd learned that she bribed them with small candies she kept in the deep pockets of the thin grey sweater she was always wearing. She would send the kids off on "errands" around the house which wound up being things like starting the washing machine or folding blankets and praise them with such fervor that they didn't seem to realize they were doing chores. Each time she came over the house was miraculously tidy by the time she left.

"Let me think about it," I said. James's face fell.

"That means no," he said forlornly.

"In this case, it means she hasn't said yes yet," Jessica said in a confidently triumphant tone. I had to admit she was right, and she could see it in my eyes.

The front door slammed and a little boy's voice yelled, "James! I see your mom's car! Where are you?"

"Brayden! I'm here!" James yelled back as he let go of Jessica and ran out of the kitchen. Children's voices started talking over and around each other so fast that I wondered if they even knew what each other was saying. Their footsteps pounded up the stairs and a distant door slammed shut, muffling the noise of horseplay and laughter. A second later, I heard what sounded like excited puppy barks. Over it all, Maria yelled up the stairs, "Ten minutes, Brayden! That's it! I'm just dropping off some papers and we're leaving!" Then she called Kelly's name, and her footsteps headed down the hallway toward the office.

"Ok, you're right," I admitted, listening to the sounds of the boys roughhousing. "He does need to stay here. I just don't want to impose on you or anyone else."

"It's not an imposition if we offer," Jessica said. "And I know I'm right." She smiled as if to show she didn't mean any offense but was just offering facts. Her phone dinged and she pulled it out of her pocket to check her texts. "Gotta go. Hannah and I are going to play glow-in-the-dark putt-putt. Like normal teenagers." She made an "Are you happy?" face at me and walked out of the kitchen with a wave over her shoulder.

I wandered into the den and plopped down on the couch, pulling out my phone. I pulled up a cash transfer app and sent twenty bucks to Jessica's account with a note, "Have fun." A moment later Jessica sent back a heart-faced cat emoji. Trying to ignore the multi-species yelps coming from upstairs, I opened a browser on my phone and started scrolling through a website I had pulled up earlier.

"Herbal supplements don't seem like your thing," Xavier said behind me. I jumped and dropped my phone in my lap. "Sorry," he said, coming around and sitting next to me. "I forget your hearing isn't as good as ours." From the grin on his face, I very much doubted that he'd forgotten or that he was sorry. "Why exactly are you looking up elderberry pills?"

"I landed a couple of short-term copywriting gigs," I explained. "Little stuff for now, but if I can build up a portfolio I think I can make a decent enough amount freelancing remotely." I didn't add that the reason I was looking for remote jobs was because I still felt completely out of my element figuring out how to raise a child who could transform into a wolf at random times, and I wasn't sure about getting a job that required me to be away from him on a consistent basis.

"And the elderberries are for... I don't know what elderberries do. Make you a better writer?" he asked.

"Ha ha," I said, rolling my eyes at him. "This company posted a job for someone to overhaul their website and create a social media page."

"I can see why they want an overhaul," Xavier said, leaning over to see my phone screen. "I'm pretty sure Trevor can write better than that. At least he can spell 'alternative.' And why is there so much yellow?"

"That is the beginning of a series of excellent questions," I said, raising an eyebrow at the animated lucky cat gifs that seemed randomly dispersed across the site.

"Is this particularly pressing, or do you have some time on your hands?" he asked.

"Call it reconnaissance. Officially I'm starting this job on Monday," I said. "Why? Do you have other ideas?"

"Just lunch. Thought you'd like a break. You haven't been further away than a few rooms from James in a while. Which I completely understand," he added, raising his hands and cutting off my protest, "but I thought a totally child-free break would be good for you."

"I can't just leave him," I started.

"You're not just leaving him," Xavier said. "Kelly's in the office and I ran this by her first. She thought it was a good idea. And Kyle's here, also. You've got brains and... whatever you want to say Kyle is here to watch over him. James is good. And you need a change of scenery." I still hesitated. I wasn't sure what exactly I thought would happen to him here, but being away from him at all made me uneasy. On the other hand, this was probably the one place he was safest, and eventually, I would have to actually be in a different building than him.

"Ok, lunch it is," I said reluctantly.

"For the sake of my ego, I'll make what I think is the correct assumption that that tone is about leaving James behind and not about the proposed company," Xavier said, giving me an exaggerated wounded look.

"I promise, it's not about the company," I assured him.

"Good, because I was worried you might want to invite Kyle instead."

"I'm pretty sure Kyle still doesn't like me."

"That's because you didn't call him a good boy when he shifted. Next time rub him behind the ears. He needs positive reinforcement." Xavier winked and I laughed, although

I wasn't sure how serious he was. Would it be considered rude to pet a werewolf?

"Lunch with the present company sounds fabulous," I said, putting my phone in my pocket.

XAVIER DROVE us downtown to a place that served what he said were his favorite Philly cheesesteak subs in the tri-state area.

"Are any of you vegetarian?" I asked as we sat at a table by the wall with our baskets.

"Percentage-wise, probably fewer of us than in the typical population, but yeah, it's happened. Why?" Xavier frowned at me, confused.

"That first night, Kelly asked if I was vegetarian," I said, frowning

"It wasn't a test or anything if that's what you're wondering," Xavier said, understanding the real question. "She really was just trying to be polite." I took a bite and chewed thoughtfully. "Look, none of us were testing you at any point. Usually, it sort of goes the other way. New people test us out until they're comfortable enough with us that they let us know who they are. You didn't notice any of the stuff someone normally would and you lasted longer than anyone else without telling us about yourself."

"How long does it usually take someone to tell you?" I asked.

"A few days. Maybe a week at a stretch. By then they've usually noticed little signs about who we are. But you," he stared at me for a second. "You hadn't noticed anything. And that never happened before. We've never had... someone like you spend so much time with us, and certainly haven't had them stay at the house."

"Like before you figured out they weren't a shifter or at all?" As I said the word "shifter," I could see Xavier go on alert, scanning the room around us quickly. When he looked back at me, I nodded, understanding. Better not to discuss specifics out loud where we could be overheard.

"At all. We're very protective of our family, as I'm sure you can understand," he said. I nodded. Since finding out that James could become a wolf, I'd gotten paranoid about other people seeing him when he shifted. What would someone do with that information? I didn't need the others to tell me that this was dangerous territory.

We ate in silence for a few minutes. He was right. The subs were delicious. Back in the car, Xavier only drove about five minutes, then pulled over and parallel parked in a residential neighborhood.

"Where are we?" I asked.

"Let's walk. We don't have to go back to the house yet. There's a little park here. Hidden gem thing. Lots of trees, winding walking paths, flowers," he paused. "And not many people on weekdays usually. It's pretty private." He scanned my face to see if I caught his meaning. It was somewhere he considered a safe place to talk openly. I nodded.

"Sounds perfect," I said.

"So Jessica tells me James will be joining the home-school group," Xavier said as we walked down the sidewalk.

"I said we'll see," I replied.

"Isn't that mom-speak for 'no?'" Xavier laughed. I sighed.

"James said the same thing. But in this case... I think the answer might be yes," I said. "I mean school starts in a couple of weeks and I haven't figured out how to register him for kindergarten yet anyway." Xavier turned us off the sidewalk and onto a small path into the underbrush on the side of the road I hadn't noticed. I eyed it warily. "Are you sure this is an actual park and not just someone's yard?" I asked.

"Do you trust me?" He asked with a smile, holding out his hand.

"Did... did you just quote Aladdin?" I asked.

"Lots of people say that," He said, the grin on his face widening.

"Not with the right inflection and holding their hand out like that, they don't," I said. He shrugged but didn't stop smiling.

"Maybe," he said. "Question still stands. But I'm not asking you to jump off a balcony, so you're taking much less risk than Jasmine did." I laughed and took his hand.

"I trust you," I said. He squeezed my hand as he pulled me off the sidewalk and started us toward a downward slope. After moving through some branches that had blocked the view of the path, we came to some stairs built into the pathway. At the bottom of the steps, it opened out into wide footpaths demarcated by ferns, flowering bushes, and small trees. To one side the path went under a bridge holding up the road we had been walking along and to the other side a small wooden bridge went over a creek that wound throughout the area. We heard an occasional car roll over the road above us, but otherwise, the only thing I heard was birds and the leaves shifting in the light breeze. Pink and white flowers dotted bushes in every direction.

"You were right," I said, looking around. "This is a gem. It's beautiful."

"This is my favorite place in town to come when I need a quiet space to think or just be alone," he said. "The house gets busy." I thought about the constant rotating door of people that seemed to always be coming and going, the nightly family dinners, the fact that there always seemed to be kids—including my kid—somewhere in the house or yard, and if there weren't, they'd be there soon.

"It would be nice to have an escape," I agreed. I realized that although I'd spent years relatively alone, I'd already gotten used to being surrounded by people now. It was nice having my own apartment to go back to though. "Why do you live at the house?" I asked. "It seems like most people have their own place."

"It's my home." He shrugged. "I was with Devon when the pack started. It's where I belong. And we do need some adults to live there or Jessica and Hannah would decorate the whole place in... I don't know. Whatever teenage girls are into. Probably murals done in glitter pens and printouts of memes or something." I laughed. "But seriously, Kyle, Devon, and I are the pack members most trained in combat, also. If something goes wrong... You know we call it a safe house." I nodded. "Part of that is that we make sure it's well-guarded and always available for the pack. We're basically the in-house staff."

"But Kelly's part of your staff, right?" I asked.

"She doesn't want to live there. Says the three of us are too much to handle 24/7. I have a purpose there, but I do have a choice. I'm not trapped."

"I didn't mean to suggest that..." Xavier waved a hand to cut me off.

"I know. Just trying to answer the question." Then he smiled mischievously. "Plus if I didn't live there I wouldn't have had the pleasure of being the first person you ran into your first morning with us," he said, winking. I blushed, remembering almost walking in on him in the bathroom.

"I must have looked like a disaster," I muttered.

"I live with a bunch of wild animals," Xavier laughed. "Trust me, you were fine."

"Well when you put it like that, I guess I was doing ok," I said.

"You'd make a great wolf, though," Xavier said. His tone made me turn to glance at him, and the intense look he was giving me sent a shiver up my spine. I froze in place, eyes locked on his. After a moment, he tilted his head toward the path. "Let's walk," he said. "This goes a few blocks. It feels like a completely separate world down here." He turned to start walking, and as he looked away I realized I'd temporarily forgotten to breathe. I took a deep breath again as I fell into step beside him and we walked in silence for a few moments.

"For what it's worth," he said finally, "you aren't trapped here either, but I do hope you decide to stick around for a long time."

We wandered through the park for a while then sat on one of the scattered benches next to a small waterfall and chatted for hours. Some of the conversation was about werewolves. Turns out the whole transmission-by-bite thing was made up, thank goodness. I'd been worried about the month-long biting phase James had gone through as a toddler. But mostly we talked about life in general.

He told me about some places around town that he enjoyed, and I told him about what drove me to move to a new town to start over. When I choked up a little talking about James's dad disappearing, he reached out and took my hand, and continued to hold on once the difficult part was over. We compared answers to theoretical questions like where we'd travel if we could go anywhere (he wanted to visit Egypt. I said Barcelona) or who we'd have a conversation with if we could speak to anyone at all. I said I wanted to talk to my grandparents now that I was wondering about James's heritage. He wanted to talk to

Anne Rice. He was curious how much she actually knew about werewolves.

WHEN WE GOT BACK to the house, James and Trevor were sprawled on the couch watching cartoons with popcorn bowls and plates of pizza pockets.

"Hey, hun," I said. James waved at me, his eyes glued to the television screen.

"Why haven't you let him watch Miyazaki movies before?" Trevor asked.

"I... didn't think about it?" I said, shrugging. "I didn't *not* let him watch them, it just never came up."

"Well I'm fixing it," Trevor said, turning back to the screen. "He needs some culture." From the kitchen doorway, Xavier made a snorting sound and I turned to see him trying to hold back a laugh, his head nearly purple with the effort. I followed him back into the kitchen and sat down at the table. He grabbed a couple of sodas from the fridge and brought me one.

"So if you start that job Monday, will James be hanging out here getting cultured?" Xavier asked.

"Yeah, I suppose he will," I said, chuckling. "It's like he has a big brother now. It's great. I always..." I dropped off. I didn't want to follow that line of thought. We were building a new life now and I wanted to move forward, not dwell on what might have been. Explaining my past was one thing. Thinking about what could have been different if our lives hadn't turned upside down was a whole deeper layer. Xavier sensed my darkening mood and reached over to squeeze my hand.

"Brothers, sisters... he's gaining a lot of people," Xavier said. I smiled. I had to admit that for what I had expected when we moved here, I hadn't expected to find a whole group of people who were here for us like this.

"You have no idea how much of a relief that is," I admitted.

"I may have some idea. Most of us here do. We all come to it from different backgrounds, but we generally know that feeling."

"What about you? How did you wind up here?" I asked and immediately wondered if I'd overstepped. To my relief, he smiled. He squeezed my hand one more time then let go and leaned back in his chair.

"Pretty typical for a lot of us," he said. "My parents weren't shifters. I realized what I could do when I was eleven. I was young, but I'd seen enough movies to be worried I'd wind up trapped in a laboratory somewhere, so I kept it quiet. When I was fifteen, I told my parents. I don't remember why. I just wanted them to know. They freaked. They weren't even religious and my mom seriously suggested I get exorcized, and it went downhill from there. I packed a bag that night and left.

"I called on occasion but as soon as they knew who it was they hung up. A year later I decided to try to go see them and they had moved. I didn't try to find them, just let it drop. In the meantime, I'd been wandering around taking odd jobs, jumping around towns, trying to find somewhere that felt right. I ran into Devon at a bar one night. We started chatting and he said some stuff that made me think he knew about me. At first, I was worried he wanted to hunt me down, but then he shifted a hand for a moment and I realized he was like me. It was the first time I realized I wasn't alone, that I wasn't a freak." He spread his arms to gesture at everything around us. "And here we are."

"I just don't understand how all of your parents just..." I trailed off, frowning.

"It's going to be a common story here because that's what our pack is. Devon and I started building this pack because we wanted to help other people like us. People who lost everything and needed somewhere to land. But it doesn't always go that way. There are others out there whose parents don't turn on them. They stay in their families and live happy, if somewhat secretive, lives. Some people never tell their families and live a double life. That would personally drive me nuts, but it works for some people, I guess. And there are whole shifter families out there. Since the gene is recessive, it's about guaranteed that if shifters have kids together, the kid winds up a shifter. There are whole communities out there where kids grow up knowing what they are from the beginning and have a culture and identity their whole lives that fit who they are."

"How have I never heard about this before?" I asked. "You make it sound like there are shifters all over."

"Think about how you reacted when Kyle shifted," he said, staring at me. "Now transfer that feeling into someone who has a proclivity for violence. Or someone who thinks their child is in immediate danger. Or someone who doesn't like anything that doesn't fit their worldview. Think about the stories you've heard before you knew we were real. The myths and legends. Think about how many stories you've heard where we were the good guys."

"Remus Lupin," I said immediately. Xavier shook his head.

"He was only a good guy as long as he suppressed his wolf side. The instant he shifted he was evil." Xavier looked almost sad, like he felt sorry for the fictional character. I went quiet, realizing that most of the stories I'd read or seen involving werewolves were similar or depicted werewolves completely as monsters.

He studied my face. "There's a lot of us, but not that many. We're stronger and faster than non-shifters, but not enough to face down armies. Plenty of people in history have been persecuted and murdered for being different even when they were still human, and what we've often suffered when we were found out has been horrific. You were there when we were bombed so you know the lengths some people will go to. We hide to survive or else we would be wiped out."

I started feeling sick to my stomach. It must have shown on my face because he reached over and took my hand again.

"But we're not alone," he said. "We have each other, and we'll keep finding others who need us and bringing them in, giving them a place to belong and be safe." He met my gaze with an intensity that was equal parts fierce and compassionate as he reached for my hands again. "That includes you and James."

7

Kindergarten felt intimidating. I'd always read that it was emotional putting your oldest in school for the first time, but I wasn't prepared for how strongly it hit me. It didn't make sense. He wasn't even going to a real school. He'd be in an office space in the house with five other elementary shifter kids and a couple of high schoolers. In many ways, it wasn't much different than what he'd been doing already.

Most weekdays, either I dropped him off at the house or Kelly, Jessica, or Xavier picked him up in the morning. I'd been making good headway with the few small jobs I'd picked up. I'd work at the apartment the first half of the day, have lunch with Xavier or Kelly, then work a bit more at the house until everyone showed up for dinner. We'd gotten into a comfortable routine, and I was starting to feel settled and, dare I say, happy.

My day-to-day life probably wouldn't change when he started school. The only real adjustment would be that he would be doing lessons during the day instead of watching anime and playing in the yard (and he would probably still be doing quite a bit of both of those). Maybe because he wasn't just my oldest but my only child, maybe because of how much else had been upended in our lives in the recent past, but I was increasingly nervous and antsy in the week leading up to his first day.

"Ok, that's it," Kelly announced one day when I had brought James to the house and settled in the kitchen for a cup of coffee. "You're taking a day off work. You're going to drive me crazy with how crazy you're acting."

"I'm not doing anything!" I protested.

"You're all fidgety. You look like you'll spontaneously combust. You need to get your mind off James for a day. For real, not just work. That doesn't distract you enough."

"Plus you smell nervous," Kyle said, coming into the kitchen and heading for the coffee machine.

"What does that even mean?" I demanded.

"You know how they say dogs can smell fear?" Kyle asked. "So can werewolves, and you're distracting this week. If you love us at all, please, go get your mind off James growing up and chill out so the rest of us aren't on edge."

"She at least loves one of us," Kelly teased, and I blushed. Kyle burst into actual laughter and I glared at him as he grabbed his coffee mug and left the room, winking suggestively at me. Xavier and I had spent more and more time together the last couple weeks and apparently, Kelly had picked up on it.

"Nothing's happened," I mumbled.

"I know," she said, smirking a bit. "But that doesn't mean you don't want it to. I've seen the looks from both of you."

"There aren't any looks," I said.

"Yes, there are, and I'm pretty sure everyone except you and Xavier know it, and both of you probably know it and are in denial."

"I don't know if I'm ready for that sort of thing yet," I mumbled.

"Ready for what?" Xavier asked, coming into the room. I wanted to sink into the floor, and when I felt my face flush hotter he gave me a bemused look.

"I told her she needs to take a vacation day to stop thinking about her baby starting school and she thinks she shouldn't because she hasn't had these jobs that long," Kelly said, shooting me a look that could either have been communicating "I've got your back" or "you owe me." Probably both.

"Sounds like a good idea to me," Xavier said. "My schedule is suddenly clear. What should we do? Day trip to Barcelona?" Kelly smirked at me again and this time I rolled my eyes at her.

"I have no idea," I said. Kelly suddenly ran over to Xavier and whispered something in his ear. He grinned.

"Good idea," he said, squeezing her shoulder. Then he turned and left the room and I heard him heading upstairs.

"What?" I asked.

"It's a surprise," Kelly said. "Give me a minute. I'll be right back. Drink your coffee."

"You can't just..."

"Yes, I can," Kelly said. "As a matter of fact, I'm exceptionally good at planning things and then making them happen. Now sit." She pointed at me. "Stay." And then she left the room. I rolled my eyes again but did as I was told, looking out the back door window at the clouds as I waited to be told what my new plans for the day were. I didn't particularly enjoy having things upended. I didn't necessarily have to be the one making plans, but not knowing what was going to happen made me anxious on the best of days. On top of my already heightened restlessness, it sent me into overdrive. By the time Xavier and Kelly came back less than five minutes later, my foot was tapping so much I thought it might start digging a hole in the floor.

"You ok?" Xavier asked, looking a little worried for the first time. "We can stay here."

"No, you absolutely cannot," Kelly said, shoving a small backpack toward me. "She's going to make all the rest of us as twitchy as she is. Out."

"We're not going somewhere overnight?" I asked nervously, eyeing the backpack.

"Nope, it's a day trip. Just packed you some supplies. Don't open it until you get there," Kelly said, holding up a hand to shush Xavier as he started to say something. "Now go. The rest of us have stuff to do."

Xavier motioned toward the door leading to the garage. "Shall we?" he asked. I nodded and headed toward the door. I could swear he was trying not to laugh, but since Kelly was still standing there I didn't say anything or glance his way, especially not after her comment about "looks."

As soon as we pulled out of the driveway, I said, "Ok, spill it. Where are we going?"

"Natural spring," Xavier said, grinning. "She packed you a bathing suit and towel."

"Oh... that actually does sound nice," I said, settling back into the seat.

"It's a couple hours away and I didn't want you to wind up crawling out a window before we got there," he said, giving me a sympathetic grin. "She's right. You're twitchy."

"I can't help it. It's stupid, I know. I mean, with every-thing else we've been through, you'd think this is no big deal but it's just such a huge thing. I feel like this is the official 'not a baby' milestone."

"Definitely a bigger deal than him learning he can have puppy ears and a tail whenever he wants?"

"That's different," I grumbled.

"I'm kind of glad you're more anxious about this now than about him being a shifter," Xavier said.

"That's not a milestone. That's just him. Kindergarten is like a rite of passage," I said. The look Xavier sent me then was so intensely happy it would have made my knees buckle if I weren't already sitting down.

"What?"

"The way that you accept who he is. It's what we all would have wanted. What we all still want from a lot of people. I don't think you understand what a powerful thing that is," Xavier said.

I didn't know what to say to that, so we rode in silence for some time, but the conversation had dispelled some of my nervous energy, and it was a comfortable silence. Eventually, Xavier turned on the radio and we rode the rest of the way singing along with 80s and 90s rock music. By the time we pulled off the paved roads onto a dirt road through the trees, I was feeling more relaxed than I had in weeks. Maybe longer. Xavier navigated through an increasingly wild-looking path until I was starting to think that we were cutting our own trail. Eventually, we made it to a small clearing where he parked and opened his door. I hopped out also and looked around.

"Springs are water, right?" I asked. "I don't see any water."

"Listen," he said. I went quiet and listened as hard as I could.

"I just hear birds and bugs," I said after a minute.

"Really?" he asked.

"Yeah."

"Huh." I'd have thought he was messing with me except that he looked genuinely surprised. "The spring is that way," he said, pointing. I looked in the direction he pointed but couldn't see any sign of water or even a path.

"I'll take your word for it," I said.

"It's a short walk," he promised, grabbing both our backpacks from the car and handing me mine. He led me to what at first looked like a random spot, but upon closer inspection appeared to be a game trail. "This way." He led me down the trail, moving branches out of my way as we went. If he hadn't been leading I didn't think I'd be able to follow the trail, the path was so overgrown with trees and bushes.

Eventually, I did start hearing running water, and a moment later we came out next to a pool of crystal clear water that fed into a river flowing a little further away from us. On one side of the pool the ground sloped gently into the water, and on the other side, it rose up about twenty feet above the water, forming a short cliff face. The greenery surrounding the pool and the clouds were reflected in the clear water, and the absolute lack of human noises made it seem almost magical.

"How did you ever find this place?" I asked. For the first time, he looked a little sheepish.

"I, um... I didn't think about the fact that you couldn't shift when Kelly suggested we come here. I don't think she did, either. I've never walked here as a human. We usually all shift after we park to run down the trail. The kids love this place."

Oh. That explained the game trail. He pointed to a spot thick with low bushes to the side of the swimming hole. "You can change over there if you want. It's about as private a space as you can get out here. I'll head over to the other side," he said and turned to walk in the opposite direction. I ducked behind the bushes and tried to change as quickly as possible. I hadn't thought about what kind of bathing suits Kelly went for but the bright yellow and white polka dots did seem to fit her personality. At least it wasn't a bikini or I might have been obliged to sing.

I stepped out of the bushes to see Xavier sitting on the sloped edge with his feet in the water. "Ready?" he asked, grinning. He looked like a little kid, bursting with excitement and ready to jump in.

"Yeah, it's hot out here," I said, heading for the slope.

"Wait," he said. He got up and grabbed my hand. "This way first."

"We're not swimming yet?" I asked, following him.

"Do you trust me?" he asked, his eyes twinkling.

"Yes, Aladdin," I said laughing. He somehow grinned even bigger.

"Wrong answer this time," he said. I suddenly realized where we were. He'd led me up to the twenty-foot drop into the water.

"No," I said, backing up, "Oh, no..."

"You said yes," he said and picked me up in his arms and leapt. I clung to him and screamed for the split second before we hit the water, then held my breath as we sank beneath the surface. I was sputtering and shivering as we came up. The water was far, far colder than I had expected of a small pool in the middle of the summer.

"Seriously?" I demanded, wiping water from my eyes. "Oh god, it's freezing!" He laughed harder.

"Give it a minute to get used to it. Once you adjust it feels good. Promise," he said.

"Promise all you want. I haven't decided if I take back trusting you or not," I said, splashing him. He took a deep breath and ducked underwater. The jump had kicked up some silt, but the water was still pretty clear, and as I watched him dive, I started to realize how deep it was. He was descending so long I thought surely he would be out of air soon when his hand hit bottom. He rooted around for a moment, then turned and shot back up to the surface, gasping when he broke out into the air again.

"Forgive me?" he asked, holding out a small, dark triangle rock. I looked closer.

"Is that... is that a tooth?" I asked.

"Shark tooth," he said.

"In a river?" I looked around nervously.

"Long dead shark," he said. "It's a fossil. Also, it wasn't initially in the river. Trevor threw a bunch of them in here once and now the kids like to see who can dive and find them when we come." I picked it up and turned it around in my hand.

"It's so small. How did you find it down there?" I asked.

"Shifter-enhanced senses," he said, wiggling his eyebrows at me. I narrowed my eyes at him. "And... Kyle and I came out here not long ago and stashed them all in one spot to mess with the kids next time we bring them out. We sifted them all out of the dirt then made a pile between some branches that they probably won't think to look under," he admitted. I laughed.

"So which kid will be maddest?" I asked.

"Probably Hannah."

"Seriously?" I raised my eyebrows.

"She seems sweet and innocent, but that girl has a will of iron and a competitive streak that would put most professional athletes to shame," he said. "I do have to put this back before we leave. If we bring it back to the house and one of them sees it, I'll catch an earful. But I thought you'd like to see."

"Yeah, it's cool," I said, looking at it closer. When I was done, I handed it back to him and he ducked under the water again, heading back to the same spot.

I was still cold, but the shivering had lessened at least. I figured treading water probably had something to do with that. When he came back up, we swam around the spring. Xavier pointed out assorted fish, turtles, and strange-looking plants under the water. When we'd circled back, we went to the slope and sat on the water's edge, our feet submerged. He had been right. The water felt cool but not freezing now and felt nice compared to the heat of the afternoon.

I tilted my face back and closed my eyes, enjoying feeling the sun warm my skin. I listened to the animals around us. Now that we'd been here a while, in addition to the birds and bugs, I could occasionally hear the skitter of small feet or a splash in the water as a fish or turtle broke the surface. But no sounds of cars, machinery, planes. No sign of people. No wonder they liked it here, where they didn't have to be careful or worry about who might be watching.

I heard Xavier stand up and I started to get up too, but he put his hand on my shoulder.

"Wait here. I'll be right back," he said. I decided not to press the matter and just nodded and sat back down, closing my eyes again to enjoy the clashing feel of the sun on my face and the water on my feet. I heard bushes rustling behind me but didn't turn around, figuring whatever he was doing he wanted privacy for. Then I realized that the breathing I heard behind me sounded distinctly different suddenly. Less human and more animalistic. I opened my eyes and glanced back, then caught my breath.

Behind me, there was a huge wolf. Its reddish-brown fur shone in the sunlight and it stared directly at me, not moving, seeming to track my reactions. My fight-or-flight instinct kicked in and it took everything in me to stay still. Slowly, I turned my body and got to my knees. The wolf watched me warily, then laid down on its belly and tilted its head to the side. Its eyes were familiar.

"Xavier?" I asked. My voice was shaking, and I mentally cursed. When the wolf nodded its head twice, I let out a breath and tried to smile at him. It was one thing to know theoretically that he could turn into a wolf, but this was the first time I'd been confronted with one of them fully shifted. I'd thought I was ready, but my body was reacting as if I were about to be eaten, and I was pretty sure he could sense it. After the conversation in the car about accepting James as he was, right now I felt like a pretty big hypocrite, but I couldn't control the adrenaline coursing through my blood or the way my heart pounded so hard it felt like it was trying to escape from my chest.

Xavier got to his feet and watched me for a moment. He ducked his head and tail, as if trying to show that he wasn't a threat, then slowly and deliberately walked toward me. I stayed frozen, not trusting what my body would do if I let it move. When he got close, he nudged my hand with the top of his head and without thinking, I started petting him. He rubbed his head against my hand as if enjoying it. I suddenly realized what I was doing and pulled my hand back. He took a step back, also, as if trying to gauge my intentions.

"Is..." My mouth was dry. "Is that ok? It's not rude or something?" He shook his head, then nudged my hand again. This time I smiled and reached for him, rubbing behind his ears and on his head. "This is the part where I tell you you're a good boy, right?" I teased. He made a sound that was as close to laughter as I imagined a wolf could get and licked my hand. I could feel my tension evaporating as my instincts caught up to the thinking part of my brain to realize I wasn't actually in danger. When I was smiling again, Xavier backed up and jumped around yipping, like he was playing. I couldn't help but laugh. Then he herded me back toward the water.

"You want to go back swimming?" I asked. With that, he shoved against the back of my legs until he had pushed me back in. I wasn't as used to the water temperature as I had been and yelped at the cold. Xavier came bounding into the water, swimming next to me and using his head to nudge my hands onto him. When my arms were over him, I quit treading water and floated, holding onto him. He swam around for a while with me floating behind him, going further out into the river than I had dared when I was swimming under my own power. At the entrance where the spring met the river, the water swirled as it changed colors between the clear spring water and the browner water flowing downstream. When we came back, we climbed out of the water and he shook himself off, showering me with water droplets.

"Hey, watch it!" I said, only half joking. In response, he came closer and did it again. "Ok, ok, quit it," I said, waving him off. "I'm going to change. I'm starving." He nudged my hand again and I gave him a quick pat on the head, then headed back toward the bushes I had changed behind before. When I was in dry clothes, I came back out. He was sitting on a fallen tree, human again and dressed in black shorts and a grey t-shirt, waiting.

Before I could say a word, he stood and had me wrapped in a hug. I froze, stunned for a moment before putting my arms around him and hugging him back. As we stood there, I thought about how many years it had been since the last time I was hugged like this. I hadn't realized how much I missed this feeling, how much I missed being held and feeling someone against me, feeling protected and wanted in someone's arms, just being with them in the moment. I melted against him a little and he hugged tighter, his chin resting on the top of my head. I lost track of time as we stood there, and when he finally released me and pulled away, I let him go reluctantly.

"What was that for?" I asked, my throat threatening to close on the words.

"For accepting us—accepting me—for what we are." He seemed to be having trouble speaking, too. "That was... I didn't expect..." at this, he did stop speaking and reached out and hugged me again. I squeezed him back. "Just... thank you," he whispered, his voice muffled in my hair. He lightly kissed the top of my head and then stepped back.

"And in return, I'm apparently going to starve you to death," he said, his composure back. "Let's go. I know a place on the way home that does really good fried catfish, and if there's one thing that tastes amazing after swimming, it's seafood."

WE PULLED into the garage at the house late that night. I could see the TV light flickering in the den windows, but the rest of the house was dark. I put the styrofoam boxes of leftover catfish and coleslaw in the refrigerator while Xavier took our backpacks into the laundry room to dump out our damp towels and bathing suits. I glanced into the den as I passed through and saw Devon watching the news. He nodded to me and I waved back as I headed upstairs to check on James. I peeked into the room we had slept in the first night we'd been here and found him sprawled across the bed, taking up as much space as possible and snoring lightly, his tail out and wrapped around his waist. I smiled and closed the door before heading back downstairs.

Xavier was sitting on the couch now, deep in discussion with Devon. I went past them back into the kitchen to grab two cans of soda then came back out to the den. I sat on the couch and offered Xavier one of the cans, then settled back next to him to watch the news program. Out of the corner of my eye, I saw Devon glance over at me then give a pointed look to the can in Xavier's hand and raise a questioning eyebrow toward Xavier. Xavier was facing away from me so I couldn't see how he reacted, but I pretended I wasn't aware of the interaction, keeping my eyes on the screen as it switched to a weather forecast and popping open my own soda.

"I'll see you in the morning," Devon said, standing up. "Paige, Kelly said to tell you that she brought over an overnight bag for you and put it in your room upstairs."

"Oh, did she?" I asked.

"She said you'd probably get back late and it would be easier for you and James to sleep over," Devon said. When I opened my mouth again, he held up his hands before I could say anything. "I'm only the messenger," he said, backing up toward the stairs. "You two have a good evening." I caught a look pass between Xavier and Devon before Devon turned and went up. I leaned back on the couch again and Xavier settled next to me.

"Is the weather super interesting, or do you want to watch something else?" he asked.

"Surprise me," I said. He flipped channels until he found

a cheesy 1960s science-fiction show about robots from an alien planet.

"This good?" he asked.

"Looks good to me," I said. He set the remote down on the coffee table and settled back, and a moment later his arm settled hesitantly around my shoulders. I snuggled against him and he relaxed at my reaction, pulling me a little closer. Four years. Four years since I'd been around anyone who made me feel like this. Who made me feel happy and safe and wanted. Four years of waiting, searching, hoping for James's father to magically show up again before I'd finally given up. I felt a slight pang of guilt, but I'd moved here on purpose. I'd wanted to move on, to start over, make new connections and a new life. And, despite some very unexpected turns, it was turning out better than I'd dared hope.

"You all right?" Xavier asked, giving me a concerned look. I guess I'd been lost in thought and I wondered how I'd been reacting. I smiled at him and laid my head down on his shoulder.

"Absolutely," I said. "I'm doing great."

8

The next morning, James and I headed to our apartment. He said he wanted to be with me and promised to play in his room while I worked. I made a big deal about it, telling him he'd have to be extremely responsible and let me work, but the truth was I wanted a day with him anyway. The day with Xavier had, as Kelly said, chilled me out. I wasn't nearly as anxious about the upcoming school year, but I wanted to spend some time with him while he didn't have an obligation to go study.

True to his promise, James went into his room and played relatively quietly for the morning. Toward lunch, even the small sounds I'd been hearing quieted down. I went to check on him, expecting him to be napping, but instead found him sitting cross-legged on his bed, Barksie in his lap, holding a photograph.

"Hey, what do you have there?" I asked, sitting next to him. He showed me and my heart skipped a beat. He was holding the last picture I'd taken of his father and me, holding a toddler James between us. Since it was the most recent picture I had of James's dad, I had printed out hundreds of copies when he disappeared and handed them out everywhere, asking everyone I met if they'd see him.

"Where'd you get that?" I asked.

"When we were packing at the old house I found it." He looked worried. "Is it ok that I kept it?"

"Of course it's ok," I said, hugging him.

"Can we put it in a frame?" James asked.

"Sure. What brought this on?"

"We have all our new friends, and that's good, but I don't want to forget Daddy," he said. He took a deep breath. "Even if he's gone forever." He turned to look at me, starting to tear up. I pulled him into my lap and hugged him tighter, my own heart constricting.

"Oh sweetie, I don't want to forget him, either, even with new friends," I said. "Let's go get a frame for this right now."

I texted Kelly and Xavier that James and I were having lunch just the two of us today and grabbed my keys. We went to a drugstore nearby where he browsed the picture frames near the photo center and picked a dark wooden frame that he said "looked wolfy because that's me and Daddy." I glanced around nervously at the comment and made a mental note to talk to him later about what he said in public. I comforted myself with the thought that if someone did overhear this one, he was five and the comment would probably be interpreted as a five-year-old's explanation of something completely ordinary.

After stowing the frame in the car, we walked nearby to a pizza place and ordered slices and sodas. Since we paid for the frame, his stoic mood had passed, and he chatted happily the entire time about the new movies he and Trevor were watching, the frogs he'd found in the backyard and how he'd started trying to make drawings of them whenever he saw new ones, a video Greg showed him about how cat claws extended and retracted and how he wished his claws could do that (again, I crossed my mental fingers that anyone around us would take this as totally normal five-year-old conversation), and how once he learned to read he would teach Barksie, too.

As soon as we got home, I helped him put the picture into the frame, mainly giving directions while he did the actual work. When he was finished, he held it out and looked at it for a long time, smiling in satisfaction at his accomplishment.

"Let's put it here," he said, pointing to an upper shelf on the bookcase. I picked him up and he set it in the middle of the shelf in front of the books. He went to the couch and sat down and looked over at the picture, making sure that he was happy with the view from his seat. He nodded happily and went back to his room to play. I knew I should get a little more work done, but I sat down at the table and stared at his door, flooded with emotions that I didn't know how to start untangling.

I stood up and went to look at the picture again. I hadn't looked at this picture in nearly two years. Seeing it used to send me into anxiety attacks, remembering the panic and fear that had accompanied printing out all those copies and the constant look of pity on strangers' faces as I handed them out. For the first time, I didn't start hyperventilating looking at the image. It still made me sad, wishing things had been different, but it was more distanced, calmer. More wistful than despairing. I thought that was probably a good sign that I was moving in the right direction, that I was starting to heal.

· · ·

THAT EVENING we headed to the house for dinner. James was unusually quiet on the trip over, but as soon as we parked he bounded out of the car as his normal, high-energy self, his ears already shifting to the top of his head before he got in the front door. Xavier was finishing putting food on a plate as I came into the kitchen and handed it to me with a smile that I couldn't help but return. I wandered over to the table and sat next to Kelly.

"Looks," she whispered, grinning at me and shooting a knowing look toward Xavier's back. I kicked her lightly under the table and she grinned wider. Xavier came and sat next to me, and I had to admit that the smile I couldn't wipe off my face now suggested she had probably been right. And what's more, I was genuinely happy about it. We chatted about mundane topics as more and more people showed up to eat and socialize.

When we finished eating, we gave up our seats to a new wave of diners and went out back to sit and watch the mixture of human children, young wolves, and half-human-half-puppy kids play. I'd come to realize that partial shifting was popular among the elementary kids. All five kids who would be doing school lessons here were part human, part wolf. Different kids seemed to prefer to have paws rather than feet, to always have a tail, or, like James, to keep their wolf ears at all times.

"Do all shifter kids do that?" I asked after noting my observation.

"The ones I've met do, but I mostly see kids here," Xavier said. "I don't know if it's mainly our foundlings that do it or if shifter kids everywhere do that. I never thought about it." He turned to Kelly. "You'd have a better idea than me."

"It's a shifter kid thing all over," Kelly said. "Playing with how things feel different, how to build your own identity with something that's completely under your own control. I had a tail and fuzzy ears pretty constantly from ages five to ten. The fact that I could hear better with my shifted ears was a bonus, also."

"Your senses change when you're shifted?" I asked. "I thought you could always hear better than other people, stuff like that."

"Oh, we can," Xavier said. "But it's more pronounced when we're shifted. As a wolf, we can hear better, see better, smell better." He grimaced. "Although honestly, that last one isn't always a good thing."

"So James wants wolf ears so he can be a little snoop?" I asked with a chuckle. From across the yard, I saw James's ears perk and he glanced our way for a second before turning back to kicking a soccer ball around. Kelly and Xavier both burst out laughing.

"Yes, I'm going to say that's a big benefit for him," Kelly said, gulping for air as she tried to stop laughing. I made a mental note that maybe I should start being more careful about what I said when I thought he was in a different room.

Others soon joined us and as we continued to talk, Xavier casually slid closer to me on the picnic table bench we were sitting on and put an arm around my waist, never breaking the conversation. When I saw Kelly watching the move with interest, I leaned into him and her eyes absolutely sparkled. The sun set and I reluctantly called James over and told him we had to get going soon.

"Could I get a ride?" Kelly asked. "I rode over with someone else earlier."

"Sure," I said, but I saw Xavier raise an amused eyebrow toward her, and she wrinkled her nose back at him. I got the feeling this was less about the ride and more that she wanted information.

As we pulled out of the driveway, James pointed and said, "Hey, Kelly, there's your car!"

"So it is. Really I wanted a sleepover with your mom. You can bring me back to the house tomorrow." She grinned at me and I shook my head. It felt good, though, having a real friend again. We were halfway home when I remembered I didn't have milk for breakfast.

"You run in. I'll stay in the car with him," Kelly said as we pulled into a mostly empty grocery store parking lot.

"No, I want to go in! If she leaves me here she won't get any chocolate milk," James protested.

"Sure, I will," I said.

"No, you won't. I need to watch you," he insisted, folding his arms over his chest.

"Group trip then?" Kelly said, unbuckling.

"I guess so," I said. By the time we checked out, between Kelly and James we had the requested chocolate milk plus two cartons of ice cream, a frozen pizza, barbeque chips, and a bottle of wine.

"You're a bad influence," I said as I loaded the groceries onto the belt.

"No, I'm the cool aunt," she said, grinning as she threw three chocolate bars on top of the pizza.

"That works, too," I laughed. Maybe that's what this was. I'd never had a sister, but I imagined this is what it must be like. The manager was waiting by the door as grabbed our bags and headed out. We were apparently the last shoppers.

"Have a good evening ladies," he said, nodding to us as we left.

"Thanks," I said. He locked the sliding glass doors behind us and walked away as we exited.

"Um, Mommy? Kelly?" James asked hesitantly as we started to step off the sidewalk.

"I see it," Kelly said, her voice suddenly deadly serious and her body stiff as she pulled us back onto the sidewalk. I looked toward the car where two men I'd never seen before were leaning against the driver side doors, staring directly at us, and smiling. Behind us, there was no sign of the store employees. They were too far back into the store now to see us. As the two men stood and started walking toward us, Kelly cursed and grabbed my hand, walking down the sidewalk away from them toward the side of the building.

"Is this a good idea?" I asked nervously. "If we're back there they can do anything."

"I can't shift out front. There's cameras," Kelly said, looking toward the security cameras near the doors. "If I can shift I can take them down with no problem. If they follow us back here, they won't come out of it in one piece." I'd never heard her talk like this and it reminded me that all of them, even Kelly, had gone through experiences that I never would have dreamed of.

I swallowed, wishing Xavier, Devon, or Kyle were with us, too. She squeezed my hand. "They won't lay a finger on you or James, Paige," she said. I nodded and followed her, holding James tight against my side. As we went around the corner, Kelly set down her grocery bag and I did the same, just before I realized what a huge mistake we'd made. Around the corner were six more men, each looking like they could easily crush us. And scattered among them were five wolves. Wolves whose eyes were much more sentient than any wild animal.

Before I could blink, Kelly had shifted and jumped in front of me and James, growling and snarling at the group surrounding us. The two men from the parking lot came up behind us, blocking us in, and I backed up from them too, pulling James close to me. When I felt my back hit the brick wall, I drew in a breath. We were completely trapped.

"We have no quarrel with you, shifter," one of the men said, looking at Kelly. "Get out of the way and leave us to it. These two aren't your problem anyway, are they? They aren't shifters or they would have done it by now. Look after your own kind." She growled and bared her teeth at him. He didn't flinch.

One of the wolves suddenly leapt at Kelly from the side, jumping on her back and aiming for her neck with his teeth. She spun at the last minute and he missed, catching her dress in his teeth and ripping it to pieces, exposing her brown fur. He came after her again, getting a quick bite on her back leg before she turned and bit down hard on his ear, yanking it until he yelped and backed away, blood streaming down his face.

He was posed to pounce again when the front man yelled, "Enough!" The wolf glared at him but moved back into formation, hatred blazing in his eyes as he stared at Kelly, who now looked fierce with blood dripping from her teeth as she positioned herself for another defense.

"Really, this is unnecessary." The man frowned at her. "Why defend them? Their kind has never been anything but cruel to you." Kelly snapped her teeth and growled, and the man sighed as if he were talking to a petulant child. "Have it your way, then," he said, and held up two fingers, pointing at us. The entire group started closing in, slowly this time. They knew there was nowhere for us to go and they had no need to hurry. My heart was in my throat as I clutched James to my chest.

"When I tell you, you run. You shift and you run as fast as you can and you don't look back. Hide. Find the others," I whispered in his ear.

"No," he whimpered, his eyes wide.

"James, you escape, you hear me?" I whispered, trying to sound as fierce as I could, although I felt like I was going to collapse from fear. My heart plummeted as I realized that every wolf there could hear the whole conversation, and if the human-looking ones were shifters, they likely could also. As I looked at their faces, I knew without a doubt that they weren't going to let any of us leave.

"No," James repeated. But he didn't sound afraid. He sounded angry.

NO! I heard James's voice in my head this time, screaming, almost knocking me to my knees. How was he doing that? *Get away from us! DON'T TOUCH MY MOMMY!*

Around us, the expressions on all the shifters, human and wolf alike, seemed to go blank. They stopped advancing toward us, then stopped moving completely.

GO AWAY! I heard his mental voice, felt its force wash over and around me. When it hit the shifters, they turned and started walking away from us slowly. I looked down at James in my arms. His little face was a mask of fury as he glared at the receding line of wolves and humans.

I felt a furry head butt my hip, and I looked at Kelly who tilted her head in a "let's go" gesture. I nodded and followed as she led me along the wall and back out to the parking lot, where we headed toward my car, keeping one eye behind us. I clutched James tight against me and could feel his body relaxing like he was falling asleep.

"Hey, you ok baby?" I whispered to him. Kelly looked up at us, concerned.

"Yeah. I'm just tired," he said, yawning.

"What did you do?" I asked.

"I don't know," he said, sounding confused. Then he sat up in my arms and looked into my eyes. "But they can't take you, too. I won't let them." He put his head down on my shoulder and hugged my neck, and I choked down a sob as I squeezed him back. By the time I got the car door open and we'd all piled in, Kelly limping in on her bitten back leg, he had fallen into a deep sleep.

XAVIER, Devon, and Kyle were at my apartment when we got there. Kelly limped into my bedroom to shift back to human and borrow some of my clothes. James hadn't so much as blinked his eyes open when I changed him into pajamas and tucked him into bed, and I was trying not to panic at what that might mean, tried to convince myself that he was only exhausted and that he hadn't slipped into a coma. When I came out of his bedroom, Kyle and Kelly were sitting at my dining table, Devon was sitting in the armchair, frowning as if lost in thought, and Xavier was standing in front of my bookcase staring at the framed picture James and I had put there that afternoon. His expression made me self-conscious. What did he think about a family portrait showing up now?

Slowly, Kelly looked at me, her expression fixed into something I couldn't identify. "Paige," she said, quietly. "What was James's father's name?"

I blanched. No. This couldn't be happening. After all these years, I couldn't be finding out what happened to him like this. "Julian." My breath caught on the word, on the name I hadn't dared say again out loud, had even stopped trying to think of because of how much it hurt after I'd been told to stop looking, to stop hoping.

"The name isn't what I'm concerned with. He would have been smart enough to create a new identity," Xavier said. He picked up the framed photo. "Is this him?" he asked, holding out the picture so that it was visible to all of us. I nodded, a lump in my throat.

"Shit. *Shit*," Devon said, leaning forward and slamming his hands down on the arms of the chair as if he needed to hold himself up. Kelly had turned white, and Xavier was staring at me, wide-eyed.

"I'm going to need someone to start explaining why you're asking me about him," I said shakily. Devon rubbed his eyes with his palms. Kelly bit her bottom lip so hard I expected to see blood, and Xavier's eyes stayed frozen on me. The only one who seemed somewhat composed was Kyle. "Now," I insisted.

"The man you knew as Julian was part of our pack," Kyle said. "Years ago. He was gone by the time I showed up, so I didn't know him myself. But I knew about him."

"What exactly do you know?" I asked. I was starting to feel light-headed and my heart was starting to race. "And what do you mean 'the man I knew as Julian?'"

"If that's Julian," Devon nodded toward the picture, "We knew him as Nathan. But I'm pretty sure that wasn't his first identity, either, or even his second. Some of us can communicate mind to mind unshifted, with varying abilities. Nate was more powerful than anyone I'd ever met. He could communicate from a farther distance than anyone else I knew about who wasn't an alpha, he could communicate fully telepathically with other pack members while in human form, and if he were in close contact he could do something he called compelling others."

My mouth went dry. "What does that mean?" I asked. My knees were starting to give out. Xavier noticed and moved me to the couch and lowered me down, sitting next to me with an arm around my waist.

"The difference between telling someone to do something and making them do it," Devon said. "As far as I know, no one else has ever had that ability. It made him…"

"Dangerous," Kyle interrupted.

"Valuable," Devon finished, glaring at Kyle.

"Both," Kyle said with a shrug.

"Valuable, like…" I was glad I was sitting down now that possibilities were running through my head, reasons he had disappeared, what may have happened to him. In the past, I would have told myself to stop being paranoid and over-imaginative, but I was currently surrounded by semi-telepathic werewolves who were telling me that Julian had a secret identity or two and could control other people's thoughts, so nothing I was thinking seemed out of range, and some of it had my stomach curdling.

"Like there would be people out there who want to control him for their own reasons," Devon said grimly. I dropped my head into my hands as I started shaking. "No, no, no," I whispered. Xavier started rubbing my back.

"Breathe," he said softly next to my ear. I gasped, not realizing I'd started holding my breath. I took measured breaths, counting in and out until I felt in control again. I looked up at Kelly.

"He's the one you told me about that first night. The one who left and you didn't hear from him again," I said faintly. She nodded, face still white.

"Paige, I think you and James should move into the house for now," Xavier said grimly. "Whoever that was may not have been looking only for you. If they were looking for Nate's child, he just confirmed what he can do. We can protect both of you better there." I felt like I might faint. His arm moved up around my shoulder and he hugged me to his side. "We won't let anything happen to either of you, ok?" he said. "You're family. We protect our own."

I nodded but could still feel panic welling up inside me. Someone was after James. Probably the same people who had taken Julian... no, Nate apparently, and done who knows what with him. They were after my baby. Our baby. At that thought, I felt my resolve come back, my spine tighten. They couldn't have him. They had ripped our lives apart, stolen James's father and my partner, but they weren't going to get a second chance. "And I protect *my* family," I said, fire in my voice again.

"Atta girl," Kelly said, nodding encouragingly. "Xavier, go pack a bag for James. I'm going to help Paige get what she needs."

"Kyle, you and I are going to do a perimeter sweep before we leave," Devon said. Kyle nodded. Devon turned to me. "Ten minutes. Preferably five," he said. I nodded and headed into my bedroom with Kelly. Behind me, I heard Kyle and Devon deciding on responsibilities. Then I heard someone shucking off clothing and a moment later a canine whine before the front door opened and closed again.

"Come on," Kelly said, nudging my shoulder. "Let's give him his five minutes and get out of here." I mumbled agreement and started shoving things into a duffle bag.

WE RODE in Xavier's car to the house, me sitting next to him in front, with Kyle sitting in the back next to James, who didn't wake up when being transferred from his bed to his booster seat. I had wanted my own car, but Xavier said it could make tracking us down easier, and I immediately agreed to leave it behind. When I had started to get into the back with James, Xavier said he wanted each of us in grabbing distance of him and Kyle "just in case."

My stomach was in knots thinking about both why he

was being this cautious and at the realization that he was acting like this wasn't the first time he'd been on guard duty. I tried not to think about what else he may have had to defend against in the past, and by extension what Nate hadn't been able to defend against. Kelly and Devon took my car to park in a random parking lot somewhere to throw off whoever was looking for us and said they would meet us back at the house.

As we pulled up in the driveway, I saw that every room was lit up, with slivers of light coming through closed curtains.

"It's past midnight. Why is everyone awake?" I asked. A young-looking wolf with grey fur and a dark streak on its head sat by the front door scanning the yard. It nodded as we pulled into the garage.

"Kelly let Devon see what happened through the link while she was shifted, and he filled everyone in before we left. We have watches set up and people out looking for the shifters who attacked you," Xavier said.

"Who is that?" I asked, pointing toward the door as we went past and into the garage.

"Hannah," Kyle said from the back. He started to gently unbuckle James. I felt a little queasy again. Hannah was a teenager. She should be worrying about math homework and what movie to go see this weekend and college admissions essays, not guarding a safe house. Guarding me.

"Don't. Don't do that," Xavier said, turning toward me as he shut off the engine.

"What?" I asked.

"I can see where your thoughts are going. She's been through worse than guard duty. She knows what's at stake. None of this is your fault, so there better not be a shred of guilt in your mind about this," he said.

"But..."

"Would you rather he not exist?" He nodded toward James sleeping in Kyle's arms.

"No!"

"And we wouldn't, either. So you will protect him, and we will protect him," His eyes softened and he brushed a strand of my hair away from my face. "And we'll protect you."

And with that, I finally broke. My face fell into my hands and I started sobbing. Xavier's arms went around me and I buried my face in his chest and cried. I felt him nod over my head and the door to the house opened and closed as Kyle took James inside. I lost track of time as Xavier held me, made shushing noises, stroked my hair, and told me over and over that everything would be fine, that we'd never, ever let anyone get their hands on James, that it would all turn out ok. I wished with all my heart that I could believe any of it.

9

The next afternoon I sat at the kitchen table, poking miserably at some leftover lasagna Kelly had heated up for me. "Eat," she said, glaring at me across the table. "When he wakes up, he's going to need you, and you won't be a lot of help if you're passing out from hunger." I sighed and took a bite, raising my eyebrows at her as if to say "happy?" She nodded in satisfaction and went back to scrolling on her phone.

"Keep going," she said, reading the news. She'd been scouring headlines for anything that sounded like a clue as to who had attacked us. Gang activity, packs of dogs running the streets, anything that sounded like it could lead us somewhere, but so far, there had been nothing. I felt a wet nose nuzzle my ankle and looked down at Xavier who had situated himself in wolf form next to my chair.

"I'm eating!" I said, waving my fork at him, and then very purposefully took another bite, keeping eye contact while I chewed. He laid his head back down and made a sound like he was laughing. Kyle was out on patrol around town with some others, and Xavier was currently assigned to be our contact point, which meant he needed to stay shifted to hear what the rest of the pack was saying through their link.

"Morning," Hannah muttered, wandering into the kitchen rubbing her eyes. She started a cup of coffee in the Keurig and yawned.

"It's two in the afternoon. But you did great last night. Thank you," Kelly said. Hannah didn't respond, but she beamed at the praise. I noticed her hair dye only covered the ends of her hair now, the top of her head a dark blonde instead of the purple it had been yesterday. It occurred to me then that the dark streak I'd seen on her head last night had actually been that same shade of purple. When her coffee was done she brought it to the table and warmed her hands, staring blankly out the window, as if she were still trying to wake up.

"Moooooooooommy!" I leapt to my feet as soon as I heard the wail, running up the stairs to the bedroom I was sharing with James. He was finally awake, sitting straight up in bed breathing hard and trembling, his terrified face white and streaming with tears as he clutched Jessica who had been sitting with him while the others tried to coax me to have lunch.

I sat on the bed and he threw himself at me, his arms around me squeezing tight enough that I had trouble breathing as I hugged him, crooning reassurances until I felt him start breathing regularly again. Kelly came and sat on the other side of James and rubbed his back, Devon hovered near the door, and a moment later Xavier appeared behind him, human now and dressed in sweatpants and a black t-shirt. Jessica had quietly slipped out the door when the rest of us showed up.

"Hey, it's ok. We're all here. You're safe. I've got you," I said when he had let go a bit. I pulled him away so I could look him in the eyes and wipe the tears away from his cheeks. He sniffled and looked around at the others in the room, as if reassuring himself, then looked back at me.

"I saw where Daddy was," he whispered. I blinked, thinking I hadn't heard him right.

"You mean you remember when Daddy was with us?" I asked.

"No. After he was gone. I saw where he was. But he's not there anymore. He..." He frowned, concentrating. "It's going away! I can't see it anymore. But he's not there. He's gone dark now." The blood drained from my face and my heart felt like it skipped a beat. I felt panic rising in me and tried my best not to let it show, but I knew James could feel the sudden tension in my arms from the concerned way he looked at me. Xavier walked up beside me and put his hands on my shoulders, squeezing gently.

"James?" Devon asked slowly. "Would it be ok if you showed me in your mind what you saw? Maybe I can help you figure it out. Can you shift right now? All the way?"

James looked at me and I nodded. "Only if you want to, but it's your decision, ok?" I said. He took a deep breath and nodded, then looked at Devon hesitantly. "Yes," he said, his voice wavering but decisive.

"When we both shift, you're going to hear my voice, but inside your head," Devon said, sitting on the floor and pulling his shirt off over his head. "We can talk that way, but you can also show me pictures. Think of what you want me to see and I'll see it, all right? You show me whatever you want to. If it gets scary, remember I'm right there with you, and your mom and everyone else is still here, too. We won't let anything happen to you." Despite his usual no-nonsense manner, I was reminded that a big part of what Devon did was work with scared kids. While he didn't completely relax,

James did look more confident now. Devon turned his gaze to me.

"I need your consent to this, too," he said. "And I need you to understand what this is. This isn't only a momentary thing. He's untethered right now, a lone shifter. But once we join minds, if he accepts the link then he's officially part of our pack, and that's a hard thing to break away from. It can be done, but it's not easy. I know we talked before about you being part of the family, but this will make it official. After this, he's bound to us unless he actively and willfully decides to put the effort into breaking the connection." Devon searched my face intently. "After this," he said, "he, and by extension you, will fully belong to us and we to him. It's your choice, but I want you to know what this will mean." His gaze went to James. "I want you both to understand, and to know that you don't have to do this if you don't want to."

"I want to," James said immediately. I could see a look in his eyes I hadn't seen before, almost a hunger, a longing. I thought about Kelly and how she'd watched over us; about Jessica, Hannah, and Trevor and how they had immediately adopted James as a new little brother; about Devon and Kyle always working in the background to make sure we were taken care of as if we were already theirs. And Xavier and whatever was growing between us. My heart already belonged to all of them. The choice had been made before he asked.

"We want to," I said, giving James a squeeze. Xavier's hands tightened on my shoulders.

"Can I stay in your lap?" James asked.

"Of course, baby. You can be wherever you want." After I said it, I realized what he meant. He wanted me to hold him while he shifted. It occurred to me that I hadn't ever seen him fully as a wolf. I'd seen him partially shifted plenty of times now, especially once he realized he could have a tail whenever he wanted, but that was it. I wasn't sure he ever had shifted completely, and from the concerned look on his face, it seemed to me that this might be the first time. I gave him a big squeeze. "You've got this. You can do this," I said. He nodded again and closed his eyes. I let go to give him space but let him stay seated in my lap. He opened his eyes.

"Do I have to take my shirt off, too?" he asked, frowning.

"Only if you want to," Devon said. "It might feel tight once you're a wolf, but it's your choice. Your body will be a different shape so your clothes might feel funny."

"Ok," James said and closed his eyes again. His feet changed quickly and his tail sprouted up out of the waistband of his shorts. His nose shifted into a muzzle and his ears moved up and covered in fuzz quickly, too. After that, the transformation went slower. A fine fuzz sprouted all over his body, but his arms and torso remained clearly human. He opened his eyes and scowled at his arms. "It's not working! Why isn't it working?"

"Have you ever shifted that part of your body before?" Xavier asked.

"No, I like having my hands," James said, confirming my suspicions.

"Remember how it felt the first time you shifted your feet? Was it quick and easy?"

"No, it took a long time to figure it out," James admitted.

"This shouldn't take as long because you know how to do other parts, but it might be hard since you haven't practiced. Think about what it feels like when the rest of you shifts. Then tell your arms that you're in control," Xavier said, smiling encouragingly then reached over me and shifted his hand into a paw in front of James's face. He playfully batted one of James's ears. "Come on, pup. You can do this."

James nodded, fixing a look of determination on his face, and closed his eyes again. The change was almost instant this time, and his eyes flew open. He looked down at himself, fully wolf now, and gave a triumphant yelp, then leapt to the floor and spun in a circle. His fur was a brown so light it bordered on yellow, and he looked like a golden retriever as he tried to catch his own tail. After a moment, he whined and turned his head to nip at the shirt that was now tight across his back.

"Do you want that off?" I asked. He nodded.

"Shift back and take it off," Kelly said. This time James didn't close his eyes. He kept his gaze fixed on Kelly and easily shifted back to human.

"I did it! I can do it!" He cried gleefully.

"Told you you could," Xavier said, grinning. Then his face went serious again. "You ready for the next step?" he asked.

"Yeah, ready," James said, his voice coming through the t-shirt he'd managed to get tangled halfway off his head. I pulled it over his head and arms and he grinned at me and shifted back into a wolf, tilted his head back, and gave a low howl. He looked at me with eyes that were shining with triumph. I had thought seeing this for the first time would terrify me, but I was bursting with pride, seeing how happy he was.

Suddenly, his eyes went wide and his body stiffened. I sat straight up, wondering if something had gone wrong, but Xavier sat next to me and squeezed me against his side reassuringly. "He's fine," he said. "Devon's making contact. It's really weird the first time you experience it." I thought about James's thoughts coming into my mind during the attack and nodded. Slowly, James turned to look at Devon, who was now sitting in wolf form, attention fully on James. After a moment, James nodded and sat down in front of Devon. They stared at each other for what seemed like an eternity. I didn't know what I expected, but watching from outside, nothing was happening. Then James began to whine and laid down on his belly, putting his paws over his eyes. Beside me, Kelly nodded at Devon.

"Devon wants me to join them," she said. "James is fine. I'm just going in to help him feel some extra support." She squeezed my hand. "You know we won't let anything happen to him." I nodded, a lump in my throat as she shifted and went to lie beside James, putting her full length against him. He put his paws down and leaned his head into her side. She licked his nose and he relaxed into her. Then she looked at Devon and perked her ears and they all went still again, Kelly resting her head on top of James's.

"I don't like this," I muttered. Xavier squeezed me again.

"Are you changing your mind? Consent can be taken back. If you don't want him to be part of the pack..."

"No, that's not what I mean," I said. "I can't help him. I can't do anything. He's only five and already he's having to deal with whatever is happening to him without me. I should be able to do something for him!"

"But he's not alone," Xavier said. "And he's never going to be alone again, now. He'll always have us. No matter what happens, he has the full pack behind him." Another squeeze. "Yes, there's going to be some stuff you can't help with. But we're here for him, too." I didn't feel any better about my own sudden uselessness, but I did stop worrying as much for the moment about James. I leaned into Xavier and waited. Occasionally James trembled or whined and Kelly nuzzled him or licked his nose again and he'd quiet down. Every time it happened I tensed and Xavier rubbed my arm until I relaxed again.

"Isn't it kind of weird seeing wolves in clothing all the time?" I asked, trying to distract myself. If I weren't so tense about this whole situation, seeing wolves in shorts and a sundress would have had me laughing.

"We don't usually."

"Do you go to different rooms to shift so you can change clothes first?" I asked. Xavier started chuckling and I looked at him and raised an eyebrow.

"We don't usually worry about changing in different rooms all that much when we're shifting. Comes with the territory. We've all been acting fairly prudish in front of the human lately," he said.

"Oh," I said. Then I remembered who "the human" was and blushed. "*Oh.*" Now Xavier was actually laughing as I studiously avoided eye contact. Devon glanced at us and let out a quick, low growl. Xavier nodded at him and made a motion like he was locking his lips together, but I could see his shoulders still shaking. Devon rolled his eyes and focused back on James. The momentary distraction was gone as I brought my attention back to the three wolves.

"What's going on in there?" I asked, keeping my voice low this time.

Xavier shrugged. "Without shifting I couldn't tell you specifics, and even then I'd need to be invited into whatever they're doing. It's not like we can see everything each other is thinking all the time. The rest of the pack will have been alerted that we have a new member, so the first few minutes was probably everyone who's a wolf right now dropping in to say hi. After that, I imagine Devon is trying to figure out the dream. When we're sharing something we've experienced or what's happening in the moment we think back over the situation and send the images and it can almost feel like we're experiencing it again, but I don't know how it will go with a half-remembered dream."

As if on cue, James suddenly sat up and let out a howl that sounded like his heart was breaking. Kelly and Devon went to either side of him and pressed against him as he howled and howled. I started to jump up, but Xavier gently held me back.

"I know, I know," he soothed me. "Give them a minute. There's as much going on inside his head as there is out here right now. He's ok. They've got him. He's ok."

By the time James finished howling and hung his head, I was trembling. I wanted to hold him, fix whatever was tearing him up inside. Devon and Kelly finally moved away from him and looked toward me, and I fell to the floor, pulling James into my arms. He nuzzled his furry head into my chest and whined as I stroked his head, his back, feeling at a loss. Kelly shifted back to human and put one hand on my shoulder and another on his head, rubbing behind his ears.

"I think we found something. But I was there for James to mentally lean on, not to be part of the process, so I'm not sure what it was. Devon's staying with him until he can calm down enough to shift back," she said. I nodded, hugging James tighter. Devon came and sat next to us, occasionally making sympathetic sounds and lightly touching James's ear with his nose. After a few minutes, James started to slowly shift back, his fur receding, his ears moving down and shrinking, his tail slowly disappearing. As his muzzle changed back into a child's face, the puppy whimpers changed into sobs.

After James had completed the shift back to little boy, Devon shifted back, also. He pulled his shirt back on over his head and wordlessly motioned to the others to leave the room. Kelly gave my knee a squeeze and James's back a pat before she followed the others out and closed the door. I didn't say anything, but rocked him and hugged him and kissed his hair until he cried himself out. When his breathing finally stabilized, he wiped his face on my shirt and gave me one more hug, then turned around so his back was to me and leaned back against me, tracing patterns on my arm with his fingers. I waited. Finally, he took a deep breath.

"They took him. They took him and they wanted him to do bad things, but he said no. I showed Devon the room where he went dark. I didn't want him to... I didn't want him to go again..." he took a deep, shaky breath like he would burst into tears again and I hugged him to me, taking deep breaths with him until he was calm again.

"You showed Devon?" I asked. He nodded. "If you want to talk about it, we can. But if it's too hard to talk about we don't have to. I can talk to Devon if that's easier." Wordlessly, he nodded again and restarted tracing shapes on my arm. He took another deep breath, and this time it felt like his thoughts were drifting in happier directions.

"We're in the family now, for real this time. I got us in the pack. He asked me and I said yes and then he asked the others and they all said yes. And after we all said yes, I could hear all of them! There were so many people, Mommy. And they were so happy that we're with them now." He turned and hugged me, his eyes shining with happiness instead of tears. "I have so many brothers and sisters!" At that, I nearly started crying myself.

His joy was contagious, and as it sank in what he had done—what we had agreed to together—I realized that a burden had lifted from my shoulders. No matter what happened to me now, I knew that James would always have someone to fall on, would be taken care of. I had no intention of leaving him for any reason, but the weight that was lifted by knowing we had the safety net forever now almost floored me.

"Want to go find Jessica and tell her she's your big sister for real now?" I asked.

"Yes!" He leapt up and ran out the door, not bothering to grab his shirt, and as he ran ahead of me, I saw his ears pop back on top of his head. I shook my head. I officially had my own little anime character.

Jessica, Hannah, and a young wolf with dark brown fur were waiting in the kitchen. James barreled into the wolf and cried, "Trevor, I can do the whole thing now! Come see!" And he ran out the door, the other three hot on his heels, his feet and hands already transforming into paws as the door slammed behind them.

"In here," I heard Kelly call from the den. I grabbed a soda out of the fridge and headed in, sitting next to Xavier on the couch.

"Could we..." I motioned to the TV. Kelly nodded and got the backyard camera showing. There were no children, but we could see a pile of clothes on the picnic table and four young wolves racing around the yard and tackling each other, wrestling, nipping, and yelping. I smiled at that, then turned to Devon, preparing for bad news. "James said you found Nate. Or found where he was," I said, my voice tight.

"Sort of," Devon said. He sighed. "It would be so much easier if I could show you," he muttered. I flushed, acutely aware of my status as an outsider here.

"Devon," Xavier said, a note of caution in his tone.

"Right, sorry," Devon said, and I had a feeling that there had been a conversation about me while I was upstairs.

"Just... what was it?" I asked, trying to temper my own rising feelings of both irritation and inadequacy. I'd deal with that later.

"First, and this is most important for now because it's the most immediately relevant, they were after both of you. James was able to see a glimpse of their intentions when he... when he stopped them. Both of you were targets. He didn't know why and I'm not sure if that's because he couldn't see deeper than immediate thoughts or because the attackers themselves didn't know." I sucked in a breath. I wasn't sure what I had been expecting on that front, but that wasn't it. I had halfway been hoping that it was a random attack, but I knew the likelihood of that was pretty much zilch. It had been far too coordinated.

"Second, this is definitely related to Nate." Devon continued. "When James was sleeping he apparently sent out mental tendrils. I don't know what he was searching for or why, but what he found... well I don't know if it was a message someone sent, a memory he ferreted out of someone, or what it was. It was pretty vague."

"He went searching for... what, the people who attacked us?" I asked, eyes wide.

"Not on purpose, not consciously," Devon said. He leaned back in his armchair and sighed. "And that in itself is another problem we're going to need to address sooner rather than later. The boy has more power than I've ever felt, even from his dad, and that was pretty impressive. Now that he can fully shift and access it, we're going to need someone to teach him how to harness and control this."

"Can he be traced? Is that something someone could use to track him down?" I asked, my mind already racing.

"Not by anyone I'm aware of other than maybe Nate himself," Devon said. At that, I sucked in my breath.

"What are you saying?" I whispered.

"I honestly don't know," Devon said. "What James saw was definitely in the past. It was more feelings and intentions than language and solid visuals. Nate was with someone who wanted to use his powers, get him to use coercion to reach whatever their goals were. He fought back, tried to escape, and then everything went dark. The vision ended." Devon's gaze was sympathetic. "Paige, I don't know if that means they knocked him out or that was the end of the message or what happened."

Dead. Or if he's dead. I could feel my mind reeling, the words repeating on a loop like they did the first time it was suggested that he'd been killed and not simply run off. When the searches hadn't come up with a body, the police changed their guess, but the possibility had always been there. Kelly was gripping my hand so hard I thought it might break, and I remembered that they had known him, too. I wasn't the only one who had lost him.

"The good news is that we did get some visual of his surroundings. The bad news is that it was an interior room and we didn't really have any hints about the location. Tile floors. Cinder block walls. There was a skylight. It's not much to go on."

"He didn't leave us," I said, my voice wavering. "He didn't abandon us like everyone tried to convince me. He fought back." Tears started building up in my eyes and Kelly squeezed my hand again.

"We knew him too, remember. He would never have done that. I know the kind of man he was, and he wouldn't have left you and his son alone if he could have prevented it," she said.

Xavier put his arm around my shoulders and I leaned into him, trying to control the flood of emotion threatening to pull me under. "We'll get answers, Paige," he said. I had never heard his voice sound so harsh. I glanced up at him and saw that his face was fixed in a look of iron determination, the look of a warrior readying for battle. "Wherever he is, we'll find him and bring him back. And we'll make sure that whatever happened to him never happens to you or James."

"He may have left us, but he's still our packmate," Kelly said, her eyes fixed on Devon now.

"The first time, he left of his own free will. We won't stop that. But we damn sure won't let anyone kidnap one of our pack," Devon said.

"If he left... you said it was hard to break away from the pack once you were connected. But he did it?" I asked.

"No," Xavier said. "He left the family but never left the pack. He walked away and never shifted again. If he had, we'd have been able to hear him. And if he'd broken away or died, we'd have felt that, too."

"You'd have felt if he died...?" I whispered. Now I really did feel like I might faint.

Devon looked at me as if realizing I didn't have the same information they did. "Yes, Paige, we'd have felt that," he said. "He's alive somewhere. And we're going to find him." My breath caught in my throat.

In the momentary silence, the front door burst open and I stifled a scream. Xavier hugged me to him, trying to keep me from bolting as Kyle strode in, kicked off his hiking boots, and dropped into the other armchair. He looked around at all of us, grinning. "I hear we're going on a wolf hunt."

10

Over the course of the afternoon, members of the pack flooded the house. It became the routine for them to head to the backyard first and give an official welcome to James, then head into the den to start discussing the recent attack. It didn't take long for James to be absolutely preening from the attention. Kelly stayed in wolf form for much of the afternoon so she could give each new person an overview of the attack through their link. She said sharing the experience was faster and more effective than trying to explain it.

Rather than food being prepared at the house as usual, different pack members brought something to share so by the time dinner rolled around, there was a full potluck available. Someone brought a store-bought ice cream cake that said "Welcome to the pack!" on it in pink and green candy letters in James's honor. I forced myself to eat, but I was too distracted to taste any of it.

Everyone was preoccupied, it turned out. Instead of the usual relaxed, extended mealtime that we usually had, everyone ate quickly and then found their way into the den.

Soon not only were the sectional couch and armchairs full, but people had brought in chairs from the kitchen and office, and more people were leaning against the walls or sitting on the floor. Some stayed in wolf form and sat around the room.

There was an unorganized buzz of noise as everyone talked, coming up with theories, making threats toward the unnamed attackers, and questioning if the bombing and this attack were connected. To my intense relief, not a single person leveled accusations toward me or James or blamed us for putting their family at risk. Rather, every time James was mentioned, there was a distinct tone of protective possession, and I was grateful for that, even as I felt my own guilt at unwittingly putting all of them in the line of fire between us and whoever wanted us.

At some point when everyone seemed settled in, Kelly gave a quick but loud howl and everyone stopped talking and turned their eyes toward the front of the room. Xavier had been wandering the room talking to different people, but at this he came and motioned for the woman next to me to scoot over, and he sat down beside me. Devon stood in front of the television, flanked by Kyle on one side and Kelly in wolf form on the other.

"Last night, we were attacked," Devon said. "Members of our pack were targeted and attacked by shifters. You've all seen Kelly's memory now. We don't know who or why, but we have some theories. Some of you remember Nate from before he left. Many of you remember him through our shared memories. But you all know him as a member of our pack, even though he left us some time ago. We have come to find out that James," as he said the name, Devon's eyes got softer for a moment, and I saw others around the room smile approvingly. "Is Nate's son." The looks turned from smiles to confusion. People started to whisper to each other. Thankfully, everyone seemed more curious than suspicious, but I found myself squeezing my hands together nervously. After a moment, Kelly barked and everyone's attention went back to the front of the room.

"We have also learned that while Nate initially left us of his own volition, some time later, he was abducted." Angry murmurs. Devon nodded toward me and eyes turned to me. I couldn't understand the intention behind them yet, and I found myself holding my breath. "Paige searched for him for a long, long time. We know Nate and we know that the chances he'd abandon a partner and child are slim to none. We're assuming at this point that he was captured by someone and is being held against his will."

At this point, Kyle took up the overview. "Based on how the attack went, it's safe to assume the attackers know Nate and know Paige and James's connection to him, as they were clearly targeted. We don't know for sure if they know that Nate has extra abilities, but they now know what James can do. While it was important for us to protect our pack members before we knew about James's abilities, it's even more vital now that he be protected at all costs." At the mumble of vehement agreement that went around the room, my nervousness dissipated. They were on our side. They'd make sure he stayed safe.

"Because the attackers were shifters, we can't send out a wide-range call for help from other packs on this one," Kyle continued. "We don't know who was involved yet. You've all seen the faces Kelly had a good look at, and we'll be searching for those people in particular. We have two goals right now. First, to find out who attacked us and why and make sure they know never to try it again. And second, to recover our packmate who was stolen." A cheer went up and

I let out a breath. Xavier grabbed my hands that were still clasped together and squeezed, his eyes on the three standing up front.

"Do we think this is related to the bombing?" Greg asked from his position near the back of the room.

"My instinct is no, but we can't rule it out," Devon said. "From what we've found so far, the bombing seems to be the work of AWL." I snuck a glance at Xavier.

"The Anti-Werewolf League," he whispered. "I'll explain later." I nodded.

"Since the attackers were shifters, it doesn't seem like AWL was involved," Kyle said. "However, as Devon said, we can't rule anything completely out yet. We have our networks still looking for their local chapter and their new national base. As some of you know, when Charlotte's pack in California discovered AWL's headquarters a few weeks ago, they abandoned that location and ran, but we don't know where to yet. The pack network is still looking for clues to where they went. We have a team working on that still, but right now we need to focus on this new, direct threat."

"We should ask Melissa's pack for help. She's always stood by us," someone said from across the room.

"Byron's pack, also," someone else said. "I know a few of them, and they're good people." The room erupted into discussions of who could be trusted to help with an investigation and how much information we were willing to share. As the quiet murmurs shifted into a full-blown group discussion and brainstorming session, I found it increasingly hard to pay attention, and my eyes began closing against my will.

"You need to go to bed," Xavier whispered in my ear as

the conversation continued around us. "You look like you're going to fall over."

"James was almost taken. I need to fix this," I whispered back.

"We will, but you didn't sleep at all last night. You can't think clearly if you're exhausted."

"I'm fine," I insisted. What felt like only a second later I blinked and when I opened my eyes, Kyle was standing in front of me.

"Go to bed or I'm going to shove some melatonin down your throat, throw you over my shoulder, and take you up there myself," he said. I felt Xavier's grip tighten on me as he gave a low growl. Kyle rolled his eyes.

"You know she needs to rest. She's not contributing by falling asleep down here," he said. I could see others glancing at us out of the corners of their eyes but not wanting to get involved. "Paige, go sleep," Devon said gently from across the room. "We've got this. We'll update you as soon as you wake up." Kelly gave an encouraging whine and nodded toward the stairs.

Xavier patted my knee and stood up, moving himself between me and Kyle. "Come on," he said, pulling me up. "Let's go" I quit protesting and followed him.

I glanced back once at the TV where I could see Jessica and Hannah once again human (and dressed) and sitting in the grass with their legs outstretched, chatting. Two young wolves were asleep with their heads on the girls' laps, stretched out in the fading sunlight. I looked at Devon again and he nodded once in acknowledgement then continued talking, debating our next steps. Kyle had sat back down and didn't look at us, seeming content with me leaving the room. Xavier put his hand on my back and guided me up the stairs.

When we got to my room, I absentmindedly picked up James's shirt from the middle of the floor and dropped it in a corner. We didn't have a laundry basket but at least we could consolidate. Then I stood staring at the duffel bags, at Barksie lying on the bed. Maybe I should unpack. But then I'd be accepting that we weren't safe at home anymore, that we were officially on the run, needing protection from something I didn't understand yet... I started shaking, the events from last night running through my head again in excruciating detail.

"Hey, hey, you're all right," Xavier said gently, pulling me to him.

"I couldn't do anything when Julian disappeared. I tried to find him. I tried so hard. Then I was convinced he was dead, that there had been some freak accident and it turns out he was probably abducted. Abducted! And I didn't find him! I gave up. I can't lose James, too, I can't! And I don't know what to do. There's nothing I can do. I'm just waiting and useless and can't protect either of them..." I broke off in sobs as he held me.

"You're not useless, and you're not alone. Sleep will help," he said. He bent his head like he would kiss my hair then stopped and hugged me tighter. And for some reason that set me to crying harder. He sat us on the bed and let go of me, rubbing my back. He lifted my chin so I was looking at his face and rubbed away tears with his thumb.

"Right in this moment, nothing is changing," he said. "You're both here and there are almost thirty combat-trained shifters downstairs between the two of you and anyone stupid enough to come here and attack us on our own territory. You need rest and there's nowhere safer to be right now. Sleep."

He gently pushed me down toward the pillow and I

nodded and laid down. He pulled the covers up from where they'd been bunched when James woke up in a panic earlier and tucked me in. Then he laid down hesitantly behind me on top of the covers, putting an arm around me and humming. I didn't know the song, but before I could ask what it was, I drifted into unconsciousness.

I WOKE up to morning sunlight streaming into the room and a small wolf snuggled up against my back, breathing heavily in its sleep. I started at first, then looked over my shoulder at the yellow fur. James. This was going to take some getting used to. I wondered if he preferred sleeping as a wolf. He certainly seemed snuggly. As I rolled over to get out of bed, James yawned and stretched, and I smiled when I saw Barksie under James's front paws. Even a werewolf needed his stuffed animal. He looked up at me and yipped, then rolled out of bed. A few seconds later, he stood up as a human boy, shoving his legs into the shorts he'd left lying on the ground.

"Kelly says breakfast is ready," he said, climbing back into bed and hugging me.

"You're good at going full wolf already," I said. He pulled back and studied my face.

"That's... good, right?" he asked. I grabbed him and kissed him all over his face, eliciting squeals of protest and a partial shift that made me lose my grip so he could slip out of my arms before shifting back.

"It's good," I laughed as he sprouted his wolf ears. "Let's get dressed for the day,"

Downstairs, Hannah was making pancakes as Kelly leaned on the counter nursing a cup of coffee. Kelly saw me and poured another cup and handed it to me. I took it gratefully and sat down at the table as James grabbed a plate and started piling pancakes from the finished pile onto it. "That's enough for now," Hannah told him sternly when he grabbed his fourth pancake. "You can have more later if you're still hungry." James scowled at her but brought his plate to the table, and I smiled at their banter. Then Devon came into the room and my smile faded as the previous night came flooding back.

"Good morning to you, too?" Devon said, noting the change in my expression.

"It's not you," I sighed. "It's just..."

"I know," he said, sitting next to me. "Trust me, I know. You're fine." He reached over and nabbed a piece of pancake from James's plate, earning an adorably ferocious growl.

"Why doesn't anyone want me to eat pancakes?" James wailed as we both laughed.

"I'll get my own, ok?" Devon said. James scooted over to the bench on the opposite side of the table anyway, just in case, as Devon stood up to go grab a plate.

"We have some trustworthy packs helping us keep a lookout for any signs of the shifters who attacked you," Devon said as he sat back down. "I don't know how long this will take. We've never had to try to track down our own kind like this. I've heard of others having turf wars, that sort of thing with their packs, but we generally aren't the territorial kind here and the next closest packs are a ways away, so I've never dealt with this." He seemed tired, but I could also see determination in his eyes. Kelly had stopped talking to Hannah and came and sat between Devon and James, who eyed her warily while trying to position himself between her and his pancakes.

"I've had some experience with inter-pack politics," Kelly told me.

"And thank god for that," Devon said.

"It can get messy. The packs that are territorial tend to be much more closed off and paranoid. I'm trying not to be biased based on past experiences with them, but honestly, they're the ones that I suspect most in something like this. Although the fact that they came into someone else's territory makes that more complicated. If it was one of them, their willingness to wander out of their own zone sends up a lot of red flags, making this a more serious matter than we thought. I know," she held up a hand as I opened my mouth. "I know it's already serious. I'm just saying it potentially adds another layer to this. Most packs have much more common sense than that, and we know some that have always had our backs. Half a dozen packs that we've worked with closely across the states are on the lookout for us. Plus every member of our pack is looking, and we're spread pretty wide. Those guys can't have gone far yet, and if they really do want you, I don't think they'll run away."

I nodded. I had more questions but didn't necessarily want to ask them in front of James. Kelly's eyes flitted over to him and she nodded back her understanding. "I have to get some work done this afternoon. Want to join me in the office to work on some of your own stuff?" she asked.

"Yeah, that sounds perfect," I said gratefully. For his part, James was focused on Devon, who seemed to have started running interference for us by pretending he was going to steal more of James's breakfast. When he noticed we were done, Devon stood up, announced he had work to do, and left the room. Kelly soon followed suit and James wasn't far behind them, running back upstairs to wake Trevor up to play video games. Hannah had finished cooking a large stack of pancakes, and I went to clean up the dishes that had been dropped in the sink, grabbing the pan from her as well as she took a plate of her own to the table.

We made comfortable small talk as I rinsed dishes and stacked the dishwasher, Hannah making plans for meals for the family for the week and talking about her plans for the school year. She was only fifteen but over the summer had started taking on more of the cooking responsibilities herself, claiming that she had plans to open a catering business when she turned eighteen and wanted to see if it was something she could keep up with. I had to admit, she probably had a good future ahead of her in the field based on how she'd been coping with feeding a few dozen people on a regular basis. I left her in the kitchen making shopping lists on her phone.

I went upstairs and poked my head into Trevor's room. James hadn't succeeded in waking up his friend but had gotten the video games started anyway, playing them at low volume while Trevor slept on as if nothing could wake him. I grabbed my computer from my bedroom, told James I'd be in the office with Kelly, and went back down.

Kelly was sitting at a large L-shaped desk, frowning at a computer set against the wall. I sat down in a seat facing her across the portion of the desk that stuck out into the room, searched for a plug, and settled in. I figured I might as well actually do something productive if she was busy.

I couldn't focus though, and soon gave up on work to start searching through old missing person bulletins from when Nate had first disappeared, going over the details in my head again. I steeled myself and went down a maze-like trail to a folder I hadn't opened at all in over a year: the folder where I'd kept every detail of the day of his disappearance, every person I'd talked to, where all I'd handed out pictures and flyers, a running description and commentary of the conjectures and eventual dismissals from the police.

My heart was racing faster and faster as I looked through everything again, all the details flooding my mind as if it were only yesterday I'd given up the search, and I were still mired in the details and the uncertainty and the desperation.

"Paige," I looked up at Kelly, who had abandoned her computer and was staring at me now, concerned. "What are you looking at? You look like you're going to pass out." I stopped thinking about the case details and focused back on myself, realizing how I probably looked. My heart felt like it would thump right out of my chest, I was near hyperventilating, and I could feel that my face was likely pale. I didn't trust myself to speak, so I wordlessly turned the computer in her direction. As she scanned the screen, her eyes got wide.

"Would you be ok sharing this with the pack?" she asked. I nodded as she started flicking through windows, opening different files. She whistled. "You really kept good records. This is impressive."

"Desperation is the mother of invention and all that. Or something else. I don't know. There must be a phrase that matches this," I muttered. I was rambling. Kelly looked up at me again.

"Is there anything in here you don't want the pack knowing about?" she asked. I shook my head.

"Whatever it takes to find the people who attacked us and to find Nate," I said. "I'm an open book. Take it all."

"So you know, we didn't tell the entire pack your full story," Kelly said. I blinked.

"Why not?" I asked.

"As a general rule, we don't tell each others' histories. I mean it's not an official rule or anything, but we all have things in our past that we don't necessarily want aired out for whatever reason. We told them enough to explain the situation, but that's it. If you want to give details you can, or if you want us to tell what we know. But we won't give everyone your full history without your consent."

"Thanks," I said softly. I thought about what parts of my story I wouldn't be comfortable sharing. Right now I was willing to give everyone everything if it meant completing our goals, but maybe that meant this wasn't the right time to make that decision.

"Morning, Kelly," Xavier came into the office, walking full speed for a metal file cabinet in the back of the room. He suddenly stopped short and did a double take. "Oh! Morning to you, too," he said, looking at me. Then he frowned. "Are you ok?"

"We were going through her notes from when Nate disappeared," Kelly said. She glanced at me questioningly for permission then turned my laptop toward Xavier when I nodded. He sat in the seat next to me and started scrolling and flipping through the windows on the screen, frowning. When he was done, he leaned back in his chair and let out a deep breath.

"Does the pack know all this?" he asked me. "This is going to give us some good starting points." He paused and looked me over. "If you're ok with that."

"They don't know yet. But she said to distribute what she has," Kelly said, taking the computer and typing. She turned the computer back to me and pointed toward a new folder marked "Nate" on the desktop. "Everything you want me to send out, make a copy and put it in there." I nodded, then copy-and-pasted the upper-level folder that contained everything. The fact that there was so much in there that it actually had a countdown to finishing unnerved me a little. I told myself I should be grateful I had that much, that this could help, but instead it felt like it forced me to face how much I'd done and still come up empty-handed. But not this time. This time I had support. This time I wasn't alone.

As if he could hear my thoughts, Xavier gently squeezed my shoulder. The countdown ended and I turned the laptop back to Kelly, who pulled it over next to her desktop and started moving back and forth between the computers. "Only our pack, or are you ok sending this out to our allies? I won't until we all decide together but I'm asking you first," she said, not taking her eyes from the screens.

"Anyone who can help," I said. Kelly nodded and continued typing for a minute, then pushed my laptop back toward me.

"Done for now," she said. "So what did you not want to talk about in front of James?"

I hesitated for a moment. "When he's shifted, how much of this is he privy to?" I asked.

"It's like having a conversation in a different room. He shouldn't see anything we don't intentionally show him," Xavier said. I let out a breath at that.

"What's the Anti-Werewolf League?" I asked.

"A hate group," Xavier said. "They're a group of non-shifter humans who have made it a mission to exterminate us. They've been around a long time but aren't extremely big and are generally seen by other humans as crackpots if they talk about us, which is probably our main saving grace. They make it a point to sniff out shifters and do what they can to run us off or, when they can get away with it, completely do away with us." His eyes glared.

"That's awful," I said. "Who would join a group whose main purpose was to kill people?"

"And yet it's happened time and time again throughout

history and here we still are," Kelly said, shaking her head. "But you can see why it would be implausible that shifters are working together with AWL?" I nodded.

"So what are our chances of figuring out what's going on and finding Nate?" I asked. Xavier and Kelly glanced at each other.

"Honestly? Finding who attacked you is possible. Not easy, but possible. But then we have to hope that we're right about them being connected to Nate, because otherwise... well, four years is a pretty hard trail to pick up," Kelly said.

"But the documents you gave us will up our chances," Xavier said.

"So what do we do now?" I asked.

"We keep sending out scouts locally," Xavier said. "We see if we can nab security footage from that store, see if they had some kind of vehicle that can be traced. We watch the news. We keep in contact with our allies."

"Also," Kelly said, "maybe we move you completely out of that apartment."

"What?" I asked. "Why?"

"Devon and I went back to try to get a few more things for you and James, to help you feel more settled here since you had to pack in such a hurry," Kelly said. "And we found this." She pulled a piece of paper from her pocket and pushed it toward me across the desk and I felt the room tilt.

We're waiting for you, Paige.

Xavier snatched it up. "Where was it?" he demanded.

"In the picture frame that had that family picture in it," Kelly said. I laid my head down on the table, feeling ill.

"If we had stayed..." I said into my arms.

"Hey, look at me," Kelly said, putting a hand on each of

my arms. I looked up. "You. Are. Ours." She almost growled the words. I swallowed and smiled weakly at her. Xavier knelt down next to me with one arm behind my back and took one of my hands with the other.

"They can wait until hell freezes over. They aren't getting you. Either of you," he said, and I could hear in his voice that he would tear apart anyone who tried. I grabbed Kelly's hand with my free hand and we sat there for a moment as I savored the connections, reminding myself that things were different now.

"The apartment isn't important," I said. "Let's go pack it up."

"You aren't going anywhere near that apartment again until we have answers, unless you're planning to use yourself as bait. Which you most definitely are not," Kelly said, and Xavier nodded his agreement. "If there's anything you want brought here, let us know. We'll find a new storage place for the rest of it for now. Once this is sorted, we can find you a new place if you want." I had to admit that she was probably right, but it didn't sit well with me.

Xavier squeezed with the arm he had around me. "I guess now I can officially say 'welcome home,'" he said. "So welcome home."

11

"We've got a potential lead." Devon didn't announce his arrival as he burst into the kitchen where Trevor, James, and I were eating breakfast a few weeks later. "St. Louis."

I dropped my fork onto my plate of scrambled eggs and stared at him. "Already?" He nodded.

"Lead on what?" Trevor asked, looking between me and Devon.

"On Daddy?" James asked.

"Yep, on your Dad." Devon went to the table and sank down to eye level with James. "We can't promise anything, ok?" he said. "This means we have an idea. It doesn't mean he's there now or that if he is we'll know what to do. But it's a second step. You were the first." James's eyes shone with pride.

"But," Devon added, "it's time to leave this to the grownups for now, ok? We'll keep you updated but from here out, trust us to move forward." James nodded, but I could see that he wasn't fully convinced. Devon stood and ruffled James's hair and pulled on one of his fuzzy ears, then stood and turned back to me.

"I'm calling a meeting tonight to figure out our next steps," he said, turning to me. I nodded, my heart racing. Even with James's vision, I hadn't thought we'd get anywhere after all these years. I thought for sure the trail would have run cold.

I didn't want to continue the conversation in front of the kids, so I said, "Sounds like a plan." From the look Devon gave me, he seemed to know I had more to say, but he turned and left the kitchen.

"We're going to get him back!" James said, turning to Trevor. "We're going to find him!" I couldn't interpret Trevor's look.

"Just... don't get your hopes up too early, ok?" Trevor said, looking down at his bowl of cereal. I wondered what experience was going through his mind right now, and my heart broke all over again for how much he'd lost at such a young age.

THE DEN WAS ONCE AGAIN PACKED with people and quite a few wolves. I sat on the couch next to Kelly while Xavier, Devon, and Kyle stood at the front of the room talking with other pack members. All around me, people chatted while occasionally shooting me glances like they expected me to crack under the pressure. At least every time I met some-one's eyes directly they smiled at me and it felt genuine.

I still didn't understand how I'd been so quickly accepted into their group, even though I was clearly an outsider. I told myself it was because James was so adorable that no one could say no to him. I did have the feeling, however, that if it weren't for me, the room might have more wolves than people. I hadn't asked, but it seemed like this sort of planning would go better with the instant communication of the pack link, and I was self-conscious about the fact that I might be the one slowing things down.

"Melissa contacted me this morning," Devon started, and the chatter immediately died down, eyes focusing on him. "Her pack thinks they found a lead on Nate near St. Louis. A few days ago, they found one of the shifters who attacked Paige, Kelly, and James. They started following him and found he's been spending a lot of time in an abandoned building near the outskirts of town, along with some others. There aren't many of us left who are willing to live in those conditions, and Melissa says they don't seem like the feral type, so we don't think this is actually their permanent base. For now, her pack has been watching, waiting for our decision to make a move. Nate belongs to us, and we'll be the ones to get him back." At this there was enthusiastic agreement from around the room from both humans and wolves.

"I won't ask Melissa to risk her pack on this," Devon continued. "Her part is done if she's ready to step back. They've agreed to keep an eye on the building until we get there and then she'll call a pack meeting to discuss further involvement. We owe her for finding the shifters who attacked our family, and if Nate is there, we'll owe her more. For now, we prepare to move. I'll be leading the search and rescue team for Nate, Xavier and Kelly will lead a team providing local support in St. Louis, and Kyle will be in charge of pack protection here. Those of us traveling, we leave in the morning."

As Devon, Xavier, and Kyle started circulating around the room and assigning roles, I turned to Kelly. "I'm going," I said.

"Paige, you can't..."

"I know I'm not as strong or fast as you and can't shift, but I can help," I said. "He's part of your pack, but he was my partner and James's father and I won't sit and wait and do nothing if he's out there and needs me. I failed him once already. I gave up on him. I won't do that again. And," I added, cutting her off as she tried to reply, "James is safe here. I don't have to worry about protecting him if he's here with the pack. You aren't leaving me behind."

Kelly's eyes shifted to behind me and I twisted around to see Devon standing there.

"It's not a good idea," he said. "You said it yourself. You're not as strong or as fast as us. If something were to happen, you wouldn't be able to fight off a shifter, much less a group of them."

"You think I don't know that?" I snapped, standing up. His eyes narrowed and I backed off a bit. "I'm not asking to be part of the search and rescue. I'm fully aware I would slow you down. But at least let me help with local support up there. Let me do something other than sit here and wait. I did that for years. I'm done with that part," I said.

Devon stared at me for a long time, searching my face. He looked like he would argue with me about it, but when he spoke he said, "Pack a backpack for a few days. We leave at eight tomorrow morning. If you're not in the car when we pull out, you aren't coming." He turned and walked away to speak to someone else before I could say anything.

From across the room, I noticed Xavier and Kyle were both glancing in my direction. Kyle looked almost impressed. When I met his eye, he gave me a nod and turned back to his conversation. Xavier, on the other hand, looked anything but impressed. I couldn't tell if he was worried or angry, but he had completely stopped talking to the others and had clearly been giving his full attention to us during the conversation. I raised my eyebrows at him questioningly and he was by my side in a few long strides.

"This isn't a good idea," he said.

"Yeah, Devon already told me."

"If shit hits the fan, I don't know if I can... if we can protect you," he said.

"Let me worry about that then," I said. "I deserve this for everything they've done."

Xavier's eyes clouded over briefly. "You know I won't leave you on your own if something happens," he said, more fiercely than I had expected. I felt Kelly look back and forth between us before slipping off to talk to other people around the room.

"I know." I took his hand and his eyes softened, but his expression remained determined. "I know you won't abandon me. But I've done the part where I sit and wait for news, for him to come home, for any sign that he was alive. I've been doing that for four years, and I don't want to do it anymore."

"Besides, Devon already said yes." I jumped at Kyle's voice from behind me.

"Local support is mine. I have the final say on who's part of the team," Xavier said.

"Local support is you *and* Kelly," Kyle said, shrugging, "and I have a feeling it won't be a unanimous vote if you try to force the issue. Besides, she's part of the pack now, even if she can't shift. She has as much right as anyone else to join the team. She's not one of the kids." I shot him a surprised but grateful look and he winked back at me. Xavier rubbed his face with both hands and sighed.

"Ok. Ok, you're on the team. But," he fixed me with a

penetrating gaze now, "the instant, and I do mean the very instant that things go sideways, you do exactly as you're told. You get out of the way and let us do what we need to do to keep all of us safe."

"Absolutely," I said. He sighed again, but it was a sound of defeat.

"Go get packing and get some sleep. Spend the evening with James. Don't give him any more details than absolutely necessary."

"He's five. I wasn't going to recruit him," I said, raising one eyebrow.

"I know that, Paige. I'm just saying..." he broke off and squeezed my hand then put his hand on my back to steer me toward the stairs. "Go have your time. We aren't going over any new plans right now. We'll talk more during the drive."

"We're driving? Isn't it a really long way?" I asked. I don't know why I had assumed we'd fly.

"We need vehicles and our own resources while we're there. Plus we don't know what we're going to find. He may not be able to board a plane to get back."

I swallowed. Xavier wrapped me in a hug. "Go," he said. "Let me finish up here and I'll come say goodnight." I nodded and hugged him back, then headed for the stairs, planning what I would say to James.

THE NEXT MORNING, I was packed and in the kitchen with the rest of the group that was headed to St. Louis. We had all eaten breakfast and Kyle and Jessica were pouring coffee into disposable to-go cups and handing them out as people moved through the house gathering supplies. Hannah and

Trevor had loaded ice chests full of sodas, water, and sandwiches and were helping to load backpacks and coolers into vehicles. James was in my lap. He had agreed last night that he wanted me to go, but this morning he hadn't left my side. I understood how he felt. The idea of being separated from him for any length of time was almost unbearable, but I was going to make sure no one else ever tried to take him from me again. For now, though, I held him tight as I sipped on the coffee I'd been handed, and he tried to nestle as close to me as he could.

Eventually, people started heading out, climbing into vehicles in groups of three or four. We were leaving in waves so as to not look like a full caravan as we made our way north. We'd all drive up today and settle into our temporary homes, then start assessing the situation tomorrow. Finally, it was time for Kelly, Xavier, and me to head out. James, who had been clingy but silent all morning, finally burst into sobs. I hugged him tight until he quieted.

"You're coming back, right?" he asked through tears.

"Of course I'm coming back," I said, kissing his head.

"We won't come back without her," Kelly promised.

"Our pack sticks together," Xavier added. At that, James took a deep breath and sat up straighter.

"You keep her safe," he said, frowning at both Kelly and Xavier. They both made motions crossing their hearts and then he turned to me. "And you..." his voice broke and I hugged him again. "Please come back," he whispered.

"Promise," I said. I handed him over to Jessica and kissed him one more time, waving at him with a smile as we left. As soon as the front door was closed, I slumped, my smile gone.

"God, I didn't expect that to be this hard," I mumbled. "Can I go back to being worried about kindergarten?" Xavier put an arm around my shoulders as we walked to Kelly's car then opened the front passenger door for me.

"He'll be fine. We'll call and update him, he'll be able to hear what's going on when he's shifted, and he's surrounded by the best security and emotional support you'll ever find," he said, ushering me into the seat. I nodded and grabbed for the seatbelt as he closed my door and climbed into the back. Kelly jumped into the driver's seat and started the ignition. Pop music started blaring from the speakers, and Xavier growled in the backseat.

"Is this what we're stuck with the whole trip or do you take requests?" he asked.

"Driver picks the music, passengers shut their pie holes," Kelly said cheerfully as she put the car in drive. "Except Paige." She smiled at me. "You can give suggestions as long as they aren't his suggestions," she said, nodding her head toward the backseat. I laughed.

"Maybe we should take my car," Xavier grumped, crossing his arms.

"Too late," Kelly said, and we pulled out of the driveway, leaving half of my heart behind us in the care of teenage werewolves.

THE DRIVE TO ST. Louis was agonizingly uneventful and my anxiety over the whole situation built by the hour. The three of us took shifts driving with minimal breaks, and we arrived at Melissa's in what Xavier assured me was record time. I had expected her to be on the town outskirts, like our house, but she was right in the middle of the city.

We drove downtown and into a parking garage below a skyscraper, then rode the elevator up nearly to the top floor.

When we knocked on the apartment door, it flung open and an older woman with dark brown skin and dark curly hair streaked with grey threw herself onto Kelly arms in a tangle of multi-colored sequins, flowing muslin scarves, and delighted squeals. Kelly, for her part, squealed right back and they both hugged and laughed in the doorway until Xavier cleared his throat.

"Oh, yes, hello to you, too," Melissa said, rolling her eyes at him with a fond smile before she pulled him into a hug. Kelly laughed at his expression of tolerant amusement as he hugged her back. "And you must be Paige!" She turned her attention toward me and I was engulfed in a glittery rainbow as she flung her arms around me. "You poor, poor dear! We'll get this all straightened right up. Come in, come in!" She took my arm and led me into the apartment where I froze in disbelief.

"That's the Gateway Arch," I said, stunned at the view of the monument lit up against the night sky out the floor-to-ceiling windows.

"Indeed, it is," she said, patting my arm like I was a child being praised for a discovery that all the adults already knew about. Xavier chuckled and I shot him a sideways glare.

"This view is spectacular," I said, looking around the huge apartment. In contrast to Melissa herself, whose outfit was now reflecting rainbow sparkles all around the room from the overhead lighting, the minimalist design didn't include much color. The room consisted of light wood floors, white furniture, and black side tables and was a stark contrast to its occupant.

"Yes, well, the outside view has to make up for my wife's stubborn insistence on blandness in here." She gave a long-suffering sigh.

"You're married?" I asked.

"Yes, Yasmin will be back soon. She wanted to meet with Devon and get him all settled in. He's nearby at the Marriot. He was planning on staying at some dinky little motel but I always say just because the world sees us as wild animals doesn't mean we have to live like them."

"Most packs aren't run by stubbornly single people," Kelly told me. She turned to Melissa. "She hasn't met any shifters outside our pack yet. Well, beyond being attacked."

"Oh! Well, you've certainly chosen an interesting pack to introduce you to our world," Melissa said, cocking an eyebrow.

"You're the one that looks like a glitter bomb," Xavier said, eliciting a laugh from our host. He was smiling and looked more relaxed than he'd been the entire car ride, although I had to admit, that might have been because he was finally free of Kelly's musical choices. I suddenly yawned.

"It's been a long day," Kelly said.

"Of course!" Melissa took my arm again and led me down a hallway. "Let's get you to bed. We have plotting and planning to do tomorrow and you must have a good night's rest for that!" She waved toward the first two doors, motioning for Kelly and Xavier to take those rooms and steered me toward the third door. "Here you are. Bathroom's across the hall." She gave me another hug, wrapping me completely up in her arms and squeezing tight. "We're going to get this all squared away and keep your little pup safe, ok?" she whispered in my ear. I hugged her back, tears pricking my eyes as I was newly overwhelmed that more people were willing to help us. She patted me on the arm before leaving and closing the door behind her.

I turned to look at the room and whistled. The same

view from the living room was outside my own window. I couldn't begin to imagine what this place cost. I stripped off my travel-worn outfit and slipped on a t-shirt and leggings. I'd shower tomorrow. I laid down but was simultaneously exhausted and too keyed up to sleep. After some time, I heard a quiet knock on my door. I got up and opened it to find Xavier standing in the hallway.

"You ok?" he asked.

"Yeah. I mean as ok as I can be in the circumstances. Why?" I asked.

"You were moving around a lot."

"How do you know that?"

"We have exceptionally good hearing, remember? You sounded like you were flopping around like a fish. Sound travels well when there's no carpet."

I didn't say anything, just stared at the bed. I hadn't heard a sound. I was too tired to formulate a response, although I felt like I should.

"Hey," Xavier rubbed my arms. "It's going to be ok." I leaned into him and his arms went around me.

"But what if it's not?" I asked, my voice cracking. I'd managed to hold it together all day, but alone in the quiet, my mind had gone to all the darkest places, had dredged up all the old feelings of abandonment, fear, terror, and loneliness that had come to define my days before moving to Florida. Feelings that I had hoped I'd left behind when I moved.

"Then it's not for a while. And we get through that until it is ok again," he said, squeezing tight.

"I don't want to go through it again," I whispered. He hesitated, then pressed his lips to my forehead.

"You won't be alone this time. No matter what happens, you won't face any of it alone again," he said. "Ever." I looked up at him then, and the gaze he was fixing on me made me catch my breath.

"Ok," I said. My mind was stubbornly refusing to cooperate with participating in conversation tonight.

"Bedtime," he said, letting go, and I went back to the bed and laid back down.

"It's been bedtime. It's not working," I grumbled as he tucked me in. And like before, he laid down behind me on top of the covers, put an arm around me, and started humming.

"What is that?" I managed to ask this time.

"What?"

"The song."

"I'm honestly not sure," he said. "My mom used to hum it when I couldn't calm down when I was young and it helped. I thought... well I thought you might need the same sort of thing."

I nodded. "I did. I do. Thank you," I said and settled deeper against him, yawning as he resumed humming. "You'll stay?" I asked, half asleep.

"Of course," he said, his arm tightening around me. "For as long as you need me."

THE NEXT MORNING I woke up and felt a warm presence behind me on the bed. Xavier. He was asleep, breathing deeply with one arm still draped over me. It felt nice to wake up next to someone again, even in these circumstances. I laid there and tried to keep my mind clear, savoring the feelings of safety and calm stillness before the day jumped into action. Dawn light was starting to peek through the heavy curtains and my mind drifted to our mission. What did "local support" mean, anyway? What was I going to be doing here? It occurred to me that I might still be sitting around waiting, but that now I was doing it from a new city. Useless again. I mentally shook my head. Xavier and Kelly wouldn't have created an actual team of people to do this if all it involved was sitting around and waiting for something to happen. They'd have more plans than that.

I felt some movement behind me and then a sharp intake of breath as Xavier woke up and realized where he was. After that initial movement, he went completely still and seemed to hold his breath, like he was waiting for something, or maybe didn't know I was awake and didn't want to disturb me.

"Good morning," I said, not moving. He let out a breath.

"Good morning," he replied. He rubbed my arm then moved his arm off of me, and I flipped over to face him. The feeling that flooded me then caught me off guard. Seeing him lying next to me, his hair tousled, sleep still in his eyes... I mentally shook myself. Nate was alive and we were here to find him. I tried not to think about what had been building between me and Xavier over the weeks before the attack, when I had thought Nate was gone forever and that I was moving on. A pang of guilt hit me then, and the mix of emotions left me confused and growing depressed. Xavier picked up on my mood shift and raised himself on an elbow, looking down at me.

"Hey, you all right?" he asked softly, his face suddenly a mask of worry. I swallowed.

"Yeah. Just... a lot to think about," I said. He brushed some hair back from my face.

"It is. But we've got this."

"'We' as in you and the pack, or 'we' as in you and me?" I asked before I could stop myself. He smiled at me, but there was a guardedness behind it.

"Both. I know you still feel like an outsider, but you're part of the pack too, not just James. It's a different dynamic than we've had before, but everyone agrees that you're one of us. 'We' always includes you." I leaned my head forward on his chest and took a deep breath. I didn't miss that he didn't address the two of us, but the confirmation of my place with the pack was comforting. He rubbed the back of my head gently, then said, "Come on. Let's get some coffee."

He got up and headed out the door while I sat up and stretched. When I came out into the hall behind him, Kelly was standing by her own door, looking at Xavier with one eyebrow raised. He, for his part, ignored the look as he walked past her, so she turned the assessing look toward me. "Morning," I said, giving her a smile that I wanted to look nonchalant but that felt sheepish instead. Not long ago, that look would have been more conspiratorial as I gave her a look that promised details later, but now I was too confused about what I should be feeling. She seemed to sense the same thing Xavier had. She came and looped her arm in mine and led us toward the kitchen where Xavier was pouring cups of coffee.

A woman I hadn't met yesterday was sitting at the table that looked out on the gorgeous view of the sun low in the sky over the Mississippi River, the Gateway Arch illuminated in a way that almost made it look like it was glowing. I wondered if you ever got used to a view like that.

She smiled at me over her coffee mug, her brown skin seeming to glow in the early morning light just like the Arch. As colorful as Melissa had been, this woman exuded sophistication in her black silk robe tied perfectly over a crisp white silk nightgown. Streaks of gray peeked through her black hair, similar to Melissa's. But where Melissa's hair was a cloud of tight curls, this woman's hair was straight, in a shoulder-length clean cut. She seemed like a woman who knew exactly how to get what she wanted.

"Sleep well?" she asked with a smile. I nodded and she stood up and came to clasp my hands. "You must be Paige. I'm Yasmin. I'm so glad to meet you, although I know we both wish the circumstances were different."

I felt my throat close up, but managed to reply, "It's nice to meet you, too." She sat back down as Kelly handed me a mug and sat down at the table. I sat next to her. Xavier didn't come in, but I heard the sounds of someone cooking in the kitchen.

"I like that boy," Yasmin said, smiling toward the kitchen. "I never have to cook when he's here. Melissa tries, but..." Yasmin let out a long-suffering sigh that matched Melissa's from the night before during the discussion about decor and I smiled at that, my mood finally lightening.

"She's not much of a cook, I take it?" I asked. Kelly stifled a laugh.

"She's good at leading people and earning loyalty, but with anything domestic she's completely hopeless," Yasmin said, with a note of fondness. I heard a phone ring in the kitchen and Xavier's voice over the sound of something cooking in a pan. Kelly, Yasmin, and I chatted for another few minutes, then Xavier brought out plates of eggs, bacon, and toast and set them on the table. After giving the three of us plates, he brought out his own and sat down.

"Devon and the others will be here at ten to meet with your pack," he said to Yasmin.

"Will we all fit in here?" I asked, looking around the apartment. It was big for an apartment, but didn't seem big enough to fit all of us plus their group.

"Oh, not in the apartment," Yasmin said. "We'll meet upstairs."

"They don't only own the apartment," Kelly said at my confused look. "They own the building." My eyes widened as I reassessed what I knew of our hosts. I'd already been impressed with this apartment's view.

"Not us personally. It's the pack building," Yasmin said. "Most of our pack lives here. It allows us to be close together without attracting a lot of attention. It's like our own little mini town within these walls where we don't have to hide. We can be who we are, talk freely, shift freely without worrying about what others see." I nodded, thinking of how relieved James had been when he had finally told me what he was and could stop hiding his shifting from me, the relief on his face when I'd accepted him in the kitchen that day. "We cleared out the top floor to be a meeting space for all of us. If you think this view is impressive, you'll love it up there. Three hundred sixty degree views of the city." Apparently she'd noticed my appreciation, or Melissa had told her I had commented last night.

"I can't wait to see it," I said. We made small talk as the sun rose and eventually Melissa came wandering out in an Asian-style silk bathrobe covered in rainbow koi fish, her hair looking like she had stepped out of a wind tunnel. She kissed Yasmin on the head and plopped into the seat next to her as Xavier disappeared into the kitchen and reappeared with another plate of food and a fresh cup of coffee for Melissa, who patted his arm in thanks as she started gulping it down immediately upon taking it from him without a word. Yasmin and Melissa spoke in quiet tones to each other as Melissa started eating, and it started to feel like we were intruding on a private ritual, so Xavier, Kelly, and I headed back to our rooms to get showered and dressed.

By the time we came back out, Melissa had not only eaten breakfast, but gotten completely dressed and ready herself. The stark contrast between her and Yasmin from the morning was still there, with Yasmin dressed in crisp , dark blue dress pants and a white button-down shirt while Melissa was wearing what seemed like every imaginable shade of blue and purple in a multitude of layers of flowing fabric.

They led us out of the apartment and up a staircase to what looked like a ballroom. As Yasmin had promised, the walls were all glass windows, providing a full view of the city in every direction. Some people were already there, setting up chairs in rows facing a half-circle of chairs situated at the front of the room. Yasmin, Xavier, and I moved to help them as Kelly chatted with Melissa near the entrance. Melissa greeted everyone by name as people filed in the door, including everyone from our pack when they arrived. I had no idea how she remembered them all.

"Amazing, isn't she?" Yasmin's voice behind me made me jump. "She can make anyone she meets feel like the most important person in the world. It's what makes her such a great leader."

"You both lead, right?" I asked, thinking of the responsibility that Devon, Kelly, Xavier, and Kyle shared.

"Oh, no. I know you only really know Devon's pack, but most of us aren't as democratic as they are. They're actually pretty non-traditional. This is Melissa's pack, not mine. She's the alpha here. She listens and cares what everyone else says, but in the end, she makes the decisions and no one questions her. She seems all rainbows and sparkles, but she's also an amazing strategist, negotiator... all the things a strong leader needs to be, and she has the strength of will to back it all up. The glitter and smiles draw people in, and she inspires loyalty like no one I've ever seen. But she's always watching the pieces, too, always looking a step ahead."

Yasmin's voice was almost reverent, and Melissa glanced over at us and met Yasmin's eyes, giving her a matching look before blowing a kiss. The love and pride shining in both their eyes made my heart ache. But for what or who, I wasn't sure anymore.

12

As relaxed as Melissa seemed, she somehow had everything running on a strict timetable. Even our pack knew to be there on time, and right at ten o'clock, everyone was sitting in their seat as Melissa called the meeting to order. This was a much more formal situation than the meetings in the den back home.

Our pack members sat interspersed with Melissa's pack in the rows, while Melissa and Devon sat in the middle seats of the front semicircle, with me and Xavier flanking Devon on one side and Yasmin and Kelly by Melissa. I assumed that Kelly was sitting with Yasmin to keep the group around the leaders visually evened out, but I did wonder if there was more to it than that based on what I'd seen of her relationship with Melissa.

I felt extremely self-conscious, sitting there in front of a new pack of werewolves, right next to their leader. I could feel them sizing me up, assessing me. Most of them were looking at me with a mix of curiosity and pity which I didn't like, but more uncomfortable were the few that were looking at me with open distrust. I was the only human in the room and, I was starting to get the feeling, maybe the only human who had ever set foot in this building beyond perhaps pizza deliveries. Xavier and Kelly seemed perfectly at ease and confident, so I tried to copy them, sitting still with my head held high, not showing the new pack how much their stares made me want to squirm. I needed to earn their trust, and acting fidgety wouldn't help my case.

Melissa started talking and immediately everyone else in the room went silent. "A small group of you are already privy to this, as we've been working with Devon to discover more information. I know the rest of you may be wondering why a large number of Devon's pack have arrived in our city. Years ago, one of Devon's pack set out on his own. Many of you who have been here a long time knew Nate. He was a good ally and friend. He left his pack willingly, and while he didn't sever himself from Devon, he never shifted again. We have recently discovered that since he left, he found a partner and fathered a child."

Melissa looked toward me and smiled. I smiled back at her, then faced forward at the packs watching me, making sure to make eye contact with those who seemed most unsure of me. "After establishing a family, Nate disappeared again four years ago, leaving his partner and child behind." At this, there was some murmuring, but Melissa glowered and it died down quickly.

"We have good reason to believe that the second disappearance was forced. Those of you who knew Nate will have trouble believing he'd leave a family behind without making arrangements for their protection." There were nods around the room but no one spoke up again. "In addition, Paige and her son were recently attacked. From the nature of the attack, it is clear that they specifically were being targeted. Paige here is not a shifter, but their son is."

She paused. "They were attacked by an unknown shifter pack, and members of that pack, specifically members involved in the attack, have been discovered in St. Louis." More murmurs broke out and this time Melissa let them go. Her expression didn't change, but it was clear she was listening carefully to the reactions. Thankfully, so far I didn't hear anyone making a "not our problem" argument. Rather, they all seemed livid that a hostile group had encroached on their territory.

After a moment, Melissa cleared her throat and the talking immediately died down again. "We've been running surveillance for the few days since we discovered the attackers are here. They don't appear to be feral or untethered. Therefore, their settling here without contacting us can be seen as an act of hostility, as they have recently committed an act of aggression against one of our allies and now seem to be in hiding." She nodded toward Devon, who didn't take his eyes from the packs facing him. His expression briefly flashed with anger at the mention of the attack, but mostly he looked determined. The members of Melissa's pack seemed to approve of whatever they saw when they looked at him, and I was grateful.

"We're here today to determine our level of involvement in this situation. We haven't been attacked ourselves, and based on the nature of the attack in Florida, we likely won't be. However, our territory has been invaded without consent, and Devon's pack has always been our closest allies. Devon, Kelly, and I will be shifted for the next hour for anyone who wants to link across packs for more information. Lunch will be up here at noon. Immediately after lunch we'll discuss this together, and I'll decide on our next steps."

That seemed to be the clear signal to disperse, because

everyone immediately started talking. I noticed a large number of people shoot me glances during their conversations with each other, and while it made sense, I started to get the feeling that it was about more than my role in all this. A short woman with pale skin and long brown hair from Melissa's pack went to where Devon, Xavier, and Melissa were talking and said something under her breath, looking my way. Devon nodded and Xavier came over and looped my arm in his.

"You've never been to St. Louis, right?" he asked, louder than was probably necessary.

"No, but..." I didn't know where this was going.

"We have some time. Let's go see the Arch. It's close by and we can be back for lunch," he said, again, louder than I thought was necessary. I looked over at the woman who had spoken to Devon and Melissa and she gave me a sheepish smile before turning to speak to the person next to her.

Once we were down in the apartment again, I turned on Xavier. "What was that about?" I demanded.

"Melissa's pack didn't want to shift in front of you," he said. At the look on my face, he added, "Not because they don't trust you. You already know about us. They're worried you'll freak out if they all shift together and you're suddenly surrounded by wolves. They've never had a non-shifter among them like this. Most of us haven't. They're concerned about your reactions."

"Oh." I didn't know what to say to that. It occurred to me that I hadn't been around when a large number of the pack shifted all at once, and I honestly didn't know how I would react to that. I'd gotten used to seeing wolves hanging around and an adult or two shifting. I was very used to kids shifting back and forth. But to be in a whole room of shifting adults... I could understand their hesitation.

"They all heard that you and I will be leaving for a while so they won't be as on guard and can focus on deciding what to do," he said.

"Well, let's go be tourists," I said, trying to sound casual and failing. Xavier grabbed my hand and squeezed.

"Melissa already wants to help us and what she decides goes here. But she'll give everyone a fair hearing before announcing any decision."

"So alpha werewolves are really a thing?" I asked. "I mean, your... our pack is more like a family than a monarchy." When I corrected myself, Xavier's eyes lit up and the smile that he gave me seemed like it would split his face apart, it was so big.

"They're a thing," he said. "Technically, Devon is our alpha. It's not something you're going to notice because you aren't part of the pack link. But," he said, squeezing my hand again at the look on my face, "we don't bend to our alpha. We decided in the beginning that we weren't going to run the same way as other packs. If he wanted to, Devon could take control, but that's not what we've built."

"They said Devon is non-traditional."

"Yeah, as far as I know, we're the only pack that works the way we do," he said.

"Why?" I asked.

"We wanted a pack where shifters who felt like they didn't have somewhere to go could be welcomed. When we met, we felt alone, and we wanted to fix that for others. Most packs don't take in just anyone. They vet their members. And if you want to join a pack, you usually have to be ok with giving up your autonomy in some way. Most shifters are ok with that because it gives them a place to belong, some protection. Plus shifters who grew up in a pack are used to the hierarchy and the stability that can bring. But we didn't want to force anyone to choose between joining a family and having their own freedom." He hesitated long enough that I sensed he was holding something back.

"What?" I asked. He didn't say anything and I poked him in the arm. "What aren't you telling me?" He sighed and rubbed his face.

"I told you about when I met Devon," he said. I nodded. "There wasn't a pack yet at that point. We were the ones who started it, but he... well, Devon and I weren't the only ones in the beginning." He watched my face carefully, watching for my reaction. "There were three of us."

"Who..." I frowned, then my eyes went wide. Only one person would make him this nervous to tell me about. "Nate?" I asked. Xavier nodded. I let out a breath. I knew Nate had been part of the pack but hadn't realized how close they'd been.

"We decided on Devon to be acting alpha because of his ability to communicate with the rest of us unshifted, even in a limited capacity. That's not an alpha thing, that's a Devon thing. Nate didn't necessarily want everyone to know what all he could do, so he didn't want to be the central link for a full pack who would all be looking to him."

"But you said you set this up without an alpha."

"To have a pack link, there has to be a central person. Like the center of a wheel that all the spokes are connected to, and that's the alpha. When we started, not many people would have been willing to trust an alpha-less pack. But the three of us knew we weren't running like that, and as more people joined and we were able to attract more people, we gained trust. Plus Melissa knew us and vouched for us, and she was already a respected alpha. Once we were established, we didn't have to pretend to be an alpha-led pack anymore. A lot of shifters don't understand why we work like this, but we've built a large, strong community fairly quickly this way. We're one of the biggest packs in the country, even if we aren't as centralized as some others."

My head was swimming. Nate hadn't only been part of the pack. He'd been a founder and part of the core group with Devon and Xavier. "Why didn't you tell me this earlier?" I asked.

"I honestly didn't mean not to tell you," Xavier said. "It didn't come up amidst everything else we had going on. And I..." he swallowed, then hugged me. "Well, it's still hard to talk about Nate sometimes. He left a pretty big hole in the pack when he left," he finished. I hugged him back, nestling against him, and he rested his cheek on top of my head.

"It's ok," I said. "It's just every time I think I have a handle on things, something else comes up. I feel like I'm treading water and keep getting pulled down." He pushed me away a bit then and lifted my chin so I was looking at him.

"I may not be able to tell you everything at once, but I'm going to be here to help you through all of it, and I will always answer anything you have questions about," he said. "I'm not going to let you drown, ok?" My breath caught in my throat so I couldn't speak, but I nodded. He pulled me in for another quick hug, then stepped back. "Let's go sightseeing," he said.

We walked a few blocks over to Market Street and wandered toward the river, walking through a series of parks and sculpture gardens. In one of the parks, we stopped at a coffee shop and grabbed a coffee for Xavier and a hot chocolate for me. The line at the Gateway Arch was long, so we decided not to go up inside but wandered along the path around the park, watching boats float by on the river. We talked about movies we were interested in seeing, James and Trevor's latest video game obsessions, what we knew of Jessica's plans for college, Hannah's budding cooking skills and her newest hair color choices. Safe topics that could be overheard without drawing suspicion. As we walked, Xavier put his arm around my shoulders, and I tried not to think about what was going on back at the apartment building.

Xavier suggested we have lunch on our own to give the others more time to chat freely, so on the way back up Market Street, we headed into a small pizza place across the street from one of the sculpture gardens. We ordered slices to go then headed back out to the park to eat outside. The weather was too beautiful to stay indoors. We ate on a bench looking back toward the Arch, then tossed our packages and headed back up the street toward Melissa's.

After turning off Market Street, we'd gone a block when Xavier suddenly stiffened and tightened his arm around me.

"What?" I asked, looking around.

"Don't look around. Keep walking," he said. He was scanning the area but keeping his face aimed straight ahead as if trying to look like he wasn't on alert. I shivered. Ahead of us, an elderly woman was walking toward us carrying a small dog and talking to it, but I didn't notice anyone else on the road with us. I tried to listen to see if I could hear anything amiss, but all I could hear was the regular sounds of a mid-day city. People talking behind us back on the main road, cars, birds. I wished I had better hearing like Xavier. Not knowing what was setting him off had me bristling.

As the woman got closer to us, she looked at me and smiled. I smiled back and as she passed us, she tripped on the sidewalk, falling toward us. Xavier automatically put out an arm to catch her, and she threw her little dog into his arms and fell with her full body into him, knocking him off balance.

Just then, someone grabbed my arm and yanked me away from Xavier. I screamed and lashed out at whoever was grabbing me as Xavier tried to get away from the woman and her dog to grab me back, but the woman had tangled her dog's leash around him. Two other huge men suddenly appeared from across the street, grabbing Xavier and dragging him away from me as whoever had grabbed me put an arm around my throat and dragged me backward as I kicked and screamed.

We were in broad daylight in the middle of the city! Surely someone would see this and come help us. Then I realized with a sinking feeling that these people may be relying on witnesses. When we'd been attacked before, Kelly had led us somewhere private so she could shift without being seen. There was no way for Xavier to safely shift here without putting both our pack and Melissa's pack at risk of discovery. I fought harder with the realization, but whoever had me was strong. I felt his other hand go into my pocket to pull out my phone and throw it to the ground. No chance the pack would be able to trace me through that.

I saw with horror that Xavier and I were each being dragged toward different vans. The men clutching him dragged him to the open back door of a cargo van and threw him in, slamming the door behind him and pulling down a lock. I heard him pounding on the door, trying to break through, screaming curses and threats that then turned to growls and barks. The men ran back toward us as I was pulled into the back of a passenger van with blacked-out windows. One of the men climbed into the driver's seat and the old woman climbed into the front passenger seat with her dog.

"That's enough, Paige," a deep male voice behind me said, shifting his hold to pin my arms to my sides. I froze in surprise. How did they know my name? Had Xavier said it? Were these the same people who had attacked us in Florida? As the door closed and the van pulled away, the other man who'd captured Xavier grabbed a clear breathing mask that was connected to a tank and moved toward me.

"Sorry about this," the man behind me said. I screamed again and tried to move my head away from the mask, but the man holding it grabbed the back of my head with one hand and pressed the mask over my nose and mouth. Someone behind him must have turned the tank on because I heard a hiss and then felt a cold rush of something hit my face. I tried to hold my breath, but eventually, my lungs started burning and I took a big breath of whatever they were pumping into the mask. The grip on me loosened as my body went heavy, and I felt someone gently sit me in a seat and buckle me in before everything went black.

13

I woke up with a massive headache. I kept my eyes squeezed shut against the pain, but I must have made a noise because a voice said "She's waking up." Someone walked up next to me and I flinched when I felt something touch my face. "It's just a cold compress for your head," the voice said. I recognized it as whoever had used my name in the van, the man who had yanked me away from Xavier and held me still while the gas mask was put on. "I imagine your head is pounding."

A cold cloth was laid across my forehead and eyes, blocking out what light had been coming through my closed eyelids. I laid still, trying to be compliant so they wouldn't knock me out again. I could hear an air conditioner blowing, a stand-up comedian coming through what sounded like phone speakers, two other people talking about what to get for dinner. Their conversation was general enough that it didn't give me any clues about where we were exactly, mainly debating between burgers or Chinese food. Chinese won out and a door opened and clicked closed. I guessed we were in a hotel room somewhere. Maybe there would be some hints around the room, stationery with the address or something.

Someone walked over to me again and the same voice said, "Here, this will help." The washcloth was removed from my face and I opened my eyes. A man with close-cut light brown hair and arms the size of small tree trunks was holding out two white pills and a glass of water. I had tried to fight this man off of me and he probably could have won a professional wrestling match. I glared at the pills. "They're Tylenol," he said gently. I sat up and put my hand to my head as it throbbed, then picked up one of the pills and flipped it over to see the name etched onto the back. The man smiled and encouragingly held out the water glass. If they wanted to drug me, they'd already proven they didn't need my cooperation, so camouflaging something more nefarious seemed unlikely. I took the glass from him and swallowed the pills.

He sat on the bed next to me and took the glass when I was done, setting it on the bedside table. I moved away from him as far I could get without falling off the other side of the bed and glanced at the table. No stationery. Damn. He noticed my movement away from him and raised an eyebrow.

"I'm not going to hurt you," he said.

"You snatched me off the street, shoved me in a van, and drugged me," I snapped.

"But didn't hurt you in the process," he said.

"What about any of that is supposed to make me believe it's not coming?"

"Look," he started to reach across the bed to touch my arm and I jerked it away. He sighed and pulled his hand back. "Someone who cares very much for you thought you might have been taken by those... those mongrels." He snarled the last word and it took everything in me not to lash out, but then the words sunk like a lead ball in my stomach. "And they wanted you out. We've been looking all over to find out which of them were holding you hostage, and finally found you."

"Who?" I choked on the word. "Who told you to kidnap me?"

"I've been put under strict orders to not say," the man said. "But you'll find out soon."

The door opened and without thinking I leapt up and ran for it, but tree-trunk man was fast and had me around the waist before I got more than a few steps. I kicked and tried to hit him, but he lifted me off my feet and held me out like a child as I flailed, not able to connect with anything except his rock-hard arms. The man who had opened the door came in and set four plastic bags with "thank you" printed on the side in red curvy letters onto the dresser. He was smaller than the man holding me but still huge, and his haircut and the way he was dressed reminded me of the military, none of which boded well for my plans to escape.

"I take it your welcome chat didn't go well?" he asked with a smirk. Tree Trunks laughed.

"I owe you twenty bucks," he said.

"Me, too," said the man lying on the other bed watching his phone. I'd completely forgotten about him. I couldn't escape from one of them. I had no hope against three. The man who had brought in the food stood in front of me barely out of arm's reach and looked me over as I glowered at him, folding my arms across my chest and hanging from Tree Trunks's arms like a grumpy toddler.

"You going to play nice now or do we get to knock you out again?" the man in front of me asked, raising his eyebrows.

"Dan..." Tree Trunks said with a warning tone. Dan looked at Tree Trunks.

"It was easier when she was unconscious."

"That's only for transition. She needs to eat."

"A couple of days without food wouldn't hurt her," Dan said, looking me up and down. At that, I swung my legs out as far as they would go and kicked him in the thigh. He hissed and raised a hand to hit me, but Tree Trunks swung me behind him, blocking me.

"No one touches her," he said, towering over Dan.

"She kicked me!"

"Because you're an ass!" I spat at him from behind my human shield.

"She's not wrong," called the man from the bed, finally looking up from his phone. Dan scowled at me and I scowled right back. Tree Trunks sighed and rubbed his face. "Why don't you take watch outside," he said to Dan.

"Fine," Dan said. He grabbed one of the plastic bags then turned and looked at me again. "Watch yourself, wolf lover," he snarled and slammed the door on the way out. I tried to get a glance out the door over his shoulder but could only see a worn-looking parking lot and a sound barrier wall blocking what I assumed was an interstate. Outside the door, a familiar van blocked most of the view before the door shut. Not many hints about location, but it looked like it was late at night. I suddenly realized that there wasn't an alarm clock or telephone in the room. They must have thought ahead and removed everything I could use to get hints or communicate. So there went that plan.

Tree Trunks turned to look at me and raised his eyebrows. "If I feed you, are you going to try to run again?" he asked. I kept my arms folded.

"I'll stay put during dinner," I said, scowling.

"Good enough," he chuckled. It infuriated me that he apparently only found me amusing and not any sort of a threat. Objectively I could understand why, but I wasn't interested in being objective. "Sesame chicken or General Tso?" he asked, looking into the remaining bags.

"I don't care," I grumbled. He handed me a bag.

"Well surprise, then," he said, grabbing another bag for himself. He pulled out the chair at the desk by the dresser and motioned for me to sit. I did and he pushed the chair in as I set the bag on the desk.

"Why are you acting nice?" I asked. He tilted his head and regarded me with genuine curiosity.

"You're one of us, Paige. You always have been. You've been brainwashed a little, but that's not your fault. You were taken advantage of, and we're going to set that right." He smiled at me, and I felt nausea rising in me as I thought about the implications of what he was saying. What were these people planning on doing to me? "Eat," he said gently, setting a hand on my shoulder. It was everything I could do not to jerk away from him. *Play along. Make him trust you. He already wants to.*

I couldn't bring myself to speak, but I pulled a metal container of sesame chicken and a plastic spoon out of the bag and started forcing myself to eat. I wondered briefly if the restaurant had been out of chopsticks or if they considered me so much of a threat that they thought I could use them as a weapon. That got me thinking about what exactly I could do with a pair of chopsticks before they incapacitated me again. Not much, probably, I begrudgingly admitted.

The man from the bed got up and grabbed the last bag, then went to sit cross-legged on his bed again with his food, turning his video back on. Maybe if he went to sleep I could swipe his phone. Tree Trunks sat on the other bed and opened his own food, and we all ate with only the sound of one-liners and audience laughter coming from the small speakers to break the silence.

"Do you have drinks?" I asked eventually.

"Oh yeah, here," Tree Trunks said and opened a door in the dresser to reveal a mini-fridge. He pulled out twenty-ounce bottles of ginger ale and orange soda and offered them to me. I took the ginger ale, hoping it would calm my rebelling stomach, although I had a feeling that was more to do with nerves than anything ginger could help with.

"Where's the woman who was with you?" I asked.

"She's a local contact. We left her in St. Louis," Phone Man said.

"So where are we now?" I asked, trying to sound casual.

"On our way back to the people you belong with," Tree Trunks said quickly, before Phone Man could say anything. Phone Man seemed to take the hint and went back to watching his video. I'd thought his hair was slicked back, but now his ponytail flopped over his shoulder as he leaned forward again. So they weren't all military types, maybe. I went back to eating in silence. I finished and stood up, and Tree Trunks immediately went on alert, watching me closely.

"Am I allowed in the bathroom alone?" I asked, narrowing my eyes at him. He waved a hand toward the back of the hotel room.

"Be my guest," he said, but he didn't take his eyes off me as I dropped my dinner container in the garbage and closed the bathroom door behind me. I sat on the edge of the tub and put my head in my hands, allowing myself to fall apart a little without my kidnappers as witnesses. I started shaking and closed my eyes as tears welled up.

What the hell was happening? How was I going to get back home to James and Kelly and... I felt a twist in my gut when I thought about Xavier. What had they done with him? Had they left him locked in that van and walked away, or had they hurt or... I stopped that train of thought. I'd been down that road before and right now was not the time to start letting my imagination run wild.

I turned on the shower so they wouldn't hear me hyperventilating or wonder why I was in here for so long. I looked at the little toiletries and at least found the name of the motel chain we were staying at, but no indication of what city, and there were so many of these that that information didn't help. I did strip down and take a quick shower since I figured if I came back out with dry hair they'd have questions. I didn't have anything else to wear, so I put my old clothes back on, but I did feel a little better. As I stood drying my hair with the towel, I heard voices and realized that Tree Trunks and Phone Man were talking. I tried to listen in.

"... and he'll be glad to have her back," Phone Man said.

"He never should have let her go like that in the first place. He should have protected her better," Tree Trunks replied.

"He couldn't have known what she'd get into."

"He knew the risks well enough. There's no excuse."

"Look, don't get too attached, ok? We don't know the full plan yet. Who knows what she'll..."

"She should have been with us this whole time! She'll come around."

"Are you sure?"

"She never had the whole truth before. Once she..." Tree Trunks broke off and they went quiet and it occurred to me that they'd both realized I'd stopped making noise. I flushed the toilet to try to explain why I'd been staying in there after the water turned off, wrapped my hair in the towel, and came out into the main room. They were both watching the bathroom door and I raised an eyebrow at them.

"Couldn't wait for me to come back?" I asked. Phone Man snorted and went back to his phone, but Tree Trunks smiled at me.

"Feeling better?" he asked.

"Would be better if I had clean clothes," I said. He tilted his head, looking me all over. I shuddered, not liking the scrutiny.

"If you tell me what sizes you wear, we'll get you some clean clothes for tomorrow," he said.

"Can't I go pick out my own stuff?" I asked.

"I'm not that dense," he said, giving me an amused grin. I sighed.

"Worth a shot," I grumbled. He got up from the bed and I stepped back instinctively. He raised his hands to show he didn't intend to touch me and grabbed the desk chair to drag it in front of the motel door, then sat down. He motioned toward the bed he'd been sitting on.

"All yours," he said.

"I slept for half a day," I said, frowning.

"You were unconscious. It's not quite the same."

"Thanks for that distinction."

He sighed. "We aren't your enemies, Paige," he said.

Play along.

"Then what are you?" I asked, trying not to sound accusatory.

"I'm not the one to answer that, but we'll be with people soon who can," he said.

"Well, what can you tell me?" I asked, sitting cross-legged on the bed.

"What do you want to know? We'll see if it's something I can answer."

"Do you have names?"

He blinked as if surprised by the question. "I'm Connor. That's Paul." He pointed at the bed, and Phone Man waved. "And Dan is outside."

"Why is he outside? Other than that he's a jerk." Paul laughed at that.

"One of us needs to keep watch out there and you and he aren't getting along," Connor said.

"Not my fault," I said, frowning.

"He's sensitive about..." Paul started, then cut off at the look from Connor.

"Ok, so Dan being a jerk is an off-limits topic, too," I said.

"Let's focus on what we can," Connor said, pulling out his phone. "What size clothes do you want?" I told him and he tapped his screen, and a moment later Paul's phone dinged. He looked up at Connor and raised his eyebrows.

"I'm going shopping?" he asked.

"You think I'm going to leave this to Dan?"

"Good point," Paul said, getting up. "Anything else you want?" Connor looked at me as he asked.

"How long do I get to stay conscious?" I asked.

"Depends on how well you cooperate," Connor answered with a shrug. At least he was honest, but the casual tone he used to discuss knocking me out again made me shiver.

"Could I have something to read since you took my phone?" I asked.

"What do you like?" Paul asked.

"Fantasy," I said. Paul raised his eyebrows. "What?" I demanded.

"Seems fitting," he smirked. I guessed he was thinking

about the connection with werewolves but I rolled my eyes at him.

"Magic, witches, dragons, that sort of thing." I said.

"And grab more sodas," Connor said.

"Noted," Paul said and headed out the door. I tried to see more outside than last time, but he was quick to get out and get the door closed before I could see much. At least they weren't treating me like a hostage. I didn't think so, anyway. Then again I'd never been a hostage before. This probably did count, even if I wasn't tied up or in a cell or something. I sighed and flopped backward on the bed. Connor stayed by the door, tapping on his phone.

"What did you do to him?" I asked suddenly, my throat choking on the words. This seemed like dangerous territory but I needed to know.

"Who?" Connor looked up, looking confused.

"To..." I stopped myself from giving Xavier's name. "To the man I was walking with." Connor's face darkened, and he looked angry for the first time since I woke up.

"That wasn't a man," he growled, and I wondered if I'd crossed a line I'd regret.

"What did you do to him?" I asked again, my voice barely a whisper. Now that I'd asked, I couldn't stand to not know the answer and didn't care what the consequences were.

"We didn't do anything to him," Connor said, frowning as if he regretted it. "The objective this time was to recover you. I stick to the mission, even when there are other opportunities." I felt a surge of relief that Xavier was ok, but it was quickly replaced by cold dread at the implication of his words. Despite his apparent friendliness toward me, this man was dangerous, and I needed to remember that. I couldn't let myself give him any information that would lead back to my family and James. This wasn't only about me. I swallowed, not trusting myself to say anything else right now, and closed my eyes. After a minute, I heard him clear his throat and his voice was softer.

"I know they've sucked you in and made you feel sympathetic toward them. I'm not the one to fix that. But I'm sorry you're hurting because of them. It will get better, I promise." I didn't respond, didn't open my eyes or move. I heard him sigh after a moment and glanced over at him. He was leaning over in the chair, rubbing his face with his hands, looking frustrated. He saw me looking at him and gave me a smile that seemed more pity than anything else. My stomach twisted again. At least Dan made it clear he was my enemy. Connor seemed to genuinely believe that the awful things he was doing were good, and that was terrifying.

I turned over and curled into a ball on the bed. At some point, I started shivering. I heard Connor get up and come over to the bed behind me.

"Get up," he said. I looked over my shoulder at him towering over me. He didn't look like he wanted to argue, so I stood up on the opposite side of the bed from him. He pulled the covers down, then motioned for me to lie down on the bed. I did so reluctantly and he tucked the blankets around me. "The shivering is a side effect of the anesthesia," he said. "It'll wear off, but for now stay wrapped up. The shower probably helped, too." I didn't answer, just turned my back to him again, angry that my body wouldn't listen to me and be still. He went back to his chair and I squeezed my eyes shut, trying to think.

Connor and Paul had been talking about someone who wanted me back. *He never should have let her go. He knew the risks.* They couldn't possibly be talking about Nate. They couldn't. But I didn't know who else fit their conversation.

Who else had left me and had known what he was leaving me behind to? But he wouldn't have done that. Nate wouldn't turn on the pack he had helped found to join people like this, who despised shifters, who denied that Xavier was human, and who seemed to consider kidnapping not a necessary evil but just necessary.

But he had left the pack on his own before I ever met him, had stopped shifting. Maybe he wasn't as dedicated to them as I had convinced myself. And maybe this was how Nate had been taken. Maybe he'd gone through this same experience I was going through now back when he'd vanished, and they'd convinced him to turn on his family. Had he kept me and James a secret then, only to send for us now? But they hadn't mentioned James, hadn't asked me about him. Nate wouldn't have only wanted me. Would he?

I started thinking myself in circles and eventually decided it wasn't doing any good. I started to think about the pending editing jobs I'd put out an offer for recently. I hadn't heard back yet about if the projects had accepted me or not and didn't have details yet... When would I be able to check emails again? Would not responding if they accepted my offers blacklist me? That got me sinking into an anxiety attack which under the circumstances seemed ridiculous, but then anxiety was never about logic.

"You ok?" I felt a hand on my back and jumped. I'd been so lost in my thoughts I hadn't heard Connor come up behind me. I moved away from his hand and he didn't reach out again.

"F-f-fine," I stammered, trying to get my heart to stop racing. He didn't say anything and I didn't turn around, and eventually, he went back to his chair. Somehow, against my better judgment, I fell asleep.

· · ·

"Paige? Paige, time to get up." Someone was gently shaking my arm, but my head was groggy and my thoughts clouded and I didn't want to wake up. I snuggled deeper into the covers and waved a hand to get the person to leave me alone. He chuckled and I put my head under the pillow.

"Go 'way," I grumbled.

"We have to get on the road. It's time to go," the voice said and the hand gently shook me again. Connor's voice. Suddenly my eyes flew open and my mind snapped into sharp focus as I remembered where I was. I sucked in a breath and went stiff and his hand stilled on me, as if he were afraid to spook me. He took his hand off my shoulder and I heard him take a step back. "We've got clean clothes for you, and some reading material for the trip today. There's an outfit for you in the bathroom."

"How far are we going?" I asked.

He smiled and waved his finger at me. "Oh, no. You know better than that."

"I tried." I shrugged and sat up, and he went over to his chair to sit down. Had he been there all night? Had he slept? I headed into the bathroom and pulled jeans and a blue t-shirt from the shopping bag set on the back of the toilet. I blushed fiercely when I noticed the pack of underwear in there. I hadn't told them a size, but they fit. Thankfully they hadn't tried to guess a bra size, but that meant I was left with one article of leftover clothing.

I got changed and headed back out to the room. I imme-diately wanted to run back into the bathroom and lock the door. While only Connor had been in the room when I got up, all three of them were there now, and they all turned to look at me when I stepped out.

"We talked about this yesterday, but I want to make sure we're still on the same page," Connor said, staring me down.

"You can cooperate and stay awake and have a pleasant day, or you can sleep today while we drive. Your call. I'd much rather you stay awake, but we'll do what we need to." The look on his face left no doubt in my mind that he was willing to use force, no matter how nice he'd been acting.

Dan looked like he really hoped I'd put up a fight, and I noticed that he was favoring the leg I'd kicked last night. Good. Jerk. Paul looked indifferent, but my eyes went wide and my knees buckled when I saw that he was holding what looked some kind of black cloth bindings. I stared at his hand and stepped back to hold onto the sink counter to keep my balance.

"It's just a blindfold, and only to get to the van," Connor said, his voice still non-negotiable but gentler when he noticed where I was looking. "It's a precaution. You understand." He took a step forward and I shrank away, remembering his arm around my throat. He held out his hand and I stared at it, trying to stop my heart from thundering out of my chest. "No one will hurt you. And it's only for a moment, from here to the van right in front of the door. You can take it off as soon as you're inside."

I looked back up at his face and his expression softened when he saw how wild my eyes were, the sheer panic in them as I remembered the feeling of being yanked off my feet and ripped from Xavier's arms, the fear as Paul had pressed the gas mask to my face. "I promise. It'll be alright." He said this last part so softly it was almost a whisper as he took a slow step closer. I shrank back more, but I nodded. I didn't like this, but I really didn't want to be knocked out again. Without taking his eyes from mine, he reached his hand back and Paul handed him the blindfold.

"Close your eyes, ok?" he said. I started shaking but did as he said, mentally cursing. I didn't want to seem weak in front of them. I didn't want to give Dan, especially, the satis-faction of knowing how terrified I was. It infuriated me that my body was completely betraying me, but there was nothing I could do about it. Simply standing still and not running and screaming was taking every ounce of my willpower and I had nothing left to try to squash down the physical reactions I was having to being cornered.

"I'm going to cover your eyes now," Connor said, narrating his next moves. I nodded but flinched when I felt the cloth touch my face. "Just me. No one else is near you," he whispered in my ear as I felt him secure the blindfold around my head.

I forced myself to stay as still as possible. Once he was done I tried to open my eyes, but the cloth pressed down so hard it was difficult, and when I did get them open, I couldn't see any light seeping through the thick fabric. I started to hyperventilate. If I thought being cornered when I could see was bad, being in the same situation but blind was a hundred times worse. I flinched again as hands came down gently on my shoulders.

"Breathe, Paige," Connor said.

"Oh for god's sake, it's literally going to take ten seconds to walk to the van. Can we get this over with?" Dan said.

"Shut up and get out there," Connor snapped back. I heard grumbling, then the door opened. I heard the van's sliding door open, one of the front doors open and close, and then the engine kick on.

"Clear," Paul called.

"No screaming, got it? Dan would love to gas you again and I'm trying to avoid that," Connor said. I nodded. "I'm going to pick you up now."

"Wait..." I said then cried out in surprise as he scooped me up in his arms and started walking. I felt him step into the van, and the door closed behind us. I heard the front passenger door close as Connor set me down in a seat, and then we were backing up. Connor pulled the blindfold off over my head and I blinked.

There was a thick fabric stretched taut between us and the front seat and sealed with duct tape to the sides of the van around the edges, presumably so I couldn't see out the front. The overhead lights were turned on, making small halos of light on the seats but leaving most of the van in semi-darkness. Without the blindfold and without all three of them staring me down, I was starting to get ahold of myself again, my breathing becoming more regular and my mind calming enough to let me think.

"It'll get easier," Connor said, buckling himself into the seat between me and the door.

"How many times do we have to do that?" I asked. I tried to sound stern but it came out sounding terrified.

"Only a couple, I think. We have some other pickups to do..." He stopped when he saw the blood drain from my face. "Not other people," he clarified. "But I think you know that I'm not telling you what it is. To be honest, I couldn't anyway because I don't know. Those two are the usual pick-up guys. The rest of the trip isn't my responsibility."

"You're only here for..." I trailed off.

"For you, yes," Connor said. "Our superiors didn't trust those two goons with this."

"We can hear you," Dan called. Connor chuckled and leaned back.

"Buckle up," Connor said. I did and he reached down to grab a plastic bag on the floor and hand it to me. "Paul wasn't sure what exactly you'd like so he got you a good selection," he said. Inside were half a dozen paperbacks.

"How long are we going to be driving?" I asked weakly, staring at the stack of books.

"I will tell you not long enough for you to finish all those, probably," he said, motioning toward the stack. "He wanted to make sure he got at least one thing you'd like. We're not evil, Paige." I leaned back and turned automatically to look out the window before remembering that it was blacked out. I sighed.

"Not being able to see outside feels really weird," I said.

"You'll get used to it," Connor said. "Which of those are you going to start with?"

I flipped through the stack and picked out one about witches and vampires and opened it under the overhead light as I felt us accelerate onto a highway going who knows where.

14

We drove for three days, stopping on occasion to pick up cardboard boxes that Dan and Paul shoved into the back of the van behind Connor's and my seats. Each time the van's back doors opened, Connor blindfolded me again. Eventually, I stopped having panic attacks every time the cloth came over my eyes. After that first night, we started getting two connecting hotel rooms instead of one. I guess Dan hadn't liked sleeping in the van that first night.

At all times, Connor stayed by my side, a constant guard. He remained cheerful and reassuring, but there was always the unspoken understanding that if I tried anything, he had no problem with subduing me. I tried to think of some way to slip away or get help, but they'd orchestrated the trip perfectly to make sure there was no chance for me to try anything, and any time I got snappy, Dan was there to gleefully offer to gas me again, usually earning a glare from Connor.

Paul, as if to apologize for Dan, bought me a few more books each evening, so by the end of the third day I had a small library to keep my mind busy and keep me away from complete despair. Despite Connor's insistence that I'd get used to living without sunlight, I didn't.

I was in a constant state of time confusion, and if it weren't for mealtimes and nights at the hotels, I'd have had no idea how much time was passing. Between that and having no idea where we were, I was feeling completely hopeless and depressed by the time it felt like we pulled into the parking lot of what I assumed was our hotel for the night.

"Do we need to gas her to get her inside?" Dan asked almost hopefully.

"No!" I snapped. "Let's just go in, please. I'm tired of sitting." I stretched my legs, which were crawling with pins and needles.

"I'll ask, but I don't think it's necessary. She's been cooperating. I don't think she'll start fighting now," Connor said.

"Ask who?" I demanded, sitting up straighter and staring at Connor. I'd gotten used to our routine and to my captors, but now they were talking about others being involved. Suddenly, I didn't know what was going to happen next, and I really, really didn't like that. Connor pulled out his phone and started typing, then sent a text. "Connor? Ask who?" I asked again, this time with a note of panic in my voice.

"It's fine," he said. "We're back at headquarters, but that means I'm not in charge of what happens to you anymore." I felt faint and leaned back in my chair, staring at him. He was a known quantity, and at least I was confident he didn't want to hurt me, even if he were willing to if he felt it necessary.

What exactly was the plan for me from here? Were they going to try to torture information out of me? Convert me? That sounded like what Connor had been suggesting the first night. What would that entail? I leaned over with a moan and put my head in my hands. He patted my back. "Really, it's ok. You're safe here," he said.

"Again, kidnapped," I groaned, not lifting my head. He sighed and didn't reply. We'd had some variety of this conversation every evening. His phone dinged and out of the corner of my eye, I saw him glance down at it.

"Blindfold is fine," he said toward the front of the van. "Drop us off out front and you can go unload." I started to hyperventilate as Dan drove to what I assumed was the front of the building, and I took deep breaths and counted to try to calm down. Whoever we were going to face, I didn't want them to see me completely freaked out. I tried to make myself angry to hype up my adrenaline but only succeeded in scaring myself more.

"Paige, I'm going to put the blindfold on now." Connor was speaking to me in that infuriatingly calm voice again like he was trying to corner an unstable animal. He hadn't used that tone with me since the first day. "The ground out there is a bit unstable, so I'm going to carry you in the front door. If you want to walk after that, you can. Ok?" I nodded, my head still in my hands. "You'll need to sit up," he said, his hand still on my back. I took a deep breath and sat up, staring at the blindfold in his hand with a sense of panic I hadn't felt in a while.

"Hurry up. It's late and we still have to unload," Dan said from the front seat.

"Shut up. We'll take what time we need," Connor snapped back. He looked back at me. "Ready?"

"Yeah," I said. I was proud that my voice didn't crack, but I closed my eyes as he came close and wrapped the blindfold around my head. He opened the van door and led me to it before picking me up. I couldn't hear any signs of humanity, no signals that we were in an area with any population at all. Rather, it sounded like we were in a forest. Birds chirped, and leaves rustled in the wind. But no sounds of people. My heart fell. Even if the pack was looking for me, what were the chances they'd find me somewhere like this?

"Why bother with the blindfold if the plan is for me to stay here?" I asked, trying to tamp down the rising dread.

"The plan isn't for you to stay here forever. Until we can trust you, it's a precaution."

"You trust me now, right?" I asked. He laughed.

"I like you, but I don't trust you even a little bit," he answered.

"I suppose that's fair," I said and he chuckled again. I felt him push through what felt like commercial swinging double doors. So we probably weren't at someone's house.

"You want to walk now, or do you want me to carry you to your room?"

"I'll walk. Can I see yet?"

"Not yet."

He set me down, then put one hand on my back and the other on my elbow as he led me forward. At one point, he picked me up to carry me down a flight of stairs and the sense of dread threatened to overwhelm me. Were we going underground? He set me down again and we continued walking, but we made so many turns that I quickly got lost without being able to see. Where the hell were we? At one point I could swear we were going back the way we came. Finally, we stopped and he opened a door and led me in. The door clicked shut behind us and he took the blindfold off me. I blinked in surprise.

I didn't know what I expected, but it wasn't to be in a comfortably furnished bedroom. The full-size bed was on a frame without a headboard, but it was covered in a green duvet and quite a lot of pillows. There was a desk, a bookcase, a dresser, and a framed painting of the ocean on the wall above the desk. A door in the back led to a private bathroom. It would have looked cozy except that under the plush blue rug, the floor was clinical white tile, and the door looked industrial strength, sending alarms through me. It was nicely decorated, but it was still a prison cell. I did notice with a thrill that the bedside table had a clock showing the time in bright red numbers, a luxury I had not had in days. Connor noticed me staring at it and smiled.

"I requested that since you always looked for the clock in the hotel rooms. I figured at this point you should at least have that much. You've been back and forth through so many time zones now that I don't think that'll give too much away."

Any happiness I'd felt at seeing the clock seeped away at the reminder that I was still utterly lost and at the realization of how much he'd noticed when I'd thought I was being subtle. He saw my expression fall and put his hands on my shoulders.

"Listen," he said. "I know you feel trapped for now. But you're going to prove yourself here and earn our trust and then you'll be free again. I know you can do this, and if you put your mind to it, you'll be able to earn that freedom again quickly. You'll do great."

"How am I supposed to do that if I don't know what I'm being drafted for?" I asked, putting what fire I could into my voice.

"You know I'm not going to tell you anything before you speak with..." he caught himself. "With the people in charge," he said, amused. Then he got serious, looking at me with an intensity that set me on edge. "But I think you do have some ideas about who we are."

I shivered. I was fairly sure at this point that this was

AWL, the group that had tried to bomb an entire pack of innocent people simply for the crime of existing. And if they were, then they probably had the experience and the resources to make sure I couldn't be found. And what would they do to someone who they saw as entangled with the enemy? I knew that as a non-shifter who was let into their ranks to this extent, I was unique among the packs. How much did my captors know about that? Did they think I needed to be rehabilitated? Was I a hostage, or were they planning to try to get information out of me that they could use against my family?

But I lifted my chin, looked Connor in the eye, and said "I have no idea."

He sighed and looked disappointed. I didn't know if that look was because he thought I'd be smarter or because he knew I was lying to him.

"I sent ahead your clothing sizes, so you're fully stocked if you want to shower and settle in. I'll bring your books down in a bit after I check in, but there's some stuff on the shelves that you might like. There are writing tools in the desk if you want them."

"Am I to be your resident poet?" I asked, raising my eyebrows. He smiled again. Good. Keep him in a good mood. Even if my playing dumb irritated him, I still needed to keep him on my side, whatever that looked like. I was more trapped now than I had ever been on the road trip, and I needed someone here who was concerned with my well-being.

"We could probably use one, actually. Liven this group up a bit," he said.

"Maybe we'll start up haiku Fridays."

"Sounds like a plan to me."

My stomach growled and Connor stepped back. "I'll go

get you some dinner," he said. And with that, he turned and walked out and shut the door behind him. It closed with a heaviness that confirmed my fears that I wouldn't be breaking out, especially once I heard a lock click into place. I fell backward onto the bed and covered my face with my hands. What was I going to do now? I lay there for a moment trying to think of what I could do and tried to stay calm in case they were watching me somehow.

That thought made me sit up. Were they watching me? Probably. I decided the first thing would be to look for cameras. The door was probably safe. No one would be peeking through that solid chunk of metal. Next, I looked over the walls and in the ceiling joints for holes or any other sign of something. Nothing.

I emptied the desk drawer and everything from the bookshelves onto the bed and looked over every inch of all the furniture, even inspecting the clock. There were no visible holes even for a speaker (I guess letting me hear the radio would have given too much away), but I still didn't trust it. I decided to shove it in the desk drawer once I put everything back away.

The door lock clicked and I froze, staring at the door, my heart pounding. It opened and Connor walked in carrying two brown paper bags.

"Time for..." he stopped in his tracks, surveying the room and me standing there holding the clock in front of the bed covered in books and papers. I didn't move. I had no clue how he'd react to this. I watched him warily as he slowly walked over to the desk and set the bags down, then leaned back against it, watching me. His mouth quirked in a smile that he seemed to be trying to hold back and I relaxed a bit. If he were amused that would be fine. Suspicious or irritated would be fine. I only needed to make sure he didn't get mad. We stared at each other for a minute, me holding my breath and him looking like he was trying not to laugh.

"Redecorating?" he asked, finally.

"The books weren't color coded properly."

He threw his head back and laughed. "What..." he took a breath, tears rolling down his face, "What exactly do you think is hidden in here?" The fact that he thought this was hilarious made me think maybe there really wasn't anything in here to find. Almost. I realized he was expecting an answer and decided to be honest this time. I needed to pick and choose when to hold back, and this one was something he'd probably be able to figure out anyway.

"Cameras," I said. He looked at me as if waiting for a punchline, then realized I wasn't joking.

"You won't find any cameras in here, Paige." I noticed that he didn't actually say there weren't any. Only that I wouldn't find them.

"Good, because I don't want anyone watching me change clothes or sleep or anything. That's creepy. It's bad enough being locked up without feeling like I'm on display."

He didn't say anything but watched me as if he were trying to piece together a puzzle. Then he reached behind him and grabbed one of the bags and held it out to me. "Burgers?" he asked. I stood up from the bed and took the bag gratefully, then frowned back at the bed as I realized I'd covered the entire surface so there wasn't anywhere to sit there. Connor stepped back and held the desk chair out for me. I sat down and he shoved some books into a pile, then sat on the end of the bed and took a burger out of the other bag.

"You're staying?" I asked.

"Now that we're back, unfortunately, you'll be spending quite a lot of time alone. I have other responsibilities here, and you're a big priority but not a top priority to the higher-ups right now. But I thought you'd at least like some company during dinner." I set down my burger as my stomach twisted. "You'll miss me that much?" he asked. I dropped my head into my hands and leaned on the desk instead of answering.

"Look," he said, putting his burger on the desk and kneeling next to me. "I know you think we're the evil bad guys. And I get it. I do. From your perspective, this is all pretty screwed up. But you don't know the full story yet," he said.

"So tell me!"

"Not my place."

I looked up at him and frowned. "Then who can?"

He sighed and stood back up. "You know perfectly well that I can't answer any of your questions," he said, starting to sound irritated. I took a breath and composed my expression again. *Play along.*

"I know," I whispered, trying very hard to look like I was sorry. Maybe I should take up acting after this. Or not, depending on the reactions I got. His face softened. One point for my acting.

"You'll get answers soon. Promise. In the meantime, you have books, you can write, and," he looked around the room. "You can redecorate to your heart's content." I snorted at that, legitimately amused. We finished our burgers and without a word, he started picking books up off the bed. "What order do you want the colors?" he asked, heading for the shelf.

"Rainbow today. I'll reorganize them by author tomorrow."

He shook his head and smiled but actually started putting them on shelves based on color. I went and helped and soon the books were all put back away. He put the clock back on the bedside table, grabbed the now-empty paper bags, and headed for the door.

"I'm busy most of the day tomorrow, but I'll see you at dinnertime again," he said.

"I get to eat before then, right?"

"Of course. *We* aren't monsters." The emphasis on "we" suggested a comparison to my previous companions, but I kept my mouth shut, despite the rage boiling in my veins at the half-veiled insult. "Good night, Paige." He shut the door and it clicked locked.

I waited a moment to make sure he wasn't coming back, then put the clock into the desk drawer. I looked around the room, wondering what I had missed, and I remembered the picture. I tried to take it off the wall, but it was glued down. No part of the frame would budge. That seemed like a pretty obvious giveaway.

I stripped the top bedsheet from the bed and tried to hang it over the picture but couldn't get it to stay up since the frame was attached to the wall, so I couldn't tuck it in. I looked around for other options and my eyes fell on the bookcase. It was taller and wider than the picture frame and should easily cover it. I shoved the desk out of the way and once again took down all the books, putting them on the desk. The bookcase was heavy, but I was able to shove it over in front of the picture. Good enough. I put the books back, then moved the desk to where the bookcase had been.

I considered a shower, but between the day in the van, the adrenaline rushes of arriving here–wherever here was– and the frustration of being locked up, I found I didn't have the energy left. I crawled into bed in the clothes I'd been wearing all day and passed out.

. . .

I woke up to a knock on the door and sat straight up in bed, immediately on alert. There was silence, then someone knocked again.

"Breakfast," a man's voice called out. "You dressed?"

"Yeah," I called back. The door opened and a man dressed in jeans and a button-down plaid shirt came in with an unmarked white plastic shopping bag and a large paper cup of what smelled like coffee. He didn't look particularly athletic. I might be able to outrun him. He headed toward the desk and when he noticed the furniture had been moved, he cocked an eyebrow but didn't say anything.

I glanced toward the door, wondering if I could get out and lock him in here. Another man, this one who definitely looked like he could take me down, was leaning on the wall outside the open door. He smiled and waved, and I returned a tight-lipped grin and a wave back. So much for running.

The man in plaid set down the bag and coffee on the desk and headed back for the door. Before he closed it, he turned and said, "See you at lunch." He hesitated, then added, "You're lucky you know. That they found you when they did." Before I could ask what he meant, he closed and locked the door.

I laid back on the bed, wanting to go back to sleep but also wanting the coffee while it was still warm. I groaned and pulled myself out of bed and over to the desk. At the first sip, I could feel my insides warming, and I immediately felt more awake. I emptied the bag to find individually wrapped muffins and pastries, a banana, a blueberry Greek yogurt, a bag of peanuts, and a granola bar. It looked like someone had raided a gas station. I pulled open a muffin and ate it, trying to focus on waking up.

After eating the yogurt and banana, I went to the dresser and started opening the drawers. As Connor had promised, it was full of clothes, including nightgowns. At least tonight I'd have something more comfortable to sleep in. I grabbed an outfit and headed for the bathroom. I let the water heat up the room until it was full of steam and breathed in deeply.

I needed a plan, but I didn't feel like I had enough information to make a plan of any sort yet. I got dressed and noticed an unopened toothbrush and toothpaste on the counter, so I brushed my teeth. Back out in the bedroom, I moved my leftovers to the bedside table and pulled a piece of paper and a pen out of the desk drawer.

At the top of the paper I wrote "van" and put tally marks to count the days we traveled. On a new line, I wrote, "prison" and one tally mark. I didn't know how or if tracking the days would help, but I liked having a record. I pulled a book from the bookshelf at random and headed back to the bed. I laid down to think, keeping the book next to me. If someone came in, I'd pretend to be reading and maybe they'd think I was too distracted to plot.

I tried to go over what I knew but eventually had to admit that it wasn't much. They had been extremely good at keeping me in the dark, literally. They hated shifters, clearly. They didn't think I was one. They hadn't said anything about James. Did they know about him? If not, I certainly wasn't going to bring him up. *James.* Would I ever see him again? The thought stabbed at my heart, and I closed my eyes and allowed myself to cry. If they were watching me sob, oh well. It probably worked with whatever their agenda for breaking me was, and they were free to guess at what I was upset about. Did they know where my pack was? Or did they think I had been living in St. Louis?

And where did Nate fit into all this? They wouldn't have let a shifter join them. Did they know what he was? Devon had said he hadn't shifted since he left the pack. Maybe he was undercover. He surely couldn't have been convinced to turn on his pack, on his own kind. He couldn't be involved here. But...

He never should have let her go like that in the first place. He should have protected her better. He knew the risks.

Who else could they have been talking about?

I was dying to write down my thoughts to get them straight and clear my head, but I didn't dare. I had no doubt they'd read anything I wrote down and I couldn't risk accidentally giving away something that would lead to James, Xavier, and the rest of the pack. At least they hadn't hurt Xavier. That was something, right? Unless they lied. The thought sent terror racing through me until I convinced myself that Connor may be a racist (speciesist?), but I'd spent enough time with him now to be fairly sure he wasn't a liar. He may refuse to tell me information but as far as I could tell, he'd never actually purposefully given me wrong information, and he'd been direct about not hurting Xavier.

At some point, I couldn't stay in the bed anymore and got up and started pacing. I was starting to understand how zoo animals felt. At least when we were traveling something was happening. Waiting like this was miserable, not knowing what would happen to me next or who would come in the door each time it opened or even when it would open again. I occasionally took the clock out to check the time, then shoved it back into the drawer. I tried to read but found myself reading the same sentences over and over, my mind going back constantly to wonder what was happening. I finally decided to write out some haikus like I'd promised Connor.

Trapped in this dumb room.
Can't even move around much.
When do I next eat?

Let me out of here.
At least answer my questions.
Dan can go suck eggs.

Is it Friday yet?
Who knows? Certainly not me.
What time zone is this?

I folded the paper in half, wrote "Connor" on the front, and slipped it under the door into the hallway. Let them figure that one out. By the time there was a knock on the door again, I was ready to start digging through the walls with the ballpoint pen from the desk. I called for whoever it was to come in, and the same man in plaid with his bodyguard stood outside.

"Lunch," Plaid said. Since no one was introducing themselves I was back to nicknames.

"Thanks," I said, taking the two plastic bags from him. I dumped them unceremoniously on the desk then lay on the bed with my back to him.

"What's this?" he said, and I heard paper scrape slightly on the ground as he picked up the note I'd slipped under the door. "I'll make sure Connor gets this," he said, sounding amused. I didn't reply but kept my back to him, and he closed and locked the door again. Once he was gone, I flipped onto my back, pulled a pillow over my face, and yelled curses.

By the time I'd worn myself out, I was calm again. I

checked in the bags. One was full of bottles of water and Diet Coke and the other contained a pre-packaged salad, a ham and cheese sandwich, and some Reese's cups. Maybe they really were feeding me from a gas station. Which could mean there was a gas station nearby if they were going this often. If I could get out of here maybe I could make it somewhere to get help.

I spent my lunchtime fantasizing about picking the lock on my room and sneaking out (wasn't sure exactly how, but that's what made it a fantasy), being fast enough to run past Plaid and the guard the next time they brought a meal (wishful thinking. No way I could outrun that guard), or convincing Connor to get me out and take me somewhere I could call Xavier for a ride (I had a better chance against the guard).

By the time I'd finished eating, my mind had started spiraling around what their plans for me might be, and that wasn't productive at all if my goal was not to fall apart. As promised, Connor came for dinner again, this time with plain white take-out boxes of spaghetti and garlic knots.

"I got your note," he said, grinning like I'd given him a birthday gift.

"I don't know what day it is, so who's to say it's not haiku Friday?" I said with a shrug.

"Close enough." Once again, while he didn't lie, he didn't actually answer the question, and I didn't have the energy to push it. Turns out that being frustratingly anxious and antsy all day was exhausting. "What are you reading?" he asked, grabbing the book I'd tossed on the bedside table.

"Didn't start it. I couldn't focus. I was going crazy all day," I admitted. He set the book back down and sat on the bed, facing where I was sitting at the desk.

"Do you want something else to keep you busy?" he

asked. "I could get you a TV and some DVDs maybe. Or some music. I could load up an old MP3 player." All things that couldn't access the internet, I noticed. He got a mischievous glint in his eye. "Or you could keep writing me poetry. I'd love a whole collection on your feelings toward Dan."

I smiled at that, but the joking didn't distract me from the fact that he could provide all the entertainment he wanted and I'd still be trapped. "How long will I need to be kept busy?" I asked, fully expecting him to shut me down.

He hesitated. "Not long. I think tomorrow you'll start getting some of the answers you've been looking for." I sat up straight and stared at him, wide-eyed, the thought of whatever the next step was pushing my anxiety up to the surface again. He held up his hands. "Maybe," he clarified. "I can't give you an exact yes or no. But I think it might be tomorrow and I figure you'd like to know."

"Thank you." I genuinely meant it, I was surprised to find. We finished eating in silence and he gathered the empty containers to take with him. Before heading out the door, he nodded toward the bookcase.

"I see redecorating wasn't limited to moving the books." He winked and I thought maybe that was his way of telling me I had been right. "Good night."

"Night," I replied. When he closed the door, I lay on the bed again, staring at the ceiling. Tomorrow. I had until tomorrow to come up with a plan. I had a feeling that once whoever had orchestrated this saw me, I'd be out of time. I still didn't know why I was here, but I wasn't interested in seeing what their intentions were once they had their hands on me. I showered, changed into one of the nightgowns, and went to sleep, wondering how I was going to get out of this.

. . .

THE NEXT MORNING I woke up to breakfast already sitting right inside the door. I sat up, my heart racing. Someone had opened the door and come in, at least enough to set that all down, and I didn't wake up. That was terrifying. I didn't feel like I'd been drugged again, but maybe it was something more subtle this time.

I inspected the wrapped muffin and yogurt closely before deciding they didn't look tampered with and ate them. There was an apple that I decided not to risk since it wasn't wrapped. They'd probably gas me again if they needed to knock me out, but now I was paranoid. I poured the coffee down the sink and drank water from the tap to wash down breakfast. Then I got dressed and settled in to wait.

Connor said maybe today. I still felt like I'd gladly chew my own leg off to get out of here, but even if it wasn't today, knowing I wasn't facing a totally undefined amount of time helped. I needed to escape, not just keep them away from me. I could bar the door, throw books, push furniture at them, but none of that would get me out of here. If anything, if they decided to leave me here until I broke down instead of trying to deal with me, I'd still be trapped. I was still trying to figure out what to do when I heard someone start to unlock the door. I stood up. I was out of time.

15

The door started to open and I steeled myself to leap at whoever came in to knock them over and then run for my life, but the voice that came through before I could see the person made my blood run cold and shocked me into inaction.

"Paige? We need to talk." I'd heard that voice say that phrase so many times as I was growing up that I suddenly felt like I was sixteen again for a moment.

"D-dad?" I choked out. As the door swung fully open, I felt the floor fall out from under me as he and my mom stepped into the room. "Mom? What... how..." I stammered. I fell back toward the bed, sitting down hard as my legs gave out.

"Hey, sweetie," Mom said, sitting on the bed next to me. She was tense, but Dad smiled at me and he seemed genuine. I stared at them, remembering the last time I'd seen them, when they looked like they might actually spit on me as they slammed the door shut in my face when I had come to ask them about Nate. This didn't make sense. Not that they were here, not that they were being nice and acting like the past seven years had never happened. None of it.

"I... I don't understand..." I broke off.

"Yeah, there's a lot to explain," Dad said.

"But the important thing is you're here and safe with us now," Mom said, patting my knee.

"I'm not safe!" I snapped, the shock starting to wear off a little. "I've been kidnapped and imprisoned. That's literally the opposite of safe!"

"Not kidnapped." Dad shook his head and gave me a sympathetic look. "Rescued."

"Being snatched against my will, shoved in the back of a van, freaking gassed and blindfolded, and taken to a secret location doesn't seem much like a rescue." Familiar emotions were starting to break through now, the betrayal and anger mixed with the wish that things could be different. I tried to squash that last one down as hard as I could. Not the time. I had to figure this out.

Maybe I could get information out of them if they thought I was willing to play along. But I knew I had to ease into it. If I suddenly started cooperating I knew they'd never believe it, but before Nate, I'd always eventually given in to whatever they wanted. If I could tap that, I might find a way out of here. Give them back their slightly rebellious but still pliable little girl I hoped they still could see in me.

"We know it's a lot. But it'll make sense soon," Mom said. "Promise." She gave me what I guessed was supposed to be a reassuring smile. I sighed deeply and gave her a tight-lipped grin.

"Ok. How soon is soon?"

"One of our friends wants to talk to you. She'll explain everything. She's really been here for our family. You'll like her. She should be back in a few hours," Dad said. I nodded and gave them a small smile but my blood had gone from freezing to boiling. *Our family.* Who the hell was included in that? Mom looked concerned and I wondered if she picked up on my mood.

"What's her name?" I asked. Too direct. Dad's expression didn't change, but his eyes suddenly looked wary.

"She'll tell you everything when she gets here later today," he said.

"If she'll be a while, I think I'll try to rest," I said, arching my back a bit to stretch. "And maybe have something else to eat? I'm still hungry."

"Of course," Dad said, his eyes growing warm again. "Sure. I know the food has been... unimpressive. We don't have much here yet. Easy Mac sound good?"

"Sounds great," I said, smiling at him. *Yet.* So maybe this was a new location for them. Mom patted my knee one more time then stood up next to Dad.

Dad knelt down to kiss my forehead. "Glad to have you back, pumpkin. We've missed you,"

"Me, too." I tried my best not to choke on the words. Mom still looked like she wasn't sure about me. I'd have to try harder to convince her. I laid down on the bed and closed my eyes, and in a moment I heard two sets of footsteps walking away and the door shutting and locking.

My eyes popped back open. I had a bad feeling that I needed to get out of here before their friend appeared. I looked around the room again, but unless I could beat them down in a pillow fight, I was out of luck.

Maybe I could pull a sheet over their heads and confuse them long enough to get out the door and run. How long did it take to cook Easy Mac? They'd probably be back any second. I stripped the top sheet off the bed and tried to get it ready to throw like a net. Just in time, too, as I heard footsteps outside and the handle of the door started to jiggle. I stood there posed with the bedsheet for longer than seemed reasonable. Maybe it was hard to get the door unlocked when you were holding a bowl of macaroni.

Finally, the door opened and someone hesitantly stepped through. I threw myself at them, my arms spread wide with the bedsheet, and covered the person's head, trying to use my weight to shove them toward the wall. They went stumbling, tripped, and fell on the bed. *Holy crap, it worked!*

As they fell, I avoided the hands reaching to grab onto me and ran for the door but slammed into a solidly-muscled male chest. As hands grabbed my shoulders, I started kicking and punching automatically, relying on instinct and adrenaline at this point. The hands tightened and when the man laughed, I finally stopped fighting and looked up at Kyle in shock.

"Oh my god, it's you!" I cried and threw my arms around his neck in a hug.

"Good to see you, too," he chuckled, hugging me back. Behind us, I heard Xavier cursing as he disentangled himself from the bedsheets.

"Your escape plan was to smother them to death?" he grumbled.

"Apparently it would have worked," I said, sticking out my tongue at him and then glancing into the hall. "They'll probably be back any second. I asked for some food and they said yes. That's why I was ready when you came in." I heard a low growl from the hallway.

"Devon's right. Let's get going," Kyle said. Xavier rolled the sheet up quickly and arranged it on the bed to look at a (very) quick glance like a sleeping body with its head under a pillow and then followed us out into the hallway.

Devon was shifted and waiting, using his wolf's senses to make sure no one was sneaking up on us. He led the way as we went down what seemed like an unreasonable number of hallways that looked suspiciously sterile, with white walls and white and blue tile flooring. Where had they taken me? I started feeling queasy thinking about the few horror movies I'd seen that took place in hospitals or mental wards.

We finally came to a staircase that led to what looked like a waiting room. There was a reception desk, but the space behind it was dark and clearly disused. My stomach started threatening a full revolt, but I pushed the feeling down. First, we had to escape. Then I could freak out. Through a crack between some double doors across the room, I could see sunlight. A way out. I took a step toward them when Xavier suddenly grabbed me and we all dove behind the desk. I held my breath as we heard the doors open, multiple sets of footsteps walk in, and voices mid-conversation.

"We'll decide what to do with him. He's our blood. He belongs to us," Mom hissed.

"You'd do well not to remind me that enough werewolf blood flows through your veins to infect your grandchild" an unfamiliar woman's voice snapped back. "You're lucky I've known you for so long. Your standing's in serious jeopardy already."

"I didn't know..." Mom sounded furious.

"Tami, don't," Dad said, cutting her off.

"Don't you dare!" Mom snapped. "You knew. You knew!"

"What was I supposed to do?"

"You could have said something, anything! Said something before she went and let herself breed with that *thing*. If she could have found a nice, normal man, we'd be fine."

"It wouldn't have been fine. She'd still be infected. What if she'd met another carrier?"

"Which is why you should have said something! We could have stopped her, controlled her, found someone suitable. Instead, now our family is mixed up with them."

Now I was seeing red. I knew my parents had turned on me when I started dating Nate. They'd always been aloof, but not downright cruel like that and it had been a shock, but a lot of memories were falling into place now. As much as I didn't want to admit it—they were still my parents—a lot of what I'd experienced growing up and especially since I met Nate suddenly made sense. I remembered them snubbing some of the other parents at school, refusing to let me play with certain kids. They'd never explained why. We'd always been well off, so I'd thought they were elitist.

I'd been relieved to move out when I started college, thinking that not having that constant tug would let my parents and me have a normal relationship once they weren't so directly involved in my life. I'd never realized how deep this ran. My fingernails dug into my palms as I curled my hands into fists, and my jaw hurt from how tight my teeth were clenching. Xavier, his arms still around me from the dive to hide, squeezed. I nodded. Escape first. Freak out later.

"Enough!" the woman's voice boomed, and both my parents' voices immediately went silent.

"The council will decide what to do with the child. You lost your claim on him as soon as he was born a werewolf. We'll decide how to deal with your daughter later. We'll see how repentant she is, if she can be saved. From what I hear, right now it's not looking good, and I suggest the two of you focus on your own future." The voices faded as we heard another door close behind them. Xavier squeezed once more and I realized my body was so tense I was shaking. I unclenched my fists and rolled my shoulders.

"I'm good," I grumbled. But I wasn't. I was furious. Furious at my parents for lying to me my whole life, at the pack that had stolen Nate, and at this entire, messed up world that was tearing up my family, denying James his father and his grandparents, and tearing my own heart into pieces. We stood in silence, listening for any other signs of people. I knew that anything I could hear they already would have sensed, but I found myself listening as hard as I could anyway. Finally, Devon nudged my hand with his nose.

"Let's go," Kyle said, and we slipped out of hiding and out the double doors into the sunlight and headed for the exit.

"WHERE ARE WE?" I asked as I stared at mountains out the car window. I'd finally stopped shaking. After we'd stepped outside, I'd seen that the building we were leaving was indeed an abandoned hospital where I'd been locked in the basement. We'd gone around the side of the building and headed toward a two-story parking garage out back that looked like it would crumble with a good kick, staying close to the walls and ducking below any first-floor windows, trying to stay out of sight.

Once we'd made it to the car hidden in the garage and driven away, my mind started going through every story I'd ever heard or seen about nightmarish experiments by insane doctors and then started coming up with new plots that I was sure would win an Oscar if they ever went to film. After enough deep breathing that I was getting lightheaded,

I'd finally gotten my bearings enough to realize we weren't in any locale I'd ever visited.

Kyle was driving, Devon lying on the passenger seat with his head on his paws. Xavier sat in the back with me, an arm wrapped protectively around me and holding tight as if he might never let go of me again. He kept glancing down at me worriedly, but when he wasn't looking at me, whatever was on his mind had his face fixed in a mask of rage. I didn't ask what he was thinking, because I was pretty sure that I was having similar thoughts now that the shock was wearing off.

"Virginia, apparently," Kyle said.

"How... how did you find me?" I asked.

"We put out word that a member of our pack had been taken by AWL and a pack based not too far from here tipped us off. They'd had suspicions about this location and were still watching, but suspicions were enough for us to move on," Xavier said. I saw Kyle's hands grip the wheel tighter, his knuckles whitening.

"We should be taking them out," Kyle grumbled. Beside him, Devon growled.

"I know, I know," Kyle snapped.

I frowned. "But once you were inside how did you find me? Did you search the entire building?" In the front seat, I saw Kyle and Devon exchange a look. "Don't even think about not telling me," I said. "I've been kidnapped and trapped in an underground room being told nothing but cryptic messages and then found out my parents are involved somehow and I'm not in the mood to not be told what's going on!"

"James saw you," Xavier said. Devon turned to watch my reaction.

"Like he did with Nate?" I asked. Devon nodded as Xavier continued.

"Exactly like that. We could sense you, see your surroundings. Couldn't make out any people but could sense what you could feel. We figured lower level because there were no windows in the room and when he paid close attention we were able to figure out what directions you went to get there based on sensations, even with the blindfold."

"I didn't know how to get out of there, though."

"We had the benefit of many people experiencing it and being able to replay it."

I thought hard about this. "I thought he could sense Nate because Nate was a shifter, too," I said.

"So did we," Kyle said.

"Maybe it's because you and he are so close. Maybe you're connected by genetics. We don't know," Xavier said.

"Why are we driving west and not south?" I asked, looking out the window again.

"They grabbed you from westward," Kyle said. "In case we're being followed or watched, we want to make sure they think that's where we're actually from. We'll go west for a while then head back home."

I slumped in my seat and Xavier gave me a squeeze. "James is fine," he said. "Right, Devon?" Devon gave an affirmative bark. Another squeeze from Xavier. "We're reasonably sure that they don't know we're based in Florida since we weren't there when you were taken. We're trying to make sure it stays that way," he said. I nodded.

"So would I be correct if I tried to guess who the daughter is of the members who almost caught us?" Kyle asked.

"Probably," I said. Now I was mad again. It was bad

enough they'd abandoned me, disowned their grandchild, and didn't care when we needed help. Now they'd kidnapped me and apparently wanted James after all, but I doubted it was to make up time and become doting grandparents. Something must have come through in my voice.

"Keep that anger, Paige," Kyle said, glancing at me in the rearview mirror. "You're going to need it." He put his eyes back on the road and I leaned my head back and closed my eyes, exhausted.

Xavier kissed the side of my head. "They made their decision years ago. We aren't giving you back now."

"Paige! You're back!" Trevor was in the den when we came in the front door two days later. "James! Your mom is here!" he yelled. Devon and Kyle had wanted to make absolutely sure that no one was watching us before we headed home, so we had driven further than I had expected. While I was anxious to get back, I did understand the caution and was glad they were thinking ahead more than I was.

I heard feet pounding down the stairs and then James flung himself into my arms with a wordless cry and started sobbing. I clung to him, holding him tight as if that alone would keep him safe, would keep him out of the hands of AWL and his grandparents and anyone else who might want him. Kelly came out of the kitchen right after James had leapt at me and threw her arms around both of us as James started talking, his voice shaking.

"I was scared you were gone forever, but Devon and Xavier and Kelly promised they'd get you back, and Kyle said they would..."

"And here she is, safe and sound," Kyle interrupted James loudly before James could tell me what Kyle had said they would do. Devon and Kelly looked like they might choke trying not to laugh, Xavier held his hands up in an "I'm innocent" gesture, and Kyle grinned and winked at me. I shook my head and smiled, squeezing James tight and feeling intensely grateful for everyone in this room.

When Kelly let go of us, Xavier gently led me toward the couch and navigated me down, James still clutched in my arms. He sat down and put an arm around me, holding onto both of us while I tried to convince myself I was really out, we were really here again. Home again. Together. Eventually, James stopped crying and lay against me. When he sat up again and looked into my face, there were no more tears in his eyes. There was fire.

"No one is ever taking you again," he declared. And even with his child's voice, the look on his face promised carnage for anyone who crossed him. I shuddered and hugged him tight to me again, wondering what exactly he could do. Most kids wouldn't be able to deliver on that threat, but we still didn't know the range of his abilities.

"Never again," I said, although I had no idea how to keep that promise. I had no intention of letting my son be my shield. I was supposed to protect him, not the other way around. He needed to just be a kid. That set off my anger again, at the people who were stealing his chance for innocence away from him, who had already stolen so much that he deserved to have.

"Never again," Xavier echoed me, his other arm coming around James now and wrapping us both in a hug that seemed designed to try to shield us.

"We'll protect her, won't we Xavier?" James said, looking up.

"Absolutely," Xavier said. "But not just you and me, ok? The entire pack. Remember that. You're never on your own."

James looked distant as he nodded and Xavier's eyes flew wide. "How are you..." He stared at James, whose look was now if anything more determined. James looked at me.

"The pack will never let you go again," he said fiercely. I hugged him to me so he couldn't see my face, then looked at Xavier over his head, trying to make a "what was that?" face. He silently mouthed, "later" at me and I nodded and put my cheek down on James's head and breathed in deep, savoring the little boy scent that I'd been so scared I'd never smell again, the feel of him in my arms, and the sound of his breathing as he clung to me. He was still five though, and it didn't take long for him to get wiggly. I loosened my grip and kissed his forehead.

"You want to go play?" I asked. He gave me a worried look.

"You'll stay here, right?" he asked.

"Not going anywhere," I said, giving him another squeeze. He nodded his agreement and went running up the stairs, yelling, "Trevor! Let's play Mario!"

I waited until I heard a door slam upstairs then turned to Xavier. "What did he do?" I asked. At the same time, Kelly came in from the kitchen, and Devon and Kyle appeared from down the hall. They had apparently been waiting until James was out of the room. Devon was pulling a shirt over his head, so I assumed he had still been shifted.

"What in all the hells was that?" Kyle asked.

"Was he shifted?" Kelly asked.

"Can someone please tell me what happened?" I demanded.

"He communicated with the entire pack," Devon said.

"He wasn't shifted," Xavier said, looking at Kelly. "We already knew he could do some things while human, but I'd assumed it had a limited range."

"That wasn't limited," Devon said. "At all. I was still shifted so I could hear wide range. He got to everyone in the entire pack." He turned to me. "We're one of the biggest packs in the U.S. because we don't discriminate in who we'll take in. We have a lot of people locally, but we have pack members all over the country, even a few in other countries now. Paige, he got to everyone in the pack. Not just those who are shifted right now, either. All of us." I felt the blood drain from my face.

"Did he... what did you call it? Compel them... you... in some way?"

"Not this time," Devon said, sighing and rubbing his hands over his face.

"Would you know?" I asked, frowning.

"Yes," Kelly said. She glanced at Xavier and Devon. "We experimented some with Nate when he was trying to figure out what he could do. Voluntarily, of course. But with him, when we were being compelled, we knew what was going on, but couldn't stop it. Like he'd get someone to get him a drink from the kitchen, little things like that. And you'd do it and you'd want to do it, but you also knew that you weren't really in control. You could feel it, like a veil over your thoughts."

"What James did this time was basically shout at us," Xavier said.

"Loudly," Kyle grumbled.

"Which wouldn't be concerning except for the fact that normally we can only do what he did when we're shifted," Xavier said.

"And we can usually only hear it when we're shifted, also," Kelly added.

"What does this mean, exactly?" I asked. I looked around at each of them. "What do we do?"

"This means that we don't have any idea of what his limits are, but it doesn't change anything. It means we raise him right," Xavier said. "We raise him to be a good man who understands right and wrong and the consequences of abusing power."

"You're not alone in this, remember," Kelly said gently, seeing the overwhelmed look on my face. "You're his mom, but we're all your family. We're all responsible for making sure he grows up happy, loved, and a good person."

"And we keep him out of anyone else's hands at all costs," Devon added grimly, looking at me. "Even your parents."

"Especially my parents," I agreed, the anger flaring again. Xavier took my hand and squeezed.

"And," Xavier said, steely resolve in his voice, "It means we find Nate and get him back, whatever it takes. James needs someone who understands what he's going through. Because as much as some of us can do, none of us have ever been through something of this magnitude." I squeezed his hand again and he squeezed back, but I could see something in his eyes I couldn't identify. Something that made me feel like things were moving in a direction that I might not be fully prepared to deal with.

16

A week later, we had mostly settled back into some semblance of a routine. James started school lessons and made me promise not to leave the house while he was in the classroom at the back of the house. He had tried to create some sort of mental link with me so he could check in, but we hadn't made any progress. He didn't know why I could hear him the night of the attack, and we didn't know what he was doing differently other than that now he wasn't trying to compel anyone, but he promised not to try that until we had a practice plan. It rankled me, but I tried to hide my anxiety from him. I wanted a link between us so we could check in with each other as badly as he did, and I had to admit I was jealous that the rest of the pack could keep tabs on him when I couldn't.

I somehow focused enough to finish up the two editing jobs I had in the pipeline (one of them two days late. I explained the delay as a family emergency involving my son and they had been understanding). Xavier convinced me not to take on anything new. I was anxious about not pulling my weight financially, but the others all insisted that my main focus should be on James and the continued search for Nate, and I couldn't say no to that.

When I'd disappeared, Kelly and Kyle had immediately found flights to swap places. Kelly had come on the initial mission as the political contact between packs. Her primary job had been to try to gain full cooperation from Melissa rather than just free range of her territory, and it had been a slow discussion with her pack, who was unconvinced it was their problem... until I'd been kidnapped. Once a direct attack happened on their territory, apparently all bets were off. They were now fully on our side, ready to take action with us. With Kelly's job done and Kyle more trained for a search and rescue, Kelly had gone home and Kyle had joined up with Xavier and Devon.

The three of them and two other groups of our pack members had gone looking for me, following different leads. Others had continued the original mission, finishing the stakeout of my previous attackers. The shifters they captured did confirm that the aim was to capture both me and James, but they didn't know why. They'd been told targets, not reasons. When I asked how we were sure they weren't lying, Kelly told me that Melissa hadn't only earned alpha status by being nice, and the look on her face made me stop questioning. Based on Kelly's reaction, I wasn't sure I wanted to know exactly how the information had been dragged from the captives or what had been done with them afterward.

Kelly and I were in the office discussing details I remembered from my time in captivity. I'd written down everything I could remember as soon as we'd stopped driving the day I'd been found, but Kelly and I kept going over it again and again, trying to make sure that any small details were included. I kept remembering more and more, but at this point, I felt like we were hitting the limits of what I could remember, what had happened, or both.

"This is definitely AWL, right?" I leaned back in my chair, staring at the notes scattered across the desk between us.

"I can't see how it's not," Kelly replied, frowning. "But knowing that doesn't help. Devon got a report back from the surveillance team this morning. They're gone. Again. He doesn't know how they got past us without us noticing."

"If we had attacked when we found them we'd have..." Kyle said behind me, making me jump. He came into the room and leaned on the desk, looking down at our papers.

"Then you'd have all probably died," Kelly snapped, cutting him off. "We were not prepared for a full invasion. It was search and rescue only."

"I know, I know!" Kyle was frustrated, but he did sound like he agreed. He just didn't like it.

"Any news?" Kelly asked.

"Yeah, actually. Melissa is on her way here. She'll be here by dinnertime."

I sat up in my chair, suddenly on alert. "Did something else happen? Is something wrong?" I asked.

"Nothing's wrong." Kyle waved his hand dismissively, but he looked wary. "She wanted to touch base in person." He paused. "And Devon wants her to meet James." I could hear how close he came to growling the last bit.

"Be nice," Kelly warned. In what was to me a surprising turn of events (but that seemed to surprise no one else), Kyle had become James's champion since we'd gotten back. He had become nearly as protective of James as I was and fiercely guarded him against any outside-the-pack interactions. I completely agreed with him most times, even pausing outings with Jessica and Hannah to parks or movies for now. I hadn't anticipated him as an ally in this, but I was grateful for it. In this case, though, I didn't know if we were on the same page.

"Why does Devon want them to meet?" I asked. Maybe Kyle knew something about this visit I didn't know yet, because he was clearly upset about it.

"Devon wants to tell her what James can do and wants her to see it for herself." Kyle's eyes glittered with barely contained fury now. Kelly stared him down, challenging him.

"But she already knows about his abilities," I said, confused. "Doesn't she?"

Kyle shook his head. "Devon only told her that Nate's child had joined our pack and been attacked, and we thought it was connected to Nate's disappearance."

"But they knew what Nate could do." I was thoroughly confused now. "Melissa said some of her pack knew him."

"Her pack knew Nate but didn't know what he could do," Kelly said. "Melissa knew he could do some things but didn't know the extent of his abilities. He was careful to keep that inside our pack, and even within us it was well-contained. Some of the core group from when the pack first started knew, but once we started growing, he kept it close."

I was starting to understand Kyle's hesitation a little more. I turned to him. "Did Devon already tell her about either James or Nate?" I asked.

"Not yet. I actually came to tell you that Devon and Xavier are waiting to talk to you both so we can all plan this together."

Devon suddenly appeared in the doorway, as if he'd been summoned. "You could have started with that. How long does it take to say 'Hey, come to the kitchen?'" He glared at Kyle.

"Trying to warm them up before you bombard them." Kyle pushed himself up from the desk and shoved past Devon into the hallway.

"If you hadn't warmed them up, the coffee wouldn't be cold now," Devon called after him. Kelly and I got up, and Devon gestured for us to go ahead of him. In the kitchen, Xavier was sitting at the table with a cup of coffee and Kyle was sitting down. Kelly poured herself a mug, then stuck it in the microwave while I grabbed a soda can from the fridge. When we were all sitting, Devon looked at me first.

"I want to be clear, you have full veto power here," he said. "Pack business is a democracy, but decisions about James aren't. If you don't want Melissa to know about his abilities right now, we won't tell her." After I nodded, he turned to the others.

"So do we tell Melissa about James and Nate's full abilities? I think we need to," he said. "Considering how long she's known Nate, that one may sting a bit once she realized how long we kept it under wraps, but I think she'll understand our reasoning, especially considering what happened to him in the end." My stomach twisted but I reminded myself that at the very least we knew he wasn't dead. Then again, was that better or worse than whatever did happen to him?

"Why tell her now?" I asked. I trusted her so far, but I was still hesitant.

"We need more than someone who will have our back," Devon said. "We need someone who will fight alongside us. We're being attacked on two fronts. One of them is AWL, and we have that enemy in common with all other packs. But we don't know who our other enemy is yet other than that it's other shifters. This is bigger than our pack can handle alone." He looked at me intently. "We can't protect James and we can't find Nate without help."

I nodded, thinking. "If we tell Melissa, how many people will find out? If we ask her to keep this to herself, will she?"

"She will," Kelly said at the same time that Kyle said, "She might." They glared at each other across the table.

"I feel like I'm missing something here." I looked back and forth between them, frowning. Xavier took a drink, looking amused, and Devon rolled his eyes and rubbed his temples.

"Kyle has no filter, as you well know," Kelly said, keeping her eyes locked on Kyle.

"Melissa's a..."

"Good friend to this pack who just happened to call you on some of your bullshit and you can't manage to get over it," Kelly cut off Kyle's protest.

"It wasn't bullshit." Kyle crossed his arms and leaned back, scowling. But he seemed to have retreated from the fight.

"Do you really think she would ever hurt our pack?" Kelly stared intently at Kyle. He stared back defiantly for a few heartbeats before his tension drained away marginally.

"No." His voice was quiet and still frustrated, but he sounded sure of the answer. Devon looked irritated and Xavier looked like he might laugh. I'd have to ask him later what exactly had happened between Kyle and Melissa.

"Can we get back to the current situation now instead of rehashing your grudges?" Devon asked, glaring at Kyle. I looked at Kyle also and waited until he met my eyes to ask my next question.

"Whatever happened between you before, do you

believe she would do what she can to keep James safe if she knew?" I asked.

Kyle studied my face and took a long time to think before finally answering, "Yes."

I leaned back and sipped my soda, thinking. The others watched me but didn't press. My immediate instinct was to keep James on lockdown, keep others from knowing about him, keep him from becoming more of a target. But I had to admit that we were past that stage. He was already a target, and so was I, and whoever wanted us had some idea of what he could do. If our enemies had that knowledge, then we also had to trust our allies with it. I looked at Devon.

"We need to tell her."

DINNER THAT NIGHT was more subdued than usual, with fewer people coming to the house to eat. I guessed Devon had asked for only a small showing so that we could shoo people out after eating to allow Melissa a private audience. Once most of the pack had wandered home, Kyle stayed in the backyard chatting with James while Xavier and I cleaned the last messy bits of the kitchen. Kelly and Devon chatted with Melissa in the den. I couldn't make out what they were saying, but from Xavier's expressions, he could hear every word. At some point, I elbowed him in the ribs.

"What was that for?" he asked, rubbing his side.

"You can hear them and you aren't sharing the intel."

"It's not my fault your hearing sucks."

"That's what I have you here for, right?"

He grinned at that, then went silent, listening. "They've mainly been going over what we learned in the last week and strategies for the teams that are still out hunting..."

"If you're going to eavesdrop you may as well come in here!" Kelly called.

Xavier grinned at me. "I'm not the only one with wolf hearing, you know." I threw the kitchen towel at him and he caught it and hung it on the dishwasher. "Do you want James yet?" He yelled into the den from the kitchen, and Devon yelled back an affirmative.

I peeked my head out the back door. "James, hun, come on in here. Melissa wants to meet you."

"I met her at dinner!"

"You waved as you ran past her to get out back."

"That's meeting!"

"No, it's not. Come on."

"Can I bring a truck?"

"Not one covered in dirt."

"Whyyyyyyy?"

Kyle, fortunately, came to my rescue then, grabbing James and throwing him over his shoulder, then spinning in a circle as James squealed in protest. "You want me to put you down, pup? Get away from me!" James suddenly shifted while spinning his body around and shot out of Kyle's arms, running across the yard in wolf form. He paused on the other side and hunched to wiggle his butt, then launched himself back across the yard and toward the back door.

"Wipe those paws!" I said, blocking him. He dutifully rubbed his paws on the mat before running through the kitchen to the den, still as a wolf, yipping. Xavier followed him into the den.

"I've been teaching him some ways to escape from someone grabbing him, among other stuff," Kyle said, grinning. "He catches on quick."

"That's... not something I want him to need to know but something I know he does need. Thank you." Kyle nodded his understanding and we trailed into the den. James was partially shifted back now, keeping only his customary tail and ears. He had gone shy and was peeking out at Melissa from behind one of Xavier's legs in the middle of the room.

Xavier stayed put, letting James use him as a shield while Kyle sat in an armchair furthest away from Melissa and I went over to hug her hello. James watched us intently, focused on my reactions to the new woman. Kyle didn't act out at all, but he and Melissa completely ignored each other's existence. I raised an eyebrow at Kelly, then looked between Melissa and Kyle. Kelly rolled her eyes.

"I'm so glad you're back safe! We were all so worried when Xavier sounded the alarm," she said, hugging me tight. She held me out at arm's length, looking me all over. "Devon said you weren't hurt. You really weren't?"

"Really. Got some bruises from trying to fight them off, but that's it, and they're mostly gone now." I flicked my eyes toward James, peeking out from behind Xavier and Melissa hugged me close again.

"We'll chat later," she whispered in my ear. I hugged her back and nodded agreement, then sat on the couch and held my hand out to James. He slowly came out from behind Xavier, then ran to me and leapt into my lap, watching Melissa the whole time with huge eyes. I'd never seen him so wary of someone, but I had to admit, recent events had made me jumpy, too.

"James, this is Melissa. She's a good friend and has helped us a lot," I said.

"I know," James said quietly.

"It's lovely to meet you, James. I've heard quite a lot about you. Everyone here loves you a great deal." Melissa smiled at him and held out her hand. He looked at her hand for a moment, then looked back up and studied her, his eyes roving over every inch of her standard colorful attire.

"You're like a glitter rainbow."

Melissa laughed. "That is the look I tend to enjoy, yes," she said. James smiled at her and finally reached out and shook her hand.

"Is your fur rainbows, too?"

"Alas, if only it were." Melissa sounded genuinely aggrieved. "But I'm pretty solidly gray."

"You could dye your hair colors. Then some of your fur will be that color. That's what Hannah does," James said.

"I'll take that into consideration," Melissa said, smiling and sounding for all the world like she seriously might think about it. James quieted again, studying her more.

"What did you hear?" he finally asked. "About me."

"Well, I've heard that you're a very brave little boy. I know you've been through some scary things in your life, losing your dad and then being in an explosion. I know you're a shifter like me." She smiled and tapped one of his ears. It twitched, but otherwise, he didn't react. She smiled at him and he narrowed his eyes at her, then looked at me, then at Xavier. Holding Xavier's gaze, he shifted. Xavier nodded and shifted also, and they locked eyes long enough that I knew they were having a silent conversation.

Another pang of jealousy shot through me, that I couldn't have this level of connection with my own son. I tried to shove it down, but it must have shown on my face because Melissa gave me a sympathetic look. I gave her a half smile back and waited along with everyone else. Finally, Xavier shifted fully back and James shifted back to his furry-eared human self.

"I'm not like the other shifters," James said quietly, making eye contact with Melissa.

"You do seem like one special kid." She smiled back at him, indulgently.

"No, Melissa," Kelly said from her other side. "He really is unique. That's one of the reasons we had you come in person." Melissa's gaze on James suddenly went from playful to assessing. He wiggled in my lap but didn't break eye contact with her.

"Really?" she asked him. He nodded. Melissa leaned toward him, smiling in anticipation now. "Can you show me?"

James looked at me questioningly and I nodded. "Whatever you want to show her is ok, baby. She's safe." I gave him a little squeeze. He sat up straight and suddenly all wariness was gone. He stared intently at Melissa and I saw her reaction the moment he made contact. Her eyes flew wide open, but to her credit, she didn't jump up or do anything that might startle James. She slowly looked around at Devon, Kyle, Xavier, and Kelly.

"How..." Her voice cracked. "How did he do that?"

"What did he do, exactly?" I asked.

"I just said hi," James said. Melissa's gaze moved back to him.

"That you did, James. Do you understand why it surprises me though?"

"Devon said not everyone can do what I can, and right now we have to keep it a secret because if people are jealous they might be mean to me." James's voice went quieter. "I think he means they'll attack me again or try to kidnap me like they kidnapped Daddy and Mommy."

Even as my chest constricted at the last bit, I glanced at Devon with a grateful smile. I hadn't heard this explanation before and I was reminded again how good he was with kids. He nodded once at me in recognition then turned his attention back to Melissa and James.

"It's very wise to keep something like this to yourself," Melissa agreed. I appreciated that she was having this conversation with James instead of talking over him, and he seemed to understand that he was being included in something significant. "Is there anything else you can do, besides link with someone outside your pack or link while you're not shifted?" The way she said it made it clear that those on their own were significant.

"I can..." James frowned. "Make people do things. Com... Comp..."

"Compel people," Xavier said.

"Yeah, that. Compel people," James said. Melissa frowned.

"Can you show me that one safely?" She asked.

"I'm not supposed to do it anymore," James said. He looked at me, but I looked toward Kelly, Xavier, and Devon. They were the ones who had helped Nate figure it out. I was out of my depth with so much of this.

"Melissa, are you ok with him showing you if it means you're out of control for a moment? We're all here standing by," Kelly said. Melissa looked wary but nodded at James.

"James, can you have Melissa go get a Sprite from the kitchen?" Kelly asked.

"I... I don't know," James admitted.

"Try, hun," Melissa said softly, taking one of James's hands in hers. "I'd like to understand it if you can show me."

James let out a deep breath and nodded. He stared at her intensely, face blank at first, but then his brow furrowing in concentration, then in disappointment. Eventually, his entire face scrunched up like he was putting serious effort into something, until he went limp and leaned back against me, looking defeated.

"I can't." He squished his eyes closed, looking like he might cry.

"That's ok." I hugged him tight until I felt the tension drain away from him and he was left frowning, but looking much less like he might have a fit.

"He's only ever done it one time. During the attack, he turned away the entire group of shifters attacking us, about a dozen of them. That's how we got away," Kelly said. At this Melissa's eyes snapped over to Kelly.

"Yasmin thought maybe you edited your experience of the attack at the end because it was gruesome or something traumatic happened to you. We were worried about what it meant that you cut off the actual escape and communicated that part in words." She sounded thoughtful. "But I can understand why you did."

"One more thing," Devon said. "We think these abilities might be inherited." Melissa looked at me with a new, assessing gaze, looking for all the world like she was trying to read my mind. I shook my head.

"Not from me."

She frowned, and then her eyes grew wide. "You did say his father is Nate?" she asked. I nodded. Melissa looked around at Devon, Kelly, and Xavier again. "I knew Nate could mind-speak with your pack as a human, but you're saying Nate could do all this?" she asked. The three of them nodded.

"We don't know if he could do everything James can do, exactly," Devon said. "James feels more powerful than what we felt from Nate. And Nate only had limited outside-the-pack communication abilities, not like what James can do. But the compelling, yes. He could do that. And there may have been more we didn't know of." That last admission sounded tight, as if Devon didn't want to believe that Nate would have kept something like that from them, but he was starting to doubt whether he had a full picture. I knew exactly how he felt.

Melissa leaned back, frowning. "I've known you all since you were teenagers, and you were able to keep this from me since then?"

"We know, and we're sorry it took this for us to tell you," Devon said, sounding sincerely apologetic. "He didn't tell us," Devon gestured toward Xavier, "Until we had made the final decision to begin our pack and started discussing who would be alpha." Melissa's gaze didn't soften until James reached over and put his hand on her arm.

"They just want Daddy and me to be safe," he said. He stared intently at her and it took a moment for me to realize that he was speaking to her mind-to-mind. She nodded at him and patted his hand.

"You're right," she said. She looked around at the others. "We all do what we can to protect our packs."

"We don't know why James was targeted," Xavier said. "If they suspected he had abilities like this or if they knew about Nate and wanted his family for some reason. We were leaning in that direction since Paige was a target, also. But if they didn't know what James could do before, they know now that he's used those abilities against them."

James suddenly let out a big yawn. "Let's get you to bed," I said.

"I don't wanna," James said, but his body was already starting to go limp against me. I kissed the top of his head.

"Mom's decision," I said. "Bedtime." I stood up with him in my arms but he looked at Melissa.

"Will you still be here tomorrow?" he asked.

"I will."

"Ok. Good night, Melissa."

"Sweet dreams, little one," she said. I could hear the others continuing to talk as I carried James upstairs. I helped him change clothes and brush his teeth, then lay in my bed with him and rubbed his back.

I thought he had fallen asleep when he whispered, "Mommy?"

"Yes?"

"I like Melissa."

I smiled. "Me, too." A moment later, he was breathing heavily, and I slipped out the door and back downstairs. Kyle had slipped away somewhere. This entire time he'd been left out of the conversation, content to watch. I wondered if that was because of his feelings about Melissa or because he was the only one who didn't actually know Nate himself. But apparently once James had gone to bed, he hadn't seen a reason to stick around.

"This won't get out," Melissa said once I had sat down. "I know your pack is a democracy, but mine is not, so I can make this promise. This will be kept to top levels for now, and no one will breathe a word of this outside our two packs unless I hear the word from you."

"Thank you," I said.

"No one is going to hurt that boy." Melissa looked fierce enough that I wondered if she were mid-shift. Then she settled back again, looking like herself and I wondered if I had imagined the momentary sharpening of her features. She grabbed her purse and pulled a small manila envelope out and handed it to me. "You need to see this," she said. I blinked at it, then looked up at her.

"What is it?"

"We found it in the building where the shifters had been

holed up," Melissa said gravely. I opened the envelope and sucked in a breath, my vision narrowing to the picture inside as I pulled it out. The picture of me and Nate holding little James. I flipped it over to see my name and phone number scrawled on the back in my handwriting. One of the pictures I had handed out years ago.

"If I had ever thought these would be used to hunt us down..." I choked back a sob and Xavier was immediately by my side. Kelly's eyes were huge, and Devon looked thoughtful.

"That's still your phone number," he said, looking down at the picture in my hand.

"Yeah. I never wanted to change it in case anything..." I drifted off again and Xavier rubbed my back. Devon looked at Melissa, frowning.

"Do you think they could have traced the phone somehow?" he asked.

"Tech isn't my expertise," Melissa said. "But considering how well coordinated the initial attack was, I wouldn't rule it out."

My heart sank and I must have made a noise because now Xavier's arm came all the way around me and gave me a comforting hug.

"We'll get you another phone," he said. I nodded, not able to speak for the moment. He leaned in closer to whisper in my ear, "And the phrase 'my fault' better not come close to crossing your mind. You did what you needed to do."

I closed my eyes and leaned into him, and he rubbed my arm. Although we had discussed the potential connection to Nate and had confirmed that James and I were targeted, this physical evidence somehow made it more real. This tangible connection between the darkest, loneliest days of my life and what was happening now threatened to overwhelm me again, send me back into that panic that had taken over my entire existence for far too long.

But this was different, I reminded myself. I wasn't alone. I wasn't lost. And I wasn't helpless. I took a deep breath. This time I was fighting back, and I would bring my own army behind me. This time, I wouldn't fail.

17

Devon and Melissa spent most of the next morning discussing details of what we knew, then shifting to link with other alphas they trusted to discuss the updates on AWL's latest movements. The other packs immediately agreed to set up surveillance in their own territories, especially now that we had some specific faces to look for.

I was thankful Xavier had seen Connor, Dan, and Paul since I couldn't join a link to send an actual image. I couldn't send mental images, but I did find a decade-old picture of my parents saved on my phone. My gut wrenched as I pulled it up to show Devon so he could send out the images to the other alphas, but I reminded myself that my parents were planning on trying to take my child from me and possibly had my partner trapped somewhere. Protecting my parents meant possibly sacrificing my own family, and I wouldn't take that risk. They'd made their own choices, and I was making mine.

Xavier disappeared and came back later in the day with a new phone, complete with a brand new number for me.

We moved over my pictures and contacts, then Xavier had planned to completely cancel my phone line. But not having access to that number felt like I was closing a door that might help Nate find his way back to us. When I explained this, Kyle set up an online call forwarding system so that the number could still be called but wouldn't necessarily be traced to my location. My old phone was wiped of data and reset before shutting it off completely.

At lunch after finishing his schoolwork for the morning, James watched Melissa carefully. She kept smiling at him, letting him decide when to broach a conversation Finally, he cleared his throat.

"Melissa?" he asked hesitantly. She put down her silverware and smiled at him.

"Yes?"

"Can we... I mean... can you..." He stared down at his plate and pushed his food around with his fork.

"Perhaps. If you let me know what it is," she said.

"I want to link with you," James said, finally looking up at her. "Can we?"

"Well of course. What do you want to talk about?"

James looked at me. "I want to show her what I did to save us," he said. "I can't com...comp... I can't do it again, but I can show her what I did before."

"Good thinking," I said, ruffling his hair. He beamed.

"Let's go in the den after lunch," Melissa said. She held up her fork. "But we should both finish eating first."

After lunch, James and Melissa headed into the den, James pulling on her arm and talking non-stop about the new cartoons Trevor had introduced him to earlier in the week. I grabbed my and James's dishes and took them to the sink to rinse off and put in the dishwasher.

After I'd put the dishes away, I leaned on the counter,

frowning out the window above the sink at the backyard. I wasn't sure I wanted them to do this alone. I wanted to be there to hear what was happening, hear his point of view since he'd refused to talk about it so far other than to reassure me (and himself, I was sure), that he kept us safe that night. But even if I were in there I couldn't...

"Still wishing you had better hearing?" Xavier whispered in my ear. I jumped and spun around, smacking him on the shoulder.

"Don't do that!" I said, but I couldn't help smiling. He chuckled and leaned back against the counter next to me.

"I saw Melissa and James in the den, and you're in here looking pensive. You ok?"

"Yeah, I just..." I shook my head in frustration. "They're going to be speaking through the link so even being in there I wouldn't know what was going on. I don't like being shut out."

"Do you want me to chaperone?" I looked at him to see if he was teasing, but the look on his face was completely serious.

"Yes," I said, relief maybe a little too evident in my voice. "Is that bad? You and the others trust her so I feel like..." I trailed off, not sure how to finish the thought coherently. Xavier reached over and gave me a hug.

"He's your son. It's your job to be paranoid." He gave me a quick squeeze then went into the den. I took a deep breath and trailed after him.

"Mind if I join the party?" Xavier asked. Melissa gestured for him to sit.

"By all means," she said. Her eyes flickered over to me as I sat in an armchair. I braced myself to see rebuke there for not trusting her, but she smiled, a look of understanding in her eyes. I relaxed and smiled back.

"James was about to show me what it was like when he compelled the shifters away from him and Paige," Melissa said to Xavier, turning an encouraging smile toward James. James nodded back, but he looked nervous.

"Want me to back you up?" Xavier asked, sitting down next to him.

"Yeah," James said, leaning back into Xavier. Xavier squeezed his shoulder gently, and James suddenly seemed much more confident. Something in my chest tightened and I couldn't help but smile, seeing the two of them sitting there, a little team against the world. James clearly had complete confidence in the man sitting next to him, and Xavier's affection showed through both his touch and the proud look he directed toward the little boy who had now scooted into his lap. Once James was settled, he raised his chin and looked at Melissa again. "I'm ready."

"Me, too," she said. "Do you want to shift?"

"Not yet. I want to try this first," James said. Melissa nodded, keeping eye contact, and James's eyes focused on her so fully that he seemed unaware of everything else around him. After a moment, Melissa shook her head and James slumped. He frowned at her and she shook her head again. I looked to Xavier, who was also focused on James. I was dying to know what was happening, but I didn't interrupt. Eventually, James fell back onto Xavier.

"Why can I only send words?" He frowned and crossed his arms and I almost laughed at how typically five-years-old he looked at that moment, like any normal kid who wasn't getting his way.

"Even sending words to me is very impressive," Melissa reminded him. He *harumphed* and crossed his arms tighter.

"Want to try it shifted?" Xavier asked.

"Guess so," James said grumpily. I wondered why James

was grumpy about needing to shift. As far I knew, this was the first time he'd ever not jumped at the chance. James reached down and pulled his shirt off and I saw Xavier glance at me. Oh. Right. I was why they were all supposedly prudes right now. I felt myself turn scarlet under his gaze and the side of his mouth twitched up in an amused grin. Now I might actually die of embarrassment.

"Want me to show you a trick, James?" Melissa asked. He nodded, his eyes lighting up again. Her legs shifted and she pulled her shirt up a bit to expose gray fur. "Shift all of you except your arms and head first. Then if you want to get undressed, you have your fur on." I melted into the chair a little in relief that they weren't about to go full nudist.

James looked down and his legs transformed. Then, he jumped to the floor and pulled his pants off to reveal his little wolf body underneath. Once he was undressed, he finished shifting and sat wagging his tail, waiting for Xavier and Melissa. Melissa was quick behind him, transforming most of herself before pulling off her outfit to reveal her gray-furred wolf form before shifting her arms and head. Her muzzle had streaks of lighter grey, reminding me of the grey in her hair.

Xavier looked at me and wiggled his eyebrows, then pulled off his shirt. Not a wolf. He caught me staring at his bare chest and smiled far too confidently, and if possible, I turned redder. Melissa distracted James by wagging her tail in front of his face until he started trying to catch it, leaping and nipping. She winked at me and I groaned, covering my face with my hands.

I heard a wolf-like chuckle and when I peeked out between my fingers, Xavier was shucking off his pants, to reveal (thank god) a wolf bottom half. He quickly finished shifting then winked at me and laid down behind James, who settled back against him again. I glared at him and James yipped, looking back and forth between us. Xavier tilted his head and stared me down until I rolled my eyes, crossed my arms, and slouched in the chair. Melissa shook her head like she was amused, then went and sat next to Xavier and James, nudging James's ear gently with her nose. He nodded and sat up straighter, his tail going still.

Forgetting whatever it was that just happened with Xavier for the moment, I focused on James. From my vantage point, nothing was happening. The three wolves sat still, the two adults focused on James. Then James started trembling. I leaned forward and clasped my hands in my lap so tight my fingers started to hurt. I looked to Xavier, who looked away from James for a second to nod at me as if to say, *don't worry, I've got him.* He wrapped himself tighter around the puppy in front of him and rested his head against James's side. James was stiff but stopped shaking a bit.

I hated this. I hated being locked out, knowing James needed me and being completely unable to act. Melissa moved closer to James and laid down in front of him, putting her front paws on James's paws, looking him in the eye as if trying to ground him. It seemed to be working to pull James back into an ok place.

Then James began to growl, his muzzle pulled back in a snarl. I sat up as I felt what seemed like a ghost of what I had felt from him that night again. Not the words, but the intent, the fury behind his order to those who would hurt us. *James!* I sent the thought out with all the focus I could muster, trying to reach back across that wave of power for him. I leaned forward, using every ounce of willpower I had not to leap for my son. Xavier nuzzled his head against

James's side and James calmed down again, the mental force I had felt retreating.

Kelly and Devon came running from the hallway into the den, freezing when they saw the three wolves on the floor. Kelly glanced at me and seemed to immediately realize what was happening. She pulled me onto the couch and sat next to me with an arm around my shoulder, making soothing sounds. Devon asked me if I wanted him to shift with them, but I shook my head.

"Xavier is there. James is ok," I said. *He's ok.* I repeated the mantra to myself in my head, trying to make myself believe what I had told the others. Devon went into the kitchen and I heard the sounds of him making coffee. Despite Kelly's presence, by the time the three wolves came out of what seemed like a trance, I was shaking.

Melissa shifted back first, pulling her clothes back on over her fur before becoming fully human again. James had turned around and nuzzled into Xavier, who rested his head on James, waiting for him to be ready to come back.

"What happened?" I asked, my voice sounding like I might choke. "I felt... I felt something. Something like what he did that night."

"What he did was incredible. I've never seen anything like it." Melissa shook her head, frowning in concentration. "He's got to be protected. But you already know that." She looked me in the eye. "My pack will do everything we can to make sure he doesn't fall into the wrong hands. We're with you. Completely." She reached toward me and grabbed my shoulder, and I grabbed her arm back, as if we were making a pact. Maybe we were. I didn't know how these things worked, but from the look on Kelly's face, whatever was happening was serious.

"Thank you," I said. Devon came into the living room

and handed cups of coffee to me and Melissa then went back into the kitchen for more. Melissa sat down with her mug between her hands, staring into it as if it could answer her questions. I absentmindedly sipped mine, watching James and Xavier, who now looked like they were cuddling, as if nothing had happened and it was simply a good afternoon to get cozy.

Eventually, Xavier nuzzled James until he lifted his head. James glanced over at me, nodded at Xavier, and got up. He shifted halfway then pulled his shorts back on and shifted his legs back. The ears stayed, and I smiled at that. He climbed into my lap and hugged me tight. I put my coffee on the table and hugged him back, closing my eyes and nuzzling his hair.

"I felt you," he whispered. My eyes shot open. I pulled him back just enough to look at his face.

"When?" I asked.

"When I was showing them how I made everyone go away. I was showing them and it was scary and then I felt you there." His face glowed with happiness, and he flung his arms around my neck. While I'd been focused on James, Xavier had shifted back (pulling on clothes while I wasn't looking, thank goodness. I didn't want to know how Kelly would react to seeing my own reactions to Xavier right now). I looked at him and he nodded.

"We couldn't feel you the way he did, but we felt you through his experience, his reaction to you," he said. "How did you do it?" He sounded calm, but his eyes were anything but. He looked delighted. Kelly was staring at me like I'd grown an extra arm.

"I don't know," I said, bewildered. "I just thought his name, but I didn't do anything. Wouldn't it make more sense that he heard me, rather than that I did something?"

"Maybe," Melissa said thoughtfully, watching James. He turned and peeked at her without letting go of me.

"She called me," he said, hugging me tighter. I had never heard him sound so proud. "She called me, and I heard her."

"Were you trying to find me?" I asked.

"No, Xavier was there." He said it so matter-of-factly, as if he wondered why I would even ask the question.

"I wish we could link with you so you could see if it feels the same," Kelly said.

"Me, too," I sighed. She had no idea how sincerely I meant it. It seemed like an aside to her, but to me, it was becoming a core issue that I didn't know how to move past.

"Hey, y'all, can I snatch James back yet?" Kyle was leaning in the kitchen doorway, looking over all of us. "The other kids are ready for defense lessons and waiting on us out back." I kissed James as he wriggled away from me and ran toward Kyle.

"Put your clothes back on," I called, throwing his shirt toward him. James caught it in one hand as it sailed close, but Kyle waved a hand dismissively. "He won't need clothes today," he said, ushering James into the backyard. At the comment, I couldn't help but glance at Xavier, who immediately grinned but had the decency to look away rather than stare me down in front of everyone. Kelly caught the glance anyway, and the feral delight in her eyes let me know that I was going to be interrogated later. To my surprise, Devon also narrowed his eyes at Xavier, as if realizing something, and I wondered where this was going to end up later between him and Kelly.

. . .

MELISSA DECIDED to head back to St. Louis first thing in the morning. She said she had done what she came to do and needed to get back home to talk to Yasmin and some of her other trusted pack members to figure out plans. I chatted with her in her room for a few moments, then went to my own room and laid down on my bed to go over what had happened with James. I tried to think of anything different I'd done when I thought his name, but I couldn't identify any way that that thought was significantly different from other times I'd been thinking of him.

The only thing I could come up with was that I had been more desperate to help him than usual, but we'd been in those situations before and he hadn't said anything about hearing me then. Maybe he was more attuned to it since we'd been attempting and failing to forge our own link lately. Maybe he had wanted me so badly at that moment that he imagined it but didn't actually hear me.

Xavier had said that they hadn't heard me but rather had noticed James's reaction. If James was convinced I did it, then it would make sense that Xavier and Melissa had noted his reaction, even if they couldn't sense the actual message. I decided to ask Xavier what exactly he had sensed. Since he'd been there with James, maybe between us we could figure this out. I was lost in thoughts about the link James thought we had now as I wandered down the stairs, but I stopped short when I heard Devon and Xavier's voices in the den.

"She belongs to Nate, Devon. *Nate.* And I..." Xavier's voice broke off with a groan. Devon and Xavier were sitting on the couch, looking away from the stairs, their heads close together as they talked. I froze on the bottom step, hardly daring to breathe, pressing back against the wall as if that would hide me if they turned around.

"You didn't know that at the beginning of this. You had no way of knowing. None of us had all the information we needed to make that connection until the attack." Devon said.

"I don't know what to do now. She needs someone there for her. And I can do that. I will do that. But when we find him... I don't know how I'm going to walk away."

"How far has it gone?"

"Not far, officially," Xavier heaved a sigh. "I mean we haven't made any declarations of anything, and I don't know how far she feels it's gone. But for me... I have no idea how to give her up. Pulling back as far as I have feels like torture. I mean I'll do whatever she needs, but it's killing me. I thought..."

"I know." Devon's voice was so quiet I could barely hear it. Just then the back door slammed, and James came barreling in from the kitchen.

"Hi, Mommy!" he called as he passed me to run up the stairs. Xavier's head snapped around so fast I thought it might fly off his neck as he found me, his eyes growing wide and then closing in what looked like frustration. Even Devon looked startled, his gaze bouncing back and forth between me and Xavier for a moment like he was assessing a threat.

Finally, he cleared his throat, smacked his hands on his knees, and stood up to leave the room, mumbling something about work he had to do. I came down the final step and he reached out to squeeze my shoulder and give me a small smile as he passed, heading toward the office. I kept my eyes on Xavier as I heard the office door close.

"Paige, I..." I'd never seen Xavier actually lost for words, but he couldn't seem to figure out what to say now as we stared at each other across the room. Finally, he sighed and rubbed his face, then held out a hand. I went to him and took it, and he pulled me down to sit on the couch beside him. He stared down at our intertwined hands, rubbing the back of my hand with his thumb. I waited, my heart pounding.

"I don't know how long you were standing there," he mumbled. "I didn't hear you come down."

"My turn to sneak up on you, for once," I said. He lifted his eyes to mine.

"Don't get used to it." He smiled, and I smiled back. The tension broken, he leaned back on the couch. I leaned back next to him, and he put an arm around my shoulder, pulling me against him and I snuggled up. He sighed.

"I'm sorry," he said.

"For what?"

"I shouldn't have..." he swallowed, lost for words again. "You came here having lost someone and I shouldn't have pushed you, shouldn't have..."

"Stop." I sat up and looked at him. He swallowed again, clearly nervous about what was coming. "You haven't done anything wrong," I said. "Neither of us has. I came here to start over. To get away, get over the past. I wanted to move on. I thought he was..." I still couldn't say the word. Even knowing he was alive, I couldn't finish that sentence. Xavier saw the look in my eyes and pulled me back against him.

"If I had known who it was you'd been looking for..."

"But you didn't," I said. I didn't sit up this time, staying pressed against him, nestled into the one place I felt safe. "And I didn't know, either. And frankly, I'm still coming to terms with that. With the fact that the man I thought I knew..." I sighed.

"I don't know if he really existed. In some ways, he didn't, and I don't know how much of what I knew was true or not. I'm going to keep fighting to find him, but I don't know who it is we're looking for now," my voice was shaking. I hadn't voiced these fears even to myself before now, trying to only focus on what needed to be done next and not thinking about what I might find out later.

Xavier hugged me tight, sensing that I was starting to fall apart a bit, and I pressed my face into his chest and took deep breaths, trying not to let everything I'd been studiously ignoring overwhelm me. Once my breathing settled again, his grip loosened, but he kept me held against him.

"He's a good man, no matter which one you're looking for. Whether that's Julian or Nate," Xavier said softly. "In many ways, we grew up together. We knew each other in ways that most others didn't know us. And the good parts... those are going to be true." I could hear his voice breaking, but his arms were steady.

"Lots of people are good men," I said. "Kyle's a good man. That's not the only criteria." I felt him laugh under his breath at that. "And right now, I don't know how I feel about what's going to happen after we find him. It's just..." I shook my head. "Everything about him is all too confusing right now."

"I'm not confused," Xavier said. I felt my heart drop until he said, "Paige, nothing about how I feel about you is confusing. That's the problem." I looked up at him and found him staring down at me with a look that made my breath catch in my chest. "I'll be whatever you need me to be, but I can't stop how I feel for you. No matter what happens, I don't think I'll ever..." he choked on the words.

"I don't know what I need." My voice was unsteady again. "I've felt completely lost and alone for four years now. I've had more thrown at me in the last few years than I ever thought possible and there were times I didn't think I'd get through it. You're the first person who's made me feel safe since..." I took a breath to steady myself again. I sat up, keeping my eyes locked on his. "All of you took us in, helped us, but you... Xavier, you brought me back to life."

He seemed to be holding his breath now. "I don't know what's going to happen past today, but you have been the best thing to happen to me in years." I felt myself on the verge of crying now. "You've been here for us in ways I never could have imagined. James loves you, and I..." the words caught in my throat as tears started to fall, but his eyes gleamed as he stared at me.

"You don't have to say it, whatever it is," he said softly, his hand coming up to brush my hair back behind an ear and linger in the strands as he smoothed it down. "Don't say anything you aren't ready for. But know this. I do love you, Paige. I have since your first day with us. I have never been confused, never had any doubt, and every moment with you only confirmed what I already knew. If you need me to step away, I'll do it. I'll do anything you need me to do. But I love you, and I don't know how to stop."

Now I was crying in earnest. "I don't want to hurt you," I whispered. "I don't know what's coming, and I don't want you to get hurt in whatever mess is next. I've handled myself for a long time now, but I don't know how to handle it if you..."

"Paige," he interrupted, cupping my face in his hands and bringing his eyes close to mine so all I could see was him. I lost myself in that intense gaze, in the emotions that I didn't need a mental link to feel right alongside him. "Forget tomorrow. Forget all of it for now. Right now, what do you want me to be? What do you need? If you want me to back off, I will. If you want..."

"I want you," I breathed.

At those words, something changed in his eyes. His hands moved from my face, one to tangle in the hair at the base of my neck, the other falling to my back to pull me closer as his lips gently brushed mine questioningly. Every thought, desire, emotion that I'd been suppressing since the night of the first attack surged to the surface, and any doubts or fears were swept away as I focused on this moment, on him, on what felt like everything in the world snapping into the right place for this instant.

I reached up to curl my fingers into his hair, pull him in closer, and any hesitation from him disappeared at my response. His arm went completely around me as the kiss deepened, the hand in my hair pulling just enough to tilt my head further up toward him, and I lost myself in him, pressing as close as I could get, thinking of nothing outside of the feel of his arms, of his kiss, of his body against mine. Suddenly he tensed, then broke off and kissed my forehead with a low growl, holding me as close as he could.

"What?" I asked, wondering if he were already regretting this.

"Devon basically told us to go get a room because he's been keeping everyone else out of here and he's about to open the den back up."

I started laughing as Xavier stood up, pulling me with him and keeping me close, like he couldn't bear to let me go an extra inch away now.

"I've got James for the night," Kelly's voice came down the hall.

"Busybody!" Xavier called back, but he had a bigger smile on his face than I'd ever seen from him. "Come on," he said, pulling me toward the garage. "Let's get out of here for a bit." I was only too happy to follow him out.

18

We wandered down the pathway to Xavier's hidden park, holding hands and stealing glances at each other. I couldn't stop smiling, and from what I saw each time I looked his way, Xavier couldn't, either. He led us under the arched bridge holding up the road overhead and stopped.

"You're sure about this?" he asked, turning to take both of my hands, searching my face intently.

"I love going on walks," I said. I tried to sound flippant, but the words came out as barely a whisper.

"Paige," he said, one hand going up to run through my hair. I closed my eyes and leaned into his touch and he drew in a breath. "Really, if this will be too hard on you, if it's not something you think you can do right now, you can tell me. I'll be fine."

I opened my eyes and stared back into his gaze. "I'm sure," I said, putting a hand on his cheek. I moved my hand to his neck to pull him down for another kiss, but he stayed upright and out of reach. I frowned at him.

"You're absolutely sure?" he asked again. This time, there

was no hesitancy in his voice. This was a challenge, and it lit something in my chest that had been dormant for a long time.

"I'm sure," I said again, putting all the conviction I could into my voice, willing him to see how seriously I meant what I was saying. The intent behind his eyes suddenly changed, moving from concern to something else, something predatory that made my blood sing in my veins. He moved forward, herding me backward until my back was against the wall of the tunnel. He put his hands on the wall on either side of me and towered over me, getting so close that everything else was drowned out as every one of my senses focused on him.

He leaned down and whispered in my ear, "What do you want?"

"You." My voice was lower than I expected as he pulled back enough to stare into my eyes again. "I want you."

Then there was no more hesitation, no more questions, no more stalling. His mouth came down on mine with a hunger and urgency that spoke to everything he'd been holding back, and I met him with answering passion. I thought I might burst with the sheer joy of finally, finally not having to convince myself to look away from what I knew I felt for him, of not hiding anymore. For this moment, there was only us, and everything else faded away as he pushed me against the wall and moved his mouth from my lips to trail my jaw and my neck.

I shuddered and tilted my head to give him more access, grabbing onto his shoulders as he kissed and nipped his way across my collarbone and then back up to my ear, my breath uneven as I responded to his touch. As he kissed a sensitive spot behind my ear I moaned, and he tangled both hands into my hair and brought me back in for another kiss.

My fingers dug into his hair and his neck, trying to hold him as close as I could, trying to make this moment, this feeling, stretch into forever.

Once we both were out of breath, we pulled away enough for him to rest his forehead on mine, one hand still tangled in my hair, the other stroking slowly up and down my back. I kept my trembling arms wrapped around him, curving up behind his shoulders to keep him close. I lost track of how long we stood there, holding onto each other, trying to remember that this moment, this feeling, was real.

Finally, he turned and tucked me under his arm, the other hand lifting my chin for another quick kiss before he kissed the top of my head and led us through to the other side of the tunnel and toward a bench next to the stream. We sat there holding each other in silence for a while longer until he suddenly put his face down into my hair and chuckled.

"What?" I asked.

"I enjoyed the way you looked at me before I shifted earlier."

I pulled back enough to frown up at him. "You didn't shift before you started undressing!"

"Didn't I?" At his feigned look of innocence, I poked him in the ribs, and he pulled me into a hug that pinned my arms to my sides as he laughed.

"When James first linked, you said that you were all acting like prudes with me around, and then I thought..." I stopped and he laughed harder.

"I said we were being more careful around you, not that we're nudists," he said.

"So is that what you all normally do? Shift part way then undress?" I asked. He was laughing in earnest now.

"Yes. Can you imagine Hannah or Jessica being willing

to totally strip down in front of anyone?" he asked. "Or any other teenager for that matter? We'd all have died of embarrassment before we grew to adulthood." He looked down at me, his eyes gleaming. "You've seen me without a shirt before, so it wasn't that you were dazzled by your first view of my chest. What was going through your mind?"

"It's different when you're in a bathing suit and when you're stripping," I grumbled.

"So that's what you were thinking about." His grin was full of mischief now. "Me stripping." I turned scarlet and tried to look anywhere but at him, but he pulled my chin over so I had to meet his gaze, his face serious again.

"Hey, no hiding. Not from me," he said. "Please." I nodded and he leaned down and kissed me again, on the mouth, the forehead, the nose. He pulled me against his side again and sighed, and I nuzzled into him.

"Can you tell me about what happened with James earlier?" I asked after a few moments of comfortable silence.

"What do you want to know?"

"He said I called him and he heard me. And you said you felt his reaction to me. What exactly happened?"

"I didn't hear you directly if that's what you mean." Xavier frowned, thinking. "But James absolutely did. So we sort of heard you secondarily, like when alphas link together to let their packs communicate through them. Without James, I wouldn't have known you were there, but I heard what he thought he was hearing."

"And what did he hear?"

"You calling out his name."

"Anything else?"

"Not that I could tell. Why? Did you think anything else toward him?"

"No. No, only his name," I said.

"So he probably did hear you. The question is whether that was you reaching out or him listening in."

"It wouldn't make sense for it to be me," I said, frowning. "I'm not a shifter. I can't do anything."

"I disagree. You're very, very good at quite a few things. Including this." Xavier leaned down and kissed me again and I kissed him back, holding him tight for a moment before pulling back and raising an eyebrow at him.

"You're shameless," I laughed.

"I'm just getting started."

My breath caught in my throat and I leaned against him, if for no other reason than to get out of the way of that look he was giving me before I got distracted again.

"Really though, I'm..."

"Don't say useless," he interrupted.

"Fine." I rolled my eyes. "But I'm clueless on so much. I can't link, so I'm not sure I understand what that feels like, even if I did feel it when James turned away those shifters. I can't shift, so things that the rest of you think of as obvious like shifting while undressing I wouldn't think of." When I mentioned undressing, Xavier gave a low chuckle that sent a flush through me that for once had nothing to do with embarrassment, but I tried to ignore it for now. "I can't even..." I stopped.

"What?"

I sat up and looked at him. "Teach me to fight."

"What?" he asked again, this time sounding surprised.

"I need to know how to fight. In St. Louis, I couldn't fight back at all."

"Paige, even I couldn't..." I held up a hand to stop him.

"They were specifically after me. If I had been able to do anything to get away, it may have changed things. And yes, I know how big they were, but anything at all would have been better than just getting dragged away. And if something happens while I'm with James, I need to be able to defend both of us." I looked at Xavier, expecting him to argue, but he looked thoughtful.

"I'm not the one to teach you."

"Why not?"

"I can teach you some stuff, but Kyle's got more experience with this sort of thing. It's why he teaches the kids and any new pack members."

"See, this is what I'm talking about," I said, throwing up my hands in frustration.

Xavier looked thoroughly confused now. "What? Kyle teaching you?"

"No, that you thought I knew he teaches new pack members. There's so much I get left out of because I'm not really one of you. It's like I'm constantly catching up with things everyone else already knows about."

To his credit, Xavier didn't try to smooth things over and convince me I was a full pack member or something. We both had to acknowledge that in some ways I still was and always would be an outsider.

"I'll try to fix that," he said. "I can't promise I'll get it all, but I'll try to make sure you're not left out of pack knowledge as much as I can."

"Thank you," I said. "So two things to work on. Not being out of the loop and learning how to defend myself."

"Sounds like a good plan." Xavier was kissing my neck again now, and it was slowly pushing coherent thoughts out of my head. "I can think of one more thing to add to that list." His lips had barely touched mine when my phone buzzed. I frowned and pulled it from my pocket. Kelly had texted me an address. A follow-up text popped up with a four-digit number.

What's this?

The address of a hotel downtown. If you two want some alone time. That's the room I booked. Your call. I didn't tell anyone else so if you don't want it, don't tell him and I'll see you tonight.

The text ended with a winky face.

Another text followed with a link to download the hotel's app. Then another text.

Log in with your email address. Password is Wolfykisskiss7. You don't even have to check in at the desk. Use your phone to unlock the room door with the app.

I'm going to kill you.

No you won't. You're too busy with him.

Lol. I'll think about it. Thank you.

Love ya.

I looked up to see Xavier staring at me quizzically. "That was a lot of texts, but you're not running back toward the car, so I assume everything at the house is good?"

"Yep, everything's fine." I shoved the phone back in my pocket. "Just Kelly."

"What's she up to?" Now he was grinning. He knew what sort of nonsense she might pull as well as I did.

"I haven't decided if I'm going to tell you or not," I said, wrinkling my nose at him. He laughed and kissed my nose, then nuzzled my hair.

"I think you'll tell me," he whispered into my ear, sending shivers up my back.

"Maybe."

"Would food entice you?" I realized it had started getting dark. I had completely lost track of time.

"Probably," I admitted.

Xavier's eyes shone as he stood up and pulled me to my feet. He bent his arm and tucked my hand into his elbow. "It's a date."

"KELLY OUTDID HERSELF," Xavier said with a whistle, pushing open the door to our hotel room on the fifteenth floor. He went in and set down the plastic bag with our leftover desserts from dinner on the dining table. I started to follow him in, but walking in the door, I froze. I felt my chest constrict, and my breath started to come in shallow gasps. I closed my eyes, trying to concentrate on breathing. What a stupid moment for a panic attack. I felt arms come around me and flinched, then opened my eyes.

"Hey, you're ok. You're safe." Xavier stepped back slightly to give me space, then knelt a bit to get in my line of sight, holding my face in both hands. "What's going on?"

His eyes searched my face anxiously, but I shook my head, unable to form coherent words to explain that the last time I'd been in a hotel room, I'd been trapped. I looked past him to the nightstand, where the clock and phone were sitting, to the one king-sized bed, not two—one for me and one for my guards—and took a deep breath, then another. As he watched me scan the room, a look of understanding crossed his face.

"We can go home if this feels too close to when you were taken," he said, getting right to the point. I appreciated that he didn't try to hide or soften the words. I needed to hear them directly. Somehow, hearing him say that out loud helped me remember where I was and grounded me in the present moment instead of the past.

I took another couple of deep breaths then stepped forward and wrapped my arms around him, pressing my face against his chest. His arms came around me again and this time I didn't flinch as he held me tight against him. This time my mind didn't replace the protection of Xavier's arms with the imprisonment of Connor's.

"I'm good," I said.

"You sure?" He didn't sound convinced. I looked up at him and grinned.

"Turns out there's a lot I'm sure about today," I said. At that, he finally smiled back, pulling me into the room and closing the door behind us as he leaned in for a kiss. I focused on the feel of his hands, of his mouth, and tried to ignore that closed door.

"Can we open the curtains all the way?" I asked. Xavier looked confused but stepped away to pull open the see-through layer of curtains that had been blocking the full view of outside. I went to the window and stood there, looking out over the city, at the glimpse through the buildings of Lake Eola and the fountain in the heart of down-town, and reminded myself that I knew exactly where I was. Xavier came up behind me and put his arms around me, resting his chin on my head.

"You don't have to, but if you do need to talk about what happened while you were gone, I'm here," he said. "Not to remember details. I know you did that with Kelly. But just to get it out." I leaned back, savoring the feel of him.

"I know," I said. "Not tonight, though."

"Whenever you need it." He kissed my temple and I spun around in his arms to face him.

"*That's* not what I need tonight," I said. His eyes lit up.

"And what exactly," his fingers traced patterns on the back of my neck that made me shiver. "Do you need tonight?" Instead of answering, I pulled him down toward me and kissed him. His arms came up under me and scooped me up, his mouth trailing kisses everywhere he could reach as he walked the few steps to the bed. He laid me down, then laid next to me, propping himself up on an elbow as his gaze slowly trailed over me from head to toe.

"You know you're beautiful, right?" he said. I blushed but didn't look away this time.

"You're not so bad yourself," I said, smiling up at him. And as he leaned down toward me and pulled me against him, I pushed everything else—kidnappings, my parents, James' still unexplained abilities, my own shortcomings—out of my head and let myself drown in the happiness of being with someone who at last made my world feel whole again.

WHEN WE GOT HOME the next day, James was in morning lessons with the other pack kids, so I snuck upstairs for a fresh change of clothes before he saw me. I was coming down the stairs when he barreled into me, almost knocking me down.

"Did you have fun last night?" he asked. I laughed and hugged him.

"Yep. How about you? What did you and Kelly do?"

"We ate candy and ice cream and I read a whole book to her!" He lifted his chin and beamed at me.

"You read the book yourself? Which book?"

"Hop on Pop! I read the entire thing and she didn't help me at all!"

"Well that sounds like it was a very successful evening!" I

said. I narrowed my eyes at him. "When did you learn to read so well?"

"Yesterday!"

I laughed and hugged him again. "Did you eat lunch yet?" I asked.

"Nope. Xavier said to come tell you it's ready." He hung on my arm as we walked down to the kitchen, chatting about the next books he planned on reading, how many kinds of chocolate Kelly had brought over, and how he'd finally beat Trevor at their current favorite video game. Xavier, Kyle, Devon, and Kelly were sitting at the table eating leftovers.

James grabbed a plate with a sandwich and chips off the counter and ran out back, and I sat down at the empty place on the bench next to Xavier where a plate of food was waiting for me. As soon as I sat down, he pressed his leg to mine under the table, and I smiled. Kelly's grin was so big it was a wonder her head hadn't split in two, Devon gave me a wink but he didn't say anything, and Kyle diligently ignored the whole situation.

"Hey, Kyle?" I said, and he looked up from his lunch warily.

"Yeah?"

"I have a request." He looked back and forth between me and Xavier, but Xavier put his hands up.

"Not my thing. All her," Xavier said. Kyle raised an eyebrow at me.

"I need to learn to defend myself. I want you to teach me," I said. Kyle blinked. Whatever he'd been thinking I was going to ask, this clearly wasn't it.

"That makes sense. Yeah, come out back after lunch. You can't do everything the kids can do, but a lot of it is a good start." He went back to eating and that seemed to be that.

Now it was my turn to be surprised. For some reason, I'd thought he'd be harder to win over. I'd had a whole argument built up that I suddenly found myself not needing.

"Sounds good. Thanks," I said and picked up my fork. We all chatted about the usual topics as we ate: the kids' lessons and their new group obsession with building card towers, speculations about Hannah's new crush on a guy who was working at the movie theater, debates on when and how to open a new gym (Hannah and Jessica had teamed up to push for a community theater as the new public-facing business but Devon reminded them that not only was that a more niche crowd, none of us had experience in stage productions).

When Xavier finished eating, he casually put a hand on my knee as we all continued talking, and the casualness of the gesture felt comfortable and right. Like this was exactly where I was meant to be, sitting here, surrounded by people who loved me. By my family.

19

After lunch, Kelly practically dragged me up to my bedroom and plopped onto my bed like we were about to have a sleepover.

"Ok, dish!" She was practically rubbing her hands together in glee. "How did it go? How was the room? Are you two officially together? What happened?"

"I can't believe you did that," I laughed. "You're ridiculous." She sat up on her knees and I really thought she'd start bouncing.

"So...?"

"I'm not giving you details about what we did in that hotel room." I raised an eyebrow at her and she sat back with a pout.

"Fine. But are you two a couple now, or what?"

"I... I think so," I said. She frowned. "I mean we didn't say it directly, but I'm pretty sure at this point the answer to that is yes," I said.

"I think so too, so let's officially say we are," Xavier said from the doorway behind me. I jumped and Kelly actually squealed.

"And you said she's the busybody," I said, but I couldn't help laughing.

"I have to go past your room to get to mine. It's not my fault you two aren't quiet." He shrugged, but then he came over and kissed me on the cheek. "If you need me to drag Kelly out of here, say the word," he said with a wink before leaving.

"You're welcome!" Kelly called at his back. He chuckled as he continued down the hallway. She turned back to me and raised an eyebrow. "So defense lessons with Kyle?"

"I couldn't do anything at all in St. Louis. I don't want to ever feel that helpless again. Plus I don't want to think that James isn't safe with me, and right now he isn't. If anything happens..." I sighed and shook my head. "I know I won't ever be able to take down an entire group or beat one of you in a fight, but I want to be able to have some chance."

Kelly nodded thoughtfully. "Wait, didn't Kyle say..."

"Hey, I'm supposed to be out back!" I jumped up and ran down the stairs and out the back door. Kyle was sitting at the picnic table watching as Hannah and Jessica corralled the kids into a semi-organized group.

"Just in time," he said, standing up as I burst through the door. He turned his back to the assembled kids and teens and winked at me and gave me a secretive grin, then schooled his features into the sternness of a drill instructor before turning around. Every single kid stood up straight with a stillness bordering on unnatural, watching Kyle with a focus I'd never expect children to have. Even James, who I could hardly ever get to sit still long enough to eat a meal, looked like a statue, the only thing moving his gaze as he watched Kyle stalk toward them, hands behind his back.

Suddenly, Kyle leapt toward the group, shifting in midair, snarling as he flew toward them. The children sprang into action, taking up what looked like practiced stances and positions as he attacked. For thirty minutes, Kyle attacked, choosing a different child as a target every few minutes, and the group would swarm to protect that child, fighting together against Kyle to drive him back.

This wasn't a scared or scattered group of kids. This was a trained unit, and I shivered watching my five-year-old, the smallest of the pack, take what was clearly his assigned place in every maneuver. Sometimes they fought as humans, sometimes as wolves. Some of their tactics, like the one I'd seen James perform to escape from Kyle before, involved shifting mid-move. Sometimes Kyle would get through to his target and give them a quick swipe on the top of the head with a hand or paw. When that happened, everyone would stop and they'd go over what happened and what could have changed, then start again.

At the end of the half hour, everyone was breathing hard but still looked ready to take Kyle on if he came at them again. He shifted fully back to human and it seemed to be a signal because every child who was wolf or part wolf also shifted to fully human again with him. He smiled at the group and they all relaxed as he went around to each individual kid to tell them what they did well and what to practice for next time before dismissing them. The little kids ran to the toys in the back of the yard and Hannah and Jessica headed inside. When everyone had scattered, Kyle turned back to me and grinned at the shocked look on my face.

"Impressive, aren't they?" he asked.

"I had no idea…" I was at a loss for words and he seemed to be enjoying my reaction.

"Think you could take them on?"

"Not a chance."

"Let's work on that, then."

For the next hour, Kyle worked with me on some basic defense, mainly ways to twist away and escape if I were grabbed from different directions. Half of it seemed like stuff I probably should have known when I was living on my own in a college dorm, and I felt ridiculous after watching what the kids could handle. Throughout the lesson, I noticed James was keeping a close watch on us from the back of the yard.

"I want to know how to defend myself against a wolf, too," I said afterwards, when we were sitting in the kitchen, dripping with sweat and chugging down water. Kyle nodded.

"We'll get to that." The look he'd been giving me since we came inside was analytic, assessing what he'd seen and trying to figure out how else to push me. "But first you need to build up some basic strength. You're kind of pathetic."

"Gee, thanks." I rolled my eyes at him.

"You couldn't take on James if he came at you in earnest right now," he pointed out, and after what I'd seen, I had to admit he was probably right.

"So how did you get tapped as the pack battle instructor?" I asked.

"I've been in battle." He took a swig of water and I raised my eyebrows at him. That wasn't the answer I'd expected. "I was a Marine Raider. Being a teenage werewolf in Georgia was... not great. I was mad that I had to hide what I was, even if I knew why it was necessary, and I was stronger than everyone around me and needed an outlet. So I went for the most dangerous thing I could think of as soon as I was old enough to enlist. I didn't want to have to hold myself back anymore. Eventually, something went wrong in a mission, and if I'd have been human I would have been dead or at least permanently injured. I got a medical discharge that technically I didn't need, but I knew if anyone found out I was actually healing there'd be questions I didn't want asked. And now here I am teaching elementary schoolers how to fight for their lives." There seemed to be quite a bit missing there, but I hadn't expected Kyle to tell me this much.

"Do you regret leaving it?" I asked. He didn't answer right away, and I wondered if anyone had ever asked him that before.

"No. I was there for a stupid reason. I don't regret joining or my time there, but I don't regret leaving, either." He didn't offer any other information, and I didn't push. He finished his water and stood up. "I'll have an exercise schedule ready for you tomorrow. If we're going to do this, we're going to do it right." As he left the kitchen, I wondered what exactly I'd gotten myself into.

As the weeks turned to months, I improved in my lessons with Kyle. I'd even managed to fight him off once. Not beat him, but I was able to slip away from him and then run halfway across the yard before he caught me, and he limped for a good five minutes afterward. That seemed like a step in the right direction.

Devon had managed to find a new space to set up another, smaller, gym, and we spent a lot of time picking out equipment and getting things set up. It seemed the fight with insurance was finally over, so now the focus was on getting something open again, both for the income and to have a place to draw in any shifters who wandered into town.

Xavier and I slipped into our new relationship easily, as if it had been inevitable. James moved into Trevor's room at his own insistence the day after his sixth birthday, which had been a blowout celebration that the entire local pack showed up for, bearing more gifts than either James or I had ever seen in our lives and the most impressive multi-layer cake I'd ever seen, showcasing characters from various cartoons Trevor had gotten James hooked on.

Apparently six meant he was a big enough kid that sharing a room with mom wasn't cool. That meant Xavier and I had more privacy, and we started spending our nights cuddling in one of our bedrooms talking and joking together until we passed out in each other's arms. My heart still skipped a beat every morning that I woke up next to him, when he was the first thing I saw when I opened my eyes, but it also started to feel ordinary in the best way.

I was beginning to think maybe our searches were all a lost cause. We hadn't found any new information about the attackers, AWL, or Nate. And if I was honest with myself, I wasn't sure if that was good news or not. Everyone seemed to have gone to ground, but the thought of running into either the shifters who had attacked me and James or AWL again was sometimes enough to send me into a spiral of panic, although none of the pack would let me fall out of control if they were there. I still felt like I should be able to do everything on my own, but I learned to seek out Xavier, Kelly, or one of the others when I could feel myself start to lose it, and I was as proud of my ability to actively lean on them as I was of any of the other progress I had made here.

"You good?" Kelly asked one afternoon as we sat in the office at the house designing and printing flyers for the gym's grand opening that was coming up.

"Yeah," I said, but she gave me a look that suggested she knew otherwise.

"What's on your mind?"

"What are they waiting for?" I asked. "They can't have given up."

"These things come in waves," Kelly said, frowning at her laptop. "It's unfortunately something that you get used to after you've been through it a few times. They won't do anything again until they think we've let our guard down."

"So what do we do?"

Kelly looked up at me. "We live our lives, but we stay vigilant. We move on and we watch and make sure that the next time something happens, we're ready." She waved a hand at the computer screen. "And we do what we can to keep making the world better for those we can reach."

At that, I smiled. "I'm really glad that's part of your mission," I said. Kelly smiled back and reached across the desk to squeeze my hand.

"Our mission," She corrected. I nodded.

"Our mission," I repeated.

Kelly looked me over like she was deciding whether I was starting to have a panic attack but seemed to decide I was safe and went back to frowning at her computer screen. I'd never seen anyone agonize this much over exactly which shade of teal to use on something, but she was dedicated to making the flyers perfect, and she would probably get it there.

I had learned that in addition to being the pack's political expert, she was a fantastic graphic designer, and she was putting all her efforts into the advertisements for the gym. As we came up to the end of fall, she'd been pushing hard for the gym to open up soon to catch all the people who would make New Year's resolutions, and it looked like it might actually happen.

"How's the social media stuff coming?" she asked.

"Good," I said. "I've got accounts set up on a few

different platforms. Working on linking them together now."

"I've almost got the logos for those ready. Give me a minute and I'll send you the images to..." Kelly stopped and sat up straight, her eyes unfocusing for a second, and I recognized the sign of Devon contacting her.

"What is it?" I asked.

Kyle stuck his head in the office to answer my question as he walked past. "There's been another attack. Pack meeting tonight," he said. Kelly nodded, then grabbed her phone and started typing. A second later my phone dinged with a group text message for everyone to meet at the house, then Kelly pulled up a website to order pizza. Hannah cooked most nights, but she wasn't prepared for this number of people on short notice.

"That was quicker than I expected. Looks like you're a prophet," she said, raising an eyebrow at me.

"Anxiety is a sucky superpower," I grumbled and went to talk to Hannah and Jessica about readying a movie night for the pack kids and to set up more chairs in the den. By early evening, the house was full of shifters, kids playing out back, and pizza disappearing quickly as everyone ate then settled into the den.

Devon stayed in wolf form as people arrived, and everyone shifted to link with him for a quick update before grabbing dinner then finding their place. After helping the girls shoo the kids up to Trevor and James's bedroom for a movie night complete with popcorn, sodas, and chocolates, I settled onto the couch next to Xavier, in the spot that seemed to have become mine during these meetings. He put an arm around me and filled me in as we waited for the meeting to start.

"There were some tornadoes in Mississippi last night,"

Xavier said. "During the storm, a pack there was attacked. Direct attack on the shifters this time, not indirect like what happened to us. Some of the pack members who escaped were able to send memories so we could identify faces." I swallowed.

"When you say some of the pack who escaped..." I whispered, scared of the answer.

"There weren't many of them there at the time. They ran a mechanic shop, and some of them had gone to pull things inside for the storms overnight. They were ambushed there. They lost five people. Two escaped. The attackers destroyed the building in the process to make it look like the victims were killed when the roof collapsed."

"Do we know who did it?" I asked. The look on Xavier's face chilled me to my core.

"We didn't recognize everyone. But our three friends from St. Louis were there," Xavier said. The world spun and I was glad I was already sitting down, because otherwise I'd have collapsed. He squeezed me with the arm that was already around me and held my hand with the other as I tried to focus on my breathing and on the feel of him to ground me. Devon, still a wolf for now, glanced over at me and I nodded to him that I was ok, leaning into Xavier. Devon nodded back and turned back to the other wolves around him.

"Kelly said there isn't usually another attack this quickly," I said.

"There's usually not. At least not on this scale. It might be that they saw an opportunity with the storms coming through, but this feels like it's connected to something bigger now. Especially with those three assholes involved." He growled the last few words and squeezed my hand, and I wondered what he'd gone through between the time I'd been taken and when they'd found me. Right now he looked like he'd gladly rip them limb from limb. I just felt terrified. Hopefully it would change into anger soon because that seemed like it would be much easier to deal with.

Devon shifted, pulling on some pants and a shirt. Since Melissa's visit none of them had hidden to shift in front of me anymore, and it had finally lost its awkwardness once I realized that I wasn't going to be faced with a room full of naked people. Devon's phone dinged and as he read the message, his eyebrows raised almost to his hairline.

"We're going to wait another few minutes to get started," Devon said, looking around the room. "I've gotten notice that we'll have a surprise visitor. Melissa will be here soon." His gaze settled on Kyle. "I expect everyone to extend her the courtesy due an ally and friend." Kyle glared back at him and sniffed, leaning back on the wall where he'd been talking to some other pack members, but he nodded. Next to Devon, Kelly rolled her eyes. I had to find out what happened between them sometime.

As we waited, everyone chatted, speculating and going over details together. Xavier kept hold of me and talked about things that suddenly seemed unimportant, like the gym equipment that was on backorder and the science museum we'd taken James and Trevor to recently. I knew he was trying to distract me, and I went along with it, knowing that I needed to be settled enough to focus when Melissa got here.

Finally, everyone went quiet and a few seconds after everyone else seemed to have heard it, I heard the vehicle pulling up in front of the house, then multiple car doors slam shut. It wasn't only Melissa here, and I tensed. "Who all came?" I asked. Xavier shook his head, frowning. Kelly was at the door opening it as they came up the porch, and Melissa, Yasmin, two men, and a woman strode in the door.

Melissa looked furious, Yasmin and the two men looked grim, and the woman looked terrified. I recognized her as the woman who had suggested I shouldn't be there at Melissa's when they were all going to shift to trade information, and I felt my stomach drop. Whatever was going on, it didn't look good.

Melissa positioned herself next to Devon at the front of the room, Yasmin went to stand near Kelly, and the other three went to stand by a wall near the hallway, the two men looking almost like guards, with the woman between them looking like she was going to try to bolt at any second.

Melissa whispered to Devon briefly and he aimed a look that could have melted steel toward the woman, who shrank under his furious gaze. She looked around the room as if to find someone who might sympathize with her, but when her eyes landed on me, they widened in what looked like fear. I wondered what I could possibly have done to have inspired that reaction from her.

"You've all been caught up on the news from Mississippi," Devon started. "And we now have some additional information that may or may not be connected, but that is extremely..." he glared at the new woman. "Concerning." The woman started trembling. "When Paige was kidnapped in St. Louis, we didn't know how AWL found her. Some of you know we suspected that her phone was being tracked. However, Melissa has discovered the real reason that AWL knew exactly where to be. I'll let her explain." He stepped to the side and motioned toward Melissa, who stepped forward.

"First, I must apologize to all of you. It's unforgivable that I allowed this to occur within my pack and I beg your forgiveness, especially you, Paige." She nodded toward me and I nodded back, my heart hammering in my chest so loud I was certain she could hear it. "When we heard about Mississippi, we got the same information as you, including the faces of the attackers. When those faces went through my pack, one person recognized one of the men involved and her shock was so strong she wasn't able to hide it from me." She glared at the woman.

"Amber here knew one of the men. She'd met him before and had been told he was looking for a human woman who had somehow become part of a shifter pack." I couldn't breathe. Xavier was holding me tight and it felt like he was both trying to keep me grounded and keep himself from launching across the room. Melissa spoke loud enough for the room to hear but was focused on me as she continued.

"When you showed up in St. Louis, Amber notified them that you were there. She suggested that you leave during our meeting, a time she knew that you would be relatively unprotected because we'd be distracted, and then she notified them when you left the apartments. Nothing about the attack was a coincidence. It was premeditated, planned, and assisted by a member of my pack, and I throw myself on the mercy of your pack."

Everyone in the room was sitting up straight and focused on either Melissa or Amber and there was a palpable threat of violence in the room. I could feel Xavier growling next to me and held onto his arm to keep him focused on me and not on tearing out Amber's throat. Melissa kept her eyes locked on mine, but I had no idea what was expected of me. I looked to Devon and he noticed my panic and put a hand on Melissa's shoulder.

"Normally this would be taken care of in a pack link.

However, Paige can't join us in that." Devon said. He looked to me. "Paige, if we shift to link and then come out to discuss it with you before making a final decision, is that ok?" I nodded, relieved to have someone else take over.

Melissa nodded. "Agreed." At that, the entire pack began to shift and soon I was surrounded by an entire room of wolves. Xavier shifted last, kissing my temple first and squeezing my hand. Amber and her guards stayed human and I wondered if that was standard procedure or if they were worried about what she'd do if allowed to shift while I were still human.

I shivered and Xavier, sitting by my feet, put his head in my lap. I absentmindedly put my hands on his head, tangling my fingers in his fur as I waited for the pack to finish their discussion. We all sat there for a while, the wolves occasionally growling or baring their teeth at Amber. After some time, Xavier and Devon shifted back to human form.

"Melissa pulled Amber's memories earlier. Amber was able to keep the entire thing secret from her pack until last night, when she gave herself away by recognizing Connor. No one else in her pack was involved. We believe Melissa, but the responsibility for her pack's behavior falls on her as the alpha. If this breaks your trust with her and her pack, then we'll move on that and make a decision accordingly."

I looked at Melissa, who had laid down on her front paws and was looking up at me in what looked to be supplication.

"I trust Melissa," I said. I looked to Xavier. "I trust her, but how do we trust her entire pack?"

"You know alphas are the central link for the pack," Xavier said. I nodded. "They can also exert a certain amount of control on their pack members. Most alphas use that to some extent. Some are extremely controlling, some less so. Melissa only uses it when she deems it necessary but doesn't have a problem doing it when she needs to." He glared at Amber again. "This is a time it's definitely necessary."

"Melissa, can I hear from you?" I asked. Melissa immediately shifted back, pulling her dress on as she became human. She knelt in front of me so we were at eye level with each other and took my hands.

"I swear to you this will never happen again," she said. "No one from my pack will ever be able to do anything to harm you again. That I can promise you."

"I believe you," I said. "So what do we do now?"

Devon put a hand on Melissa's shoulder and she rose to her feet. "If we decide to put our trust in her, then it'll be her responsibility to deal with her pack member," he said.

"I agree to that," I said. Melissa nodded at me and turned toward Amber, her expression turning icy.

"Your memories will be stripped. You will not remember any information about our pack or Devon's pack that could harm us in any way. We will be erased from your mind." Amber looked like she might faint, an expression on her face as if she were looking at her own death coming for her.

"Second," Melissa drew herself up taller and her presence seemed to fill the room. Cold fury emanated from her, and every wolf in the room bristled and growled, their fur standing on end as they all focused their attention on Amber. "You will be untethered, your link cut. You will be packless and marked as a pack traitor. You will be a lone wolf for the rest of your life." Amber fell to her knees. Melissa stared her down. "Every shifter will know that not only did you betray your pack, you betrayed us to AWL. You will never, ever harm a member of our packs or any pack ever again."

"Please, no." her voice was barely audible and tears poured down her face, but not a single person or wolf in the room looked at her with any pity whatsoever. If possible, Melissa, Devon, and Xavier looked more furious.

"Shift," Melissa said, her voice taking on a tone of such authority that even the guards, who she wasn't speaking to, trembled. I wondered if that was from her tone or from some power she had over them as their alpha. Amber whimpered as she shifted, falling to the ground and twisting onto her back to expose her throat and belly once she was in wolf form.

Melissa shifted, and Devon, Xavier, and the guards followed suit so that I was the only human left in the room. Every eye was on Amber as she cried out, howled, and writhed on the ground. I shuddered, wondering what was happening through the link, wanting to look away but feeling that I shouldn't. After a few moments, Amber quieted and went still, her breathing the only sign that she was still alive. I hardly dared to breathe myself.

Xavier shifted back first and pulled me into his arms. I realized I was shaking. Slowly, the others shifted back to human form one by one. The last to shift back were Melissa and Devon. Before becoming human again, Melissa stared at Amber who shifted to human without otherwise moving. One of her guards lifted her unmoving form in his arms, and Kyle gestured for them to follow him to his room down the hallway past the office. The guards stayed with Amber as Kyle returned to the den.

"Now," Devon said, "we need to decide what to do about the Mississippi attack." As everyone was settling in again, my phone dinged. I pulled it out, frowning, and I took a strangled breath as I saw the notification from the online voicemail service Kyle had set up from my old phone number. I clicked on the notification and Xavier reached over to press the speaker button. A voice I recognized filled the room as everyone went silent to listen. A voice from behind a grocery store, from the night that changed everything.

"Hello, Paige. Julian's waiting for you. See you in Mississippi."

20

The room was so quiet I wondered if any of us, human or wolf, were breathing. I looked at Kelly and saw that her eyes were wide with recognition, too, and I wondered how many of the others had made the connection, if the memories she had shared in the link had gotten that across. I looked around and realized yes, they had. While I was sitting there in shock, the rest of them looked ready to attack something. I took up that mood also, and I was grateful to be feeling something other than fear finally.

The fear was still there under the surface, especially when I thought of what these people might want to do to James. But the main emotion overwhelming me now was pure, bloodthirsty anger. I had tried to build a family and we had been torn apart. Then I finally found another family, and someone was trying to destroy us here, too. People who I had never done anything to had taken Nate, tried to take James, hurt Kelly, attacked Xavier, and kidnapped me. I was done wanting to hide.

"We're going to Mississippi," I said. I was amazed at how

steady, how cold and determined my own voice was. It wasn't a question. I was ready to take them down. All of them. And now they were inviting me to do just that.

"Yes, we are," Devon said. He was still looking at the phone in my hand. He slowly looked up to meet my eyes. "But we're going to make a plan first. They're expecting us to come, and they'll be ready for us."

I frowned but nodded. I was ready to jump in the car and lead a mob straight to wherever we were being drawn, but I knew that wouldn't get us anywhere except maybe killed. As painful as it was to admit, I knew that my own methods hadn't worked in the past and there were people here much more experienced with this sort of thing than I was. I glanced at Kyle and the look on his face as he locked eyes with me suggested he was already strategizing. Xavier squeezed my hand twice to get my attention, and when I looked at him, I noticed he was looking toward the stairs. When I looked myself, my heart dropped.

"Sweetie, you're supposed to be upstairs," I said, crossing the room to James where he stood near the bottom of the staircase.

"I want to go get Daddy." I hadn't seen him this angry since the night we'd been attacked, and I frowned at him.

"You don't get to tell anyone to do that, got it?"

"Mooooom. I'm not doing *that*." Then he rolled his eyes at me. Apparently turning six had given him a stronger attitude. Rooming with Trevor probably didn't help this particular issue, either. I heard a snicker behind me but didn't turn to see who it was, keeping my focus on James.

"We're going to get him. But *you're* not going to get him," I said. "You're six and you're staying here."

"But I can..." he stopped suddenly, then looked toward Devon and narrowed his eyes but stopped talking, and I sent up a silent thanks for that intervention. In front of the entire gathered local members of our pack plus a few from Melissa's in the house, this wasn't the time to discuss what only some of us knew he could do.

"We can talk about it later," I said. "But right now, go back upstairs. Does Jessica know you're down here?" At that, he had the decency to look sheepish.

"She thinks I went to the bathroom," he muttered, looking at his feet. I felt someone walk up behind me and then Kyle knelt down to get at James's eye level. James looked up at him, his eyes starting to fill with angry tears.

"We're getting him back," Kyle said. "We won't let them win. We're a pack and we take care of each other. All of us, even if someone hasn't been around a while. But we all have to do our own parts to make that happen, and right now your part is to wait for the pack leaders to make decisions. And I know that sucks. I've had to wait lots of times for orders. But that's your job right now."

Tears had started to fall now, but James dashed them away with a furious swipe of his hand and lifted his chin to look Kyle in the face with determination.

"When you make your decisions, I'll be ready," James said. Kyle ruffled his hair and smiled at him.

"I know you will. Now get your butt back upstairs, pup. And keep your mouth shut up there."

James looked at me and I wanted to hug him, but I knew that that wasn't what he needed right now. This wasn't my baby boy standing here, ready to fight. This was a tiny warrior starting to realize what he might be capable of, and I knew I needed to let him have this moment to stand on his own. Even as guilt twisted my gut at the thought that I should have protected him more, that at six years old he shouldn't be considering himself as an asset in a battle, my heart swelled with pride watching him stand there and hold his ground against an entire room of adults.

"We'll let you know when we're ready," I said, smiling at him. He nodded once, with a seriousness that belonged to a soldier rather than a kindergartener, and turned back up the stairs. We were all silent until we heard the door to his room click shut. "Thank you," I said to Kyle.

"He's a good kid. One day he'll have his place defending the pack. But not yet."

We returned to our places in the den, but I kept glancing over at the stairs to be sure James didn't get it in his head to sneak back down again.

"So what are we going to do?" Kelly asked.

"They're clearly expecting us to come investigate the attack," Devon said.

"This doesn't make sense, though," I said quietly.

Devon stopped and looked toward me. "Explain."

"We know AWL was behind the attack. But this," I held up the phone, "was shifters."

"Would they work with shifters if they had a common goal?" Devon asked. Everyone was staring at me, and I came to the uncomfortable realization that as the only person who had actually interacted with both groups, I might be the resident expert. I shook my head.

"Connor might. He wouldn't like it, but I bet he'd do it if he thought he needed to. But Dan absolutely wouldn't, no matter what. And from the feeling I got from the few other people I saw there, I'm willing to bet that there's more like Dan than like Connor." More like my parents. I felt sick to my stomach, but I squashed it down, telling myself that after everyone went home I could panic to my overactive heart's content. I felt Xavier put his hand on my back, lending support without making too big of a visual statement that would suggest I needed to be coddled. I took a deep breath.

"Since Dan was there, I don't think the AWL attack is directly linked to these shifters calling me now. If Nate's in Mississippi in the same area, I think it's one of three things. It's a coincidence, which doesn't seem likely. Or they've moved Nate there after hearing about the attack themselves to lure us, hoping we'll slip up somehow. Or he isn't there at all. They're lying to get us to come to them." I had a sinking feeling that last one was probably the case.

"We need to send out scouts," Kyle said.

"We have people we can send ahead," Devon said, nodding in agreement.

"Who do we know in Mississippi?" Kyle asked.

"We can always reach out to the pack who was attacked. Offer our support in tracking down responsible parties," Greg said.

"Except that's not who we're tracking down, and we know it. And if we follow through on our own plans, they'll know it, too," Kelly said, shaking her head. "That's Tyler's pack. We're cordial but not friends, and we don't want to make a full-on enemy out of this if they think we're double crossing them or taking advantage. Even if it gets Nate back now, politics is a long game and we'll still have to deal with our actual enemies later. We'll need allies for that. We can't alienate anyone. If we do contact Tyler, we need to be direct about who we're hunting and why." Melissa nodded her agreement with Kelly, looking at her with what seemed like pride.

My phone dinged again. Everyone went silent and looked to me as I stared down at the new notification. Another voicemail from the same number. I looked at Xavier wide-eyed, the panic starting to creep in. He put a hand on my leg and squeezed as I tapped the notification and then the speaker button.

"We tried to text you, but you aren't receiving texts. Shame. We took some lovely pictures." It was the same shifter who had called the first time. I felt sick. The voice mail continued. "In lieu of pictures, you can listen." He stopped talking and we heard a series of beeps and other familiar sounds.

I frowned, then sucked in a breath when I realized what it sounded like. Medical equipment. "We've kept him alive all this time, hoping he'd cooperate. He hasn't, so we're hoping now that you will. We're unhooking him... now."

Another pause and the sounds of someone moving around and pressing buttons in the background. "I don't know how long someone can survive without any nutrients or fluids, but I'd say you're on a clock now. Don't let us down, Paige. We're waiting for you, but we're losing patience." The voicemail ended and I found that I was shaking. *We're waiting for you.* And they had been since they broke into my apartment all those months ago. At least now I was fairly confident it wasn't AWL that had planted that note, although I wasn't sure this was better.

I looked at Devon, trying to keep my voice steady but failing. "We may not have time to scout first."

"Devon, you want me to bring in some of my teams?" Melissa asked. Devon nodded.

"That's a good idea. We can use all the backup we can get for this," he said. Melissa pulled out her phone and started tapping out messages.

"Tyler has a cousin in our pack. I'll talk to him and make sure he's ok with us nosing around his territory. As long as we stay out of their way as they recover, I think he'll be fine."

"Should we... I mean, is there anything we can do for them since they lost people?" I asked.

"Tyler's far more traditional than I am with how he runs his pack," Melissa said, shaking her head. "He'll interpret an offer of help as an insinuation that he's weak."

"He's got a macho complex," Kelly added, rolling her eyes.

"Yes, that," Melissa said, looking down at her phone as texts started coming back in. "If he asks, we'll step in to help. Until then, we'll make sure not to step on his toes." She shot off another text and got an answer back nearly immediately and looked up at Devon. "Tyler's fine with us coming. He said we can even look at the mechanic shop if we want to if we need somewhere to start. I've got two teams who will be on their way south within the hour."

Devon nodded. "Good. Kyle, Xavier, set up teams. Xavier, you're search and rescue. Kyle, combat. We don't know what we're up against, so be prepared for a serious fight. Kelly, Paige, find us a home base." He looked around and seemed to make eye contact with everyone crowded into the room. "We leave in an hour." At that, the room exploded into action.

"You are not going," Devon said again. I crossed my arms, looking across the yard at the vehicles that were getting loaded with supplies and shifters.

"I can help!"

"You can't shift."

"I can do other things..."

"Look, I know you've been training with Kyle, but you aren't ready for a full-scale battle yet, and that's probably what we're going into. Paige, I know your heart is in the right place, but you'll be a liability in the field that we can't afford right now."

I bit back a retort. I knew he was right, although everything in me was screaming to jump into one of those cars. Kyle saw the look I was sending across the yard and came trotting over to me.

"When we got you back from AWL, I told you to hang onto that anger, right?" Kyle asked, coming up to us. I nodded and he put a hand on my shoulder. "Keep it going. You have a part to play in this, too, even if it's not in the field yet. Stay angry. Keep the fire burning. This isn't over, and we need every person."

"I know," I said. And I did want to keep the anger going, if for no other reason than that for now it was pushing out the pure terror that kept threatening to close in on me. Kyle squeezed my shoulder and gave me a dazzling grin suddenly.

"And don't worry about us. You can't get rid of me that easily," he said before turning and heading back toward the vehicles to bark orders.

Devon sighed. "Look, I'm sorry. I really, really am. I know the stakes for you and James. But you have to trust us." Something in those words finally broke through the wall of determination that I had constructed since the meeting.

"I do," I said with a sigh. Devon nodded, sensing that I'd acknowledged defeat.

"Good," he said. "Now please go help Kelly get us set up, ok? We do need you, but we need you here."

I sighed again but headed back inside, then stopped short when I came back in the house. Xavier was sitting on the bottom few steps with James, who looked like he was as ready to explode as I was. He turned furious eyes to me.

"Xavier won't let me go rescue Daddy," he said, and I

suddenly found myself in Devon's position from seconds before. I went to sit on the other side of him.

"You and I need to stay here to support the pack from headquarters," I said. Xavier reached over to take my hand and I squeezed, all too aware of what all I could be losing today. I felt a lump in my throat. *Keep the anger. Drive out the fear.* "We aren't going to let the bad guys get away with this. We're sending the best shifters in the world to take them down, ok?"

"But none of them can do what I can do," James said.

"Compel Xavier to go get you a Twizzler from the kitchen," I said. James moved his attention to Xavier, who schooled his expression into blankness. James focused, frowning, his face turning red, first from effort and then from anger when nothing happened. Finally, James slouched back against the step, almost in tears again. Xavier put an arm around him.

"You'll learn to control it, and then we'll talk about you joining missions, ok?" he said. James nodded but didn't reply.

"Head back upstairs and make sure the other kids are doing all right," I said. "That's your job tonight. Help them. They need you."

"I guess that's important, too," James said, then turned and trudged up the stairs. As soon as he was up. I moved over and threw my arms around Xavier who hugged me back tightly.

"You better come back," I said, pressing my face against his chest.

"We'll have a whole pack coming back to you," he said, putting his cheek down on my head. I squeezed tighter.

"You bring them all back. Even Kyle," I said. He chuckled and lifted my chin for a kiss.

"Even Kyle," he promised. I didn't dare mention the actual reason they were going. We didn't know what they would find, and we had no idea what we'd do afterwards if the phone call had been honest about Nate's condition. And, as selfish as I felt thinking about it in the circumstances, I didn't know what came next for me and Xavier once Nate was back, or what was next for me and the man who I had once thought I knew everything about. I pushed those thoughts out of my mind and focused on my last moments in Xavier's arms before he climbed into one of the vehicles outside and rode away from me.

KELLY, Yasmin, Melissa, and I sat on the couch in the den that evening eating leftovers while Trevor and James sprawled on the floor with popcorn and sodas watching the latest superhero movie. Hannah and Jessica had gone out to meet with some friends, promising to be back before midnight. We'd rented a few houses for everyone for a week near Natchez, Mississippi, and Melissa's teams were meeting them tomorrow after everyone had a chance to rest after the drive.

I wasn't eager to send them all into a fight, but I hated the waiting, too. Melissa had sent Amber and her guards back to St. Louis in their car and booked a flight for the next morning to join Devon in Mississippi. If her teams were going to fight, she said she'd be there leading the charge, but she didn't feel the need to ride eleven hours to get there.

"They'll be driving all night," Yasmin said as I looked at my phone again. Xavier had turned location tracking on for me and I'd been obsessively watching my phone as they made the drive north and west.

"I know. But this is the only thing I can do right now," I said. Yasmin smiled at me sympathetically.

"It gets easier. I'm never happy when she has to go handle things like this obviously, but it does get easier." She smiled at Melissa and reached over to squeeze her leg affectionately.

"You trust them, right?" Melissa asked. I took a deep breath and nodded. "Then trust them to come back. Otherwise you'll drive yourself crazy."

"Do you have to deal with stuff like this a lot?" I asked. "You both seem way too calm about this whole thing."

Yasmin shrugged. "There's a lot I have to stay calm about when it comes to Melissa," she said with a smile. Melissa snorted and rolled her eyes. "But she can handle herself, and the teams she has picked out would follow her to the ends of the earth and then right over the edge if she asked them to."

"And if I needed them to do that, I'd haul them back up over the edge myself afterwards, and they know that," Melissa added. "Devon and Xavier are the same way. They'll come back and bring the others with them."

"I can't decide if I wish they weren't going so far away or if I'm glad the danger isn't close by," I said.

"This doesn't mean there's no danger closer. You need to stay careful," Yasmin pointed out. "We thought you were safe in St. Louis, too. I'm not trying to scare you, just point out that we need to be alert since you're a target."

I frowned, something not quite connecting suddenly. "Wait... why are they waiting for me in Mississippi?" I asked.

"We were assuming because they knew our attention would be there because of the murders," Yasmin pointed out.

"Yes, I know, and I know they said they'd be waiting

there..." I sucked in a breath, a new realization hitting me. "Shit."

"What?" Now Melissa was sitting up and staring at me. "I can't link with you, girl. I need words."

"Why would they go to Mississippi and tell us to meet them there when they know I was living here? Even if they don't know where exactly I am now, they knew I had an apartment in Orlando a few months ago. Why would they try to lure me somewhere else? Why assume I'm not here anymore?"

"You think they lied?"

"I think most of the pack's best fighters aren't here now," I said, my voice coming out as a whisper. Trevor and James had stopped watching the movie and were looking at me.

"Paige?" Trevor asked, his voice trembling.

"What's up?" I asked.

"I want Jessica to come home now."

"Good idea. I'll tell her, ok? You watch your movie. She'll be home soon."

I pulled out my phone and texted Jessica and Hannah.

Hey, sorry about this. Go ahead and come home now, please. We need to talk.

After sending the text, I called Xavier.

"How are you all holding up?" he asked when he answered.

"I don't know. I think we've made a mistake," I said.

"Hold on, I'm patching in Devon and putting you on speaker," Xavier said. The phone went quiet as he put me on hold to add Devon to the call, then I could suddenly hear multiple voices clearly speaking and Xavier yelling, "Hey, quiet! Ok, Paige. We're all here. What's up?"

"We missed something. These shifters knew I was living

here before. They were in my apartment. Why would they try to get me to go to Mississippi?" There was a brief silence on the other end of the line.

"It may not be you they were trying to get out of town," Devon said. "We left you unprotected in a town they know you have a history in."

Xavier started swearing.

"I'm sending over more pack members to the house. Is everyone home?" Devon asked

"Jessica and Hannah went out with some friends. I just told them to come home now," I said.

"Have you heard back?"

"Not yet... hold on, getting a text." I tapped on the notification to read the message from Jessica.

Paige?

Yes?

At the next text, my heart dropped. I looked at Melissa and nodded toward the boys on the floor then got up. Melissa signaled for Yasmin to keep an eye on them and she and Kelly followed me to the office.

"Devon, the girls are in trouble," I said, switching to speaker so Melissa and Kelly could hear once the door was closed behind us. In the living room, I noticed that the television's volume had been turned up.

"We're turning around now," Devon said. "But we're almost three hours out. Paige, what did the text say?"

"It says 'these young ladies seem like sweet girls. Come collect them soon while you still can.'" I could barely say the words and the other end of the phone burst into multiple voices yelling and cursing. Kelly's eyes were huge and

Melissa looked like she was going to start spitting fire. I sat down hard on the chair by the desk.

"Kelly, you there?" Devon asked.

"Yep," Kelly said.

"Text the local pack and tell them to shift. I'm shifting now to link and give them instructions."

"While you're driving?" Kelly exclaimed.

"It's fine. He doesn't need thumbs to drive," Kyle said, at the same time that Devon said "Obviously I'm not driving if I'm shifting. Get the word out. Don't include Jessica or Hannah in any texts right now. They're compromised."

"On it," Kelly said, her phone already out and her fingers flying across the screen. I felt sick.

"This is my fault. I shouldn't have let them go out. I should have..."

"Paige, quit it," Xavier said sternly. "Melissa, you there?"

"I'm here," Melissa said.

"I'm not there to talk sense into her. You got this for me tonight?"

Melissa looked at me and grinned. "I got you," she said to Xavier, putting a hand on my shoulder and squeezing.

"Do we know where they are?" Kyle asked.

"Yes! Jessica shared her location with me a while back and never turned it off," I said. I opened the location tracking app.

"Got them," I said. "Or at least got her phone. Hopefully they didn't ditch it after they texted." I sent the location to Xavier, Devon, Kyle, and Kelly's phones, but when I looked at the location closer, my heart skipped a beat. My old apartment. My phone dinged.

"What was that?" Kyle asked. I opened the new text and almost cried out. The shifter who had led the charge that night had taken a selfie with Jessica and Hannah in the background, the girls wearing expressions that were a mixture of terrified and pissed off. Two huge wolves sat on either side of them on the floor in my old living room. Hannah looked ok, but Jessica had a bruise spreading across half of her face. I read the text out loud with a shaking voice.

> Glad I have your new number so I can send pictures now. I'm sure you recognize this room. You have ten minutes to convince me you're on the way. You personally, Paige. Alone. No more games.

The string of curses Kyle and Xavier let out were some of the most creative I'd ever heard.

21

The world spun. Ten minutes. Most of the pack was hours away and I had ten minutes to figure out how to save Hannah and Jessica. I groaned and put my head in my hands.

"I have to go," I said. "They're targeting me. If I don't go..." I trailed off, not wanting to think about what they might be willing to do to the girls if I didn't cooperate. The other end of the phone was silent and I knew they'd come to the same conclusion.

Kyle's voice started giving me instructions. "Paige, there's a burner phone in the desk. Top right drawer, near the back. Don't take your own phone with you. If they get ahold of it, we don't want them getting any more information than they have now. Get location sharing set up on the burner."

With shaking hands, I opened the drawer and found the phone. I turned it on and sent location sharing to Devon, Xavier, Kyle, Kelly, and Melissa's numbers. "When you go, keep this phone on so we can hear. We'll stay muted. Keep the phone in your pocket and don't bring attention to it," Kyle continued.

"Got it," I mumbled.

"I don't like this," Xavier said.

"She's just bait. We aren't sending her alone," Kyle said.

"I know, but I still don't like it," Xavier responded.

"Melissa, Kelly, tail her. Not too close. We'll send some others also. Devon's giving out orders right now. And we're setting up a guard at the house in case this is a way to lure us into leaving James unguarded," Kyle continued. I felt sick. My phone dinged and I looked down and read the text out loud.

Six minutes. You coming?

"Tell him you're leaving now," Kyle said. I did.

"Then I have to actually do it, don't I?" I asked quietly.

"Yes," Kyle said. "But Paige? We've got you. We've got James. Things might get bad for a bit, but we're going to fix them. Ok?"

"Ok." My voice was barely a whisper.

"Paige?" Xavier asked.

"Yeah?"

"In three hours, I'm going to be there and if you aren't home, I will burn down the city to get you back, you hear me?" He paused. "I love you."

"I love you, too." It was the first time I'd said those words out loud, and I wondered if it was the last.

"Now go get our girls," Kyle said.

I DROVE to my old apartment, shaking the whole time. I'd sent a screenshot of the arrival time on the GPS to Jessica's phone number, careful to crop out any information that might suggest where I was coming from. I furiously wiped tears from my eyes. I didn't want them to see me cry.

I'd barely had a minute to say goodbye to James, and Yasmin holding him back as he sobbed when I walked out the door broke me. I didn't calm myself down completely, though. I needed to seem non-threatening, and while I didn't want them to know how broken I was inside right now, I also needed to appear as if I believed I'd lost. There was no way I could fight them, and I knew it. Kyle told me to stall until Melissa, Kelly, and the other shifters from our pack could get to me, but until I got there, we didn't know what we were walking into.

I pulled over before I got to the complex and called Xavier. He connected to Devon's and Kelly's phones also, and they put me on mute. I turned off the screen, then drove into the complex parking lot. My hands were shaking as I pulled the key from the ignition and set it in the cupholder before getting out. The stairs up to my apartment had at one point been welcoming, but now they were foreboding. I went up and stood outside my old door, taking a deep breath, then knocked.

"Come in," the man who had been texting me called out cheerfully.

"There's four of them! Don't..." Jessica's voice called out, and then a pained cry cut off the words. If I could have shifted I would have leapt through those doors and ripped out the throat of whoever had touched her, but instead I was reduced to hoping the others had heard that and were there to back me up soon. I pushed open the door.

As I came into the room, I saw the two wolves on either side of the girls and the leader standing in the middle of the room. I wondered briefly where the fourth was when the door slammed shut behind me and another man positioned himself between me and the door. Found him.

"I'm so proud of you. You did the right thing." The man's smile was pure canine delight, his teeth a touch sharper and more animalistic than they should be.

"You wanted me and you have me now. Let the girls go," I said.

"Fine with me," he said, shrugging. He nodded at the wolves and they stepped away from Jessica and Hannah. Jessica faced me, blood from a busted lip dripping down her chin. Anger roiled in me at the sight of her injuries.

"We aren't leaving you," she said.

"Yes, you are," I said, putting every ounce of parental authority I had into that command.

"Why would he let us go?" Jessica said.

"I don't have any bones to pick with you or your pack," the man said. "Paige here, though. Oh, she hasn't done anything herself, but she has such a rich family history. She's going to be very, very useful to us, whether she wants to be or not." He grinned at me.

"Jessica. Go," I said. She looked like she was going to argue more, but I glared at her. "Get her out of here." She glanced over at Hannah, who was white with terror, and finally nodded. She turned a glare on the man in the center of the room.

"Give me my phone back," she snapped.

"Teenagers," he sighed, handing her the phone.

"Now go," I said. The man behind me grabbed my arms and pulled me away from the door as the girls filed past me. They each looked over at me as they passed, Hannah looking scared but livid, Jessica looking like she would fight them all if she could. I nodded to them and the wolves growled as they walked out and the door closed. I heaved a sigh of relief. I hadn't expected that part to be this quick and easy. I wondered how far behind me Kelly, Melissa, and the others were.

"I'm not evil, you know," the man (Number One, I named him) said, looking at me with disdain.

"You kidnapped children," I snapped. "You let your goons hit a teenage girl." One of the wolves growled and snapped at me and I bared my teeth back at him.

"My, my, you have gone feral," Number One said with a grin.

"Whatever it is you want me to do, I'm not doing it," I said, glaring at him.

"I don't actually need you to *do* anything," he said, his voice ice cold now. "I need you to be collateral. I have multiple people who care about your welfare not cooperating with me." I shivered and Goon chuckled at my reaction.

"Who?" I asked. Keep him talking.

"Your despicable parents for starters," he said. I laughed.

"They don't care what happens to me," I said. "They abandoned me years ago. You're barking up the wrong tree."

"You're wrong, Paige. If they didn't care, they wouldn't have tried to get you back in St. Louis." My blood ran cold. How did he know about that? "And," he continued, smiling at whatever reaction he noticed in my expression, "There's our dear friend, Julian. Or have you figured out his real name yet?" He held up one of the pictures I'd passed out with my contact information years ago.

I didn't try to hide my reaction as I felt the blood rush from my face and my legs wobble. "Where is he?" I whispered. "What have you done?"

"He's nearby," Number One said dismissively. "He's been asleep a very long time. So long, in fact, and with no medical reason for it that we can figure, that we've decided he's probably doing it on purpose. That's where you come in. If you're threatened or hurt, we hope he'll snap out of it and come to understand that he needs to play by our rules. We're going to see him now, and you won't give us any trouble." Suddenly, Goon twisted my arm up behind my back so hard I cried out as pain stabbed through my shoulder. Number One smiled. "Understand?"

"Yes," I gasped, my eyes watering. I wondered if he'd wrenched my shoulder out of the socket because it felt like it was on fire.

"Time to go see Julian," Number One said, and the two wolves took up guard positions around me as Goon pushed me forward. We went down the stairs and to a sedan parked a few spaces away from me. Number One opened the back door of the car and one wolf jumped in. I went to follow, but my arms were yanked back. Number One pulled a black piece of cloth out of his pocket. I felt myself start shaking, staring at it. Dammit, why did everyone insist on blindfolds? He smiled bigger.

"You didn't think I was going to let you see where we're going?" he asked. I prayed he didn't notice the phone shoved deep into the back pocket of the men's jeans I'd changed into before leaving. There's no way I would have snuck a phone in one of the stupid pockets in a pair of women's jeans. I sucked in a breath.

"I don't like being blindfolded."

"Do tell," Goon whispered in my ear. *I hope Xavier rips you apart*, I thought. But Number One chuckled.

"This will be fun, then," he said. Goon twisted both arms behind my back, not as hard this time, but enough that I couldn't move without pain lancing up the shoulder he'd already injured. I held as still as I could while the blindfold was put around my eyes and another piece of cloth tied around my wrists behind my back.

"You know anyone could look out their windows and see this, right?" I asked.

"Let them," Number One snarled. Now real, unadulterated fear took root. What was his plan if he was this confident about abducting me in plain view, even if it was the middle of the night? I was shoved into the back of the car and I felt the second wolf settle on my other side. The two men climbed into the front seats.

"I'd behave back there if I were you," said Goon. "They bite." Growls sounded on either side of me, and I tried to make myself as small and still as possible as the car pulled out.

We didn't seem to have been driving that long when the car slowed and pulled to a stop. A door opened and one of the wolves jumped out. I tried to focus on my breathing and slow down my heart. The blindfold had stayed on the entire drive and I'd moved into full panic attack mode, hyperventilating until I was dizzy and feeling like my heart would burst from my chest.

No one said a word to me the entire drive, so I stayed quiet, too. The silence allowed me to imagine what we were driving toward, which was what had led to me completely freaking out. I'd never expected to miss Connor, but this was already making the St. Louis kidnapping feel like a luxury vacation. I briefly considered that I'd also never expected to wind up in one hostage-like situation, much less enough of them to be able to compare experiences.

Hands grabbed at my sore arm and pulled, and I bit my lip as I tried to move myself out of the car on my own to alleviate the pain. When I was out, whoever had me kept a grip on my elbow and steered me forward. It felt like we were walking on gravel, and while I could hear cars, they sounded like they were distant. Someone took out keys and unlocked what sounded like a heavy-duty door. Where were we going? And why hadn't Melissa and my pack stolen me back yet?

I tripped on the door's threshold and a hand gripped the back of my neck to steady me. The floor seemed to be concrete, and our footsteps echoed in a large space.

"About time. What took so long?" a new man's voice said, footsteps coming toward us.

"She took a while to initiate contact," Number One said, and I realized he might not actually be in charge based on how the new guy was speaking to him. What was above Number One? Captain? My heart started racing again as I wondered how many shifters might be between me and safety now.

"He's in the back. Bring her over there so he can hear her," Captain said. Hear me do what? I stumbled as I was pulled forward again.

"Don't do too much to her yet," Number One said. "We still need her in good enough condition to lure her parents in." My mind started threatening to succumb to terror completely.

"If we can get him to cooperate, they won't be a threat anymore and we can stop this whole charade with AWL," Captain said.

"But until we know..." Number One started, then cut off with a pained cry.

"Don't question me," Captain said in a calm, terrifyingly threatening voice. Oh god, if they were willing to attack each other, what were they planning to do to me? I had to get out of here. I started running through my lessons with Kyle in my head. I didn't need to be able to take them down, just get away enough to run. But where to? I hadn't seen where I was at all yet. We came to a stop, and I started trembling so hard it was a challenge to stay standing.

"Oh, Nate?" Captain crooned. I almost collapsed then. Nate was here? My mind whirled. I couldn't run and leave him. What would they do to him if I tried to escape? But what would they do to me to try to get through to him? Where the hell was our pack?

"Nate, we have Paige here to see you. I'm fairly sure you can hear us, and I don't think you want anything happening to her, right?" Silence. "Paige, say hi." My arm was wrenched up behind me again so hard I yelped from the pain.

"I said, say hello. Make sure he knows it's you," Captain said. My blindfold was yanked off and I felt like the world moved sideways into something that wasn't quite reality. I couldn't breathe, couldn't think.

The man lying on the dirty medical cot in front of me was achingly familiar, even sallow and gaunt as his face was now, as if he had been kept alive on the bare minimum required for survival. I'd searched for him for years, had given up on ever seeing him again, and certainly hadn't thought I'd find him like this.

"Julian?" I said with a trembling voice. No response. "Julian, it's me. It's Paige." Tears started streaming down my face. "What did you do to him?" I yelled at Captain, unable to stop myself. He slapped me across the face and I tasted blood as my lip burst open.

"You don't get to speak to me. This is his own doing. We tried to work with him, and he put himself into this state. We've tried to get a response from him, get him to wake up, and he's refused. So now we're trying something new." His eyes shined with malice, and I shrank back against Goon, who was still standing guard behind me.

"Ok, Nate," Captain said, keeping his eyes on me. "I hope you're somewhat aware of what's going on, because otherwise, this is going to be very, very unpleasant for your girlfriend." And he aimed a punch at my ribs. I'm sure he could have hit harder, but the pain that bloomed was enough to make me cry out. "You'd better try to get through to him," Captain said to me. I looked toward the still figure on the bed.

"Julian! Nate! Please," I screamed. I had no reason to think he could hear me, and I wondered why they thought he was aware of us at all. I called out to him as Captain advanced on me again. Number One stood to the side watching us, frowning, not as if he were concerned about me, but as if he thought this was a strategic mistake. I was a piece in their game, and they didn't care what happened to me as long as they got what they wanted, whatever that was.

"If you do too much damage will her parents consider this a real bargaining chip?" Number One asked. Captain glared at him, making him flinch, but didn't seem to retaliate this time.

"She'll heal. And even if this doesn't get through to Nate, I'll enjoy letting Tami and Vick know what I've done to their daughter. They won't dare step out of line again if they know that we're serious." The words hit me like a physical blow. This wasn't a generalized idea that I was connected to AWL. He knew exactly who I was. I tried to turn to run, but Goon grabbed my arms again. Captain grabbed my chin so I had to look him in the eyes.

"After what your family has done to my kind, I think I deserve this, don't you?" he asked with a smile.

I was so terrified it was a wonder I was able to meet his gaze as I said quietly, "They aren't my family." His eyes hardened in anger and I flinched as he let go of my chin and stood up taller, glaring down at me. As he lifted his hand again, I saw his fingers sharpen into claws, and I bent my head down to avoid another blow to my face, wondering how long I would survive him. Then the world around us exploded.

There was a huge crash and dirt filled the air as lights flashed through the room. The sounds of screams, barks, and furious growls and snarls filled the air. I stood up as tall as I could and threw my head back hard into Goon's face, and when he reached up with one hand as he yelled curses, I slammed my good elbow back into his ribs and smashed my foot down into his ankle, twisting away from his now slackened grip. He yelled threats at me as I ran as hard as I could, ignoring the stabbing pains coming from multiple places in my body, ignoring that I was breathing thick dust, ignoring everything but getting to the source of the chaos that had taken over the room. Toward the voice that was yelling my name. Toward Xavier.

I was nearly there when something hit the back of my knees and I slammed into the floor. I turned over to see a black-furred wolf standing over me, teeth bared and snarling. I tried to crawl backward and he growled. As I tried to stand up again, he tensed to leap at me, and I threw my arms up as he left the floor. But he never hit me.

Melissa sailed past me, her gray fur catching the light, and slammed into the black wolf, biting and snarling. I froze, watching the two huge wolves fight. He tried to bite her face, her side, but she twisted around each time, kicking out at him and making him lose his balance. She circled him, and he watched her warily, tense. She finally lunged for him, going for his flank, and when he moved to protect himself, she adjusted and went for his throat.

He didn't have time to twist again, and her teeth caught in the side of his neck, ripping open a gash that started dripping blood. He staggered and she jumped on his back, her teeth sinking into the flesh of his neck, immediately over his spine. She twisted her head sharply and he fell beneath her, dead or paralyzed, I couldn't tell.

She turned to look at me and barked. My eyes wide, I tried to stand up, but my body had had enough, and I fell again. She looked behind me and I turned to see Devon in wolf form, brown fur standing on end and his teeth bared. He looked at me and tilted his head behind him as if telling me to move, but I couldn't. Suddenly, strong arms grabbed me and lifted me from the floor.

Instinctively I started flailing, but stopped when I looked up to see Greg, his blonde hair matted with blood on one side. I sobbed and grabbed onto him as he ran with me back out the hole that one of the pack's trucks had smashed into the side of the building where a bay door had been. He shoved me into the backseat of a car behind the ruined truck and yelled at the driver, "Get her the hell out of here!" before shifting and leaping back toward the building, colliding with another wolf who had followed us out, their teeth flashing as they attacked each other.

"No!" I sobbed, and watched my family fight for their lives out the back window as the car sped away.

INSTEAD OF DRIVING to the house, we wound up at a medical clinic. I was confused until Maria burst through the front door and came toward the car.

"How many, Ben?" she asked.

"Just Paige right now."

"Were you followed?"

"Nope. Nothing behind us, and I turned this off before we were too far away from the warehouse." Ben tossed her the burner phone I'd given him when he told me to turn off the location tracking and then came around to gently help me out.

I almost told him I was fine and could do it myself, but as I tried to move, a lancing pain in my side made me whimper and I realized this wasn't a time I should be insisting on independence. The look Maria gave me told me she knew exactly what was going through my head, too. Instead of helping me stand up, Ben lifted me and followed Maria into the clinic, carrying me in his arms. She had him set me on an examination table in a back room and he disappeared, presumably back to the fight.

"Let's get that shirt off," Maria said, and I nodded but then hissed in pain when I tried to move the arm that had been twisted. She decided to cut the shirt off instead, assuring me she had extras for me to wear home, and she went about examining every inch of me, gently wiping off blood and applying creams and ice packs.

My rib cage was sporting a purple and green bruise, but Maria said nothing looked broken, noting that between the gym explosion and now, she was convinced I must have ribs of titanium. It still hurt like hell, even if the bones weren't broken. She declared that my shoulder was dislocated and gave me a shot of something that immediately dulled the pain before she worked to move it back into place, then put my arm in a sling.

When she was done, she gave me some pills to take now, then handed me a full bottle of them with some instructions about what schedule to take them on to keep the pain under control and called out to someone that I was ready. Kelly came into the room and I almost sobbed with relief at seeing her. They got me into a new shirt and Kelly led me out of the clinic to her car out front. As I got into the passenger seat, it occurred to me that I hadn't said a word to Maria, and I wondered in passing if that was a sign of shock.

"You ok?" Kelly asked as she got into the driver's seat. I nodded, and from the look she gave me it was clear she didn't accept that answer. But she didn't say anything, just reached over and held my hand as she pulled out of the parking lot and drove us back to the house.

22

"They're here," Kelly said as James ran to the front window, whining, his tail between his legs. I had awakened with him in wolf form curled against my back in the bed, and he'd been stuck to my side all morning. Kelly said he was too anxious to shift back because he wanted to make sure the rest of the pack was safe, and he couldn't hear them as well from this distance as a human. Occasionally Kelly would shift to check in, then shift back to update me and keep me company.

Yasmin had gone to the clinic to help Maria as soon as we got back to stay with the kids, and she was still there. I went to the window with James and watched the vehicles pull up the drive, running outside as one car pulled right up into the yard in the front of the house rather than going to the garage on the side. Inside, I could see Devon, Kyle, and Xavier illuminated in the reddish light of early morning.

"I thought you said they had Nate," I whispered, holding my arms tight around myself. Kelly came up behind me and put her arms around me gently. James came out of the house behind me, human again, and I hugged him to my side, watching the car as Devon and Xavier got out of the front seats. When Kyle got out of the back seat door facing me, I saw why I didn't see the fourth person as they were driving. At the sight of the man's body lying motionless in the backseat, I stifled a cry.

"He's still alive," Kelly said, holding me tight. I nodded, not trusting myself to speak. I knew he likely hadn't woken up, but seeing him completely motionless like that still made me fear the worst.

"What do you need?" she called out, stepping away from me.

"Stretcher, first aid kit, and call Maria and see how far away she is," Devon said grimly. Xavier was suddenly in front of me, taking me and James in his arms and holding us tight. I hadn't registered that he'd moved.

"We got him," he said. I stepped back and looked him over.

"You're hurt!" I exclaimed, realizing that he was bleeding under rips in his shirt across his chest and arms. I looked at Devon and noticed he was limping. Kyle's face looked like he'd been in a bar brawl. "You all are."

"We're fine. We heal fast, and Maria's on the way." Xavier kissed the top of my head. "We're all fine, I promise. You on the other hand..." He held me at arm's length and looked me over, taking in the bruising, the cuts, the arm strapped to my chest to keep it still.

His eyes were absolutely murderous as he catalogued every injury, and I wondered what he'd already done to the shifters who had orchestrated this. I reached up and hugged him with my good arm and he held me tightly again, then loosened his grip when I sucked in a breath as he jostled my shoulder. I looked back toward the car and stared at Nate lying still in the backseat. Kelly came out of the house behind me carrying a rolled-up stretcher.

"What can I do?" I asked. Xavier gave me a squeeze.

"You take care of James and yourself," he said and headed toward the car.

"I'm fine," James said as Xavier walked away. He did sound ok, but I wondered what was going on inside his head and mentally cursed again at the fact that I was the only person here who couldn't link with him.

"You sure?" I asked.

"Yeah..." he sounded distracted, but not upset at least. "Is that really Daddy?"

"Yeah, looks like it," I said, trying to keep my voice level.

"What's wrong with him?"

"I don't know, baby."

We watched as Devon, Xavier, and Kyle pulled Nate out of the car and onto the stretcher, and then Kyle and Devon picked up the ends and headed into the house. As they passed by me, I felt my chest constrict and I started trembling. Xavier's arms came around me again and he led me into the den to the couch as Kelly followed Devon and Kyle upstairs.

"I should..." I shook my head. "I don't know. I should do something. I should..." I couldn't think of what it was I should be doing, but I definitely felt like I should be reacting with more than what felt like immobilizing shock. James sat next to me, leaning to look at the stairs curiously. Xavier rubbed my good arm.

"There's nothing for you to do right now. We're going to get him in a bed, and Maria's coming to see what he needs. But honestly, right now, more people would be in the way. Let them get him set up first."

I nodded and looked at Xavier's torn shirt. Underneath,

the cut on his chest already seemed smaller than it had been. He followed my gaze and sighed.

"I should probably go change now so when they need me again I'm not a wreck. Will you be ok?" he asked. I nodded.

"You should probably shower, too." I said. He laughed.

"You don't need shifter senses to smell that, huh?" he asked.

"You smell pretty bad," I admitted, giving him a small smile. He kissed the top of my head as he stood up.

"Be back in a minute," he said and headed for the stairs.

"It really is Daddy," James said, still staring at where the men had disappeared up the stairs.

"Yep. I know he looks different from the pictures, but that's him."

"It feels like him." James sounded wonderstruck. I looked over at him.

"What do you mean it feels like him?" I asked. James finally tore his gaze away from the stairs to look at me.

"He's asleep, but I can feel him. And I remember him. I didn't know I could hear him before, but now I remember how he felt in my head." It took me a minute, but when I realized what he was saying, my eyes got wide.

"You mean you can feel his mind?" James nodded. "Can you hear anything right now?" I asked.

"No. I can feel him, but he's not saying anything. He's just... there."

"Well let's not push it right now until Maria sees him, ok?" I asked.

"Ok." James sounded impatient now and I wondered if he had been planning on trying to communicate with Nate mentally.

Trevor and Jessica came down the stairs, and I wondered if they'd been kicked out while everything got situated upstairs.

"Let's go out back," Jessica said to James, looking to me for confirmation. I nodded and she held out her hand. James took it and followed her out, looking thoughtful. Without James there to keep out from underfoot, I wandered up the stairs. I wouldn't get in the way, but I wanted to know what was going on. I saw movement in the guest room across from Xavier's bedroom and went to hover in the doorway.

Now that I could look at him for more than a passing second, Nate looked worse off than I thought. He'd seemed in bad shape back at the warehouse, but now the details as I was able to study him in good light without the distraction of being threatened made it so much more intense. His hair was long and matted to his head, and his skin looked not only pale but thin. His nails were long, and a layer of grim covered him head to toe. It was as if someone had locked him away and forgotten about him.

"Should we... I don't know. Clean him up or something?" I asked as Kelly came to stand by me.

"We shouldn't do anything until Maria sees him, just in case," she said. I nodded, then the front door downstairs slammed, and someone came up the stairs.

"Where is he?" Maria called, and Devon called back to lead her to the room where we were watching Nate. I moved out of the way to stand next to the wall by the door as she strode into the room, all stern professionalism.

"Go get the stuff out of my car," she snapped at Devon and Kyle as she went to Nate's bedside, putting her stethoscope onto her ears and waving the guys out. Xavier came out of his room with clean clothes and damp hair as they came into the hall.

"Kyle, I'll get this. You grab a shower," Xavier said. Kyle nodded and at the bottom of the stairs turned down the hall toward his own room instead of heading for the front door. Kelly and I followed Xavier and Devon downstairs and Kelly went into the kitchen to start getting food and drinks ready for everyone. When Xavier realized I was behind them, he turned me around and sent me back upstairs, pointing out that I only had one good arm to work with anyway.

When they got back with the first haul, Maria was looking Nate all over, inspecting his skin, feeling his pulse, listening to his heart. She didn't say a word as Xavier and Devon set down the bags and boxes and went back for a second load. After bringing in the rest, they came to stand near me by the wall, Devon leaning back against the wall and Xavier with an arm around my waist. I could feel how tense he was and put an arm around him also, rubbing his back. None of us could take our eyes off Nate as Maria worked with practiced precision setting up what looked like a makeshift hospital room, pulling out syringes, an IV bag, and other medical implements.

"Devon, you smell terrible. Go take care of that, please," she said as she connected tubes to the IV bag. Devon huffed but left the room. Maria looked up at me and Xavier. "You two can stay if you stay out of my way and stay quiet." I nodded but didn't say a word and she nodded her approval before putting her attention back on her patient. She drew blood and put the vials in what looked like a lunch box, then set up an IV drip.

"I'm going to go to my office to run labs on these and take care of some of the others who got hurt," she said, picking up the container with the blood vials. "When I come back, we'll see how he's doing with that IV. We'll probably be able to clean him up a bit then, but let me run this first. Do. Not. Touch. Him." She narrowed her eyes at us with the last words and we promised. Satisfied, she left the room as quickly as she came in, and we were left staring at Nate hooked up to tubes and monitors that were tracking all his vitals.

"Who all does she need to take care of? How bad was it?" I asked quietly. I felt like we should whisper so as not to wake Nate, although I knew it would take more than that for him to open his eyes. "Is anyone..." I couldn't finish the question but Xavier gave me a comforting squeeze.

"No one died," he said. Then his eyes went steely. "At least not on our end. And not for lack of trying, either. But we expected this, and we were ready, even if we'd thought the fight wouldn't be until tomorrow."

"Is everyone going to be ok?"

"Yeah, they'll be fine. Greg and some others may need to stay still for a day or two while their bones set, but they'll be fine soon."

"A couple days for bones to set?"

"We heal fast." He looked me over again. "I'm much more worried about you than I am about any of them."

I looked at Nate and wondered how worried we should be about him now that he was here. Xavier squeezed me again.

"Now that he's being taken care of properly, he'll heal up, too," Xavier said. But he didn't sound nearly as confident about this as he had about Greg. Kelly poked her head into the room.

"Hey, there's food downstairs," she said. Her eyes flicked to Nate. "How is he?"

"Your guess is as good as ours," Xavier said. "We've been

given strict instructions not to touch him until Maria gets back."

"You two go eat something. I'll sit with him," Kelly said, and shooed us out of the room. We went downstairs silently. I wanted to ask more about what had happened, but from the look on Xavier's face, I didn't think he was ready to have a conversation about it yet. I told myself it didn't matter, that we all were back and safe.

Devon and Kyle were sitting in the kitchen, silently eating the chicken sandwiches Kelly had set out. Xavier and I sat down, but none of us really knew what to say right now, so we all ate quietly, lost in our own thoughts.

As the day went on, other members of the pack showed up, bringing food with them for dinner, just as they had the night we had the first meeting to discuss Nate's rescue and welcome James and me to the pack. Many of the pack who had joined in the rescue were wearing bandages or had bruises, and I tried not to think of what had been so bad that they were all still healing.

Xavier, Kelly, and I took turns sitting with Nate while Devon and Kyle fielded most of the conversation with the pack members who came to the house. When Maria got back, she gestured for me, Devon, and Xavier to come upstairs with her. In the bedroom, we sat on folding chairs that we'd brought up to use while keeping vigil.

"Other than nutrition deficiencies, which we can work on intravenously, there's nothing in Nate's bloodwork to indicate why he isn't waking up," she said.

"So what's our next step?" Devon asked.

"Without bigger equipment than I can bring here, there isn't much more I can do," she replied. "If he doesn't wake up after a while, I can figure out a way to get him into some scans after hours when there aren't others around to ask questions. But other than that, on a medical basis all we can do is wait." She paused. "Devon, have you tried to link with him yet?"

"I tried when we first found him. I thought if we could get him awake it would be easier to get him out. But it was like beating my fists against a steel wall. His mental guards are so thick I don't think there's any way I can get through to him."

"Even as his alpha?" The look she gave him had Devon fidgeting uncomfortably in his seat.

"You know I've never used the alpha abilities like that."

"This might be the time," Xavier said quietly, and Maria nodded. Devon stared at Nate as if he were being asked to torture his best friend. For all I knew, that's exactly what might happen. I caught Xavier's eye to let him know this was one of those pack things I didn't know about yet and he nodded his understanding to let me know he'd fill me in later.

"In the meantime," Maria said. "Let's get him cleaned up. I wanted that IV going first, but I think we're settling in for the time being, so let's get him set up for an extended convalescence. Clean clothes, wash him up, clean bedsheets."

"We can do that," Devon said. Maria started unhooking Nate from all the equipment and setting it to the side.

"Let me know when you're ready to get him hooked up again," she said and headed back downstairs. I slowly walked toward the bed and stared down at Nate. I hadn't dared touch him before Maria had given the all-clear for fear of doing more damage, but now I touched his face then his hair, smoothing the long strands back. I paused when I realized he was caked not just with dirt but with blood. I sucked in a quick breath at the realization, wondering whose blood it was.

I heard someone behind me move slightly, but Xavier and Devon stayed back, watching but not interrupting as I stared down at the man I both knew intimately and didn't know at all. Tears started to well up, but I choked the sobs back down and wiped my hand furiously across my eyes to clear them before turning back around.

"Let's get him more comfortable," I said, and at that, they both moved. Devon left the room, presumably to get supplies, and Xavier came and wrapped me in a hug. My breath shuddered, but I didn't let myself fall apart. Not yet. It was coming, but right now we had a job to do. He let go with one arm and turned to look at Nate, the other arm still keeping me firmly at his side, and I wondered if it was for my sake or his as he stared down at the bed with the most helpless expression I'd ever seen on his face.

"Seven years," he said so softly that at first I wondered if he'd actually said it. "It's been seven years. We thought... I didn't think I'd ever see him again. And I never in a million years thought I'd see him like this."

Xavier sounded like he was as close to breaking down as I was, and I was reminded again that the three of them— Nate, Xavier, and Devon—had grown up together, coming of age as a unit standing up against two worlds that didn't understand them to build a new family. I may have begun to build a life with Nate, but they had done it. And then he'd left them. Xavier and I stood there holding each other for a moment and staring down at the man who both of us knew so well in such very different ways before Xavier took a deep breath and pulled me away from the bed.

"Come on. Let's grab some clean clothes while Devon gets stuff to wash him up."

"That hair will need to soak," I said, frowning, looking at the blood and dirt caked on in layers. Xavier sighed.

"It might be easier to cut his hair," he said, and I had to begrudgingly admit he was probably right.

I ran a warm bath and Devon and Xavier carried Nate into the bathroom and laid him in the tub so we could wash him off. It took soaking and multiple rounds of washing before the water that ran off him finally wasn't dark grey from the layers of dirt and filth that had covered him.

We tried to wash his hair but in the end decided to cut it off since it was so matted, and then we soaped and cleaned what was left now that it was close-cropped. We changed the bedsheets and got Nate in clean clothes and settled back into the bed, then Devon called for Maria. The entire time, I tried not to think about the fact that Nate didn't react at all to any of this.

"Ready?" she asked, and we all nodded before she started hooking all his monitors and tubes back up to him. Soon the regular beep of a heart rate monitor was the only sound in the room, and the consistency of those beeps steadied me. He may not be awake, but at least he was home and stable. And that could be good enough for now.

I lay in my bed that night unable to sleep. I'd been thrown back into feelings of helplessness that were all too familiar. Even though Nate was in a room down the hall now, he was still unreachable, and there was absolutely nothing I could do to change the situation. I consoled myself with the fact that at least we knew where he was now, and that was worlds better than things had been for four—no, almost five now—years.

After an hour of lying in the dark, I went to peek into

James and Trevor's room. The boys were passed out, snoring lightly, and I went to tuck them both in and kiss James's forehead before tiptoeing back out. As I closed the door, I sensed someone behind me and whirled around.

"I couldn't sleep, either," Xavier said, handing me one of two mugs he was carrying.

"What's this?"

"Warm milk with vanilla."

"Thanks." I held the cup close to my face, feeling the warmth seep into my fingers as I sniffed the sweet drink.

"Want to talk?" Xavier asked.

"I don't know... but I'd like not to be alone," I said. He nodded and put an arm around my shoulders as we wandered into his room. We sat on the bed, sipping the milk and watching Nate across the hallway through the open doors, his monitors blinking and occasionally softly dinging. I finished the milk and set the mug on the bedside table and leaned against Xavier with a sigh.

"He's here, but I still don't know what to do. I still can't fix it," I said.

"How did James do seeing him earlier?"

"I couldn't tell, honestly." I sighed again, thinking of James standing by Nate's bedside, staring at his father with a mixture of curiosity, longing, and shyness. "He was a baby back when Nate was taken. I don't know much he actually remembers and how much he only knows from pictures and stories. But James said he could feel his mind and that he recognized him from that. I don't know what to make of that."

Xavier was silent for a moment. "Did he try to link to Nate?"

"No, he said he didn't. I told him to wait until the adults talked about it to make sure it was safe."

"If Devon tries to link to him tomorrow we'll see what happens."

"Devon's never used the alpha abilities before? Ever?" I asked.

"Never. It's something we all agreed on when we founded the pack."

"Do you think he can get through?"

"I don't know. I've never been in a pack where the alpha controlled me like that. Devon hasn't either, so all our knowledge of this is secondhand. Seeing what happened to Amber wasn't firsthand because we were only spectators." He shuddered. "I don't even know if it will work without Nate shifted, and I don't know how to get him to shift without waking him up."

"Amber shifted."

"She was fully conscious." This time I shuddered, thinking of the lifeless, blank look in her eyes that night.

"Full circle," I mumbled. "Can't do either one without the other."

"We can at least try," Xavier said. "But it's going to be hard on Devon, especially with it being Nate, after we all agreed in the beginning that we wouldn't be that sort of pack, that we'd never use the alpha to command anyone. It's for a good reason, but..." He trailed off and I nuzzled my head against his shoulder. He leaned his head on mine.

"You sure you're ok?" I asked.

"Me?" Xavier sounded surprised. "Fine. Why?"

"One of you crashed a truck into a building." I reminded him.

"Ah, yeah..." He rubbed the back of his neck. "James kind of screamed at us that you were dying when we were still a few minutes away and it didn't seem like we had time to figure out how to get in there with any more stealth than that."

"Oh, god. He didn't say anything... How much was he aware of?" I asked. I felt sick thinking of James knowing what I'd gone through. I couldn't even protect him by leaving him behind.

"We aren't sure. He didn't really send any more than that, just started yelling at us to hurry." He pulled me close. "We should probably talk to him about not spying in the future, but right at this moment I'm glad he did it."

"Let's get some sleep," I said. Xavier nodded, lost in thought as we laid down as we had most nights for months now, snuggled up together. And with his arms wrapped around me, I was finally able to fall into oblivion.

"WE *SWORE*, Xavier. We swore to each other that we wouldn't do this, that we wouldn't be that sort of pack. When I agreed to be acting alpha, we all agreed I wouldn't ever use this part of it." We all sat around the kitchen table the next morning as Devon and Xavier debated whether Devon should tap into his alpha status to pull Nate awake.

"We never thought we'd be in a situation like this," Xavier said. "You might be able to command him to consciousness."

"It's still going against everything we stood for, every-thing we founded all this on." Devon waved his hands out to encompass everything around us.

"We've got to try, though. We've got to try to bring him back. And we don't have any other way."

Devon's eyes briefly flicked over to me but moved back to Xavier quickly. We'd already all agreed to keep James out of this for now. He may have powers we didn't totally understand, but he was still six and this was his father. We didn't know what it would take to get past Nate's shields or what sort of trauma might come through if James did connect with Nate's mind. Kyle, Kelly, and I were at the kitchen table also, but this conversation was between Xavier and Devon. None of the rest of us had been there in the beginning, and without discussing it, we all acknowledged that this was between the three pack founders.

"If I do this..." Devon paused, then shook his head, frowning and pinching the bridge of his nose.

"If you do this, it doesn't break our bond. You aren't forcing him to do anything. You aren't controlling. This sort of situation wasn't covered in that decision. This is triage, not command," Xavier said. Devon leaned back in his chair and took a deep breath.

"Fine. But I don't know how to tap into alpha control. We've never done it before."

"Ask Melissa."

Devon nodded, his expression going to thoughtful rather than frustrated.

"I'm going to link with her. Give me a few," he said, then stood up and left the room. When he was gone, Xavier leaned back and rubbed his face with his hands.

"At least he agreed to try," I said.

"I never thought he wouldn't," Xavier said. "This is about making sure he's ok with it, that it doesn't make him feel that he's broken his word to all of us and destroyed the trust the pack has placed in him. In all of us." I nodded and leaned forward on my elbows.

"He knows we would still trust him, right?" Kyle said, and he sounded worried. "Devon knows that we all understand the situation?"

"He does. But he has to convince himself he's right," Xavier said.

I wandered back to the den, where Hannah was scrolling on her phone and Trevor and James were watching some show that involved a girl riding what looked like giant bugs. James looked up at me when I came in, sitting up straight.

"Is Devon going to try to link to Daddy?" he asked. I nodded.

"Yep. We don't know if it's going to work, but we're going to try to wake him up. Do you want to hang out down here or come upstairs? It's probably going to be boring up there. You'll just be looking at Devon sitting there staring at Daddy."

"I want to come," James said. I nodded and held out my hand.

"All right. Come on."

As James took my hand, both Hannah and Trevor shot worried looks his way. I made a mental note to ask Hannah and Jessica later about what the kids thought of this whole situation. I had no doubt that James was probably more willing to talk to them about some aspects of this, especially anything that he thought might upset me.

We headed upstairs into Nate's bedroom. James looked around but didn't say a word as I led him to a chair and he sat down. Devon and Xavier were in wolf form next to the bed. Kyle leaned against a wall with his arms folded over his chest, frowning thoughtfully at the two wolves, and Kelly came to sit in a chair next to James.

"Did they start anything yet?" I asked. Kelly shook her head.

"Devon linked with Melissa for a moment, but I think that's finished. Waiting for you," she said. Devon looked toward me, and I nodded that I was ready. Then Devon looked at James, who stared at him for a moment with an expression that I'd learned meant he was speaking mind-to-mind.

When whatever exchange had happened was done, Devon and Xavier looked at each other, then simultaneously looked at Nate. I leaned back to wait. I was used to this part by now. Watching and wondering while having no way of knowing what was going on inside their heads. I still didn't like it. After five minutes, James started getting wiggly. After fifteen minutes, he was barely staying put in his seat.

"You can go back downstairs if you want. I can come get you if anything happens," I whispered to him.

"They can't do it that way," he grumbled back. I frowned at him.

"You're not linking with them, are you?" I asked.

"No, they're loud," he said, frowning at the wolves. I looked at Kelly and Kyle, but they shook their heads.

"I'm not getting anything," Kelly said.

"Me, neither," Kyle said.

"How do you not hear that?" James demanded, sounding exasperated. Xavier glanced over at us and aimed a low warning growl in James's direction. James glared back at him and leaned back, crossing his arms and frowning, and Xavier turned his attention back to Devon and Nate. Another five minutes, then ten minutes of watching the wolves stare at Nate. Devon had started breathing heavily as if he were exhausted, and every once in a while, Xavier would reach over and nudge Devon, as if trying to bring his attention back from something.

Then Devon started growling, first low but growing louder quickly. Kelly and Kyle stood up straight, looking to Xavier to see if they should shift, but he shook his head at them and focused on Devon. I tried to keep my breathing calm but could feel the anxiety building up, wondering what was going so wrong that Devon looked like he wanted to attack something.

James had stopped fidgeting, his eyes wide as he stared at Nate. Suddenly, James leapt from his seat, shifting in mid-air as he launched himself toward the bed. Kyle tried to reach for him, too late, but Xavier managed to grab him by the scruff of the neck before he reached Nate.

The wave of mental energy hit me so hard that it knocked me back into my seat. No words at first, just sheer force of will, James throwing himself with everything he had toward his father. Then the words came, so loud I wanted to throw my hands over my ears, even knowing that blocking my hearing wouldn't help.

DADDY! DON'T GO! Don't go away again! Don't run! PLEASE!

Tears started pouring down my face, both from the force of the mental wave pushing everything else out of my mind and pinning me in place, but also from the anguish, the longing, crashing into me. Most of James's life had been spent with me looking for his father, in a constant search for answers, and every emotion that both of us had felt for the last four years came pouring out of him, overwhelming all my senses completely.

James! James, I'm here! I thought, trying to replicate whatever I'd done the day he'd linked to Melissa, and he stopped straining against Xavier's hold and looked at me, panic in his eyes.

Mommy, he's scared. He's trying to run. But he won't make it back next time. He can't run! If I don't stop him now, he'll never come back.

I locked eyes with James and I stood and went to him,

taking him from Xavier and holding him close. He trembled but didn't try to get away.

Can you get to him? Can he hear you? I thought.

I don't know. I think so. I feel him. He's not talking, but... I feel him. Bring him home, James.

He nodded then turned his attention toward Nate. I didn't sense words anymore, but I felt James reaching out, as fast and as far as he could. He started trembling more and I held him tight. Xavier and Devon had turned their attention from Nate to James now, supporting him as he poured every ounce of energy he had into trying to catch his father and drag him back into the world. I could feel James's awareness of them, how he leaned on them, drawing energy from them to reach further and further. At some point, I started to feel James stretching too far, his stamina waning, and he started whining in great sobs as he realized he couldn't reach any farther, that he was at the end of his abilities.

I felt his link with Nate snap painfully, his mind reeling back into itself, and he let out a howl like he had the night he had first linked with the pack, the first time he'd truly felt his father's loss. He buried his head into me, and I held him and cried with him, wondering if the break he felt meant that we had lost Nate for good, if this was the end.

Xavier shifted back, quickly pulling on a pair of sweatpants Kyle tossed his way, and held James and me in his arms as if he were afraid to lose us too. He rocked us gently and making soothing sounds, even as his expression looked like his own heart was breaking. Devon stayed in wolf form, pressing his head into James's side. Kelly came up behind me and put her hands on my shoulders. The support surrounding us should have been a comfort, but instead, it made everything feel more final.

Then Kyle sucked in a breath. I looked at him and realized he was looking not at us, but at the bed. Nate's eyes
were wide and staring at us all with a look of shock. I let out
a strangled cry and the others all looked toward the bed,
expressions of disbelief on their faces that I'm sure matched
mine. The voice as he opened his mouth was hoarse from
disuse and barely audible.

"Where's my son? Where's James?"

Watch for book two, coming soon.

Daughter of Legacy

ACKNOWLEDGMENTS

So many people championed me as I wrote this book, and I owe my thanks to every one of them.

To my fellow Claws in the Eagle Tower: Thank you for your constant support when I got excited and just had to let people know I was writing something, even when I didn't know if it was anything anyone else would ever see. You are the best cheerleaders!

To my Beta readers, Cindy, Lesley, Elyse, and Martha: Thank you for giving me your time, taking a chance on my characters, and letting me know how to improve both the story and my writing. Your insight and encouragement were invaluable.

To my Alpha (in more ways than one) reader, Alex: You are part of the heart of this book. Thank you for listening and helping me fuss at my characters, hash through plot holes, agonize over being mean to my poor wolves, and think through exactly how everything should come together. Thank you for letting me get stupidly excited with you over writing statistics and formatting software. Thank you for loving Paige, James, and the rest of the pack as much as I do, being my sounding board when I saw things that reminded me of parts of the story, and laughing with me at memes that reminded me of Kyle.

To my family who read my book when it was still in its infancy: Thank you for getting excited about this with me as

I was taking the first steps on getting this world and these characters fully developed.

Peter and Catherine: Thank you for supporting this project even when you didn't know you were doing it. For being an inspiration, dealing with me on nights when I couldn't stop thinking about the story and needed to sit with my computer until the words were out, and getting excited when I let you stay up late because you wanted to help (you had no idea you were providing dialogue).

To Jesse: Thank you for getting excited about my story, pressing me to keep writing, and for keeping things moving on the days I needed to disappear into my own world. Thank you for helping with the non-writing, business-y stuff that made me freeze up (dealing with werewolves is so much easier than dealing with taxes and DBAs). And thank you for your constant encouragement to keep moving forward. I love you.

And finally, to you, the reader: Thank you for picking up my book and getting to know Paige and her family. I hope you enjoyed the journey so far, and I can't wait to share more of their story with you and show you around more of Orlando.

ABOUT THE AUTHOR

Carolyn Glasshoff has been obsessed with books since she discovered read-along books and records as a toddler. Her favorite genres to read and write have always been fantasy and sci-fi, and she loves all things supernatural—especially vampires and werewolves.

As a native Floridian, Carolyn always thought more fantasy stories should be set in Florida since the state is weird enough that real magic could exist there without anyone actually noticing. She lives in Orlando with her husband Jesse and their two kids, and she teaches technical writing at the University of Central Florida. She loves watching rocket launches and being a theme park regular.

Follow Carolyn's author page on Facebook at https://www.facebook.com/glasshoff for writing updates, book memes, Florida life insights, and conversation about your favorite Florida werewolf pack.